Praise for *Run the Risk*:

'. . . shows Scott Frost's blend of action and psychological intrigue is here to stay' *Daily Mirror*

'Cracking outing for Frost's LA cop heroine Lt. Alex Delillo' *Peterborough Evening News*

'Fast paced, plenty of action and a great plot. Excellent read' *Nottingham Evening Post*

'For people who like their books frantic and frightening . . . it delivers the goods' *Booklist*

'A taut, swiftly paced thriller . . . a latter-day Hitchcock would love to film' *Kirkus Reviews*

More praise for *Never Fear*:

'Edgy and enthralling' *Belfast Telegraph*

'Fear is the one thing that definitely runs through this crime thriller like an electric current, never releasing its grip' *Northern Echo*

'A thrilling introduction to a new cop heroine' *Birmingham Post*

'This is a very visual whodunit with oodles of twists and turns, terrifying secrets and personal journeys into darkness. Delillo is a character worth following' *Sun-Herald*, Australia

'A snappy and assured thriller' *Sydney Morning Herald*

'[A] pacy thriller. In a word: gritty' *Weekend Gold Coast Bulletin*

Scott Frost is a screenwriter whose credits include *Twin Peaks* and *The X-Files*. He lives in Montana.

Also by Scott Frost

Never Fear

run the risk

scott frost

headline

First published in Great Britain in 2006
by HEADLINE PUBLISHING GROUP

First published in paperback in 2007
by HEADLINE PUBLISHING GROUP
4

Cataloguing in Publication Data is available from the British Library

0 7553 3392 6 (ISBN-10)
978 0 7553 3392 9 (ISBN-13)

Typeset in Plantin by Avon DataSet Ltd,
Bidford-on-Avon, Warwickshire

Printed and bound in Great Britain by
Mackays of Chatham plc, Chatham, Kent

Headline's policy is to use papers that are natural, renewable and
recyclable products and made from wood grown in sustainable forests.
The logging and manufacturing processes are expected to conform to
the environmental regulations of the country of origin.

HEADLINE PUBLISHING GROUP
A division of Hachette Livre UK Ltd
338 Euston Road
London NW1 3BH

www.headline.co.uk
www.hodderheadline.com

For the bravest woman I know, Valerie

I'm the boy in the third row of the class photograph that everyone's eyes pass over. No one remembers my name, the color of my hair, or the sound of my voice. I'm invisible.

– Gabriel's journal

one

The auditorium had the strong perfume scent of too many roses, like the hospital room of an accident victim. That sweet, not entirely healthy air. It smells so good you just know something terrible has happened.

It's funny how the imaginary life you conjure up for your child is invariably nothing like the real thing. It's actually not that different from being a cop, except that the longer I'm a cop, the less surprised I am by the things I see. And the longer I'm a mother . . . well, I don't really need to finish that, do I?

I was watching my daughter compete in a beauty pageant. The Rose Parade Queen no less. How can you prepare for a moment like that?

How the hell did this happen?

I should be happy my daughter is on that stage, right? She's beautiful, smart. It's just that I always imagined beauty queens as girls from Texas with a missionary glow in their eyes as if they were selling a peculiar brand of

1

faith. And I always imagined they were someone else's daughters.

Maybe it's because I'm a cop that I don't buy any of it. Look at the girls on that stage. From left to right: Kimberley, Rebecca, Kellie, Grace, Caitlin. They're all hiding something – no escaping it. Doesn't take a cop's eyes to see it. Kellie had her nose done, Grace her teeth, Caitlin lips . . . God only knows what Kimberley had done. And Rebecca . . . Rebecca I think has done it all.

What isn't perfect can be hidden. Beauty queens cling to that like some ultimate, unshakeable truth.

My own daughter lied on her application for the pageant about two piercings. Bet the judges wouldn't be happy about that: I know I wasn't. I only know about them because I found the disinfectant in her bathroom.

Nothing is ever completely hidden – ever. A cop's one and only unshakeable truth.

I looked at my daughter and wondered how she'd become a stranger to me. I didn't know. It just crept up like the change of seasons.

A pageant official in a white suit started walking from judge to judge collecting the final tally sheets. I looked around for the other contestants' parents seated in the auditorium. They were easy to pick out. They all appeared to belong to a lost tribe of perfectly proportioned people. It's no mistake that their daughters are on that stage. Some have been in pageants since they were five years old. But why Lacy? I couldn't let it go. Six months ago her wardrobe didn't extend beyond jeans, T-shirts, and work boots. What is she doing in taffeta and heels?

I glanced at two of our SWAT officers wearing dark suits at the entrance to the auditorium. In the weeks before the pageant there had been whispers of the unthinkable happening. But those voices are everywhere now. In every civic gathering, in every speck of unattended white powder, in everyone's imagination. The auditorium had been made as safe as we could make it. The fact that a cop's daughter was one of the contestants seemed to give everyone involved an even greater sense of security, except me.

The master of ceremonies, a former TV actor who vaguely resembled his younger self, walked up to the mike.

'Ladies and gentlemen, it's time to crown our new queen.'

The auditorium fell silent. I looked at Lacy and began to wonder if I'd survive being a mother. She had a rope around every nerve in my body and was yanking it tight. And it never changes, not from the moment the doctor places her on your chest, to the moment you find the nipple ring and the diaphragm in the sock drawer.

My pager started vibrating and the woman next to me gave me a look like I had just crawled out of a dumpster. I pulled my jacket back just enough so she could see the gun on my waist. She stared at it with that blank look of fear that always accompanies the sudden sight of a weapon by a civilian.

'My daughter's the second on the right,' I whispered. 'Isn't she beautiful?'

The woman smiled nervously and looked quickly

3

away, not wanting to disagree with a mother packing heat.

I glanced down at my pager – my partner's cell number. I'd left word with him that I wasn't to be disturbed unless there was a body, so evidently somewhere in Pasadena, someone had died violently.

I tried to focus on the stage, but my mind drifted to the distant crime scene. I imagined the position of the body and started to work backward. I could hear the dull sound of the victim hitting the ground. The crack of a gunshot. The sound of a scuffle. Fabric tearing. Individual voices raised in anger as events spun out of control.

A flashbulb went off.

'And the 2003 Rose Queen is . . .'

'Come on, Lacy,' I whispered. 'You go, girl.'

A kid in his twenties, with long dreadlocks, wearing a knee-length jacket, jumped out of his seat across the aisle from me and stumbled, falling to the carpet nearly at my feet. He looked up at me for a second in embarrassment as if he knew me, then rushed up the aisle and disappeared. Behind me I heard the sound of movement. Out of the corner of my eye I saw one of the other parents stand up and point in horror toward the stage.

As I turned back to the stage I saw Lacy lifting up her dress and removing a dark plastic bottle that was secured to her thigh.

'You're poisoning the planet for a fucking parade!' Lacy yelled as she began spraying the audience with herbicide. 'Pesticides kill, herbicides are poison. You're all killers!'

People began diving under seats and shielding themselves with their programs as someone began screaming, 'Poison, it's poison, she's got poison!'

I jumped out of my seat and began pushing my way through the panicked audience trying to flee up the aisle. On the other side of the auditorium one of the SWAT officers was removing his weapon from under his suit jacket and rushing toward the stage thinking my daughter had a weapon.

I yelled no at him but my voice was lost in the shouting and chaos erupting throughout the hall.

I took out my badge and began yelling 'Police,' hoping it would help to clear people out of my way but the only thing they were seeing were the exit signs. A woman in a pink dress with tears streaming down her face and hair sprinkled with herbicide ran into me and briefly looked me in the eye before pushing past with the rest of the crowd.

Someone seeing the other officer holding his gun screamed, 'No, no, no. He's got a gun.'

I reached the stage as the SWAT officer took the steps on the other side, his weapon at his side. An usher tried to stop me so I grabbed his hand and twisted it just enough to move him quickly out of my way. Onstage one of the contestants was crying and shaking her hands as if she had touched something hot. The SWAT officer was twenty feet from Lacy, his gun coming up from his side.

'No!' I yelled, but he didn't hear me.

Lacy saw the SWAT officer moving toward her and began to turn toward him and raise her spray bottle.

'Lacy!' I screamed.

The SWAT officer froze and raised his weapon to a firing position just as two pageant officials grabbed her from behind. The spray bottle was knocked from her hand and seemed to hang suspended in midair for a beat, then fell to the floor with a dull thud.

There wasn't a sound in the auditorium. All movement stopped.

The officer stared at the bottle on the floor for a moment then looked across the stage to me, took a breath, and quickly slipped his weapon back under his jacket.

Someone said, 'It's over, it's over,' as the two officials quickly walked Lacy offstage. I took a breath, then another.

The master of ceremonies, apparently confusing the pageant with the first space shuttle disaster, stepped up to the mike and said, 'Ladies and gentlemen, we've had a malfunction.'

Backstage Lacy was seated on a folding chair surrounded by a half dozen gray-haired men in white suits who appeared on the verge of heart attacks. The man in charge was standing over Lacy trembling with rage and repeating himself.

'You're in big trouble, young lady! You're in big trouble.'

Lacy saw me approaching and straightened up in the chair, trying to give the impression that she was still in control. I walked up and made brief eye contact with her, then turned to the men in suits.

'I'm her mother.'

6

The man standing over her turned to me, the veins in his neck pumping like fire hoses. He stared dumbfounded for a moment then yelled, 'She's disqualified!'

'I think she knows that,' I said.

He shuddered like a tree about to topple. 'In all my years—'

'Yes.'

'I've never—'

'I know.'

'Someone could have been hurt!'

'Only if they were beneficial insects!' Lacy said.

I looked at Lacy and started to shake my head.

'That's enough out of you, young lady,' the official said. He turned to me in a rage. 'What kind of a mother are you?'

The question caught me off guard. Who would really want to know the answer to something like that? I took out my badge and held it up in front of his flushed face. 'I'm Lieutenant Delillo, Pasadena Police.'

He stared at the badge as if confronted by a puzzle. 'A policeman?'

'-Woman . . . lieutenant . . . mother.'

The white suits all glanced at one another, looking for some sort of direction.

'I'll handle it from here,' I said.

'You damn well better!' yelled the man in charge.

I took Lacy lightly by the arm and led her toward the stage door. In case there had been any misunderstanding of his previous words the man in charge yelled at us one more time, 'She's disqualified!'

'Asshole!' Lacy yelled as I guided her out the door.

* * *

Outside, a full moon lit up the parking lot with an almost unnatural blue light. As we walked silently to the car, I promised myself I wouldn't say any of the dozens of parental clichés that were fighting to come flying out of my mouth.

'I . . .'

I managed to stop the first outburst.

'What?' Lacy said.

I took a breath and tried to stuff the words back down my throat. 'Nothing.'

'Right.'

'Did you—' I bit down on my lip.

'Go ahead, say it, I know you want to.'

It was frightening how well she knew me.

'I hope you're proud of yourself.'

'Yes, I am,' Lacy said, displaying none of the weakness of character I had just succumbed to. She turned to me though I kept my eyes straight ahead.

'I did something I believed in. That can't be wrong.'

To the east, the snow-covered San Gabriels loomed over us like a brightly painted backdrop on a sound-stage. Jasmine was blooming somewhere and the air held its sweet, delicious smell. Someone had covered the roof of their house with fake snow and strung a palm tree with Christmas lights. It was one of those perfect nights that sell the California dream without a word being spoken, but my mind couldn't hold on to it. Lacy had seen to that. It was fiction as surely as the notion of judging beauty.

The truth, or the only truth I was willing to confront

head on, was the call I'd gotten on my pager. Somewhere below these mountains on the alluvial fan that spread out below Pasadena lay a body that had been ravaged by violence.

We reached the car and got in. Lacy removed the rose-colored pumps she was wearing and took a deep, relief-filled breath. There were a dozen things I wanted to say to her, a few that I should have . . . *You're really something. I don't agree with your methods, but I'm proud of you. I wish I believed in something as strongly as you do.*

I said none of them.

'I have a call I have to take. I'll drop you at home.'

Lacy nodded, looking straight ahead. 'Sure, Mom. Why should tonight be any different? Go take care of the dead.'

As we drove away, Lacy opened the window and casually dangled her pumps out under the moonlight. She spun them once on her finger, then I heard them hit the pavement and skitter across the curb like rats racing for cover. I stole a glance at my daughter, who was staring straight ahead, the faintest hint of a smile showing at the corners of her lips. It was a perfect moment. Her moment. I turned my attention back to the road, and somehow managed to keep my mouth shut.

two

The yellow crime-scene tape was already strung by the time I arrived at Breem's Florist at 1360 East Orange Grove. Four black-and-whites and two motorcycle units were parked on the street. Two of the squads had their yellow flashers working. A uniformed officer recognized me and lifted the tape so I could pull into the small parking lot where there was one more black-and-white, two unmarked squads, and the van from the ME.

As I stepped out of my car I glanced at my watch. 11:19. The scent of jasmine in the air had been replaced by the rich smell of smoked chilies from a taco stand down the block.

'Lieutenant.'

It was a young officer I recognized by the name of Baker, the kind of straight-backed kid who looked like he had come unglued and fallen off a recruiting poster.

'You take the call?'

He nodded.

'Tell me.'

'Received a shots-fired call at . . .'

He checked his notes; Officer Baker was a very thorough note taker.

'. . . Eight thirty-five. I arrived at eight forty-two. I waited two minutes for backup, and then entered. No sign of forced entry. Found the victim in the shipping garage, facedown, deceased from apparent gunshot. I set up a two-block perimeter when other units arrived.'

'And?'

My mind drifted back to the scene in the auditorium when Lacy began opening up with her spray bottle and pageant attendees dove for cover.

'Nothing. Two male Hispanics carrying open containers were detained and released. When I returned inside I found the other owner hiding under a display case.'

'Is he the one who called it in?'

'I haven't checked. He was pretty shook up. Apparently they were robbed and the perps killed his partner.'

There are times I feel like a den mother when I listen to young cops talk like they are on a TV show, and right at that moment I had had enough of being a mother to last me several lifetimes.

'The witness inside?'

'Yeah, Detective Traver took over the scene.'

Thank God for small miracles. I left Officer Baker to his note taking and walked over to the front door. The exterior of the business was cedar with that Big Sur, 'I'm in touch with every living thing in the universe' sort of feel. Hanging on the door was a carved wooden sign that read GREEN IS OUR COLOR. I glanced at the lock; it was untouched. Print dust covered the handle where the crime-scene investigators had dusted. The salesroom had several large walk-in refrigerated display cases with dozens of different flowers in black plastic pots of water. The air was heavy with the scent of flowers, the roses being particularly distinctive at the moment. And there was another odor, barely detectable but still present, mixing with the fragrances of Dublin Boy and Queen Mother: the acrid smell of spent gunpowder.

'So, how'd she do?'

My partner, Sergeant Dave Traver, was standing in the doorway to the back room. He was a big man: six-foot-one, 220, early thirties, with the exhausted, sunken-eyed look of the father of two-year-old twin girls. He carried himself like a man who had once been an athlete, junior college football, though all evidence of it was becoming fainter and fainter with each passing year. He had a smile on his face like someone about to hear a secret. I think he thought of himself as the Skipper and I was his Little Buddy, even though I was nearly seven years older and his senior on the force.

'She won, didn't she? I can tell by the look on your face.'

'That's not the look you think it is.'

Dave has certain blind spots when it comes to anything to do with kids. The thought that tiny, perfect creatures like his daughters could actually grow up to disappoint, or worse, was beyond his field of vision. It was a trait that made him difficult to dislike, though it was not always an aid in being an effective cop.

'So, come on. Did she do it?'

I pictured people ducking behind seats as Lacy shouted the last words of her beauty pageant career. 'You're all killers!'

'She did "it" all right.'

Dave's eyes grew as large as silver dollars with excitement. I longed to just walk past him and examine the victim. Some people, civilian people, escape their own lives by going to the ocean or taking long Thoreau-like walks, or jogging until every last ounce of body fat has been sucked dry. I prefer crime scenes. The minutiae of my own life vanishes as soon as I step beyond the yellow tape. There's only the silence of a victim and a story to discover.

I looked through the doorway leading to the shipping room where the violence had occurred. Sanctuary.

'Are you going to tell me?' Traver asked impatiently.

I finally managed to look at him and say it. 'She didn't win.'

He seemed to take my reticence as profound disappointment and he put his big arm around my shoulder and gave me a squeeze. 'She still gets to be in the parade, right?'

There was no way in hell I figured he was ever going to survive twin teenage girls.

I stepped up to the door into the large shipping and receiving area. It was maybe forty by seventy feet, a large roll-up loading door closed at the far end. Four-foot-high stacks of flowers took up most of the available floor space; half appeared to be roses of every imaginable color, the other half, exotic flowers I had no idea even existed. The overhead rows of fluorescent lights drained just a shade or two of color from every flower in the room, giving some of the wild tropical plants the appearance of plastic.

Protruding around the end of a large sorting table stacked with cut roses, the feet of the victim were visible on the concrete floor. He had been wearing sandals and bright orange socks. One of the sandals had fallen off and lay upturned on the floor several feet from him. Winding out through the stacks of flowers, a stream of blood had found the floor drain in the center of the room. Strangely, it was the only thing in the room whose color wasn't muted by the fluorescent lights: a bright red stream working its way downslope to join the shopping carts, plastic bags, and empty milk cartons on their way to the Pacific via the LA River.

'Why the hell would you shoot someone wearing orange socks? It's not right,' my partner said.

Traver had an unusual sense of justice that was difficult to disagree with. Looking down at the body, I couldn't imagine what threat someone wearing orange socks could possibly present that would require a bullet to the back of the head.

'You got an ID?'

'Daniel Finley, co-owner.'

I slipped some surgical gloves on, knelt down, and looked over the body. He wore jeans and a yellow polo shirt, the collar stained red with blood. He had sandy-colored hair that was matted with blood over the back of his head where the round had entered his skull. When he had fallen he landed facedown, arms at his sides, breaking his nose so it was pushed to the left side of his face. The streams of blood from both the head wound and the broken nose met about three feet from his body to form the larger stream that flowed to the floor drain. I imagine he never felt the cartilage and bone in his nose snap. The force of the round entering his head had knocked him flush out of one of his sandals as he tried to run from his killer. By the time he hit the floor the last conscious sensation he would have felt was terror, and even that would have been disappearing into the ether.

'Forty-eight years old, married, lives in South Pas.'

I inspected the front of his skull as best I could without touching it.

'No exit wound.'

Traver shook his head. 'None that I saw, but I didn't poke around too much. I was thinking thirty-two and it ballooned or splintered inside the skull.'

I leaned in and examined the hole in the back of his head. It was smaller than the tip of my little finger, and I have small hands – it wasn't a .32. It had likely traveled through his head and bounced off the other side of his skull, making mincemeat of his brain in the process.

'Thirty-two's too big. I would guess a twenty-five or a twenty-two.'

'A fifty-dollar popgun,' Traver said.

Three kinds of people use guns like this: gang-bangers, addicts, and wealthy white women in gated communities who keep them in their nightstands next to the bed. If I remember correctly, Nancy Reagan kept one in the White House.

'Where's the other owner?' I asked.

'He's sitting in the office.'

16

I glanced once more around the room to make sure I hadn't missed anything. I noticed another door next to the roll-up marked FIRE EXIT that I hadn't noted before.

'Both rear doors locked?'

'Yep.'

Above the door, right up against the ceiling, fifteen, eighteen feet up, nearly obscured in shadow was a small video camera. If I hadn't noticed it in the relative order of a crime scene, then it was a good bet that the shooter may have missed it.

'Do we know if there's tape from the camera?'

Dave glanced up to the corner where the camera hung. It was clearly news to him. He looked like a kid caught stealing cigarettes.

'We're checking.'

We started walking back toward the office. Halfway there I noticed a smile forming on Traver's face.

'Goddamn shadows.'

'Right,' I said.

It was a game we played at crime scenes: who saw this and who missed that. It was harmless and lacked the kind of competitiveness that the same game would hold if played by two men.

'How'd Lacy take it . . . not winning,' Traver asked, sticking the missed camera firmly in the past.

How was she taking it? Jesus. What kind of question is that to ask a mother who had just discovered her daughter lived an entirely different life from the one I had imagined? Not that I actually 'imagined' her life at all. She had managed to become a stranger while I stood by and let it happen.

'She took it pretty well,' I said.

'It's quite an honor to be a member of the queen's court. There's important duties and responsibilities. Being a member of the court can lead to things.'

It was the thing I liked most about Traver as a cop. His failures were mostly small ones, and they never penetrated the skin. I should do so well as a mother. I hardly knew where to think Lacy was headed at that moment, so I didn't try.

'Lacy won't be a member of the court.'

'Of course she will. All the finalists are.'

At the end of a short hallway I could see through an open door to the office. A uniformed officer stood just inside looking bored and tired of baby-sitting the witness. Across the room the other owner was sitting on a small couch, bent over, his head in his hands. He had the physical appearance of a wilting flower slowly sinking to the ground.

I thought of Lacy standing on the queen's float spraying herbicide at parade watchers instead of waving. I thought about trying to tell Dave what had happened in the auditorium, but couldn't find a starting point to explain it to myself, let alone him.

'They changed the rules this year – no court, no float.'

I could feel the outrage in Traver building like a shaken bottle of soda. The skin in his face began to flush. The doting uncle.

'The sons of bitches can't do that!'

Every head within fifty feet turned to see what it was the sons of bitches couldn't exactly do.

'They aren't sons of bitches; they're killers,' I said,

18

smiling for the first time since walking Lacy out of the auditorium.

Evans Breem looked up from his seat on the couch as we walked in and said, 'Jesus God, oh, Jesus God.'

He was in his mid-forties with a soft, middle-aged face, green eyes, his brown hair streaked with gray. Even for a man who had just been witness to violence he had the appearance of someone who worried too much. You could see the stress lines around the corners of his eyes. I imagined he had a lot of headaches. Not the picture of a florist that Hallmark sells.

'I should have done something. I should have. We talked about having a gun in the shop, but I was . . .' His focus drifted for a second. 'The neighborhood has changed a lot since we started here.'

He looked at us like he had suddenly discovered he wasn't alone.

'I'm sorry, it's just that—'

'I understand,' I said, cutting him off. 'Tell me what happened.'

He searched his memory for a moment as if it were a five-hundred-piece puzzle that had just been dumped on the coffee table. I've seen the same look dozens of times at crime scenes. That blank look of 'How could this have happened?'

Traver looked at me and then glanced down at his watch. Breem was a man on the edge of coming undone and badly in need of direction.

'Why were you in the shop at night?'

He took a breath and seemed to focus.

'Flower shipments. We contracted with one of the float designers. It was a big break for us.'

Wonderful, I thought. I could see the headlines: MOTHER OF ROSE PAGEANT QUEEN SCANDAL HEADS FLOWER MURDER INVESTIGATION. I could already hear the nitwit conspiracy theorists tinkering in their basements.

'The flowers in the back are all for a float?' Traver asked.

Breem nodded. 'Yes, most are from greenhouses in Mexico, shipped in refrigerated trucks. Time is the critical factor.'

'Which float?'

'San Marino's Spirit of Diversity.'

More good news for the rose officials. Spirit of Diversity Leads to Murder. A wild thought that this was all some sort of strange hate crime against florists stuck in my head for a moment.

'How much cash was in the shop?' I asked.

'Several thousand dollars. Shipments were coming in tonight and some of the suppliers prefer cash.'

'Did you recognize the gunman?'

He shook his head. 'He had on a mask.'

'What kind of a mask?'

'It was blue, no red . . . maroon, one of those ski things.'

'Did you give him the money?'

He nodded vigorously. 'Yes, yes, everything . . . that's when Daniel tried to run out the back.'

'Why did he run? Had the gunman said something? Did he say he was going to shoot either of you?'

'No, I think he just panicked. I froze and the . . . He went after him and I hid in the display case.'

Breem fell silent for a moment, sadness spreading across his face like a flush of blood. 'Then I heard the shot,' he said in a whisper.

'I know this is difficult, but sometimes this is the best time to remember events,' I said as understandingly as I could.

He nodded, trying to pull himself together.

'What did his voice sound like?'

'Daniel had a gentle—' He caught himself. 'You mean the killer?'

I nodded. 'Yes. Did he have an accent? Anything to distinguish it?'

'It was flat.'

'Like music?'

He shook his head. 'Like he didn't care what happened. Like it meant nothing to kill some—' His eyes began to drift away.

'Is the camera in the back room taping?'

Breem had apparently forgotten about it and just realized there was a recording of the murder.

'Oh, God . . . yes.'

'Why isn't there a camera out front where the register is?' Traver asked.

'It was just being installed. We had some break-ins in back so we put the first one there.'

'Who would have known you had as much cash on hand as you did?'

'We have two part-time employees, and one temp we hired.'

21

'We'll need addresses.'

He nodded sadly. 'I don't think any of them would do this.'

I looked around the office. There was a framed dollar bill; a gold plaque from the Florists Association; a chamber of commerce membership; a photo of the two partners and their wives standing on a dock in Mexico with a large sailfish hanging by a rope. This happy, sheltered world had just come apart like a rose dropping all its petals.

'Why was the front door unlocked?'

He looked up, surprised. 'I don't understand.'

'The front door wasn't forced open, so it was either open or he was let in.'

'I was in back. I thought it was locked.'

I walked outside, leaving Traver to finish questioning Breem. The temperature had dropped and I could see the steam of the gathered cops' breaths evaporate like little jets into the night. The smell of smoked chilies had been swept away with a breeze blowing inland off the ocean. A tall row of Italian cypress swayed with the wind like characters in a silent movie. As one of the coroner's men walked by heading to the scene, I noticed the faint odor of menthol they use to mask the smell of death when it's had time to ripen. I walked to the edge of the crime-scene tape and played the few facts that we had out in my head. Most killings were exceedingly simple acts. Connect-the-dots sort of puzzles. Smart people, if they do kill, usually do it stupidly. This had all the makings of a bad paint-by-numbers canvas, but I've been surprised before.

Instead of standing outside at a murder scene I suddenly wanted to be sitting on the edge of Lacy's bed having the conversation I wished we had had in the car but didn't.

When I had dropped her off, she got out of the car, then turned and said, 'So you have nothing to say to me?'

I sat silently for a moment, a thousand questions in my head, none of which I asked.

'Later,' I said. Exactly one word more than I had said to her the entire ride home.

Lacy took a deep breath, then shook her head. 'That's perfect.'

I opened my mouth to reply but nothing came out.

'You always say there's going to be a later, but there never is.' She turned and walked into the house as I sat there silently.

My heart started pounding in my chest and I had trouble catching my breath. My mind raced with questions and doubts like it had lost its brakes on a hill. Why didn't I say something to her? What harm could it possibly have done to open up to her and tell her what a complete failure I am as a mother? I wanted a drink, I wanted a cigarette, I wanted to cry. I felt a tear forming in the corner of my eye.

Traver walked out carrying the videotape from the surveillance camera and stepped up to me. I turned away, looked up at the mountains, and brushed the tear away with my sleeve.

'Shall we go look at this tonight?'

I nodded and took several deep breaths trying to regain my balance.

23

'You okay?'

I swallowed, trying to get some moisture back in my throat. 'Yeah.'

Dave nodded and took a deep breath. I could see in his face that he was thinking about not sneaking into his twins' room to kiss them good night. He loved being a father, every exhausted minute of it. Somewhere inside him I'm sure he was convinced that if something were to go wrong in their lives twenty years from now, they'd trace the root cause back to a missed kiss on a sleeping forehead.

'They won't remember if you miss a kiss,' I said.

The grainy black-and-white surveillance tape showed Daniel Finley sorting through bunches of flowers blissfully ignorant of how little time he had left to live. Was he thinking about flowers, what he was going to have for dinner, his wife's birthday, an upcoming New Year's party?

He hears something behind him and turns just as the masked killer steps in pointing a short-barreled weapon at him.

'Looks like a twenty-five auto,' Traver said.

The killer was wearing jeans, a dark sweatshirt, and white basketball shoes, the Nike swoosh visible on the side. Finley stands dumbfounded for a moment as if frozen in fear. The shooter motions with the gun toward the door but Finley still stands there as if in disbelief. The shooter's head appears to move as if he's shouting, then he steps toward Finley and places the gun against Finley's head and pushes him out of camera range.

'Didn't Breem say he was in back and Finley up front?' I said.

Traver checks his notes and nods.

On the tape Breem steps into frame for a moment as if looking for something and then walks back out.

'That could explain why he thought he was in back and Finley up front,' Traver said.

'Doesn't explain how the shooter got the front door open, does it?'

I glanced at my watch and counted the seconds before what I knew was coming appears on screen. Twenty-five seconds later, Finley rushes back into frame and almost immediately goes down like a puppet whose strings have just been cut. At the edge of the frame a tiny puff of smoke from the round's discharge is all that is visible of the killer.

We looked at each other thinking the same thing: Why did the killer stop just short of camera range? Did he know it was there, or was it chance? But if he knew the camera was there and avoided it, why had he walked into its view before?

'Probably doesn't mean anything,' Traver said.

'Probably.'

I sat back in my chair and looked out the window. The street below was empty except for a few parked patrol cars. The moon had set, and the snow on top of the San Gabriels no longer glowed with reflected light.

'Breem said he was shipping flowers from Mexico. What if they were receiving more than flowers?'

Dave turned the VCR off, stood up, arched his back,

and yawned. He looked at his watch; it was three A.M. 'I was hoping we could keep this simple.'

There was a knock on the office door. A young female officer walked in carrying a piece of paper.

'We got a hit on one of those names.'

She laid it on my desk and walked out. It was a rap sheet for the temp employee Breem had hired.

'Frank Sweeny, did thirteen months in Lompoc of a four-year sentence for forgery.' I turned to Traver, who was already playing out the implications in his head. All of which meant that the kiss on his twins' foreheads was getting further and further away.

'What was that you said about keeping it simple?' I said.

'It was just a thought.'

I handed him the rap sheet. He studied it for a moment then let the facts bounce around in his head as if he were jangling change in a pocket.

'How does a guy go from doing thirteen months for writing bad paper to executing a guy for two grand?'

'They don't,' I said.

'What if it was more than two grand?'

'What if it was something else?'

'Such as . . .'

'Tonight is not the night for me to make assumptions about anything.'

'Am I supposed to understand what you're talking about?' Traver asked.

'Not for another fifteen years.'

He tossed the rap sheet back on the desk. 'Could be just what it appears to be. Some kid with a twenty-five auto who gets lucky and scores, then panics and steps up to the big time.'

'Then who opened the front door?'

Traver took a deep breath and blew it out like he was expelling smoke.

'You want to wake the son of a bitch Sweeny up? Rattle his cage?'

'If he's involved, then the address he gave Breem will be worthless.'

'If he isn't, we're wasting our time and ruining his night of sleep, not to mention ours.'

I looked at the photograph of my daughter on my desk. It was from a camping trip when she was fourteen. She was standing in front of a giant sequoia in a plaid shirt and cutoffs, her arms held out to her sides, palms spread wide. She was looking up toward the sun with a huge smile on her face. It was taken two months after I divorced her father. My timing having always been impeccable in regards to matters of the heart, three months after the divorce he was diagnosed with an inoperable brain tumor. He lasted five more hideous months connected to tubes and flooded with drugs. In Lacy's adolescent mind it was all somehow my fault, which was not all that different from the way I saw it. He was the one who cheated, and I was the one who felt like I had failed. His dying after I divorced him was just further confirmation in my mind that he was the real victim through it all instead of me.

I had thought for a long time that Lacy's smile in the photograph was because she had passed through some rubicon that had set us free from the baggage her father had dumped on us. Looking at it now I realized that wasn't it at all. She looked like she was about to take flight, slowly circling up around a tree that had witnessed nearly a quarter of all of human history. What Lacy had found were kindred spirits, survivors, mute participants who silently endured all the poison we could dump on them from the moment they rose out of the soil. Not so different from being a kid.

'I should have told her I loved her,' I said silently in my head.

Dave cleared his throat. 'So what do you think? We gonna do this?'

I looked at Dave sitting anxiously on the edge of the chair.

'We'll pay him a visit in the morning,' I said. 'Go home and kiss the twins.'

three

I waited at the office until four A.M., when the coroner's investigator called and said he had cleared the body and sealed the scene. Then I cut the witness Breem loose to go home and placed the surveillance tape in evidence lockup. When I got in the Volvo, I slipped a Pablo Casals tape in the deck and drove to Lake Street, where I took a left and headed up toward the foothills, the lights of downtown Los Angeles in my mirrors.

I would give the case a rest for a few hours. I would get an hour and a half of sleep and then I would do what real mothers do: I'd make Lacy eggs, toast and jam, some orange juice, then I would sit at the breakfast table with her and say all the things to her that I should have said last night.

I turned onto Mariposa and headed for our house. A white Hyundai pulled out in front of me from the curb, nearly clipping my right front bumper, and the driver began tossing *The Star News* out the window onto driveways. I passed on the left and glanced at the driver.

In the faint light he looked foreign, maybe European, late twenties, unshaven, the tired, sunken eyes of a recent immigrant who had jumped ship for the American dream and found it contained two minimum-wage jobs and four hours of sleep a night.

Out of habit, I glanced one more time in the mirror at the Hyundai, then my lights caught the eyes of a coyote, glowing red in the darkness, standing in the middle of Mariposa. As I approached, it moved casually over to the side, then just as casually reclaimed its position in the middle of the street once I had passed.

Near the end of the block I hit the garage remote and pulled up the drive to my three-bedroom ranch. My breath caught as if I had been grabbed from behind. Lacy's yellow Honda wasn't in the garage. I sat there until I could take a breath, then got out, staring at the empty space next to my own car.

'Shit' quietly slipped out of my mouth. If I had only . . . Don't go there, but I wanted to. Why didn't I say something to her? What was I afraid of?

I heard the slap of the paper hitting the driveway and glanced toward the street. The white Hyundai sat at the end of the drive until I walked back and picked up the paper before it drove quickly away squealing its tires.

'If I had only been smarter,' I said, steam rising into the chilly air.

Over the top of the San Gabriels, the first hint of light tinted the dark purple of the sky with the warm glow of sunlight. A lizard rustled in the ivy that covered the hillside below the house. A crow sitting on top of a telephone pole croaked its first call of the day. I looked down the street and noticed that the Hyundai had driven on without tossing out any more papers. It seemed strange, but what the hell didn't at this point.

I opened the paper and glanced at the front page. The headline read: A ROSE QUEEN BY ANY OTHER NAME? Below it was a photograph of Lacy holding out the spray bottle, her mouth open in an angry shout.

I folded it under my arm and for an instant had the brief thought of running down the street and grabbing all the papers before the neighbors wandered out in their robes and slippers. Up the block the yellow light from a kitchen came spilling into the predawn. Too late. I walked inside and closed the garage door behind me.

On the kitchen table Lacy had left a note.

'How can you be so clueless . . . I'm at a friend's.'

I sighed and sat down. So much for breakfast plans. I looked at the refrigerator and then over at the stove. I couldn't remember the last time I had actually cooked a meal for the two of us. I remembered talking about it, I may have even bought groceries, but I didn't cook anything. I looked at the bowl of fruit on the table and realized I had no idea how it had come to be sitting in my kitchen. For all I know it might have grown from seed.

I grabbed a banana from the bowl, then turned the light out and walked through the dark house. I hesitated at Lacy's door and looked inside, hoping against all evidence to the contrary that she would be there. It was empty. I walked inside and lay down on her bed. I could smell the sweetness of her hair on the pillow. It reminded me of when she was a baby and her scent would linger in my arms long after I had put her down for the night. Her red taffeta dress from the pageant lay in a pile in the middle of the floor, along with some dirty socks, a bra, and a Greenpeace sweatshirt.

'Clueless,' I whispered into the dark. Then I peeled the banana, laid it on my chest, and fell asleep without taking a bite.

Four hours later I woke up. There were six messages on the phone machine that I hadn't seen when I came home; two were Lacy's friends who thought what she had done was totally radical, two were reporters from local television stations requesting interviews, and one was Lacy's school principal, who thought it might be a good idea if we got together and talked about Lacy's home environment. The last one was a fan of the Rose Parade who thought the mother of such a child must be a piece of shit, a degenerate, a slut bitch who isn't fit to raise a chimp.

On the heels of receiving such good news I walked into the kitchen to defend my motherhood and scrambled two eggs, made toast, and had half a grapefruit. I overcooked the eggs.

I left a note for Lacy asking her to call me on my cell so I knew she was all right, and then told her I would be home later and we would talk, or more precisely, I would listen and learn about the depths of my cluelessness.

Stepping outside I noticed the first hint of a Pacific storm was bumping into the base of the foothills and dropping a steady light mist. Up in the mountains the white spiked flowers of yuccas glowed in dull gray light. A low bank of dark clouds hung just over the top of downtown LA on the distant horizon.

News of what my daughter had done was all over morning talk radio. Even the local public station jumped into the fray, though their point of view weighed heavily toward the broader geopolitical side of pesticides and habitat destruction, as opposed to a teenager just acting out to get her mother's attention. One caller actually described Lacy as the progeny of Rachel Carson.

At the plaza I noticed the first heads turning as soon as I stepped out of the car in the parking lot. This was how it was going to be from now on, I figured – heads turning, finger-pointing. 'There goes the failed mother of that girl.' I would be the Typhoid Mary of the Rose Parade, the mother who let a hundred years of tradition slip through her fingers. Inside Homicide I received a standing ovation and then found half a dozen plastic spray bottles with concealed-weapon permits sitting on the desk in my office.

Traver knocked on the door and stepped in looking as solemn as a visitor to a funeral home.

'I heard,' he said, broaching the subject carefully. 'We don't have to talk about it if you don't want to.'

'I don't,' I said.

'Maybe it would be good to talk about it.'

'For who?'

'How is she?'

'She stayed at a friend's house last night.'

'That's good.'

33

'Not for me.'

'You want to talk about it?'

'No.'

Traver stood there silent for a moment, his eyes looking like they were trying to find a destination on a map. Then he nodded and said, 'If you do—'

'Thanks,' I interrupted.

'I'm here, whenever you're ready.'

'To talk?'

'Absolutely.'

I nodded. 'I'm a degenerate slut bitch who isn't fit to raise a chimp,' I said, then started for the door to go question the temp employee Sweeny.

Traver looked at me for a moment not sure how to respond. Then he smiled and started out the door after me.

'I love chimps.'

The address we had for Sweeny was one of six small white bungalows that lined a short drive off Mission in South Pasadena. They were one of the early attempts at postwar housing that dotted older neighborhoods and were now mostly filled with low-income Mexican immigrants.

There were a few plastic children's toys scattered along the drive. Grass grew in tufts between cracks in the cement. The bungalows needed paint and new roofs. A few bedraggled-looking birds of paradise were planted along the foundation. The wet weather only seemed to heighten the sense that this housing built for returning GIs had seen better days.

Traver looked at the numbers then motioned toward the back.

'He should be in the last one on the right.'

As we walked to the end, I noticed a few curtains pulled aside and suspicious brown faces watching us pass, before quickly disappearing when it was clear that we weren't there for them. From one of the bungalows came the sweet aroma of pork carnitas slowly roasting in an oven. In two of the others the tinny sound of TVs drifted out through the ill-fitting windows. We walked up to Sweeny's front door. Some yellow-stained shades were drawn over the window next to the door. A wet, pink flyer for carpet cleaning lay on the stoop, the color bleeding onto the damp concrete.

'Don't suppose they get a lot of business here,' Traver said, looking down at the flyer.

I knocked on the door. There was no response, no sound of any movement inside.

'What time was he supposed to be at work at the florist's today?'

'Not till later.'

I knocked again and said, 'Police,' and again there was no response.

The mug shot we had from Sweeny's forgery arrest placed him firmly in the everyman category: dark hair, five-eleven, features designed to blend into whatever environment he was in.

'I'm going to walk around and see if there's a back door,' I said and started toward the side of the bungalow.

Traver grabbed the handle of the door and tested it.

'Hey, it's not locked.'

He pushed it open without stepping in and yelled, 'Police!'

Through the side window I saw a white flash that was the ignition point. I started to yell to Dave but it was already too late. The explosion was shaped and directed to kill a person stepping inside. The speed with which my world changed was astonishing. A rush of hot air knocked me sideways, showering me with pieces of glass from the window. As I was falling I looked toward the front of the bungalow and saw Dave disappear in a cloud of dust and debris as the door blew off its hinges, somersaulting across the alley, where it stuck in the wall of the facing bungalow.

And then it was over. Barely the blink of an eye.

I was lying on the wet ground, the bitter taste of dust filling my mouth. Rising up to my knees, I felt the wet trickle of blood down the side of my face and out my nose, which also began to bleed. I reached up and found a nickel-sized piece of glass from the window had penetrated my scalp just above the hairline and was embedded in my skin. Though I wasn't aware of the sound of the blast itself, I was acutely aware of the silence that followed it. It was like a shroud had been placed over everything within the area of the explosion. The air itself felt dead, empty, like the blast had created a lifeless hole in space.

Unsteadily I rose to my feet and looked over at the front of the bungalow. The mist that had been falling had turned to rain as if shaken loose from the force of the explosion. The soft plops of raindrops hitting the ground broke the dull, strange silence. The acrid odor of explosives filled the air. I lost my balance for a moment then righted myself.

One of Dave's brown shoes sat on the first step of the bungalow, its laces still tied in a bow. Dave lay on his back in the middle of the drive, his shoeless foot resting on the other leg, his green sock hanging halfway off his foot like a little kid who had been playing in the yard without his shoes.

I walked over to him and knelt down. His unfocused eyes were open and unmoving. His face was covered in small cuts and thin spidery lines where blood vessels had ruptured from the concussion. Both his arms were outstretched above his head with his sport jacket pulled halfway up each arm. The buttons of his shirt had been blown off and the shirt lay open, exposing his chest. Drops of rain began to wash tiny lines of dust and grit down his stomach.

'Dave?'

If he heard me, he gave no indication. I placed my fingers on his neck until I found the faint rhythm of a pulse. His chest filled weakly with short breaths.

'Dave?' I yelled again.

The white of his right eye flooded with a hemorrhage, turning a bright, crimson red. He blinked several times, then focused on me for a moment as if I had just arrived for a surprise visit.

'Dave, can you hear me?'

A moment of understanding flashed in his eyes.

'There was an explosion. You're hurt.'

His lips moved as he tried to speak, but nothing came

37

out. He tried again and then faintly said, 'No shit.'

A frightened Mexican woman in her mid-thirties stepped out of one of the other bungalows.

'Do you speak English?' I yelled.

The woman nodded.

'Call nine-one-one, tell them "Officer down."'

'No phone,' the woman said.

I looked back at Dave, but his eyes had slipped away again. I stood up and started toward the car and the radio inside. Halfway there I heard the first sirens already on the way to the scene. I reached the car and picked up the radio anyway and called in an 'Officer down' call, just so there was no doubt about the amount of help that would be on the way.

As I started back toward Dave, I noticed that glass from each of the bungalows had shattered and littered the drive. Blood began to drip into my right eye. I reached up and painfully touched the small piece of glass embedded in my scalp. I again checked Dave's pulse and found it unchanged. His eyes had rolled back in his head.

I pulled out my Glock and moved to the front of the bungalow, where the shattered door frame hung by a single nail. I raised my weapon and scanned the inside of the bungalow to make sure Sweeny had nothing else planned. Everything behind the source of the explosion was intact, as if nothing had happened. A mug, half-filled with coffee, sat on the small dinette table. Next to the mug several empty beer bottles still stood upright. The third of the room in the direction of the blast was a shambles. The woodwork had been splintered, the plaster walls turned to dust and now lay on the floor.

As my mind began to clear from the fog of the concussion, I noticed the fragments and wires of the triggering mechanism in pieces on the scorched wood floor. I holstered my gun and rushed back to Dave as the first squads pulled up with sirens blaring. A fire truck was on their heels and a paramedic unit right behind them, and still the air was filled with sirens. Nothing brings help faster than an 'Officer down' call. And no call is more dreaded.

I stood over Dave wishing I could do something and feeling helpless that the best I could do was nothing. An officer walked up to me and said something, but I didn't hear it. Several firemen knelt over Dave and began administering to him. Another took me by the arm and walked me over to the step of another bungalow, sat me down, and slipped on a pair of blue latex gloves that were unnaturally bright in the rain.

He held up a finger in front of my eyes and moved it back and forth. 'Can you follow this?'

I nodded. 'I'm all right,' I said.

He reached up and pulled the piece of glass from my scalp and covered the wound with a compress. I looked at Dave, who was now completely surrounded by the yellow jackets of firemen and paramedics. More than a dozen officers were now on the scene securing the bungalow. I heard one of them call for the bomb squad. My head began to hurt for the first time, and there was a pounding in my ears almost as if I was finally hearing the explosion. I looked at the bungalow and tried to focus on the blown-out doorway. I sensed there was something I had to remember. What was it? My mind was stuck, unable to find a gear.

Another officer knelt next to me and began talking.

'What can you tell me about . . .'

The fireman was asking me questions.

'Are you hurt anywhere?'

More sirens arrived filling the air with sheets of sound. I stared at the doorway, trying to remember, trying to escape the swirl of voices flooding my head. The fireman helped me to my feet and put a silvery space blanket over my shoulders.

'You may have a concussion and you'll need some stitches.'

He began walking me toward one of the ambulances. And then it struck me. I turned and looked at the shattered doorway. How did a man whose criminal history extended no further than forging signatures on checks manage to build a sophisticated explosive device? It didn't fit any more than the possibility that he was the man in the mask pulling the trigger at the florist's.

A group of firemen carried Dave strapped to a backboard and wearing a neck brace past me toward a waiting ambulance. I watched them load him into the ambulance, then I looked back at the bungalow.

If Sweeny didn't have the ability to build the device, then who was the bomb for? Us . . . or was it for him? The only things that were clear were right in front of me: the officers stringing yellow evidence tape, Dave's brown shoe sitting on the stoop as if waiting to take its next step, the rich aroma of the carnitas, and the rain washing away the sickening smell of explosives.

* * *

'If Traver had stepped in through the door instead of stopping on the threshold and calling "police" he would have been killed instantly,' the bomb squad officer said. 'The device was designed for a very specific purpose with a very small kill zone. His leaving the door open and not stepping in dissipated the effect of the blast over a much wider area than intended.'

It was five P.M. – seven hours after the explosion. Dave was in intensive care with a hairline fracture of the skull as a result of being struck by the door as it was blown off the frame. He was heavily sedated but no longer unconscious. He wouldn't know whether the vision in his right eye would be the same until the swelling went down. The attending physician suggested that for a man who had been blown across a driveway by a flying door, he was lucky. I suggested to the doctor that he stay away from Vegas if that was his understanding of odds.

I had four stitches in my head, ringing in my ears, dirt all over me, and blood-soaked cotton stuck up one of my nostrils. It was the nightmare my mother had always feared when I became a cop – not that I would be killed, but that I would become unattractive and therefore an unsuitable wife. If she had only understood that I was an unsuitable wife long before I ever had cotton stuck up my nose, our relationship would have been a lot easier.

I called Dave's wife from the emergency room and told her what had happened and that he would be all right. She asked for specific details as if trying to find a

41

hole in the story because I was avoiding the really terrible news. I could hear her holding back tears.

'I thought when he left patrol he would be safe . . . Detectives aren't supposed to get hurt.'

After that I left a message for Lacy that I was all right, in case she had heard something on the news.

I wanted to curl up in an afghan and lie down, but instead I was back standing in the middle of the bungalow wearing plastic booties over my shoes and talking with Detective Dylan Harrison of the bomb squad. He was thirty-seven years old and I suspect a genius who liked things that went bang in the night, day, or anytime in between. Like most of the men on the bomb squad he had found a home there because he never quite fit in anywhere else in the department. He was good-looking, though he didn't seem to know it. In fact at times it appeared a burden to him, almost like he was embarrassed by it. He moved through a room like a deer that is being stalked, each step carefully considered to arouse the least suspicion or attention. He had blond hair, green eyes, and an unimposing but strong body that he inhabited as if it were a stranger's that he was temporarily in custody of. In these times of dysfunctional body image, he reminded me of many women I've known.

Though there was nothing on his department record, I imagine he was once severely wounded or traumatized either physically or emotionally, maybe both. He masked the pain with his good looks. And everything else he hid by working with explosives.

I walked over to the door where Traver had stood at

the moment of the blast and looked back in. Both the walls and the floor of the bungalow were covered with tiny circles made with markers where fragments of the device had come to rest after the explosion. I looked over at Harrison, realizing that I had already forgotten what he had just said.

'The point you are making is . . . ?' I asked.

'The device was designed to kill a person walking all the way in without hesitation and closing the door behind them.'

He studied me as if waiting to see if I could complete the puzzle he had just laid out for me. He was giving me a test, something I wasn't used to in junior officers, but he wasn't just any officer.

'Like a person coming home,' I said.

He nodded.

'It was designed to kill the person who lives here,' Harrison said.

'He could have been expecting someone. Like us.'

I didn't believe it myself but I was curious to watch his thought process.

'Why go to all the trouble of a sophisticated device unless you are certain of the results?'

'Maybe killing wasn't the point; maybe he was making another point. Bombers have been known to do that,' I said.

'Yes, but in public places, in cars, mailboxes, department stores, bus stops, shopping malls, abortion clinics.'

'Like the Unabomber.'

He nodded. 'This was supposed to be an assassination.'

43

'I prefer the term "murder."'

'Yeah,' he said, as if the word made him uncomfortable.

I thought about it for a moment. 'So it's doubtful Sweeny made the bomb, unless he had a very dramatic flair for suicide.'

'People don't kill themselves with booby traps.'

What Harrison didn't know about the ways people were capable of exiting the planet was a lot, but I still didn't disagree with him.

'If Sweeny was the intended victim, why not just kill him with a gun?' I asked.

'Blood,' he said simply.

'You lost me.'

'It's too intimate. Bombers don't like to be close to people. The use of an explosive creates a kind of fiction for them that the pulling of a gun's trigger can't produce.'

'Fiction?' I said.

'An explosion is an act of creation. The use of a gun is an act of finality.'

'You're talking about control.'

'Exactly. Someone who uses a gun is just a killer. Someone who uses a bomb is after more than death.'

I glanced at the 9mm in Harrison's waist holster and wondered if he was in some part talking about himself. Would he be capable of using it if push came to shove? Could he point a weapon at a suspect and pull the trigger even if it meant saving his own life? I couldn't answer that.

'What can you tell me about him from the bomb?'

He knelt down and looked over the flashpoint on the floor where the device had been placed. I wondered if a part of him admired what he was looking at. You can't be an explosives expert if some part of you doesn't love it.

'He's very skilled, very dangerous, and he enjoys his work. He's also very careful; everything he used could have been bought at any hardware or hobby store, there's nothing to trace. Chemical analyses of the residue will probably tell us that he made it himself or it was a readily available explosive.'

'He?' I said. 'So you think it's a man?'

The question surprised Harrison. He even smiled. 'Women don't blow people up. It's a guy thing. A woman would have used a gun.'

His eyes darted uneasily about for a moment like he was searching for a way out of the room. I was right about Harrison. He had been wounded, probably right in the heart by Mary Jane Doe, whose eyes still locked on him in his sleep. But he was right. A woman would have pulled the trigger, not lit a fuse. For some reason I took a small amount of solace in that, though I'm not sure why.

When Forensics had finished going through the debris from the explosion, we combed through every piece of Sweeny's life that was left behind in the bungalow. But beyond discovering that he wore boxers and bought cheap clothes, there was little to tell much of a story. There were no family pictures, no letters, address books, bank statements, checks, nothing that even remotely appeared personal. No favorite pen by the phone, nothing stuck to the door of the refrigerator. Nothing on top of the small cheap dresser next to the bed. Even the food in the fridge was all prepackaged dinners that appeared designed to obscure any sense of the individual. The sum total of my knowledge about him was that he had a thirty-four-inch waist and liked bland food, which sounded a lot like most of the men I had dated in my life.

But what I did know about Sweeny and maybe all that really mattered was that he knew something about the shooting of the florist Daniel Finley, and because of that knowledge someone had tried to kill him. And if the young genius Detective Harrison was right, the man who planted the bomb was probably not the same person who so intimately put a bullet in the back of Daniel Finley's head, which meant I might be looking for two killers instead of one.

'I'm going to need a partner on this investigation to replace Traver. You want it?'

'I'm not Homicide.'

'And I'm not an explosives expert.'

I could see him working it out in his head like he was tracing the intricate wires of an explosive device: the red one here, the blue one there, don't ground this one, and for God's sake, don't touch the two leads together or that's the end of the party.

'I don't . . . I don't really like being around bodies,' he said.

'No . . . just small unidentifiable pieces of them.'

His face pained for a moment as if replaying a bad memory. 'It's just—'

'I wasn't asking if you want it . . . You're it,' I said.

'You don't have to get this approved?'

'The supervising detective of Homicide is responsible for all assignments in the division.'

'And you're the supervising detective.'

'Right.'

He was the first cop I had ever met who took being asked to work Homicide as a form of punishment. He had the appearance of a man who had just been tossed out into the light of day after living in a cave for years. The world was a big place and it was all out of his control.

'It's a temporary assignment.'

'Good,' he responded, his eyes betraying no emotion, retreating to the hideout of his good looks.

I stepped out into the drive between the bungalows and walked to the edge of the taped perimeter. The rain had stopped, though the pavement was still wet and the dark clouds still hung low on the mountains. I removed the plastic booties from my shoes and handed them to one of the forensic investigators.

Harrison emerged from the bungalow and was examining the door that had stuck in the wall of the adjacent bungalow. He looked like a man better suited for an archaeology dig than a crime scene. He didn't want his new assignment, which as far as I was concerned made him perfect for it. Beware of someone who wants something too much. I think my mother told me that, though she was talking about sex, not ambition.

I got in my car and began driving through the wet streets past old Craftsman cottages and Spanish ramblers with terracotta-tiled roofs. I would stop by the hospital to check on Dave, then go home to see if my relationship with my daughter was in any better shape than Sweeny's bungalow.

four

Lacy was home when I pulled into the garage on Mariposa. As I stepped into the kitchen, I could hear the sound of the television in her room at the other end of the house. There were the remains of a salad on a plate next to the sink. What she ate couldn't sustain a small dog, in my mind. Maybe if I cooked more. I could take a class. I could. I really could. Yeah.

I walked through the kitchen, through the living room, and down the hallway to her door, where I stood silently. I didn't knock, I didn't say anything. I just stared.

'Can I come in?'

'Yeah,' came the reply.

I opened the door and stepped in. I saw her eyes stop on my blood-encrusted nostril and then raise up to the stitches just above my temple. She opened her mouth as if she were clearing back pressure in her ears, then her face flushed and lost all color.

'It was you . . . in the explosion,' she said, her voice wavering with emotion.

'I'm fine.'

'I saw the news. They said a policeman was hurt. Was it Dave?'

I sat down on the bed and nodded. 'Yes, his skull was fractured, he's pretty banged up. The doctors say he'll be okay, though.'

'You could have called.'

'I did, I left a message.'

'There wasn't one on the machine.'

'The machine probably didn't get it,' I said.

'Yeah, whatever.'

I sat there for a moment, thinking about the phone machine, but couldn't stop myself. Had Lacy heard the message and was just turning the screws on me for leaving her the night before? I tried to push the thought aside before I said something I would regret. Lacy saved me from myself.

'I was on the news,' Lacy said. 'They interviewed me. They wanted to know why I did what I did.'

I took a deep breath. 'We might have talked about it before you talked to the press.'

'It's not about you, it's about me.'

Ignition.

'That's not what I meant. It can be tricky, that's all. You have to be careful you don't get manipulated.'

'I think I'm the one doing the manipulating.'

'You're right there.'

Blastoff.

'Meaning?'

'Nothing.'

'I'm not going to apologize for what I did because you got hurt,' Lacy said.

'No, you should apologize to me because you didn't tell me what you were going to do last night.'

'If you knew about it beforehand, you would have been an accomplice.'

'If I knew beforehand I would have stopped you.'

'Case closed. Direct action only works in secrecy.'

The words 'direct action' hung in the back of my throat like a strep virus.

'Direct action?'

'That's what it's called.'

'By whom? You sound like you were trained for this.'

'And you sound like a cop. It's just a beauty pageant, give me a little credit.'

'Credit isn't the first thing that comes to my mind.'

'Thanks, Mom. I did what I believed in and I would do it again.'

'I haven't had a very good day. I don't want to argue.'

'I'm not the one arguing.'

'You're the one who lied.'

'When?'

'Silence is just as good as a lie.'

'Well, you would be the expert on that.'

Jesus.

'Stop!' I yelled. 'Just stop!'

She took a breath and steeled herself. She was working real hard at being the tough one, but I could see the cracks showing. She had already lost a father, and I had promised her years ago that nothing would happen to me because I was a cop. Now my partner was in the hospital and I had come closer than I wanted to admit to breaking that promise today. The weight of that landed right on my shoulders. I felt like I had betrayed her trust, and had acted impossibly irresponsibly. Looking at her now, I couldn't imagine how I could take even the smallest of risks.

'I was scared,' she said.

My eyes welled up with tears. 'I'm sorry.'

I reached out, put my arms around her and held her for as long as she would let me. She buried her head in my shoulder, trying to let herself be a little girl again, and me a mom, if just for a moment. I was out of practice . . . We both were.

Lacy let go and looked at me as if she was about to say something, but instead hit the mute button on the television and stared straight ahead. I stood up thinking that if I could gather up the conversation in my hands and toss it out of the room, I would. I could start over by telling her that I love her and go from there, but instead I turned and walked out into the hallway and closed the door.

I went into the kitchen, tore a paper towel off, and blew my nose. I was hungry but too exhausted to do anything about it, so I just nibbled on the remains of Lacy's salad. And then, just because I couldn't help myself, I walked over and took a look at the answering machine. I had called, I was certain of that, but as Lacy had said the display read '0 messages.' I pressed play to be sure but just as it read, there was nothing there. It could have been the machine, but it had never done this before. Was I being a mother now, or a cop? And to what end? Let it go, I quietly told myself. Wrap yourself in the afghan, go to bed, and forget it.

Lying in the dark of my bedroom I tried to clear my head, but one thing out of all the day's events hung in my mind and pushed away sleep. Why had Lacy said 'direct action'? As a cop I was trained to find the one thing in the room that doesn't fit. As a mother, my training was clearly best forgotten. But when I looked at what she had said, it satisfied neither the cop nor the mother in me. It didn't fit. The daughter I knew, or thought I knew, had never used those words before. 'Direct action.' Where did they come from? Or more precisely, who did they lead to?

The morning radio shows were still talking about Lacy as I drove in to the plaza. Listening to the rage in some of the voices, you would think my daughter had committed an act of treason or defaced the Lincoln Memorial. Such was the level of civic pride that she had wounded. 'Never in the one hundred years of the Tournament of Roses has . . .' etc., etc. If it had been directed at anyone other than my daughter, I would have laughed at it. But underneath the absurdity of it all was an ugliness that couldn't be brushed aside when your family was the target. I turned the talk radio off and tried to clear my mind and focus on the day ahead.

The storm of the day before had moved east, spinning into the Mojave like a pinwheel. Wild sage scented the air. The blue of the morning sky had the clarity of a New England fall morning. It almost didn't feel like Southern California, until I looked to the west and saw the gray

53

line of the Pacific with Catalina floating like a cloud where the sky met the water.

Harrison was waiting in my office when I walked in. If he had slept at all, his appearance gave no hint of it. His jacket and pants were wrinkled, and his tie looked like it had been in the same knot for ten years.

'You look like you slept in your clothes,' I said.

He looked down at his suit and winced. 'We're a little informal on the bomb squad. I don't use these much.'

'Funerals and weddings.'

'Something like that . . . One wedding, one funeral.'

The words clearly held a weight I wasn't expecting and didn't want to confront before I had had a second cup of coffee. And possibly not even then, so I moved on quickly.

'You finished at Sweeny's?'

He nodded and motioned toward my desk. 'It's all there except for the lab work. Should have that later today, maybe tomorrow if they have trouble with any of the samples.'

I picked it up; it was six single-spaced pages, more words than most cops I knew wrote in ten years.

'Any surprises?'

'One,' he said.

I waited. Harrison seemed to have trouble getting hold of the thought.

'And?' I finally asked.

'I was wrong.'

'About what?'

'I thought it would be a pedestrian bit of material used. Everyday stuff.'

'It wasn't?'

'Not entirely. There were two explosives. An everyday, simple kind of powder, probably from fireworks. Inside that was military-grade plastique – very difficult to obtain in this country.'

I immediately thought of Breem shipping flowers from south of the border.

'Could they have been gotten in Mexico?'

'Easier than here, and untraceable.'

Harrison smiled like a kid who was excited about a school science project.

'How do you know it was military grade if the lab work isn't finished?'

'Every explosive leaves behind its own particular signature. If you know what to look for, you can tell a lot about the material used. The kind of energy released from the blast would have required more of the simple powder than was used, so I knew there was something else there.'

'"E equals MC squared" sort of thing.'

He nodded, though my attempt at rudimentary science pained him like a pair of tight shoes.

'Something like that.'

'Why try to hide what he's using if there is no way to trace it?'

'Because it's more enjoyable for him.'

'Enjoyable?' I said, unable to conceal my disgust.

'Bombers, if you rule out the suicide kind, are game players.'

I sat back in my chair and shook my head. 'That's a pretty twisted bit of psychology.'

'As a rule, bombers are a sick group of people. The stuff of profilers' dreams.'

A detective named North knocked and walked in. He was one of the older detectives on the squad, a divorced father who fought a long-running battle with cholesterol and Bud Light. He had thinning, reddish hair and cheeks that were flushed from alcohol.

'Got the warrants for Breem and Finley. You want us to execute them?'

'Every piece of paper in the house, cars, including the trash.' I amended that. 'Especially the trash.'

'Breem's making some noise about the business being sealed.'

I looked at him as if to say, 'Do I really need to answer this?'

'Right,' North said. He glanced at Harrison as he walked out. 'Nice suit.'

The phone rang on my direct line and I picked it up. 'Delillo.'

'Mom,' Lacy said. Her voice sounded an octave higher than normal.

'Lace, is everything all right?'

'They suspended me.'

'Who suspended you?'

'The assholes at school. Parks, the principal.'

She was in school three days Christmas week as part of an effort to shorten the school year during the air-conditioning season.

'They want to meet you and me at one in his office.'

My other line rang.

'Hold on for a second, Lace.'

56

I hit the other line. It was a patrol sergeant named Tolland.

'Lieutenant, we got a body down in the arroyo I think you should look at. May be a homicide.'

There were thirty-six thousand people in Pasadena. A second body in as many days constituted a major crime wave.

'Where?'

'Parking lot of the casting pond.'

'Okay.'

I hit Lacy's line.

'Lacy.'

'Those bastards.'

'Where are you now?'

'Starbucks.'

I took a breath; my head felt like another explosion had just gone off next to my ear.

'I'll call you at home later and we'll work this out.'

'You would think I had stolen a baby, not spoiled a beauty pageant. What's wrong with these people? Don't they know what we're doing to the planet?'

'Apparently not.'

'That's all you have to say about it?'

I placed my index finger on my temple and started rubbing in a small circular pattern, trying to stave off a headache. Have it all, be a working mom, what could be better? You're a modern woman. Jesus. My mind drifted for a second to explosives wrapped around each other.

'For the moment,' I said.

'Great,' Lacy said and hung up.

I put the phone down and stared at the door to my

office. Harrison shifted in his chair. I looked at him, almost surprised to find him in the room. He looked like he wanted to ask a question but didn't know where to begin.

'I have to make another call,' I said.

'I'll wait outside.'

He got up and started for the door.

'How are you sure the explosives didn't come from within the country?' I asked.

'I checked. They keep very good track of this stuff.'

'They?'

'I have contacts in the army.'

'When did you call?'

'Last night. I don't sleep.'

'Ever?'

'Feels like it sometimes.'

It occurred to me that he was talking about something I hadn't fully put my hands around.

'Am I missing something here? Why is this stuff so special?'

'Oh,' he said, as if he just realized he had forgotten an ingredient in a recipe. 'It produces no detectable scent.'

I thought about that for a second. 'The explosives?'

'Yeah.'

'Dogs can't smell it?' I asked.

'Nothing can, and it leaves virtually no trace after the explosion. That's why it's dangerous, and that's why they keep such good track of it.'

'Then how would it get into Mexico?'

'We didn't develop it; the Israelis did. They sold it to the Mexican military.'

The full picture of this material, or at least a partial image, was emerging like a photograph in a tray of developer. And what I saw frightened me. This was not a material used to demolish old casinos in Vegas for TV cameras, or to blow up mountainsides to extract coal.

'It was designed to assassinate people, wasn't it? Like someone walking through a door?' I asked.

He nodded.

'Or with a car bomb,' he added coolly.

Putting Sweeny in the same picture frame as this stuff didn't make sense.

'Why the hell would you use this to kill a two-bit forger?'

Harrison's eyes engaged the problem like a physics professor at UCLA would an unsolvable equation. 'That's what's interesting.'

'How?' I asked.

'He tried to mask it with the other powder to hide the fact that he used it. There can only be one logical reason for trying to conceal its presence.'

The image in the darkroom tray became clear. It was the kind of picture only a cop would arrive at. I felt a queasiness in my stomach.

'He's going to use it again,' I said.

'It's the logical assumption.'

The words left a hole in the room that was quickly filled with an uncomfortable silence. It felt much the same as when Lacy's father told me he had inoperable cancer. A future you don't want to know about has just been laid out in front of you and there's no turning away from that knowledge. Lacy and I would watch him die, and there was nothing we could do about it.

'You want me to contact the ATF?' Harrison asked.

The last thing I wanted was federal agents storming in and taking over the investigation. They're like a conservative pope. There's only one way to do things in their eyes.

'Carefully,' I said.

'Sure.'

He started for the door.

'If I understand, your only proof that he used this is by what wasn't there?'

'Proving something with a negative is accepted methodology.'

'Not in homicide.'

A faint trace of a smile flashed across his face.

'I'll let you make your call,' Harrison said, and walked out.

I stared at the phone, playing out in my mind the grim reality that had just landed in my lap. Then I dialed my daughter's school. An unhappy secretary with way too much work on her hands to be answering the phone picked up.

'Marshall High School.'

'This is Lieutenant Delillo of the Pasadena police. I'm Lacy Delillo's mother. I'd like to talk to Principal Parks.'

I'd always found that when dealing with any level of bureaucracy no matter how small, identifying myself as a cop right off always moved things along to the next level much faster. I was on hold listening to the school song for no more than two bars of 'Marshall Pride.'

'Ms Delillo. This is Principal Parks.'

He was one of those administrators who I suspected didn't actually like kids, so jumped ship out of the classroom at the first chance he got. Those who can't teach, teach gym, and those who can't teach gym become principals. He was a small-minded man whose interests lay in budget numbers instead of kids' minds. If anything, I think he saw students as the enemy.

'It's Lieutenant Delillo, Mr Parks,' I said to clearly remind him that I was the one with the gun, not him. 'I understand you sent my daughter home.'

'Yes, we did. I'm hoping we can talk about this this afternoon.'

'Why is my daughter suspended?'

'I was hoping we could talk about this in my office.'

'We will, but in the meantime, I would like some information,' I said.

'Of course. Given her recent activities, which I might add have been a great disappointment to the entire faculty and student body . . .' He let that hang in the air as if trying to draw a response from me.

'I'm proud of her,' I said, a little surprised at myself.

'Well . . . She's become quite a distraction. But that isn't why we sent her home.'

Lacy was right; he was an asshole, a passive-aggressive martinet who enjoyed wielding power over kids and parents alike. I knew cops like him who were physically dangerous to anyone unlucky enough to fall under their authority. As it was, Parks's power was limited to the squashing of a child's spirit. At that moment I wasn't sure which was the more destructive.

'Why did you send her home?' I asked impatiently.

'I no longer felt I could guarantee her safety,' he said blithely, like he was talking about the cheerleaders' new uniforms.

I could feel my jaw tighten and my face warm from the hot flush of anger. Those faceless voices on the radio calling Lacy things a mother should never hear began to echo in my head.

'Her safety?'

'Yes.'

'Has my daughter been threatened?'

'I believe so.'

'You believe or you know?'

'She was threatened.'

'From inside the school or out?'

'We're not sure. That's why we thought it—'

'You thought?!' I wanted to reach through the phone and grab him by his neck. 'My daughter is threatened and you let her leave the security of the school without talking to me first!'

'Our policy is for the safety of the entire student body—'

'To hell with your policy.'

'Now, just a minute,' he said angrily.

I could hear the trembling in his voice. I imagine it had been a long time since anyone had talked to him the way I just had.

'Did you notify the school police?' I asked him.

'Yes.'

'Before or after you let my daughter walk out of the building?'

There was a long silence on the other end of the phone. I imagine he was already working out how to cover his ass.

'Before or after?' I demanded.

'After.'

I took a long, deep breath to try to calm down. Parks opened his mouth again and put an end to the attempt.

'This is a school, Ms Delillo, we have rul—'

I had had enough of listening to him.

'And I have rules, Mr Parks, one of which is the willful endangerment of a juvenile. And that's a felony. If anything happens to my daughter I'm going to come down to that school, put you in handcuffs, and march you past the entire student body.'

I hung up and quickly dialed the school police offices downstairs. A woman sergeant named James answered. Her high, sweet voice gave me the impression that she did a lot of undercover work as a high school student.

'This is Lieutenant Delillo, Homicide.'

'Yes, Lieutenant?'

'My daughter is a student at Marshall, and there have been threats against her. Apparently it's been reported to you. I'd appreciate what you could find out about it.'

'I'll check into it and get back to you.'

I hung up and then called Lacy's cell phone, but got an out-of-service-range recording. I then quickly called home and left a message for her to stay inside and to call me as soon as she got there.

I put the phone down and sat at my desk looking at the photograph of Lacy standing in the sequoias. I'd been threatened dozens of times as a uniformed officer and as a detective; most were nothing more than hot air.

But this, a threat to my daughter, even if it proved to be a crank, shook every nerve in my body. I felt as if I had stuck my finger in an electrical socket. Nothing was going to take her away from me. At that moment I understood that I was capable of more violence than I had ever thought imaginable.

The phone rang and I snapped it up.

'Delillo.'

'Officer James, Lieutenant.'

'Go ahead.'

'The school got half a dozen phone calls.'

'What were they?'

'Cranks most likely.'

'Specifically, what were they?'

'I don't think you want to hear—'

'I can't evaluate the severity of the threat unless I hear them. You understand?' I said.

'All right. Four of them called her a bitch and suggested she be thrown out of school and that they didn't pay taxes to educate kids like that. We figure they don't mean much. It's the last two that concerned the school.'

'Go on.'

'The next one said, "Throw that fucking cunt out of school or I will take her out." '

'The last one?'

'The last one said, "Lacy Delillo will pay for what she did. I'm going to make that little bitch pay for what she did." It's possible the last two were by the same person.'

My breath caught short. I tried to swallow but couldn't manage enough spit to do even that. They had called Lacy by name and said my baby would pay.

'I understand that she left the school,' Officer James said.

'They asked her to leave.'

'We'll have a talk with that principal.'

'I already did,' I said.

'Do you know where your daughter is right now, Lieutenant?'

'She called me from a Starbucks.'

'Do you know which one she frequents?'

I was numb, as if the room had been plunged into ice water.

'No,' I answered.

'We'll check them out. Does she have a car?'

I gave Officer James Lacy's make and plate number, then looked at the picture of my daughter on my desk. I reached out and took it in my hand. 'Do you need a photograph of her?'

'We have the photograph from the newspaper.' She hesitated. 'I think everyone in Pasadena knows what she looks like.'

'Yeah.'

'That's good. She'll be safer the higher her profile.'

'Sure,' I said.

'One last thing. Does she know about the threats?'

'I don't think so.'

'Sorry about this, Lieutenant. I don't have kids but I can imagine what it must—'

'You can't actually.'

65

'No. I didn't mean—'

'It's okay. I appreciate your concern.'

'If we don't find her at the Starbucks, we'll have a squad wait at your house just to be safe.'

'Anything you can tell me about the callers?'

I was looking for the thing she hadn't thought of, the overlooked detail on a written report. I was looking for straws to grab hold of.

'Both calls were apparently made by adult male Caucasians.'

She paused for a moment. I could almost hear her forming the words in her head.

'I know I don't need to tell you this, Lieutenant, but it's probably just smoke,' Officer James said.

'And I don't have to tell you that when it's not someone blowing smoke, when the anger boils over and the trigger is pulled, it's always an adult male Caucasian, isn't it,' I said.

'That's not really my—'

'No, it's mine. Thanks, Officer James.'

Harrison was sitting on the edge of Traver's desk when I stepped out of the office. The look in his eyes told me he saw that something was wrong, but being unsure of his place either in the job or with me, he let it go. I started walking through the squad room toward the door.

'Where we going?'

'There's a body in the arroyo.'

'Is it connected?'

My mind was still on Lacy and the word 'connected' knocked me off balance for a moment.

'Connected?'

'To Sweeny?' Harrison said.

I shook my head.

'As supervisor of the homicide unit I look in on every body found if there appears cause for Homicide's involvement. They don't normally stack up this quickly.'

'What don't?' Harrison asked.

'Bodies,' I said.

'Do I really need to—'

'As my partner, it's your job to come with me.'

Harrison nodded reluctantly, the muscles in his jaw flexing in and out as he clenched his teeth. I noticed a hint of color leaving his face as we started down the marble stairs.

'Out of curiosity, Harrison, why did you become a cop?'

He narrowed his focus, his eyebrows gathering up as he came closer to an answer. There are times when words seem to have the same effect as a weapon and I regretted asking the question. I'd just asked him to go someplace he didn't want to travel to, at least not with me. I wanted very much to be walking down the stairs with uncomplicated Traver instead of Harrison.

'It's not my business,' I said.

'If I'm your partner, I guess it is,' he said.

'Forget it. I shouldn't have asked. We all have our reasons. Most of the cops I know just wanted steady work that wasn't boring.'

We reached the next landing without speaking, almost as if a sheet of glass separated us. As we made the turn onto the next flight, he broke the uneasy silence.

'I wanted to catch the man who murdered my wife,' he said flatly.

I took the next step and then stopped. For all the obvious reasons, most pointedly my own inability, I didn't need to be a mother to another person at that moment. More often than not, when someone tells you about a tragedy they're seeking something in return. In women I find it's a validation of their emotions that they haven't been able to get from the men in their lives. With men it's usually sympathy, understanding from a relative stranger that they couldn't expect from those closest and best able to give it. I looked in Harrison's eyes and saw that he wasn't seeking anything. He was putting a statement of fact out on the table. A cold, terrible truth.

'I didn't catch him,' he added self-mockingly. He even smiled slightly at his own absurd, naive thinking. 'The things we don't know.'

'I have several volumes full myself,' I said.

It did explain his difficulty with bodies, not an inconsequential problem for getting the job done in Homicide. He was also smart enough to know that I was going to ask my next question, so I assumed he already had an answer.

'If this assignment is a problem for you—'

'It's not.'

He said it with the confidence of a man disarming a bomb that could take his life with the slightest slip of the hand. Our eyes met for a brief second, long enough to tell me that the wound he carried was no longer a crippling one. I turned and started down the rest of the stairs, the intense green of his eyes staying with me a few moments longer. It was a feeling that was surprisingly unnerving. Jesus, what the hell is that about? Do not even think about it, I said silently to myself. Do not, for a second, think about it.

five

Four miles south of the Rose Bowl, Harrison and I turned into the arroyo at the old stone gates of the Casting Club. The branches of coastal oaks hung over the road like large, outstretched fingers. Acorns popped under our tires. Yellow mustard seed bloomed in bright patches up and down the arroyo's sloping green hillside.

At the floor of the arroyo was a stone building known as the Casting Club, a vestige of Pasadena's more genteel days when displaced Easterners tried to relive their days on Catskill streams by dressing in tweed, smoking pipes, and casting flies into the club's fishless shallow cement pool.

'I always wondered what this was,' Harrison said as we rounded the turn at the bottom and pulled onto the gravel where the gathered squads and ME vehicles were parked.

'It's where men used to get away from their wives,' I said.

I glanced across the seat at Harrison and regretted

saying it almost before it left my mouth. Harrison turned toward the graceful lines of the stone building, studying it as if he were reconstructing it stone by stone.

'I never understood those kinds of relationships,' he said without a trace of self-pity.

I couldn't imagine anything *but* those relationships, but I kept my mouth shut.

The body was half floating facedown at the south end of the pool, ten feet from the edge. The pool itself was maybe 120 feet long, forty feet wide. Where the body lay put it about 150 feet from the steps of the clubhouse. I scanned the perimeter of the pool and then over to the gravel parking lot, which was separated from the pool by a line of thick brush six feet high.

'No lights. Would have been dark down here last night,' I said instinctively, as if I were talking to Traver.

Harrison looked at me, unsure whether my words required a response.

'Dave and I do that,' I said. 'Think out loud.'

'Like an old married couple,' Harrison said, smiling slightly.

'Not like my marriage.'

In the pool the ME began wading out in knee-high rubber boots to have a look at the body. Harrison's eyes held the scene without turning away as the ME lifted the stiff body enough to take a look at the face.

'Male Hispanic.'

I glanced at Harrison, grateful it wasn't a woman. The victim was wearing jeans, leather loafers, and a red sweater over what looked like a white polo shirt.

'Seems unlikely a man would drown in twelve inches of water,' Harrison said.

'Unless he was unconscious when he fell in,' I said.

A detective named Foley, who had caught the call, walked up with Tolland, the patrol sergeant. Foley was my last investigator who wasn't executing the search warrants at Breem's and Finley's. He was about five-six with the build of a high-school wrestler, which he had been in the distant past. He had close-cut brown hair and a Gable-like mustache he had grown for a nonspeaking role of a detective sitting at his desk drinking coffee in an Elmore Leonard movie. His gift, if you could call it that, was a steady, blue-collar type of work ethic. He might not dazzle you with his insights, but he always worked a scene thoroughly and tracked down leads like a Labrador retriever. He glanced at Harrison and nodded as the ME began going over the victim, narrating as he went, as if it were a nature documentary.

'No wallet, keys . . . pants pockets empty . . . shirt pockets appear empty, no ID. No visible signs of bodily trauma.'

The ME pulled the body over to the edge of the pool and rolled him over in the water. It was like turning a waterlogged piece of wood. The man's arms were turned at the elbow straight out from the shoulder, his fingers bent as if he had been clawing at the water's surface. He had a black mustache, neatly trimmed. His dark hair was cut short and just as neat. The ME tested the flexibility of the wrists.

'Rigor is nearly full.'

He leaned in close and took a look at the man's face.

'Appears to be bruising just above the left eyebrow; skin appears undamaged except for slight hemorrhaging. No other facial trauma, no presence of blood on the body or in the water. There's a gold band on left middle finger, looks like a wedding ring, no watch, no other jewelry. Estimate approximate age as forty-five to fifty.'

'He'll be missed by somebody,' Foley said.

'Male, married Hispanic in his forties, he probably has kids,' I added.

'Found an empty bottle of tequila in a paper bag behind that bench,' Tolland said.

Foley held it up already bagged for evidence.

'Who found him?' I asked.

'The guy with the fishing pole, about seven-thirty,' he said, motioning toward a white-haired man in his sixties standing by a squad, holding a fishing rod.

'Any unaccounted-for vehicles?' I asked.

'Nope,' Foley said. 'He either walked here, got a lift, or came with somebody. Looks like the guy got hammered, fell, and hit his head as he went into the water.'

'If there's water in the lungs,' I said.

'Yeah,' Foley said.

'After the storm cleared last night there was no wind,' Harrison said.

We all turned to him. I didn't know where he was going with this, but he had me. I was curious to see if he could go over a potential homicide scene the same way he could dismantle a bomb. Foley looked like an annoyed high-school teacher.

74

'What's that got to do with anything?' Foley asked.

'Look at his legs. They're submerged from the hip down, dragging on the bottom. Only way he could have drifted out that far is if he would have been blown by a strong wind.'

Harrison glanced at me as if to see if he had stepped out of line. I motioned with my eyes that he most certainly had not.

'He could have walked out that far and hit his head when he fell,' Foley said.

Harrison studied the body for a moment, then shook his head.

'He looks like he goes maybe one-fifty?' he asked the ME.

The ME cocked his head and nodded like he was juggling numbers. 'Give or take, yeah.'

'Then he didn't hit his forehead on the bottom unless he did a swan dive off that bench,' Harrison said.

'How do you figure that?' Foley asked.

'At one-fifty he didn't carry enough mass to penetrate the water with enough force to strike the bottom – not unless he dove in. The water would have dissipated the energy. He would have slapped the surface and at most kissed the bottom.'

Foley looked at Harrison like he had just spoken Chinese. 'What the hell are you, Mr Wizard?'

I looked at Foley and nodded.

'That's exactly who he is,' I said.

'Well, shit on me,' Foley said.

Harrison walked over to the bench where the bottle of tequila was found. He knelt down and studied the ground for a moment, then looked out toward the pond.

'Don't tell me, you're Daniel Boone, too,' Foley said.

'Eagle Scout,' Harrison said.

'Fucking beautiful.'

'He could have fallen out here, struck his head on the cement, staggered into the water, and passed out,' Harrison said.

'But?' Foley said, sensing more was coming.

'What happened to his wallet and keys?' I asked.

'So he got jacked, then whacked on the head, he fell into the water and they took his car,' Foley said.

'Why didn't they take his ring? A petty thief wouldn't leave it behind.'

'Maybe they couldn't get it off his finger, maybe they got scared and took off.'

'Maybe they didn't want anyone to know who he was,' Harrison said.

Foley looked at Harrison impatiently. 'Now why would someone jacking a wallet and a car give a shit about that?'

'Maybe for the same reason they tried to make it look like an accident with the tequila,' I said.

'Which is?' Foley asked.

'I don't know,' I said.

'Maybe it's a crime of passion?' Foley said sarcastically.

'I doubt your idea of passion and mine are the same, Foley,' I said.

The ME leaned in close to the body and lifted the collar of his shirt to examine the neck.

'There's a gold-beaded chain here.'

Foley took out a pack of cigarettes, removed one, tapped it on the back of his hand, then stuck it in his mouth without lighting it.

'You are making this way too complicated, Lieutenant, if you don't mind me saying.'

'I got an ID,' the ME said.

He lifted a chain from around the victim's neck with his fingers. 'Couldn't see it under the shirt and sweater.'

'What?' Foley asked.

'Dog tags.'

'So we got a soldier,' Foley said.

The ME looked at the tags and shook his head in surprise. 'He's a major in the Mexican army. Hernandez. What the hell is a major in the Mexican army doing here?'

Harrison and I immediately looked at each other, thinking the exact same thing at the exact same moment.

'He missed the dog tags,' Harrison said.

'It's gold, he must have thought it was jewelry and left it.'

'How long would it take to ID a foreign national?' Harrison asked.

'Weeks, if we identify him at all,' I said. 'And by then, whatever he's intending to do will be over.'

'That's why he didn't want us to know his ID,' Harrison said.

I stared at the body for a moment thinking we had missed a piece of the puzzle. Then it struck me.

'You said bombers don't like to be intimately involved

77

with violence,' I said. 'It's why he couldn't have killed Finley. Could he have done this?'

'Drowning is a benign form of violence.'

'A bump on the head and he goes for a swim,' I said.

Harrison nodded.

'There's another possibility.'

'What?'

'He doesn't fit any of the profiles and is much more dangerous.'

'He?' Foley said. 'Who the hell is *he*?'

The line connecting the dots from Finley to Sweeny to the bomb that blew Dave into next week had just been drawn straight to the casting pond. There is no such thing as coincidence, not when murder is the result. Breem's flower trucks had come from Mexico. The explosives had come from the Mexican military. The middle-aged father whose life ended facedown in a pool where men practice catching trout was a major in the Mexican army. Dot to dot to dot, and here we are. Wherever the hell that left us. I turned to Foley.

'Consider this a murder scene.'

Foley's eyes moved back and forth between me and Harrison like the guest at a dinner table who doesn't get the joke.

'You want to tell me what the hell is going on?' he said.

'Yeah,' I said, looking down at the body. Death and the water had softened the contours and age lines on the man's face. His eyebrows and mustache were the color of freshly ground pepper. I tried for a second to imagine what his voice had sounded like. Was it deep? Resonate?

Did he talk in rapid bursts of sentences or slow, graceful arcs of words? Did he like to laugh? What was his wife's name? Did he have a daughter? Did he understand what was happening to him as he fell face first into the shallow water of the pond?

'The same person who made the bomb that nearly killed Dave killed this man.'

Connecting this man to an attempt on Traver's life immediately brought Foley up to speed, even if he didn't understand the hows and whys of it.

'You tell me what you want, Lieutenant,' Foley said.

'I want to know everything about this man before and after he crossed the border.'

Foley nodded. 'If there's water in his lungs and we get nothing more than a bump on his head from the autopsy, it's going to be hard to prove this is a homicide.'

'It's not this one I'm concerned about,' I said.

'You want to tell me what does concern you, Lieutenant?' Foley said.

'The next one,' I said.

'The next one?' Foley asked.

I walked over to the edge of the pool and looked down at the red sweater the Mexican major was wearing. It was so obvious to me that I was stunned I hadn't thought of it before. I turned and looked back at Harrison.

'What was it you said about a bomb used as a political or terrorist act?'

Harrison thought a moment, replaying the conversation in his head. 'They take place in public places – train stations, restaurants, wherever.'

'What if this, and the bomb in Sweeny's, were just attempts to cover up another act?'

'What?'

'Something that hasn't happened yet.'

'Another killing?'

'An act of terror.'

'I'm not sure I follow.'

'That makes two of us,' Foley said.

'We have two people dead for no apparent reason, and an exotic explosive designed for one purpose, to explode in places where it won't be detected.'

'What kind of places?' Foley said.

'Public places,' I said. 'What's the date?'

'Thirtieth.'

'The first is two days away,' I said.

I could see in Harrison's eyes the light of recognition going off.

'Jesus,' he said. 'The Rose Parade.'

I nodded and said, 'Exactly.'

'Exactly what?' Foley said.

'And the bungalow and this, and even Finley were just acts to cover his tracks?' Harrison said.

'It's the logical conclusion,' I said.

'But it's not one you could base on evidence,' Harrison said. 'There've been no threats, no warnings. We would have heard about them in the squad, we get those kind of warnings all the time.'

'And when don't bombers give warnings?'

He didn't even have to think about that. It was glaringly clear, even if the theory was supported by nothing more than the finest thread.

'When the device's intention is to kill, you don't warn anyone,' Harrison said.

We all know about that now. The terror that comes out of nowhere is seared into our collective consciousness.

'Devices?' Foley said. 'You're saying the guy who did this is going to put a bomb in the Rose Parade?'

I turned to Foley. I didn't want this information picking up speed and getting out of control, not until I had more than conjecture to follow. We still had four days. When time was up and push came to shove, we could send up the red flags of desperation. But until then we would do this quietly.

'What I'm doing is thinking out loud,' I said. 'And no one else needs to know any of it. Not yet.'

'No shit,' Foley said, unhappy at being on the outside of the conversation.

'You find out everything about this man's movements and maybe we'll have something to talk about,' I said. 'I don't want to start telling people that someone is sticking a bomb in the Rose Parade if all this man did was come across the border to take his kids to Disneyland.'

Foley nodded in such a way as to say he was unhappy but would do exactly as told. It was just one of the extra bonuses of being a woman on the job that when men accede to your authority, they often act as if they're doing you a favor.

'The Mexicans aren't exactly known for being real cooperative. It would help if I knew what the hell I was looking for . . . aside from everything,' Foley said.

'If he brought the explosives in, he would have been paid a lot of money for it. If we can find it, maybe it left a trail.'

'And?' Foley said.

'We need to know if he had access to explosives,' I said.

'He was in the army, how much more access do you need?'

'This is special,' I said.

'How special?'

'It doesn't officially exist, and it's your worst nightmare,' I said, glancing at Harrison to gauge if he was certain of his information.

'You're certain about this?'

'It's Israeli,' he said without hesitation.

'In Mexico?' Foley said in surprise. He let it sink in for a moment, then nodded. 'You got it, Lieutenant.'

Back in the car Harrison sat silently looking down at the pool as we drove up the slope of the arroyo. His theory had just widened the investigation to include the killing of a major in the Mexican army and, if it was correct, a possible terrorist attack on one of America's favorite New Year's traditions as it was broadcast live around the world. The weight of Harrison's deduction had just landed squarely on his shoulders and had already begun creeping into the lines around his eyes as they tightened with the tension.

As we stopped at the top of the arroyo, I glanced back down and saw the bright red sweater of the Mexican major as they lifted his body out of the water. Played against the color of the surrounding vegetation, it looked like a single, red maple leaf floating in a pond in a forest of green.

'Jesus,' Harrison said. 'I hope to God we're wrong.'

I put the car in park and leaned back in my seat.

'Why the parade?' I said. 'It could be the game.'

'The game?' Harrison said, not knowing what I was talking about.

'The Rose Bowl. A hundred thousand people in one stadium.'

'Oh, that game.'

'You don't watch football much, do you?'

He shook his head.

'I'm a failure as a man by most standards,' he said in a deadpan voice, without a trace of a smile.

'Which of the standards aren't you a failure at?' I asked.

'I don't think I know you well enough to tell you that,' he said.

He turned and looked out the window, the trace of a private smile breaking his perfect jawline as if he were remembering a moment from his past.

My mind focused on the image of a bomb being placed somewhere as we spoke. I reached out and took hold of the steering wheel with both hands and gripped it tightly like it was the seat bar on a roller coaster.

'A stadium would be easy to secure in comparison to an entire parade route. If I'm wrong, there's no way we can adequately secure both sites.'

The smile on Harrison's face vanished. He looked down at his hands resting in his lap as if questioning something about them. I couldn't help but wonder if they had held his wife as she died. Did he look upon them as failures for not being able to save her? And was that why he was in the bomb squad, to test those hands again and again against bombs that could take his own life with the smallest slip?

Harrison looked up from his hands and out the front of the car.

'It's more complicated than that,' he said.

I turned to him, waiting for him to finish the thought.

'There's no way to secure either the parade or the game, not with this explosive,' he said. 'That's what's complicated.'

We both sat silently for a moment as the reality of what we were facing settled over us like a shroud.

'Then we have to approach this from a different direction.'

'Which?'

'Why . . .' I corrected him softly. 'That's the doorway into this. We figure that out, or we don't have a prayer.'

Harrison picked right up on the thought. 'What battle is he fighting?'

'Or whose? Is it personal or political?' I said.

'Knowing how much explosive he brought in from Mexico would tell us a lot,' Harrison said.

'Meaning, if it's a relatively small amount, he could be after an individual. And if it's a large amount, he's after something bigger?'

'Yeah,' Harrison said. 'So where do we begin?'

I thought for a moment, trying to take hold of the flood of thoughts and emotions rolling through me like waves.

'We go through a list of the participants in the parade, start with the obvious targets: politicians, celebrities, prominent businessmen, work our way down.'

'What else?'

'Everything he's done so far has been to cover his tracks. That means the man in the casting pond, Finley, and Sweeny knew something that put him at risk, so he killed them. Except he made a mistake with Sweeny at the bungalow and got Traver instead. We need to find him.'

'What about Finley's partner, Breem?'

'You mean why wasn't he killed at the flower shop that night?'

He nodded.

Breem? I thought. That had bothered me since I watched the tape of Finley being shot in the back of the head. Was Breem just a lucky guy? Or was it something else?

'He either knew nothing, or he's a part of it.'

Harrison nodded in agreement.

'Let's talk to Finley's wife, and then we'll talk to Breem,' I said.

My cell rang inside my jacket pocket and I pulled it out.

'Delillo.'

'Lieutenant, Officer James.'

I suddenly forgot all about Breem and Finley and the bright red sweater in the dark water of the pond. Even the bomber vanished from my consciousness.

'Did you find her?' I asked.

'We covered every Starbucks in Pasadena – nothing. I

put out a call on her car, and have a squad at your house. I'll let you know as soon as she turns up.'

'Turns up,' I said silently to myself. 'Turns up' implies she's missing. I felt goose bumps rise on my forearm. I wanted to ask more questions to find a way to erase those words.

'She's probably just at . . .' I let it go. I didn't know how to finish the sentence. I didn't know where she would go. Which was just another item to add to the list of what I didn't know about my own daughter.

'Thanks,' I said and hung up.

I sat there for a moment listening to the pounding of my heart in my chest. I felt entirely inadequate for every task I had facing me. It was all happening too fast. I was no good as a detective, no good as a mother.

'Your daughter?' Harrison asked.

My daughter? My voice caught with just the words.

'Yeah' was all I could manage. I took a deep breath, held it for a moment, then let it slip out. 'There've been some threats because of the pageant thing. We're trying to locate her.'

'Is she missing?'

I looked straight ahead without taking in anything I was looking at. 'The principal sent her home without contacting me.'

'He shouldn't have done that.'

I shook my head.

'If there's anything I can do.'

'I'm thinking of driving over to the school and putting my gun against his head so he'll know exactly how I feel right now.'

86

'I could hold him for you,' Harrison said.

I glanced at Harrison and tried to smile, but only made it about halfway, so I turned and looked out my window. A man in a yellow running suit was jogging by with a golden retriever. I noticed his left leg swung loosely out wide as if he wasn't in complete control of where it would settle with each step. The detective in me began to construct a story about what had happened to him, but the mother in me took over and I saw Lacy as a two-year-old taking her first awkward steps.

'Why is it there's never enough time to do the things we most care about correctly and always enough time to excel at the things that don't matter,' I said, glancing at Harrison.

The look on his face told me he was unsure if a response was required.

'I'm not actually looking for an answer, Detective,' I said. 'I'm just talking. Kids will do that to you.'

I imagined Traver would have smiled broadly and said, 'Don't you love it.'

Harrison's eyes drifted away to some distant point beyond vision. I noticed the thumb on his left hand moving back and forth across the base of his ring finger as if his wedding band were still on it.

'I'm the wrong person to ask about time, Lieutenant.'

six

If it's possible for a house to take on the character of tragedy, Daniel Finley's green Craftsman bungalow appeared to have the soul of a broken heart. The blinds were drawn on all the windows. Flower boxes lining the front porch hadn't been watered in what appeared to be weeks, impatiens hung limply down the sides. The grass was long and unruly. The overhanging roof appeared to be trying to shield the occupants from the outside world.

I stopped on the sidewalk before walking up to the front door and took it in.

'Something's wrong with this,' I said.

Harrison looked the house and yard over. 'Wouldn't you expect this?'

'Finley died two days ago; this has been unattended for more than a week. Why would a man whose business was flowers let a place go to seed?'

Harrison got it. 'His mind was on other things.'

'And it worried him to the point of all this.'

We walked up to the oak front door. A small, beveled window at eye level had a green paisley curtain drawn over it on the inside. The doormat read 'Welcome. Think Green.' As I reached out to ring the bell, I noticed the wood of the door frame next to the handle had a slim, barely noticeable crack in it.

'This door's been jimmied,' I said.

I tested the handle and it was unlocked.

'Don't open that,' Harrison said, his voice flush with tension.

My hand felt as if it were holding a stick of dynamite.

'Keep your hand on the knob and step to the side,' he said, then knelt down and examined the jamb where it had been jimmied. 'It's possible you've just completed a circuit. Letting go would set it off.'

'It?' I said. Then it dawned on me. 'You mean a bomb.'

'He's used doors before,' Harrison said.

'Are we being a bit paranoid?'

'I once found a bomb inside a cookie jar. In my world there's no such thing as paranoia.'

The handle of the door seemed to be growing hot in my hand.

'You have a suggestion?' I said, stretching out as far away from the door handle as I could go.

'I could go around back and enter, but that would only delay the inevitable.'

'Which is?' I said.

'If there is a device, I doubt I would be able to disarm it without breaking the circuit.'

'I don't have a real firm grasp on electricity,' I said. 'What exactly are you saying?'

90

Harrison got up from his knees and moved to the other side of the door frame across from me.

'I think you should just run the risk.'

'The what?'

'It's what we do in the squad when we're out of other options.'

'That sounds suspiciously like being a parent,' I said.

'When you're ready, let go as quickly as you can.'

'You're sure?'

Harrison looked at me, his green eyes unblinking, his face betraying no emotion at all.

'Trust me . . . do it.'

I inched a little farther from the door and tried to let go, but my fingers wouldn't cooperate. My jaw tightened, the knuckles on my fingers holding the handle were turning white. My hand felt as if it were holding a hot coal.

'Let go?' I said. 'A boy genius like you ought to be able to do better than that.'

'Let go,' Harrison said.

I looked away, gently began to release the tension in my fingers, and then pulled my hand away as quickly as I could. In my mind I could still hear the sound of the blast that injured Dave. I could still feel the rush of air and broken glass knocking me to the ground. The silence surrounding us now felt unnatural, as strangely unnerving in its own way as the blast from an explosion. I turned to Harrison and saw him breathe a sigh of relief, then smile.

'This happens all the time on the squad,' he said.

'It never happens in Homicide,' I said, taking my first breath in what felt like several minutes.

I reached out to take a hold of the handle again and involuntarily hesitated just before my fingers touched it.

'Why don't we ring the bell,' I said.

I pushed it and heard the chime inside the house followed by the rush of footsteps and something crashing to the floor.

'The back door!' I said to Harrison as I grabbed the door handle and flung it open. Harrison had already cleared the porch and was heading around back as I drew my gun and stepped in.

It was dark inside. It took a moment for my eyes to adjust from the brightness of the sunlight. And then I saw that the floor of the living room was littered with the ransacked contents of a desk.

'Police!' I yelled.

To the left were stairs to the second floor. I listened for a moment and heard nothing. I moved inside toward a hallway lined with framed photographs, the wooden floor creaking under my weight. On either side of the hallway was a door, each closed. I stopped again and listened for any hint of sound but heard nothing. From the back of the house, I could hear Harrison trying to force open the back door. I looked at the doors on either side of me. I raised my gun, reached out, and tested the door on the right. The handle didn't move; it was locked. I looked over my shoulder at the other door and began to reach for the handle.

The door on the left flung violently open, its heavy oak knocking me back into the other door handle, which hit my ribs like a baseball bat. I felt a sharp bolt of pain spreading out across my body from the point of impact as if I had had a heart attack. My knees buckled. My gun slipped from my hand and landed on the floor with a thud. I tried to call to Harrison but could only gasp as I tried to get air into my lungs. I saw a figure move out of the closet, momentarily stepping through a ray of light cutting into the darkness from the open front door. And then the dark shape of the door swung at me again. I tried to raise my left hand in defense, but the door was already on top of me, striking me in the side of the face.

I fell back against the wall and slipped slowly down to the floor and onto my hands and knees. The side of my face was numb from the blow. It tingled like a leg that has gone to sleep. I was cut somewhere, probably the stitches I had already taken from the explosion. I could feel the dampness of blood on my tongue and slipping down my chin. The odor of aged varnish from the wood of the door hung in my mouth as if I had taken a bite out of it. I looked down and saw my gun lying within reach, but I couldn't make any part of me move toward it. The edges of my vision began to cloud as I slipped toward the tunnel of unconsciousness.

I sensed the attacker step up beside me. I saw his dark boots out of the corner of my eye and thought, This is how I die. Just like this, on my hands and knees. Shit. I wasn't frightened or angry. I wasn't searching my life for moments of regret. I was embarrassed.

'I'm sorry,' came a soft voice.

I flinched, expecting another blow, and then nothing came. Jesus, what is he waiting for? I waited and waited and then the tunnel of unconsciousness closed in on me in a cascade of colors like a child's kaleidoscope.

It was a voice that brought me back. It was distant at first, as if someone were whispering from the other end of a long hallway. I couldn't make out the words, but it was enough for me to follow. The voice called again and again, and then finally I could make it out.

'Mom,' Lacy said. 'Mom.'

The tunnel began to open. Light began to filter in.

'Lacy,' I think I said.

The light began to come faster and then the image of a face appeared right in front of mine. It was soft at first, out of focus.

I said, 'Lacy,' again.

My eyes blinked and the softness of the face began to sharpen. I could see the mouth move as if talking, but I heard nothing. I blinked again and tried to force my eyes to focus.

'Lieutenant,' Harrison said.

I slipped out of the tunnel and found myself on the floor of the hallway, propped against the wall. Harrison's hand was on my shoulder, steadying me so I wouldn't fall over onto my side.

'Can you hear me, Lieutenant?'

I looked at Harrison, and then up and down the hallway trying to orient myself. My eyes stopped on the heavy oak door of the closet.

'Oh, yeah,' I whispered, finally placing myself. I remembered the sound of the door hitting my face.

'Are you all right?'

The floor seemed to float like water for a moment, then it settled.

'They made very solid houses back then.' I looked at Harrison. 'I heard my daughter's voice . . . she was . . .'

Harrison looked at me and shook his head. 'It's just me. I'm sorry I couldn't get through the back door. I had to come through a window.'

I looked at the floor and my gun was still there.

'He left my gun,' I said, half surprised.

'Did you get a look at him?'

I tried to replay the events in my head, but it came slowly. It was like trying to put tape back in a cassette that had spilled out onto the floor. I remembered the door, the handle digging into my ribs.

'I dropped my gun when I hit the door handle . . . Then the other door hit me.'

The side of my face throbbed and I felt unsteady. I remembered the smell of varnish in my mouth. I reached up and touched my lip, and my fingers came away bloody.

'He said he was sorry,' I said. I was angry. The last thing you want from someone bashing your brains in is kindness. 'How long have I been sitting here?'

'You've been drifting in and out for a few minutes. I checked out front, he was already gone,' Harrison said. 'If he drove away I didn't see a car.'

My head cleared as if I had just stepped out of a heavy fog.

'I saw him,' I said. 'He stepped into the shaft of light from the doorway.'

'Can you ID him?' he asked.

I reached out, picked up my Glock, and slid it back into my belt holster. I then took hold of Harrison's shoulder and raised myself to my feet.

'It was Sweeny,' I said.

Harrison looked at me as if trying to decide if my judgment had been affected from the knock on the head.

'From the bungalow? You're sure?'

I nodded. 'I think he was looking for something; he rifled a desk.'

'I'll go call it in.'

'Shit.' A voice came from the front door.

We both turned and saw a woman holding a packet of information from a funeral home.

'I saw your car with the radio. I assume you're policemen.'

'Mrs Finley,' I said.

She nodded. She had short dark hair, pale skin, and wore black jeans and a black sweater that, if worn anyplace other than Southern California might be taken as a statement of mourning. She was younger than her late husband. I put her in her mid-thirties. Beneath the exhausted look of someone who had dealt with death for two days, she had the face of a free spirit, pretty, hanging on to youth with every muscle in her body.

She looked into the living room and saw the contents of the desk spread out on the floor. 'What happened?'

'You've been burglarized.'

Her shoulders sank ever so slightly, and she took a deep breath. 'That's great.'

'It's not unusual for this to happen after a tragedy.

They follow things like that in the paper,' I said, not wanting to draw too much attention to it.

She looked down at the folders from the funeral home she was holding in her hands.

'I guess they know you won't be around,' she said angrily.

'I'm Lieutenant Delillo. I'm investigating your husband's murder. This is Detective Harrison. I would have talked to you yesterday, but that wasn't possible.'

Mrs Finley walked in and tossed the packet from the funeral home onto the dining-room table with the rest of the junk mail that had piled up. She sat down and looked at me. I took a chair on the other side of the table.

'You have blood on you,' she said, looking flushed.

I reached up and wiped it off my chin.

'We surprised him,' I said.

'Looks like you're the one who was surprised, Lieutenant.'

She looked at me for a moment, her eyes reflecting someone who had used up all the emotions she had stored and had nothing left. What could possibly surprise a person whose husband had just been gunned down?

'I'm sorry. Can I get you something?' she asked.

'I'm fine,' I lied.

'You don't look fine. Trust me, I'm an expert on the subject,' she said.

She got up and walked into the kitchen, returning a moment later with a damp towel wrapped around ice cubes.

I thanked her and placed it gingerly against the side of my face.

'Have you found the man who killed my husband?' she said.

I lifted the towel from my face. 'No.'

'Is that to be expected?' she asked.

I wanted to drift away into the cool ice I was holding against the side of my face. I wanted to find my daughter, I wanted to sleep, I wanted to be anywhere but right where I was. For the first time in my entire career, the thought entered my mind that my mother may have been right about me becoming a cop. I glanced at Harrison, who saw in my eyes that I wanted him to take it.

'Did anything different happen to your husband over the last couple of weeks?' Harrison asked.

'I don't understand,' Mrs Finley said.

'Did he seem upset or talk about something unusual at the shop?'

She shook her head. 'I don't believe so.'

Throbbing pain rolled across my cheek like a wildfire. It was all I could do to stay upright in the chair.

'Why are you asking these questions?' Mrs Finley asked. 'I thought my husband was killed in a robbery.'

'We're exploring every possibility,' Harrison said.

'What other possibilities are there?'

'This happens in every homicide, Mrs Finley,' I said. 'It's part of the process of every investigation. We look into everything, regardless how small.'

'I wouldn't know,' she said in resignation.

'Do you know an employee of the shop named Sweeny?' I asked.

'I don't think . . .' She thought for a moment, then shook her head. 'No, I never met him. He must have been a temp.'

I stood up and motioned toward the door to Harrison.

'Would you let us know if anything is missing after the burglary, or if you find something you don't expect?' I said, handing her my card.

She nodded without interest.

'You can keep the towel, Lieutenant,' she said.

I thanked her and started out the door, then stopped when I looked out into the yard.

'Why is the yard in the shape it is?' I asked, turning back to Mrs Finley.

She looked at me, puzzled by the question, then made the connection to what I was asking.

'Oh . . . that,' she said. 'Daniel's philosophy was changing.'

Harrison looked over to me and shrugged in confusion.

'I'm not following you,' I said.

'He was getting rid of the lawn, going organic . . . native grasses.'

I glanced down at the doormat.

'Think green,' I said.

Mrs Finley's eyes moistened with tears as she nodded. I turned and walked out of the house and into the yard. The sun appeared unnaturally bright after being in the dark house. When I slipped on my sunglasses the frame touched the side of my face where the door had hit me, and sent another wave of pain through my head. I put the ice back against my face and the pain began to pass.

'Does it seem odd to you that in a business with only three employees she didn't know Sweeny?' Harrison said.

I glanced back at the house. 'Not if she was lying.'

'You think she was lying?'

'The other two employees are women. How did she know Sweeny was a man?'

I glanced one more time around the yard and realized there was one other thing that troubled me. He was changing his philosophy, going green, the same conversion my daughter had just 'leaped' into with both feet and a spray bottle. I searched my memory trying to come up with something that would dismiss this entire line of thinking as the feverish worries of a mother who might just have suffered a concussion. I missed the mark. I remembered the carved wooden sign on the front door of Breem's flower shop instead. GREEN IS OUR COLOR.

'Goddamnit,' I whispered to myself.

'What?' Harrison asked.

'I'm thinking too much. It's nothing.'

My heart skipped a beat. There was no such thing as coincidence, not when murder was involved. I didn't want to believe it, couldn't believe it. Every dogma eventually runs smack into the reality of the exception to the rule. This had to be it, must be it. The dots we had been connecting were not going to include my daughter.

Throw a stick in California you'll probably hit an environmentalist. Forget it.

'You don't look so good, Lieutenant,' Harrison said.

'I'm a little light-headed.'

I walked out of the yard and over to the passenger side of the car.

'You better drive,' I said.

'I think you should see a doctor,' Harrison said.

Absolutely, I thought. I wanted to disappear in a nice fat hospital bed, drift away in Demerol. I took the ice off the side of my face and looked at Harrison.

'So he can tell me I have to lie in bed for forty-eight hours? I don't think we have that kind of time.'

I tossed him the keys. 'Unless you want to lead the investigation by yourself?'

Harrison's eyes did a little dance and then he shook his head. 'I don't think so.'

I checked my watch; it was twelve-thirty. The day wasn't half over and we had already found another body, my daughter's life had been threatened, I was entertaining thoughts that she was somehow remotely connected to the rest of the investigation, and I had been hit in the side of the head with a slab of oak from the Arts and Crafts movement.

I got in the car and sank back into the seat. Harrison walked around and slid in behind the wheel. The jolt from the closing of the door went through my head like another shot from Sweeny.

'Sorry,' Harrison said, seeing the corners of my mouth wince from pain.

'Call Fraser and get them over here to execute the

101

search warrant. If Sweeny didn't find what he was looking for, I want to.'

'Where we going?'

'My daughter's school. I'm supposed to meet her there at . . .' I checked myself. 'She'll be there at one.'

seven

Principal Parks was in his late forties, with the trim build of a runner. He favored the pressed collars of Brooks Brothers to the casual dress most of his teachers wore. Whatever high-minded tone he may have contemplated using with me vanished the moment I walked into his office and he saw my bruised face and the blood on my shirt collar. Nothing kills a party like blood.

He stood dumbfounded for a moment like a passing motorist staring at a wreck.

'Have you had an accident?' he asked.

'Yes,' I said. 'I was hit with a door.'

He seemed to have trouble getting his mind around what I assumed was a first for a parent conference.

'A Craftsman door,' I said, trying to sharpen his understanding.

He sat silently for a moment, then seemed to have a breakthrough.

'I love Green and Green,' he said, as if we were on a

103

walking tour of Pasadena's most famous Arts and Crafts houses and he was trying to impress me with his knowledge of these two architects. The absurdity of his words struck him a second later and he added, 'If you would like to do this another time . . .'

'This is the only time I have,' I said.

His eyes looked as if they were pleading for me to leave his office until it dawned on him I wasn't moving.

'Did you bring Lacy?' he asked.

'No one has seen my daughter since you sent her home,' I said.

'I don't understand.'

'What part of "No one has seen her" do you not understand?' I replied.

He shifted uneasily in his chair.

'I'm sure it's just a misunderstanding.'

I wanted to agree with him, I wanted to agree with him more than I've wanted anything in my entire life.

'I'm not sure,' I said.

Parks stared at me like someone who had drifted off the map with no idea where he was headed. Rather than talk, he sat strangely quiet, shuffling papers and occasionally glancing at my gun as we waited for Lacy.

Ten minutes after one, he finally spoke up.

'Is she often late?' he asked nervously.

In truth she was chronically late, but I didn't think that was it, no matter how much I wanted it to be.

'No,' I said.

My imagination began to outpace actual events, leading me down paths every mother has visited in nightmares, but thankfully very few ever visit in reality.

Why had she spoken to me when I was drifting in and out of consciousness at Finley's? Was she reaching out to me? Was she calling for help? I began to search madly for meaning in things where none could possibly be found. I replayed the phone conversation I had had with her in my office, examining every word for something guarded or hidden. I tried to picture how much gas was in her car, what clothes she had chosen that day, what coffee she had ordered at Starbucks, as if they would all lead to her walking through the office door.

Five minutes passed and Parks began checking his watch. Two minutes after that he cleared his throat and tentatively spoke.

'Maybe we should discuss a few things before she arrives.'

It was nearly twenty after. Lacy was never that late.

'She isn't coming,' I said almost involuntarily. The sound of the words coming out of my mouth startled me as if they had been said by someone else. What remained was why? Why wasn't she here? A cop immediately assumes the worst. But I was a mother now clinging to every other possible explanation. That was unthinkable. I took out my cell phone and called home. With each ring I would silently repeat, 'Answer it, answer it, answer it,' like a mantra.

The machine picked up.

'If you're there, honey, please pick up,' I said. 'Lacy, pick up the phone, come on, it's me . . .'

I waited until I ran out of tape, then I retrieved the messages in case she had called. There were three more calls from reporters, and then a voice that sent chills through me.

'Your daughter is a cunt.'

It sounded middle-aged, white, no detectable geographical origin. The residual fog that had engulfed me since I was hit by the door was instantly gone. I turned the phone off. To Park's credit he sensed that I had not gotten good news on the other end of the phone.

'Maybe we should talk to some of her friends, in case she said something to one of them before leaving.'

I looked at him and realized I hadn't heard a word he had spoken.

'I'm sorry . . .' I said.

'Her friends . . . why don't we talk to them?'

I nodded. Yes, that was a good idea. She must have said something. Lacy always had something to say.

'Do you know which friends she would possibly confide in?'

Everything came crashing down.

I looked at Parks and shook my head. I had just failed my daughter again.

'I don't know any of her friends . . . I should . . . but I . . .'

Parks stepped in. 'Maybe just a first name? We can figure out the rest.'

I looked at him for a moment and realized that this was not the first time he had had this conversation with a parent who has just discovered her child is a stranger. I felt pathetic. I had no excuses.

I frantically searched every crevasse in my memory and finally stumbled across a name.

'Carrie,' I said. 'She knows someone named Carrie.'

Parks buzzed his secretary, who walked in a moment later.

'Karen, we need to find a senior or a junior named Carrie.'

'There're three. Only one is a senior – Carrie Jacobson.'

'Would you find out what class she's in and bring her here.'

As she walked out I called Officer James and told her that Lacy had not shown up at school.

'I'll give the surrounding departments a description of her car,' she answered.

She then tried to find something encouraging to say. 'You know how kids are, Lieutenant. She's probably at a movie.'

'I have a voice recorded on my phone machine,' I said.

There was a pause on the other end of the line as she played that out.

'If it comes to that it might be useful, Lieutenant, but for right now—'

'I'm not a civilian, Officer,' I said.

'No . . . but you are a mother.'

I turned the phone off as Carrie Jacobson was escorted in by the secretary. I thought I would be able to tell just by looking at her if she was a friend of my daughter's, but quickly realized I was clueless again. She wore no makeup, had two piercings in her left ear, and blond hair with a streak of lime green down the right side. The soles of her tennis shoes looked to be four inches high.

Parks did the introductions, but I cut him off.

'Are you a friend of Lacy's?' I asked.

Her eyes moved guardedly back and forth between Parks and me. I could only imagine what she had heard about me from Lacy. Mom the cop. A teenager's worst nightmare. Her eyes froze on the blood on my shirt and then traveled reluctantly up to the bruising on my face as if she didn't want to see the source of the blood.

'Oh, God, did something happen?' she said, her voice shaken.

Parks looked over to me with no idea how to respond. I moved my chair closer to Carrie, trying to act as much as I could like a mother instead of a cop. The blood clearly made it a stretch. That, and I was out of practice.

'I had some trouble, but it had nothing to do with Lacy.' Which as far as I knew was still the truth. I hoped to God, anyway, it was still the truth.

'You're a friend, I've heard her say your name,' I said. She nodded uneasily.

'Did you talk to Lacy before she left school today?' She shook her head.

'Is she in trouble?' she asked.

'She may be in danger. I need to find her. Did she talk to you or anybody about where she might be going?'

'What kind of danger?'

'Someone may be trying to hurt her.'

I saw hesitation in her eyes, as if betrayal was the first thing she thought of.

'Someone's threatened her, someone possibly very dangerous.'

Her shoulders sank toward the floor, the color in her face drained away.

'All she said was . . .' Her eyes darted toward Parks, then away. ' "Those fucking assholes" . . . that's all . . . Is she going to be all right?'

I looked over at Parks. The anger that I had felt toward him began to rise back to the surface. I clenched my teeth, trying my best not to say something I would probably regret later, then turned back to the girl.

'She was talking about Principal Parks?' I asked.

'Yeah,' she said, as if annoyed by the obviousness of the question. 'She just came from his office; she was really pissed. I mean, all she did was make a political statement and she was kicked out of school so the administration can look like they're doing something to the people who are pissed about what Lacy did.'

'That's enough, young lady,' Parks said.

I looked over at him.

'The time for Mr Parks to explain himself will come.' I turned back to Carrie. 'Right now my only concern is Lacy's safety.'

She nodded.

'Did she mention any other names?'

She took a nervous breath and nodded.

'What other names?' I asked.

She looked me right in the eye. 'Yours.'

'What did she say?'

Carrie didn't flinch. 'She said, "Like my mother's going to do something about it." '

I found myself liking this generation in ways I wasn't aware of before. If this girl and my daughter were

109

examples of their strength of character, I figured they'd be all right. They'd survive the piercings, the tattoos, and the sherbet-colored hair. Their parents, on the other hand, and their whole self-absorbed generation, seemed entirely hopeless. I was an expert on that.

'Did she mention any names in connection with what she did at the pageant? Someone maybe you've never heard of?'

She shook her head. 'I didn't even know about it.'

She smiled when she said that. She wasn't lying. She took pride in Lacy's ability to have kept what she did a secret. I found myself feeling the same thing.

Carrie glanced defiantly at Parks. 'I think what she did was awesome.'

'So do I,' I said to Carrie.

The ability of my daughter to inspire a friend like this only increased my sense of desperation. I could hear a clock beginning to tick away the seconds in my head. Things were spinning out of control and I felt helpless to do a goddamn thing.

'Is there any place where she would go that we should look for her?'

She hesitated, still wrestling with trusting me.

'Please, Carrie, I need your help.'

She nodded. A wave of relief flooded my body.

'Starbucks.'

My heart sank. With one word my options had vanished.

'Shit,' I said involuntarily.

Carrie's surprise at my reaction served to increase her understanding that Lacy was in real danger.

'I'm sorry,' she whispered.

'If you can think of anything else, or if you hear from her, call me at this number,' I said, handing her a card.

Her fingers tried to slip quickly out of my hand like a hummingbird darting away from a flower, but I gently took hold of her hand before she could pull away. I looked down at the flawless, smooth skin. There wasn't a line or a crack; time hadn't touched her yet. I gripped her hand as if I were holding my daughter's.

'No more secrets, okay?' I said weakly.

She looked down at my hand for a moment, then into my eyes. 'Lacy's smart. She'll be all right.'

I started to respond, but the words caught in my throat and all I could manage was a feeble nod.

'You can go back to class,' Parks said.

She glanced at me and I nodded.

Almost imperceptibly her fingers slipped out of my hand and she was out of the room. I sat motionless for a moment, my mind unable to focus on anything. It was the same sensation I remember feeling when we buried Lacy's father. A disbelief, a terrible sense that there was no one there to help me. I saw Harrison step up to the glass door and knock. His presence reminded me that I wasn't there just as a mother, there was a madman out there with a bomb.

'You have a call,' he said, holding up a phone.

I looked at the phone in his hand as if I had never seen one before. Harrison saw the confusion in my eyes.

'I think you better take it,' he said, his tone leaving little doubt that this couldn't wait.

I glanced at Parks, wanting to say something, but

found there wasn't a single word in my vocabulary that fit what I was feeling.

'I'll take it in the hallway,' I said, getting up and following Harrison toward the door.

'Ms Delillo—' Parks said.

With the sound of his voice, I found the words that had eluded me before. I stopped at the doorway and turned.

'If my daughter is injured or hurt in any way,' I said, looking him in the eye, 'I will charge you.'

I could see the color leave his face. He appeared to shrink in his Brooks Brothers as if it were two sizes too big for him. I glared at him for a moment, then turned and walked out into the hallway next to the school's trophy case.

'It's Detective Fraser,' Harrison said, holding out the phone.

I took it and answered.

'Delillo.'

'You're not going to like this, Lieutenant. I don't like it.'

I wasn't in the mood for a riddle.

'Just tell me what the hell you found, Fraser.'

'We were going through Breem's phone records. He made three calls to your home number.'

I heard the words, but they still had a quality of unreality.

'My number?' I asked, just to be sure I had heard him correctly.

'Yeah, the last one was the night Daniel Finley was shot at the florist's.'

The words hit me harder than the door that had just knocked me senseless a few hours before. The phone records had just loosely linked my daughter to the business partner of Daniel Finley, who had a bullet tear through the back of his head. I didn't know in what way or how, but another dot had just been connected. I quickly tried to play it out in my head as to why she would have talked to Breem. There had been calls from a florist about her corsage for the pageant. That could be it, that is, if I was willing to forget the idea that there is no such thing as a coincidence. But even if I did buy that, which I didn't, it didn't explain why Breem would have called her the night of the murder. How had a green revolution and a loaded spray bottle become connected to multiple murders?

My mind began to fill with possibilities, one of which stuck harder than the others. If this connection to Finley's killing was real, even if tenuous, then the threat to my daughter had nothing to do with her disrupting the pageant. There was no middle-aged white male filled with rage, at least not one who was an actual threat. If Lacy was in danger, then the threat was from a man who had already killed two people and probably would kill again.

'Where's Breem?' I asked.

There was no response from Fraser.

'Do you have Breem?' I said impatiently.

'No,' Fraser said.

'Why not?' I asked.

Fraser mumbled something under his breath that I think was 'Shit.'

'His wife said he left the house before dawn. We don't

know where he is now.' He hesitated. 'You want to tell me why a suspect in a murder called your number three times?'

I never liked Fraser. He was to police work what Hamburger Helper was to the food pyramid. He was what you used when you ran out of imagination. I ignored his question, even though it was the same one I was asking.

'See if he made any calls to the other contestants in the pageant,' I said.

I could almost hear the grinding of gears as he worked it out in his head.

'Your daughter?' Fraser said. 'She was a—'

'My daughter,' I said, 'is missing.'

I hung up and turned to Harrison, who was standing in front of the trophy case. Only then did I notice the 8x10 photograph next to the small gold trophy in the shape of a book instead of a tennis racket or a football. City debating team champs. Lacy was in the picture, second on the right, a wry smile on her face, staring at the camera as if she knew some hidden secret. She had joined the team about the same time she decided to try out for the pageant. I had missed the final debate for the championship because I had been investigating the beating to death of a transient.

Harrison noticed me staring at it, though he didn't know why.

'That's my daughter, second from right,' I said.

He stared at it for several moments, his eyes covering every inch of the frame as if deconstructing an explosive.

'She looks like you,' Harrison said.

'No,' I said, 'she's beautiful.'

My cell rang and I picked up.

'Delillo.'

'It's James, Lieutenant.'

There was a pause on the other end. 'We found her car.'

I waited for her to finish but she didn't.

'Just her car?' I asked.

'Yeah,' she said.

'What else did you find?' I asked, already sliding toward panic.

'The doors were locked, her keys were in it . . . a window was smashed.'

I tried to hang on to being a cop even as my hand began to shake.

'Which window?'

'Driver's side,' she said flatly.

'Where?' I asked.

James began to answer, but my hand dropped to my side and the phone slipped out of my fingers and fell to the floor. I moved my hand up to my mouth to suppress the urge to vomit. My knees began to sink out from under me. There was no up, no down. The one and only thing that centered me on this planet had just been wrenched right out of my arms. No door could have hit me as hard as the words she had just spoken. I was halfway to the floor when Harrison reached out and took hold of my arm to steady me.

'Oh, Lacy,' I whispered.

'What is it?' Harrison said, though the words drifted by me without understanding.

I gripped his arm and regained my balance.
'What's happened?' Harrison said.
'They found her car.'

eight

Lacy's yellow Honda was parked on a quiet middle-class residential street with neatly clipped lawns about two miles from the Starbucks where she had called me. There was nothing unusual about the way the car rested next to the curb, no indication that it had been forced to the side of the road. A gardener's leaf blower droned in the distance. The normalcy of the scene only served to heighten my sense of dread.

Harrison pulled our car up behind the squad that was parked in back of her Honda and started to get out.

'I need to just sit here a minute,' I said. The words slipped out of my mouth as if I were out of breath. 'I need to . . .' I stared at the bright yellow of her car. She called it her sunflower.

'I'll look it over. Take your time,' Harrison said.

He closed his door and started toward Lacy's car.

'Make sure the uniforms haven't compromised any prints,' I said, trying to cling to whatever cop instincts remained in me.

That was my baby's car, her shattered window, her . . . I tried desperately not to let my imagination go beyond that. Stop, don't do that, don't go there, this will not help. But it was like trying to hold back the rain with your hands before it hit the ground.

I got out of the car and walked toward her Honda. My mind flashed on the day she brought it home. I had taken a picture of her standing in front of it, holding the registration. The joy on her face was what I imagined birds felt when they discovered flight. How did that joy end up here? How do these things happen? If I had just done one thing differently. If I had just . . .

I was thinking like a victim.

I'd listened to its desperation for years as stunned casualties of crime tried to make sense out of violence by stringing a thread through time so it could be traced to a definable origin. I knew better. It was never just one thing. And even if it was, what would it matter? There was no going back, no fixing wrongs. It was a free fall in the dark with no idea when you would hit bottom.

I walked up beside her car and stopped next to the shards of safety glass that littered the pavement.

'All the doors are still locked,' Harrison said.

I tried to lean in to look through the shattered window, but my body resisted the way it does when approaching the edge of a cliff. I turned away.

'Take a few breaths,' Harrison said. 'Real slow, nice and deep.'

Across the street the large leaves of a banana plant rustled in the slight breeze. Curious bystanders were on

118

the curb watching. I closed my eyes and the sound of the rustling leaves was replaced by the shattering of glass.

'She was pulled out through the broken window,' I said.

Harrison nodded.

'God,' I whispered. My stomach began to heave and I turned and walked over to a hedge of rosemary and vomited.

'Oh, God,' I whispered.

I tried to let go of the image but it was too vivid. I could see the hands grabbing her hair and her shirt as she tried to fight them off. I could see her feet struggling to grip the steering wheel as she was pulled out.

I heard the crunch of gravel as Harrison walked up behind me. He stood there for a moment in silence, then spoke up.

'You all right?'

I nodded. I had been to a thousand crime scenes. I'd looked into the faces of countless victims' relatives whose hearts had been shattered by violence. We told them we understood, we held their hands, but we never let ourselves feel, we never let ourselves see the world with their eyes. But now I was one of them. I could see it in the way the other cops looked at me. Be wary, don't get too close. I had stepped across the yellow tape and was standing on the other side now – a victim.

Two more uniformed units pulled up. A young woman sergeant walked directly over to me.

'You're Officer James?' I said.

She nodded. 'I'm so sorry, Lieutenant.'

She motioned with her finger toward her lip. I

reached up and wiped away some vomit from the corner of my mouth.

'We need more units to canvass for witnesses,' I said.

'They're on the way. So is crime scene.'

'Put a tap on my phone in case . . .' I couldn't finish the thought.

'We'll take care of it,' Harrison said.

I looked into her face. She was probably late twenties but appeared barely older than Lacy. Her blond hair was tucked neatly behind her ears, which were pierced with a simple silver ring. She had bright blue eyes, two rings on her right hand, nothing on her left.

God, I was already a mother at her age.

'Whatever it takes, Lieutenant, we'll do it,' James said.

It was what cops say when one of their own is down. I probably said it to Traver in his hospital room, but it just didn't translate to my daughter. James reached out and gripped my hand. The sisterhood of blue. I suppose I was a role model to officers like her. First woman head of Homicide, first this, first that. But I still couldn't protect my own daughter.

'You've been injured,' James said. 'Do you need a paramedic?'

I shook my head weakly, and then she walked away to talk to the other uniforms who were stringing perimeter tape across the street surrounding Lacy's Honda.

I felt lost and out of place. I didn't know how to take the next step. What way, which direction? Some role model. I took a deep breath trying to steady myself. I felt as if the side of my face where the door struck me was glowing like a neon sign. The ground seemed to be opening up beneath me and swallowing me up. I couldn't hold air in my lungs. My heart was racing out of control.

'Work it,' I whispered. Work the scene, the witnesses, work it, work it.

I struggled to take a breath.

'We need a witness,' I said, barely able to finish the sentence before I ran out of air. 'Someone must have seen something, heard something . . . anything.'

Harrison looked back at the car. I could see in his eyes that he was working out something.

'What?'

'I was just thinking,' he said, hesitant to finish the thought.

'Think out loud . . . good or bad.'

He glanced once more at the car.

'There's no sign in the car or on the pavement that she was injured,' he said.

I swallowed heavily, still fighting for air. 'You're saying there's no blood?'

'Yes.'

'Am I supposed to feel better for that?'

He shook his head. 'I'm saying this may not be connected to Finley.'

He was pointing to something that I couldn't see, and it made me angry. I didn't need more unanswered questions. I wanted my daughter back.

'What the hell are you saying?'

'I'm saying everyone else this guy has come in contact with is dead. If this was him, I think Lacy would still be in the car.'

This was moving too fast. I wasn't ready to work a scene, not yet. I couldn't get past the fact that my daughter was gone. Someone had yanked her out the window of her car. I felt helpless. The gun and the badge felt like props, ornaments we hang on ourselves to reassure a frightened public that we know what we're doing. Tears filled my eyes and I turned away.

The street was quickly filling with other black-and-whites. Uniformed cops moved about like a useless, occupying army. I reached up to wipe away a tear and noticed my hand was trembling. I tucked it under my other arm and squeezed my fist trying to wring the fear out of it.

'The phone threats?' I said, looking back at Harrison. 'The middle-aged male Caucasian?'

'It's a possibility.'

'If that's true, then we've just gone from multiple leads to none, a voice on a phone machine . . . nothing,' I said.

'We'll know where he made that call.'

'And that will be a pay phone, if we're lucky, and the one print that will matter won't be on it.'

'The only thing that's certain is that we don't know anything yet, so there's no reason to think the worst.'

'The worst has already happened.'

He shook his head. His eyes drifted into memory for just an instant, then he looked back at me. 'No it hasn't.'

No, the worst hadn't happened. He knew about the worst.

The side of my face began to throb as if current were flowing through it. I walked over to my car, slipped inside, and closed the door and the windows.

'Think,' I whispered. 'Do your job.'

I was pleading with myself, trying to pull myself out of helplessness. There had to be an answer right there in front of me, I just had to see it. It had to be that simple. Every crime always was, it never failed. I tried to take some slow, deep breaths. I closed my eyes, but my mind still raced out of control. It was all tumbling down on top of me, every piece of information from the moment Lacy had screamed 'You're all killers' at an audience who had come to see beauty on parade. There were Breem's phone calls. Finley's orange socks, and a stream of blood. The door swinging toward me. The uncut grass of Finley's yard. The red sweater in the dark water of the pool. Sweeny saying, 'I'm sorry.' The white flash of the explosion. Dave disappearing in the cloud of dust. A car named sunflower. A young bird learning the joy of flight.

A tapping on the window pulled me back. Harrison and James were standing there. I opened the door.

'A woman saw a car driving away shortly after hearing some breaking glass.'

He motioned across the street. 'She's over there.'

I quickly stepped out and started across the street. She was standing on the other side of the yellow tape. She looked sixty, white hair, slacks and a blue sweater with puffy white clouds on it. I wished it had been a man. Men were useful for identifying makes and models of cars, like it's part of their genetic code. Unless it was a kind of car they have driven, women usually give you the color.

She had been watching *Oprah*. She smiled nervously, the way citizens do in the face of this many police.

'Oprah had on a woman who had starved herself nearly to death until she found strength in . . . . I just love Oprah.'

'What did you see outside?'

It surprised her that a discussion of anorexia wasn't germane to the investigation.

'Oh, I see, I'm sorry.'

'That's fine. What did you see?'

'I thought maybe a radio had been stolen when I walked out and saw the broken glass. Then I thought maybe it was just a broken bottle so I didn't call the police. I guess I should have. Is all this about a radio?'

'What did the car look like?' I asked.

She glanced at all the cops on the street. 'Am I in some sort of danger staying here?'

'There's no danger,' James said.

'Tell me about the car,' I said. 'What did you see?'

She took a breath and put her hand over her heart like she was swearing to the truth. 'It was going that way,' she said, pointing north. 'It was white.'

I waited for more, but nothing came.

'Is that all?'

She didn't get it.

'How big was it?'

'Oh . . . small, probably, yes, it was small.'

'Two doors or four?'

'I . . . don't . . . two.'

'Did it have a trunk or hatchback?'

She thought for a moment. 'It was square, hatchback.'

'Make?'

124

She looked at me puzzled, then understood. 'Foreign, I think. Most are, aren't they? I wouldn't know what kind. It looked cheap.'

'New or old?'

'Not new. It wasn't shiny. Could have just been dirty, I guess.'

'How many people inside?'

'I only saw a driver. He had dark hair.'

'Skin color?'

'Couldn't tell.'

'Male or female?'

'Male, I think.'

'You're sure about the dark hair?'

'I think so.'

That was it. The only witness to the kidnapping of my daughter saw a small, white hatchback that was maybe not new, maybe foreign, maybe driven by a man, who might have dark hair.

I walked back to Lacy's car and forced myself to look it over. Maybe I would see something that only I would understand because I'm her mother. Maybe an answer would jump out at me by the sheer force of love. I knew it wouldn't, but I tried anyway.

I knelt next to the open door and looked over every inch of the inside. I could still smell her presence inside, the same as when I had lain down on her bed and she was still there in the fabric of the pillow. She was so close. A plastic sunflower hung from the mirror on a braided yellow and orange cord. An empty Starbucks cup lay on the floor on the passenger side: double mocha latte. The cup was crumpled, the mat was damp

125

with spilled coffee. She had still been drinking it when she was . . . I didn't finish the thought.

Her backpack from school was on the backseat. I opened the glove compartment; taped inside was a photograph of her standing next to her father. She had her arm around him, they both were smiling. He still had his wedding ring on. But I hadn't taken the photograph. I imagined the woman he was having the affair with had been holding the camera, which meant Lacy knew about the affair before I did and she hadn't said anything, not a word to me. It was their secret.

'Anything?' Harrison asked. He was standing over my shoulder.

I closed the glove compartment.

'No,' I said.

I reached into the backseat and pulled out her backpack.

'I want to go over this, go through her phone numbers.'

'If it was the caller who made the threats, then there won't be anything in her book—'

I shot a look at him. 'I need to think that I can do something to bring my daughter back.'

I wanted to be a mother grizzly at that moment, to eliminate doubt.

He nodded. 'We'll bring her back.'

It was the sort of thing my injured partner Traver would have said, except Traver would have believed the words with every cell in his body. Harrison knew better, though he did his best to sell it.

'The description of the car went out; every department has it.'

'If it was the caller who took her, then he'll make contact. He'll make demands, or he'll just boast about it. If it's connected to Finley, we won't hear anything.'

Harrison nodded agreement.

'Then we pray it's not.'

I stepped under the perimeter tape and stopped next to the hood of my car. I had to begin to think like a cop. I couldn't help her if I was thinking like her mother. But it meant I had to let go, if just a little – let her slip through my hands to the column on the report under 'victim.' I clutched her pack in my hands and looked back down the street at her car.

'I'm missing something,' I said.

'You want to go back over it?'

I shook my head. 'What I'm missing isn't here.'

'You lost me,' Harrison said.

I thought for a moment. It was like trying to find my way through a dark room. I began to work backward. There was something I hadn't connected to, hiding in plain sight.

'The car,' I said to myself almost involuntarily.

'What about it?' Harrison asked.

'The white car was a hatchback.'

'Yeah.'

'A Hyundai.'

'She didn't ID a make.'

'I am.'

'I'm not following.'

'The morning after Finley's killing at the flower shop, I was driving home just before dawn. A white Hyundai pulled out and nearly hit me before the driver

127

started delivering *The Star News*. When I opened the garage door and stepped out of the car, the Hyundai was stopped at the bottom of my driveway. When he saw I was looking at him he squealed his tires and raced away.'

'Maybe he saw the photograph of Lacy in the paper?'

'He didn't throw another paper the rest of the street. Why didn't he finish delivering his papers?'

'You think he might have been involved in taking her?'

'We're going to find out.'

'You see him?'

I looked one more time at Lacy's car and tried not to imagine what horror she was going through. It was impossible.

'Yeah, I saw him.'

Officer James walked up with a cell phone in her hand. She hesitated a moment, not wanting to interrupt.

'Dispatch got a call for you from someone who identified themselves as a newspaper deliveryman. Said you would know him, and that he wanted to talk to you about the end of the world. They assumed it was a crank until your daughter was taken.'

'Did he say which newspaper?'

'*The Star News*.'

nine

According to the circulation manager at *The Star News*, the delivery driver who had stopped outside my house and who had apparently just made the call to me was named Philippe Genet. French, he thought, though he wasn't certain. Not many questions are asked in the off-the-books economy. He had worked for them for less than two months. He hadn't talked much. Hadn't made friends. All they really knew about him was that he would work for six dollars an hour.

He had picked up his papers as usual the morning I encountered him, then delivered only eight papers on his route, all on my block, my own being the last one he threw. Eight papers out of nearly four hundred. They hadn't heard from or seen him since. They had no phone number for him, just an address in Hollywood.

The sun was starting to set as Harrison and I drove toward Hollywood on the 134 freeway. Behind us the San Gabriels were aglow in shades of orange and pink. In front of us, the gray line of the ocean stretched across the distant horizon, the buildings of Century City rose, and the vast expanse of greater LA spread out as far as the eye could see to the south past the towers of downtown. Directly in our path Hollywood descended into shadow below the Griffith Observatory and the Hollywood Hills.

I tried to focus on facts, on the pieces of the puzzle that would bring Lacy back, but nothing was falling into place. The florist Breem was still missing. The trace on the ballistics from the gun that killed Daniel Finley had turned up nothing. The missing employee Sweeny was out there. And the Mexican army was a hopeless maze of phone calls and bureaucracy.

I called home on the slim chance and prayer that it had all been a mistake and Lacy was sitting in front of the TV. Even though I knew better, my heart still sank when the machine picked up.

There was a call from a friend of hers about what an asshole Principal Parks was. Another reporter wanted a quote from the 'Green Beauty Queen,' as he called her. And then short of the voice of the person who had pulled Lacy out through the window of her car, I heard the last voice I wanted to hear.

'Alex, it's your mother. I just saw my granddaughter on the news . . .'

There was a pause. I could hear measured breathing as she found just the right words.

'It would have been nice to have learned about this from someone other than Tom Brokaw, but I suppose you have your reasons . . . Call me, if you have time.'

I hung up. Great. I looked at the phone, trying to

figure out how to tell her that her only grandchild had been kidnapped. I punched her number out on the touch pad of the phone but didn't call. Listening to her break into tears wasn't going to help Lacy. And hearing that it was all my fault wasn't going to help me.

'Something?' Harrison asked.

'My . . . It's nothing.'

I took a breath. 'My mother.'

'Forget I asked.'

I slipped the phone back in my pocket and opened Lacy's pack. Her phone book had a black leather cover that had 'Numbers' carved into it. I began looking for the number that didn't fit, or a name that rang an alarm bell. A few names I recognized, but most meant nothing to me. The more I tried to work it, the less I was able to focus. I wanted to hold my daughter. I wanted to be a dysfunctional mother again. I wanted to say the wrong thing just one more time and spend the rest of my life repairing whatever damage I had done to her.

I rolled the window down and closed my eyes, letting the breeze wash over my face. Instead of a moment of peace, my mother's words rushed out of the past on a gust of wind.

'If you become a policeman, you'll ruin your life. I expect something more of you.'

Harrison turned onto Sunset and headed west through the east side of Hollywood. The Walk of Fame was only a couple of miles away, but no stars were remembered here, no tourists snapped pictures. Here there were storefront chapels and transient hotels. The sidewalks were littered with the broken dreams of immigrants who spent their days dodging INS agents and random street crime.

Philippe, the *Star News* delivery driver, lived in a run-down section just a few blocks south of Sunset Boulevard. We found the address and circled the block looking for the Hyundai, but there was no sign of it.

'If Philippe is in his apartment, he didn't drive here,' I said.

Harrison stopped outside the address on Wilcox. It was a three-story, mustard-yellow building with louvered windows. Overflowing garbage cans lined the sidewalk. The charred remains of a Christmas tree lay on the ground next to a dying palm tree that had been spray-painted with gang tags.

I sat there for a moment without making any move to get out of the car. A young Mexican woman was carrying a child across the street. I stared at her for a second, closed my eyes, and imagined my infant in my arms as we went home from the hospital.

'You okay?' Harrison asked.

I slipped back into the present. 'Yeah.'

I don't think I fooled him. His eyes carried the look of a fellow traveler to the 'addiction of memory.' I had known a few men who suffered from it, but not many. Women were better suited to it, I thought. The residue of nurturing.

'I'm okay,' I said.

I looked around to ground myself in the details of my surroundings. Up on the corner of the block, a hooker with a vaguely familiar look eyed our car suspiciously. God, I was sick of people willingly destroying their lives.

It was all too short. Don't we know that, or can we just not stop ourselves?

'She looks like somebody,' Harrison said.

I eyed her for a moment, then nodded. 'Jamie Lee Curtis.'

'Theme hookers?' Harrison said in amazement.

'And she's a guy,' I added.

Harrison looked at me to read whether I was joking. Not that it was a guy, just that it was Jamie Lee.

'*A Fish Called Wanda*?'

I nodded. 'I was in Vice for a month; three of those weeks I spent dressed as Jamie Lee. She has a solid fan base.'

We stepped out of the car and stared at the building.

'Does this strike you as a little serendipitous?' Harrison said.

'No, it strikes me as a setup.'

I don't think my answer was exactly what he wanted to hear since the last two times I had entered a building, one blew up, and in the other a door was slammed into my head.

'What do you want to do?'

I started walking across the street. 'Let's go in.'

Stepping into the apartment building was like walking into the Third World plunked down only two blocks from Ronald Reagan's star on the Walk of Fame.

There were no lights in the hallway. The walls were streaked with stains of God knows what. From an apartment on one side came the wailing of Middle Eastern music. From another, the crying of a baby and salsa music. The place smelled of turmeric and lard and

133

urine. I tried not to imagine Lacy's presence in a place like this. I tried desperately to cling to the image of her lying on her bed, listening to her Walkman, and ignoring my attempts to talk to her.

'Third floor in the back,' Harrison said uneasily. This wasn't territory that the bomb squad visited frequently. Bombs were a high-end crime, the product of education. Why go through the bother of blowing up a place like this when a single match would do just as well?

The second-floor landing was littered with fast-food bags and rat droppings. We moved up to the third floor. There were six apartments, three on each side.

'He's the last one on the right,' Harrison said.

We walked slowly down the hallway, the sound of Iranian and Spanish language television coming from several of the apartments. One of the doors cracked open then just as quickly closed when the occupant recognized us as cops. As we reached the last apartment on the right, I removed my Glock and held it at my side. Harrison glanced at it with a mixture of surprise and apprehension.

'I should—'

I nodded.

He reached down and carefully removed his 9mm like a person picking up an artichoke in the grocery store.

'Take the other side,' I said in a whisper, motioning to the other side of the door.

He took his position and nodded that he was ready. I started to reach for the door handle and then thought of

Dave disappearing in a cloud of dust. My hand stopped short as I looked over to Harrison and then stepped back from the door.

'Assuming the worst, how do we do this without getting blown up?' I asked.

Harrison thought for a second. 'If we had optics we could look under the door.'

I glanced at my watch. It was after five: rush hour.

'How long to get it here?'

'At least an hour in traffic this time of day.'

'What about LAPD?'

'Not much shorter. Bomb squad operates out of the Academy.'

I looked at my watch. With every second she was slipping further away.

'My daughter doesn't have an hour.'

Harrison thought about the problem for a moment, looking at the walls next to the door.

'If it's a shaped charge like the other one, the walls will offer enough shielding. Don't touch the handle. We kick it open and then hug the wall.'

'What if my daughter's inside?'

I could see in his eyes that he didn't want to answer. I'd just put him in the position of being responsible for Lacy's life if he said it was all right to go through the door.

'What was it the caller wanted to talk about? The end of the world?'

'Something like that.'

'This is my call, then, whatever happens.'

'Do you think she's inside?' he asked.

135

I looked at him and then stared at the door. Half of the number on it had fallen off. Dirty handprints lined the edges like fancy stenciling.

'No,' I said. There was no reason for her to be. It would have been much too simple. For whatever reason Lacy was taken, it wasn't to make things less complicated.

'I agree,' Harrison said.

We moved back to the door and took positions to kick it in. Echoing up the stairwell came the shouts of an argument in Spanish. The man's voice sounded drunk, the woman's carried the edge of fear. Outside a car alarm briefly wailed and then fell silent. I nodded to Harrison and counted off . . . 'One, two . . .' With three we kicked.

The door gave way with a splintering of wood and flew open, banging hard against the wall. We hugged the wall for an instant, waiting for the deafening concussion and the whoosh of air to take our breath away.

Nothing.

I swung around and stole a glance into the room with my Glock raised. The fading light barely illuminated the simple, spare room. In one corner a sink and counter served as the kitchen. Opposite that a door led to what must be the bathroom. In the center of the room, in front of the two windows a man sat absolutely still in a chair. I ducked back behind the wall and looked at Harrison. I didn't have to say a word. He could see on my face that something was wrong. The muffled sound of a voice drifted out the door. Harrison raised his gun and looked in the apartment. I could see the surprise register on his face. And then I watched his eyes as they focused in the low light at what sat in the middle of the room. He then retook his position behind the wall.

'Is that the guy you saw delivering the papers?'

I wasn't sure. 'Could be. I need a closer look at him.'

'That might not be a good idea,' Harrison said.

'Why?'

'I think he's wired.'

He took a breath then stole another glance around the door opening.

'We have a problem,' Harrison said.

'A bomb?'

'More than that. I think the opening of the door started a timer.'

'What?'

'There's a timer on his chest. It's counting down.'

He looked at me for a moment, though his eyes were already inside the room working the device.

'I think it's a safe bet he wasn't the one who made that phone call to talk to me,' I said. 'Which means whoever did wanted us in this room with that bomb. His message is beginning to make sense.'

Harrison nodded. 'You don't have to be inside.'

Before I could say anything he quickly got up and went through the door. I went in behind him and swung my weapon left and right, clearing the room, then pushed open the door to the bathroom. It was clear. Harrison went directly to the figure who sat in a chair, explosives wired around his chest.

There were two mattresses on the floor, a cheap television, a prayer mat, and some cardboard boxes with clothes. Against one wall was a cheap chest of drawers and a mirror. The floor was littered with copies of *The Star News*.

I stepped next to Harrison and looked at the frightened face of the man in the chair. He had duct tape around his mouth; otherwise there were no restraints. He could have gotten up and walked away, except that a glass motion detector the size of a double-A battery sat on his lap. It reminded me of a carpenter's level. Two wires led from that to the small plastic circuit box that served as the detonator. There were six sticks of dynamite taped around his chest. A small digital kitchen timer was taped to the center of the sticks. He was well aware that if he had tried to run he would have been blown all over the walls of the room. His dark eyes were wild with fear, pleading for help, his T-shirt soaked with perspiration.

The counter on the timer passed one minute and continued counting down.

'Is your name Philippe?' I asked.

He seemed to nod with his eyes.

'Do you recognize me?'

Again he indicated yes.

Harrison took a Swiss Army knife out of his pocket and calmly opened the scissors. He looked Philippe in the eyes. 'I know you know this, but don't move. If you move we both die.'

Philippe nodded ever so slightly, his forehead wet with sweat.

'What do you want me to do?' I asked.

'Turn on the light.'

I walked over to the switch by the door.

'Make sure the paint on the screw covering the plate hasn't been touched.'

My heart jumped. Until that moment I hadn't fully realized how entirely different someone like Harrison saw the world. Anything could be a weapon. A toaster could kill you, a lightbulb could blow you to pieces, a car could take out an entire block. Nothing was safe. It was all potentially lethal, every knickknack, every inanimate object.

I looked carefully over the cover plate of the switch. The paint was thick in the grooves of the screws.

'The paint's fine.'

'Turn it on.'

I hit the switch and a single bare bulb illuminated the room.

Harrison leaned in close to the explosives and began following the wires with his fingers without touching them.

'What else?' I said.

'I think you should leave.'

I could see panic sweep across Philippe's eyes, pleading not to be abandoned.

'We're all going to walk out of here together, no one's leaving,' I said.

I wasn't sure I believed it, but it had the right effect on Philippe. He nodded, though his eyes still had the wild look of a panicked horse.

The timer hit forty-five seconds and continued its countdown.

Harrison sat back on his heels, studying the problem, his

fingers moving ever so slightly as he traced the imaginary path of detonation.

Thirty-eight seconds.

A heavy truck passed outside, grinding its gears, setting off the wail of a car alarm. Harrison abruptly looked toward the window as the shaking from the truck's passing moved up the walls and spread out across the floor. The motion detector on Philippe's lap began to sway back and forth ever so slightly. The air seemed to disappear from the room. Philippe's already panicked eyes doubled in size. A faint squeal slipped out from under the tape around his mouth.

'Shit, shit, shit,' Harrison said. His hand quickly moved toward the motion detector and stopped just millimeters from it. The tremor in the floor subsided as the truck moved down the street. The motion detector swayed back and forth once more and then settled into place.

The air began to return to the room.

Thirty seconds ticked off.

Harrison reached up and gently took the yellow wires from the motion detector in his fingers, easing the blades of the scissors over them, and snipped them in one quick motion.

'Jesus,' I said, relieved.

The timer clicked off twenty seconds.

'We're not finished,' Harrison said.

The wailing of the car alarm outside sounded like the crazed, night-time laughter of a coyote.

Fifteen seconds.

Harrison gently eased his fingers behind the timer and examined the wiring.

'That's interesting,' he said to himself.

Ten seconds.

He took in his fingers the two wires leading to the detonator. One was black, one red. The car alarm outside fell silent. I could hear my heart beating. He placed the black wire in the blades of the scissors, hesitated for a second, shaking his head, and then snipped it in half.

The red LED numbers of the timer clicked on three seconds and stopped. Harrison looked over to me and smiled, ever so slightly, like a kid who has just aced a test in chemistry. If his blood pressure had risen so much as a point, he gave no indication of it.

'I don't think that was interesting,' I said, getting reacquainted with air in my lungs.

Harrison looked Philippe in the eyes. 'You're fine.'

He quickly cut the tape holding the dynamite to Philippe's chest and slipped it off him like a doctor removing a bandage. Philippe began tearing at the tape around his mouth as if he were suffocating, unraveling it like a turban. The last strip of tape ripped off his cheek with a painful snap. He took no notice, jumped out of the chair and backed away from the dynamite on the floor to the farthest corner of the room. He stood there, frozen with shock for a moment, then raised his hands to cover his mouth and began to sob.

He looked to be in his early thirties, thin, his eyes sunken like those of a child who has not had enough to eat; his hands had long slender fingers. Without the tape I recognized him as the man I had seen in the Hyundai delivering papers.

'Thank you, thank you,' he said between sobs in a subtle French accent.

Harrison was still on his knees examining the device. I walked over and knelt next to him. I could see a question forming in his eyes. 'What?'

He cocked his head as if finding a comfortable place for the thought. 'Given the sophistication of the other device, if he wanted us dead, he wouldn't have made it like this.'

'What are you saying?'

'I could have cut any wire in this device and it would have disarmed it.'

He looked at me with a mixture of either fear or admiration in his eyes, I'm not sure which.

'And that means something?' I asked.

He nodded gravely. 'We're being played with. A phone call to bring us here, then a bomb that doesn't go off. It doesn't make sense. Why bring us here and not kill us.'

'I don't know.'

I turned and looked around the room. The details that I hadn't had time to absorb before began to show themselves. Both mattresses had been slept on, and there were more clothes in the boxes than a single man in a place like this would have worn. Half a dozen pornographic magazines lay next to one of the mattresses. Miss August adorned the wall above the pillows. I walked over to Philippe, who was hugging the corner like a frightened animal.

'Can you identify the man who did this?'

A look of fear flashed in his eyes. He looked toward

the door, the window, any way out of the room would seem to do.

'No, no,' he said, vigorously shaking his head and badly overselling the lie.

'Who is the second mattress for?'

His dark almond eyes that had been nervously moving around the room stopped and focused on me.

'He slept here, didn't he?' I said. 'You know him.'

The truth settled into his face like a flush and he looked down at the floor.

'I wanted to be an American,' he said in a barely audible whisper.

'Did he take my daughter?' I said.

He raised his head and looked at me.

'Did he take my daughter?'

His eyes slowly registered shock as the words began to make sense to him. His mouth opened slightly as if to gasp. He didn't have to answer. He knew nothing.

His eyes filled with tears. If he had been made of glass, he would have shattered onto the floor.

'I've been in this chair all night, all day . . . all day.'

During the drive to Pasadena, Philippe sat in the back, chain-smoking Camels and talking nonstop as if the words had been unleashed from inside him when we took the tape off his mouth. He had been in the country for two years on a student visa attending a trade school to become a disc jockey. And while waiting for top-forty radio to knock on his door, he delivered papers, washed dishes, and played soccer on Saturday afternoons. He was handsome, though not in a distinctive way, or in a way that stood out in a town like Hollywood.

He said everything that was of importance to him had been taken by the man who placed the bomb in his lap. He had lost all his papers, work permit, passport, letters from home, and his car – the white Hyundai that may or may not have been connected to my daughter's disappearance. But one look in his terrified eyes told me that what he had really lost couldn't be accounted for in a property inventory.

Within moments of our return to Pasadena, LAPD had taken control of Philippe's apartment. The FBI would soon take it from them. The cat was officially out of the bag now. I would only have custody of Philippe for a short time. The full weight of law enforcement and intelligence was descending on Pasadena like an occupying force. Terror was loose.

Philippe finished another cigarette and snuffed it out in the nearly full ashtray in the interrogation room. I handed him the pack and he took another one out. He tried to light it, but his hand shook so much he couldn't, so I did it for him. He inhaled deeply and held the smoke in his lungs for a moment and closed his eyes. He had been sitting in that room with the explosives strapped to his chest, watching the motion detector on his lap shake with the passing of every truck, for over ten hours.

'We're bringing you some food,' I said.

He smiled at some private thought. 'My mother wanted me to study to be a doctor. But I love rock music.'

'Tell me about him.'

He took another long drag on the Camel. 'If I do, I die.'

'No, you won't, you'll be protected.'

He smiled at me and shook his head as if everything around him were part of an absurd circus act. 'Is that what you tell people who have been through what I have?'

'I've never met anyone who's been through what you have.'

He leaned his head back and took a breath. When he began to speak, it was in a whisper, as if his tormentor could hear every word.

'I met him in a bar, said his name was Gabriel. We got to talking like you do. He said he had been living in Europe for several years and had just come back.'

'He was an American?'

'Yes. He said he was an actor.'

'You invited him to stay with you.'

He nodded. 'I'm not gay . . . just lonely. He seemed like . . . I was wrong.'

'Describe him.'

'He was tall, over six feet, dark hair, strong. He had these eyes, light-colored, they made you feel like he was looking through you, like you weren't even there.'

'When did he come back from Europe?'

'Five days ago.'

'Do you know from which country, or where he came through customs?'

'No.'

He began to raise the cigarette to his mouth again, but his hand began to tremble and he lowered it back onto the tabletop.

'You must find him.'

'Did he make any phone calls?'

He shook his head.

'Do you know who he saw or where he went?'

'Until yesterday he only slept there once, the first night. He just kept his things there. Said as soon as he found what he was looking for he would move on.'

'What happened yesterday?'

'He asked to come with me to deliver papers.'

He took a long, nervous drag on the cigarette, then lowered his head and blew the smoke out toward his feet.

'That's when it began. He took out a gun and . . .' He shook his head, a tear slid along the edge of his eye then fell to the floor.

'What happened?'

'He put the gun to my head and pulled the trigger.'

His eyes began to betray a feeling of shame. And then he spoke in a whisper.

'He laughed at me, said it was empty. Then he put a bullet in the empty chamber, spun it, and put it back to my head . . . and pulled the trigger again, and again.'

Philippe winced with the memory as if he could still hear the hammer falling on the chamber. He dropped his face into his hands.

'I felt like an animal begging for its life. I would have done anything he told me to.'

He looked up from the floor and deeply exhaled with exhaustion.

'When you were delivering the papers, why did you

pull your car in front of me and then stop at my driveway?'

'He told me to wait until we saw your car, and then I was to pull out so you could see my face, I don't know why. I just did what he told me to do.'

'He knew where I lived?'

'I think so.'

'But he said nothing about why, or anything about my daughter?'

'He said nothing to me.'

'After you drove away from my house, what happened?'

'He put tape over my eyes and mouth and tied my hands. Then he held something over my nose and made me breathe.'

'And you passed out?'

He nodded. 'I think I was in the car for a long time, I remember him walking me back into my apartment.'

'Did he mention the names Breem or Finley or Sweeny?'

'No.'

'How about the name Lacy?'

Again, he shook his head. I took a picture of Lacy out of my wallet and handed it to him.

'Have you ever seen her?'

He stared at my daughter for a long moment, then started to hand the picture back to me.

'Wait.'

My heart seized up as he looked closely at the picture again.

'The TV, the one in the beauty pageant. Is that her?'

I took the picture back and slipped it into my wallet. There was nothing here.

'An artist will be coming in to get a description of Gabriel. Tell them everything you can in as much detail as you remember.'

I got up from the chair and started for the door.

'Is that your daughter?' Philippe asked.

I stopped and turned back to him. His presence barely registered in the room. It wasn't part of the deal when we're brought into this world to have explosives strapped to your chest. How could anything, even the simplest acts of living, ever be the same after that? What dreams of rock and roll he had brought with him from halfway across the world were faint memories now. It was as if everything had been taken from him except his own shadow, and even that barely registered. His sunken, exhausted eyes were those of a ghost's.

'Yes, that's my daughter,' I said.

'Did he take her?'

'Someone did.'

'She's very pretty. I'm sorry.'

'Is there anything you can think of that I haven't asked about, someplace he went, something he said, could be anything, something unimportant he said to you?'

He nodded. 'He said everyone will know who he is . . . and everyone will fear him.'

I stepped out of the interrogation room and leaned back against the door and closed my eyes for a moment. When I opened them, Harrison was standing there. 'You hear everything?'

He nodded. 'Gabriel.'

'He either thinks he's an angel doing God's work, or he took the name from the San Gabriel Mountains.'

'It may be something else.'

'What?'

'In Hebrew, Gabriel means "strong man of God,"' Harrison said.

His eyes held mine for a moment, then he looked away as if in apology for what he had said. I looked around the squad room. Every desk was occupied by a detective or a uniform working the phones. The din of their conversations added together seemed to suck the available air out of the room.

'Send in the artist,' I said.

'On the way.'

'What else have we got?'

'The other clothes in the apartment checked out as he said. They were for someone well over six feet. Two or three inches taller than Philippe. There were no papers, everything was taken just as he said. We've put an APB out on his car.'

'Any prints?'

'Just partials on the other box of clothes. That's it so far, crime scene's still there. The bomb was clean. The explosives were industrial, nothing exotic, tracing them would be beyond a long shot. The electronics could have been bought at any hardware store. He's very careful.'

'So we have nothing.'

'A name and a description – that's something.'

I shook my head.

149

It didn't matter. He wouldn't be on record anywhere. There would be no pictures, no fingerprints, school records, nothing. Whatever twisted plans Gabriel had, for whatever reason, whether some form of twisted faith or fanatic political agenda, it was as secret as his true identity.

I started toward my office, but Harrison didn't follow, so I stopped. Something else had happened. I could feel it the way you feel a storm approaching just over the horizon. My skin felt cold.

'What is it?'

The skin around the corners of his eyes tightened. 'There was a call to your house,' he said.

I was suddenly back in Finley's hallway, the door swinging violently toward me.

'And?' I asked, nearly inaudibly.

'They've made demands for Lacy's release.'

My knees buckled. Then Finley's door hit me again.

ten

The voice on the tape was devoid of emotion. It could have been reciting a grocery list – demanding milk and bread, corn flakes, Coke, and lettuce, instead of money for the return of my daughter.

'We have Lacy Delillo. She has a small mole on the back of her neck, and one on her left ankle. We want two million dollars or you will never see her again.'

That was it. I listened to it a dozen times, and with each listening she slipped further and further from me.

'Two million dollars,' I whispered to myself in disbelief.

My daughter's life was now attached to a dollar sign. It could have been four million, ten, a hundred, it didn't matter. Whatever sum was demanded, there was no guarantee I would ever see her again.

After hearing the tape I looked around the conference room, stunned. Harrison stood by the door. Chief of Pasadena PD Ed Chavez was at the head of the table. He had been the only man in the department who believed in me when believing in women cops wasn't fashionable. He had given me my detective's shield. He put me on Homicide and eventually put me in charge of it. He also had known Lacy since she was an infant, even thought of himself as her proud Latino godfather. He commanded a room like the aging ex-Marine that he was. You just deferred to him because to do otherwise was unthinkable. He was a year from early retirement with one foot already striking out toward his sailboat at Catalina.

The FBI was present – a special agent named Hicks, who was in charge of an antiterrorism task force. He looked like the prototypical FBI agent. Polished, not a hint of doubt in his demeanor. I envied that confidence. To be without doubt. I couldn't remember a moment in my life when it wasn't present. Was the absence of doubt a gift men got when they were born, or was there just some genetic coding in them that didn't allow them to acknowledge its presence? Whichever it was, Hicks was its poster boy. Each hair on his head appeared to have been cut with a razor and assigned a place from which it would not move. A forty-year-old hotshot with a master's degree. He would have been just as at home in a corporate boardroom as he was in a police investigation. At the other end of the table, detectives North and Foley rounded out the room.

We reran the tape again then sat back and tried to put whatever pieces of the puzzle we had together.

'I think it's the same voice that called my home and made the threats to Lacy before,' I said.

Chief Chavez looked at me and then turned away when tears welled up in his eyes.

'We can run a match on it,' Hicks said.

'Where was the call made from?' the chief asked.

'A phone booth on Colorado in Old Town. We're checking to see if any security cameras picked up anything, and we're watching it in case they use the same phone again.'

'I wouldn't count on it.'

'I'm not,' I said.

Chavez sat back in his chair, the muscles in his square jaw flexing. 'So where do we stand?'

'We're looking for two suspects for questioning in the killing of Finley: his partner, Breem, and an employee named Sweeny.'

'I understand you saw Sweeny,' Agent Hicks said.

It was a loaded question.

'Yes, he hit me with a door.'

Hicks glanced at the report in front of him. 'And he said he was sorry? Why do you think he did that?'

I wasn't in the mood to play any passive-aggressive games with the FBI. He wasn't here to assist in an investigation; he was here to take control of it.

'I'm taking him at his word that he felt bad about it.'

'What about Finley's business partner, Breem?' Chavez asked.

'He left the house before dawn and hasn't been seen since.'

'The body of the Mexican major in the casting pool?'

I turned to North, who sat upright in his chair and cleared his throat.

153

'We just got the prelim from the ME. The victim's blood-alcohol level was six times the legal limit. His prints were all over a bottle of tequila found at the scene. Water was present in sufficient quantity in the lungs to result in death. The guy got smashed, smacked his head, then staggered into the pool and drowned. End of mystery.'

'We're still trying to determine if he brought explosives across the border. The Mexican army has been less than helpful.'

'I may be able to expedite that,' Hicks said. He began tapping his index finger on the report in front of him. 'Does your daughter belong to a radical environmental group, Lieutenant?'

'Not to my knowledge.'

'But she did interrupt the proceedings at the pageant with an act of environmental political protest.'

'I think she acted like a seventeen-year-old.'

'You understand I have to ask this?'

'I understand.'

'Is there any reason to believe that your daughter would be in collusion with a radical group to fake her own kidnapping to obtain funds?'

'No.'

'But she did keep her acts at the pageant secret from you?'

'A spray bottle is a far cry from faking a kidnapping.'

'I'm just following an obvious thread, Lieutenant.'

'You track those groups. Do you have any reason to believe there's one operating in Pasadena?' I countered.

'We're checking that.'

I glanced over at Chavez. His eyes were pleading with me not to do what I was about to, but I couldn't stop myself.

'Is there any reason to believe that the FBI screwed up by not having Gabriel on a terror watch list?'

Hicks at least had the grace to smile at the question. 'If he was on a watch list, someone messed up.

'Tell me about Gabriel,' Hicks said.

'He's a white male, probably American, may have spent the last few years in Europe. He's highly competent with explosives and the means to deliver them, which could indicate a military background. If he is self-trained, then that would indicate a very high level of intelligence, and possibly education.'

'It could also mean he was trained overseas. We'll look into that,' Hicks said.

'The fact that he's taken the name Gabriel indicates he sees himself as very powerful. He told Philippe that everyone will know his name, and everyone will fear him.'

'Is there anything that directly links Lacy's kidnapping to the bombing this Gabriel carried out at Sweeny's, and the attempted one in the apartment belonging to this Frenchman Philippe?' Chavez asked.

What the chief was doing was easing me into the idea that the FBI would be taking over the hunt for Gabriel.

'Finley's partner, Breem, made at least three phone calls to Lacy.'

'I understand he called all the contestants,' Hicks said.

'Lacy was the only one he called more than once, including the night of the pageant.'

'Three phone calls from a florist to a beauty pageant contestant is not a connection to acts of terrorism.'

'A car similar to Philippe's was seen leaving the scene of Lacy's abduct—'

'A white car was seen – no make, no model.'

'Gabriel had Philippe stop his car outside my house. That puts him outside the house of a kidnap victim; that sounds like a connection to me.'

'If Gabriel was responsible for attempting to kill you and your partner with the first bomb, then wouldn't it make sense that he appear at your house? You had already been a target once. I think he was watching you, not your daughter.'

'I don't think he was trying to kill Traver and me. I think the bomb was intended for Sweeny.'

'Why?'

'He's killing everyone who can identify him.'

'You think that's why your daughter may have been kidnapped – she saw him?'

'That's a possibility.'

Hicks shook his head. 'That doesn't track. He could have killed Philippe at the apartment. Why didn't he?'

'We either got lucky or he's playing some sort of game.'

'Why the ransom demand? What would be the purpose of drawing more heat on himself? If Gabriel is who he appears to be, he's here for one reason: to plant a bomb. The kidnapping just doesn't follow.'

'I think the only thing we can predict about Gabriel is that everything he does will surprise us.'

Hicks glanced at Chavez, who looked back uneasily for a moment, then turned to me.

'You need to find Lacy, Alex—' He paused and sadly lowered his eyes. 'We need to find her. Everything else is unimportant.'

'Terrorism is our job,' Hicks said. 'I'll have over a hundred agents working on this by tonight. Double that by tomorrow. If the two cases do intersect, we can help each other and share information. But otherwise, this isn't up for debate. It's my job to find Gabriel. You have to find your daughter.'

There was a knock on the door and Officer James stepped in. 'We have the likeness, Lieutenant.'

'I'll take that,' Hicks said.

James glanced at him for a moment, then walked directly to me and handed me the drawing.

'I'll have copies in a second,' James said, glancing around the room.

Gabriel was clean-shaven with dark, neatly cut short hair. His face was wider than I had expected with full lips and nose. A small scar at the corner of his right eyebrow extended downward in a half-moon curve. And as Philippe had described, he had light, penetrating eyes that even in a drawing had a fierce defiance to them. I held those eyes for a moment, trying to imagine the cold heart behind them. But even in my imagination, it was territory I couldn't fully grasp. I had arrested countless individuals who had committed almost every act of violence on another human being imaginable and except for the rare occasion, there was often no dark secret inside them, no evil force at work. They were husbands, brothers, wives, parents, or someone's child who just lost control. Events and emotions – love, hate,

157

and fear – had taken on a life of their own. And when it was over and they looked at the wreckage they had caused, they were like viewers watching a television show, clueless as to how it had happened.

Gabriel didn't look clueless. And if there was a window into his heart, nothing he had done so far pointed the way. I slid the likeness across the table to Hicks, watched him as his eyes searched over the drawing. If he was surprised by anything, it didn't register in his face.

'Does he look familiar?' I asked.

He studied it a moment longer, then sat back and shook his head. 'I would remember that face.'

With that, Hicks got up and left the room, calling a number on a cell phone as the door closed behind him. The room was silent for a moment, as if we had all just stepped off a plane in a foreign country and didn't know which way to customs.

'You disagree with Hicks that Lacy is somehow caught up in all of this?' Chief Chavez asked.

His words passed by as if they had been shouted from a speeding car. In my mind I was trying to hold Lacy's smooth, perfect hand in mine and tell her that I was there, that it would be all right, not to cry, not to be afraid. I was also trying to tell myself the same thing.

'Alex.' A hand reached over and took hold of mine. Chavez had moved around the table and was sitting next to me. 'Can you do this?'

I nodded. I had to do it; there was no choice. Nothing would stop me from finding my baby, nothing.

'You remember the first thing you taught me about investigation?'

He smiled. 'Always promote people who are smarter than you.'

The corner of his mouth tightened. He was holding his heart together with all his strength.

'There's no such thing as coincidence,' I said.

The muscles in his jaw began to relax. He wanted to ask another question but couldn't find a way to say it. How could any decent person find a way to say it?

'What about the . . .'

'I'll pay it. I'll mortgage the rest of my life if that's what it takes to get her back.'

'Okay,' Chavez said. 'You let me and the department worry about the money. Where do you want to begin?'

There were so many steps to take. But which direction pointed to my daughter? And what if I chose wrong?

'I want taps put on Breem's and Finley's phones.'

'I'll get the court orders myself,' Chavez said.

'I want each of their wives watched.'

North and Foley both nodded.

'And this stays out of the press. Not a whisper, nothing.'

'Not a word,' Chavez said.

I looked at Harrison. 'We'll start in Lacy's room.'

I needed to know her secrets, and to do so I'd have to break whatever thread of trust there was between us. I stood up from the table and looked over at Harrison as the room began to clear.

'I'll need a few minutes first.'

Harrison nodded and held back as we walked out of the conference room. Walking across the squad room toward my office, I noticed Hicks and two other FBI agents escorting Philippe toward the door. Philippe glanced in my direction and briefly made eye contact as Harrison stepped up behind me. Philippe should be dead but wasn't. Hicks had been right about that. If his continued presence among the living wasn't a result of luck, then it would follow that Gabriel wanted us to make a composite of his likeness. But why? To what end? Philippe smiled at me as if to say thank you, then was led out the door.

'Do you think we got lucky,' I said to Harrison, 'or do you think Gabriel wanted us to see his face?'

Harrison looked at the empty doorway where Philippe had just exited.

'I've been thinking about that . . . The best I've come up with is that Gabriel couldn't have known that I would be one of the people to walk through that door. If I didn't, or someone like me, that bomb blows out the corner of that apartment building. And you're dead.'

'Why did we have that minute to disarm it then?'

He turned to me. 'A timed device multiplies the terror.'

The words hung in the air demanding attention.

'Multiplies the terror?' I thought about it for a moment. 'You're talking about suspense, aren't you?'

He nodded. 'Yeah, like a Hitchcock movie.'

'It's not just about the victim, it's about the people you frighten?'

'It makes more sense than us seeing his face.'

I started to step into my office.

'Lieutenant.'

I stopped and turned back to him.

'Whichever it is, this is the first bomber I've ever been frightened of.'

I looked into Harrison's eyes for a moment. They appeared older; there was a weariness I hadn't noticed before. They were the eyes of a man who had buried a young wife, who knew the results of terror. I stepped quickly into my office. I wondered if he would have shared that bit of information with me if I had been a male officer. And in truth I could have used a bit more locker room bravado than honest emotional intimacy.

I closed the door behind me, locked it, then walked over to my desk and looked down at my phone. My mother had already found out about the pageant fiasco on TV. And now it would only be a matter of hours before the news media had the story of Lacy's disappearance, and I couldn't let her hear about it that way.

I looked around at the walls of my office. They were lined with commendations, awards, service medals, plaques, photographs, every kind of knickknack that records a successful career. And now I would have to admit the truth to the one person who had always been able to inspire doubt in me. I hadn't been able to protect my daughter. I felt like such a terrible failure.

I reached out to pick up the handset. As my fingers touched it I was sixteen again, geeky, never right, never perfect, never quite good enough. I was no longer any of the things my career suggested I was. The evidence on the walls of my office belonged to a stranger.

My mother's phone rang three times. On the fourth ring I ever so subtly began to move the handset away from my ear, as if there was an involuntary reflex to hang up before she answered. The line clicked as we were connected.

'Hello.'

'It's Alex, Mom.'

'Alex, I have been calling. What time is it?'

I had forgotten about time. I checked my watch. It was already after midnight.

'It's late, Mom.'

'Why didn't you get back to me? What is going on with my—'

'Mom.'

'I don't understand why one phone call—'

'Something has happened. I need you to be quiet and listen.'

'I'm always here to listen, you know that. Not that you call . . . Oh, God, is she pregnant?'

'Stop. Just stop and listen.'

There was silence on the other end. I could hear her take a wounded breath. 'Fine.'

I started to speak, but before I could form a word my eyes filled with tears.

'Alex?'

She always had that ability to sense my emotional balance. Normally she used it like a shark sensing blood in the water to undermine me. But not this time. Her voice was different – softer, tender. It touched a place in my memory where all there was was love between us. A six-year-old daughter and a proud mother. Soul mates.

What had happened to that? Was it my father leaving her when I was seven? Was it her quest to make sure I was never going to be as vulnerable as she had been to the musings of a man that made her push and push until we were strangers to each other?

Tears fell from my face and soaked into the pages of a report on my desk. I wiped them away and closed my eyes.

'Lacy's been kidnapped.'

There was a short gasp as if all the air had just been forced out of her lungs. 'I . . . I don't understand. What do you mean—'

'She's been kidnapped. It's exactly what it sounds like.'

'But . . . you're not joking.'

'No.'

'You're not rich. Wealthy people are kidnapped. This doesn't make sense. You must have made a mistake. I don't believe—'

'Listen,' I yelled into the phone before her emotions got out of hand.

'Don't talk to me like that.'

'Just listen.'

I heard her take a deep breath, then I continued.

'This is different. There's more that I can't go into, but I don't think it's about the money.'

'What then? Why?' Her voice was rising as the shock began to settle in. 'Oh, God.'

'Mother, you need to call a friend, have them come over, don't be alone right now.'

'I'll come out there.'

She was in a retirement community in Arizona called Sun Estates.

'No, there's nothing for you to do here, and I'll be too busy. You'd just be alone.'

'You don't—'

'Mother, I have to think of Lacy and nothing else. Your being here won't help her. I'm going to find her, I promise you. She's going to be all right.'

'This can't be . . . It just . . .'

There was a long silence on the other end of the phone, then a barely audible whisper.

'Oh, Alex . . .' Her voice trailed away in heartbreak. Then she whispered, 'I'm so sorry.'

It was the voice I remembered from my childhood, as gentle as a song. As she hung up the phone I could hear her holding back sobs.

A Pacific breeze had blown in, clearing the sky and dropping the temperature into the mid-forties. As Harrison drove us up the gradual slope into the foothills, I rolled down the window. Even this far inland, there was the subtle briny scent of the Pacific in the breeze. Taking in the air, I looked up into the dark sky – the stars sparkled in the blackness like luminescence in a tide pool. And somewhere underneath it all was my daughter.

'They'll be camping out tonight,' I said.

Harrison looked across the seat not understanding.

'The parade. Families will be wrapping themselves in blankets and sleeping bags and camping out all along Colorado. I know of families that have been doing it every year since I was a kid. It's a family tradition like Fourth of July fireworks. And that's just the people on the actual parade route.'

A shudder went through me. I could still feel the rush of air and then the deafening concussion of the explosion in the bungalow.

'Worldwide, they estimate that two hundred million people will be watching on TV.'

I could tell from the look on his face that the number was news to Harrison.

'Two hundred million,' he said in surprise. 'I had no idea.'

'Next to the Super Bowl, it's one of the most-watched television events of the year.'

I looked at the dark road ahead for a minute.

'What was it that Philippe said Gabriel told him?' I said.

Harrison thought for a moment. 'Everyone will know who I am, and everyone will fear me,' he whispered.

That was it. Everyone will fear me. A dream come true.

'There're kids out there waiting for a parade . . . Gabriel's going to kill children, and two hundred million people will be watching.'

The lines around Harrison's eyes tightened.

'The more innocent the victim, the more effective the terror. That's the idea, right?' I said.

Harrison stole a quick glance at me, then looked straight ahead.

'We have his face; he won't get close.'

'Does he have to? Has anything he's done up to this

point struck you as the work of someone who plans on martyring himself?'

Harrison thought for a moment and then shook his head uneasily. 'No.'

'And that makes him even more dangerous, doesn't it?'

Harrison didn't have to answer. The truth settled over his face like a mask. Things just kept getting worse.

We turned onto Mariposa and headed down my block past houses I had been driving by for twenty years. There were ivy-covered hills sloping up to perfect lawns. There were plastic reindeer on roofs and white Christmas lights made to look like icicles hanging from gutters. The Kellys lived there, the Geotzes there. Lacy had taken her first steps on this block. In that house, she kissed her first boy. In that one, my husband had had the affair with a dentist's wife. Everything about it was familiar, except now it had the appearance of a studio backlot where only make-believe happens. The houses were facades, the happy, safe lives merely scripted. If a Santa Ana came blowing down out of the desert, I was sure it would all be swept away.

I noticed an unmarked car parked on the street outside my house. Harrison pulled up the incline of the drive and stopped. He opened the door and began to get out, then noticed I wasn't moving.

I didn't want to walk into that house knowing she wouldn't be inside. I didn't want to step into her room and go through her things as if she were just another victim whose secrets were now public property.

Harrison slipped back into the seat and looked

straight ahead, his eyes seeing far beyond the garage door toward some distant point in time.

'My wife was missing for six days before she was found.'

He turned to me as if looking away from the past. 'You have to fight doubt as if it has a face.'

He held my eyes for a moment, then looked straight ahead and took a deep breath.

'What face did you give it?'

The corners of his mouth turned up slightly in a smile, then he looked down at his hands as if something had just slipped through them. He shook his head.

'I never managed to.'

Harrison hesitated at the door to Lacy's room as I stepped inside. As if by instinct, I picked up a T-shirt lying on the floor, folded it, then laid it on her bed. Mustn't let a visitor see how messy your daughter's room is.

'Does she have a diary?' Harrison asked, still standing in the doorway.

'Journal,' I said, remembering how Lacy had corrected me years before with the same question. 'A diary is something nineteenth-century women used to remember who they had tea with. A journal is for writing, a record of your life.'

I glanced at Harrison, who was puzzled by the words.

'Teenagers are very specific about some things.'

I looked around the room. I wanted to touch every object, as if they would bring her closer to me. I wanted to hug her worn-out stuffed bear, as if it could whisper to me where she was.

'The journal wasn't in her backpack, so it should be here,' I said.

Harrison was still standing in the doorway, hesitant to violate my daughter's space and turn her bedroom into an evidence search.

'You want to do this alone?' he asked.

I looked around the room. Memories began rushing out of the pale yellow paint of the walls like oncoming traffic. A seven-year-old with a missing tooth came flying by. A five-year-old with a fever dream. A sleepover. Laughter. Loud, bad boy-toy music. The faint whiff of cigarette smoke filtering out from under the door.

I gripped the painted iron of her bedpost as if to pull myself back to the present. I then looked over to Harrison.

'Being alone is the last thing I want right now.'

'Okay.'

He stepped across the threshold and looked around. I could feel something change in the room. Lacy had just slipped a little further away.

'How about her desk?' he said.

I nodded and walked over to it but didn't reach for any of the drawers. I just stared at it, unable to lift my hand.

'I think I'd like you to do this,' I said.

'Sure,' Harrison said. He stepped up beside me and began opening drawers.

I looked away. I didn't want to be a part of this. I thought I could, but I couldn't. I had to hold my daughter closer than this. I wanted her secrets to remain hers now more than ever.

'Anything that seems out of place, whatever, take it out,' I said.

I turned and walked over to the window, listening to the sound of drawers sliding open and papers being searched. The window looked out onto the backyard, which consisted of a square patch of grass and a border of bougainvillea along a split-rail fence line. Lacy had always said it would be a perfect yard for a dog, a golden retriever. But we never got one. I always came up with a reason why we shouldn't.

'You ever have a dog?' I asked Harrison.

The rustling in the desk stopped. 'Sure, growing up. We always had dogs . . . I think this is it.'

I turned around and Harrison was holding Lacy's journal. A blue, leather-bound volume with a sunflower painted on the cover.

'Yeah, that's it. I've seen her carry it.'

He held it out to me. 'You want to—'

'No, you do it. Work back from the last entry. A number, name . . . you know what to look for.'

He stepped back to the desk, sat down, and opened the journal to the last entry. 'Dated yesterday.'

He began reading backward, turning pages quickly. As he read more passages a faint smile became visible on his lips.

'What is it?'

'It's about the pageant.' He looked over at me. 'I wish I had been there,' he said.

'I wish I hadn't been.'

I heard myself say the words and swore my own mother had just said them. God, why did I say that? Have I learned nothing?

'No, that's not true, it was great,' I said. 'To have done

169

what she did in front of all those people, knowing the trouble she would be in and what people would think of her. I'll never be that brave, ever.'

Harrison glanced back at the journal and nodded.

'You have a very cool daughter, Lieutenant.'

He looked at me, but I couldn't hold his eyes. My heart was in my throat. My voice broke when I tried to speak. All I could manage was a weak 'Yeah.'

Harrison returned to the journal, carefully dissecting each word for any hidden meaning or misdirection. The room felt unnaturally silent. I desperately wanted to hear some very bad music, or the ringing of her phone – any noise to mask the emptiness. My breathing began to increase, though I couldn't seem to take in enough air. Where was my daughter, where?

'I think I'll step outside,' I said, starting for the door.

'Does the name or letter D mean anything?'

I stopped. Harrison was holding out the journal toward me. 'There's a phone number next to it.'

I reached out and took her journal in my hands. For a moment I just looked at the writing on the pages. The graceful loops and turns of ink looked like extensions of her long, thin fingers. I had always marveled at it. Where did she get this natural grace? Certainly not from me. Was it possible that along with red hair and certain genetic maladies, grace skipped a generation or two?

The letter D and the number were centered on a page between two widely spaced paragraphs.

'It doesn't reference the paragraph before or the one after.'

'What do you think D stands for?'

'The obvious choice would be Daniel.'

'Finley.'

'Yeah . . . but that's not his phone number. I remember it from the report.'

I picked up Lacy's phone and called the number. Each ring felt like a jolt of electricity traveling through the line to my hand. I gave it ten rings and put it down.

'Let's get an address on the number.'

Harrison jotted it down and then left me alone in the bedroom.

I resisted looking in the journal for a moment but was gradually drawn into it. How could I not be? I wanted to put my arms around it and hold my daughter's thoughts as if I were embracing her. I began skimming pages looking for another reference to D, but found nothing. I tried not to read specific passages, but it was like trying not to love something you gave life to. Every other entry was a question. *Why am I . . . Why do I feel . . . What did I do . . . Why is ____ such a shit.* Being seventeen was like riding an insane carnival ride with no direction and no foreseeable end. God, I'd forgotten.

As I skimmed, my eyes settled on a passage and refused to move on. I tried not to read it, but it was already done. Shit. I read it softly out loud.

'What do I have to do to make Mom proud of me? What do I fucking have to do?'

There it was.

The journal sank to my lap. I stared into the pale yellow of the walls and silently repeated the words.

'What do I fucking have to do?'

Somewhere over the foothills the *thump, thump* of a

171

department helicopter broke the silence. Out the window I saw the beam of its night sun arc across the darkness toward the ground. The helicopter turned to the west and moved away, the thumping of its rotors fading away, only to be replaced by the rhythmic beating of my heart in the empty room. I was holding the journal so tightly the knuckles of my fingers were turning white. Tears began to flood my eyes. What had I done?

Harrison knocked on the door and stepped in. I closed the journal and slipped it carefully back into its drawer exactly as we had found it. I didn't want her to know we had violated it. It would be the last lie between us.

'Tell me something good,' I said, wiping away the tears.

'The number's in Azusa. From the address, I'd say it's a residence.'

I started for the door, but Harrison didn't move. His eyes were seeing beyond the walls of Lacy's room and held a look of apprehension or disbelief. The beeper on my belt went off. Harrison appeared to be expecting it.

'What is it?' I asked.

'The Frenchman Philippe – we found his car,' Harrison said.

'Where?'

I could see the muscles in his neck tighten.

'It's across the street from headquarters. I think you could see it from your office window.'

A chill went up my spine.

'Gabriel's playing more games with us? What is he trying—'

I didn't have to finish the thought to know the answer. Terror. And that meant there was more to it than just the parking of a stolen car across the street from my office.

'It's not just the car, is it? There's more,' I said.

Harrison nodded.

'Finley's missing partner, Breem, is inside.'

eleven

Garfield Avenue was blocked off at either end with the same stanchions that would be holding back parade-goers in a little over twenty-four hours. Nothing moved on the street other than a few dried magnolia leaves that blew across the pavement in the breeze. The central plaza in front of the grand Spanish city hall building was filled with emergency vehicles instead of tourists looking at the thousands of Christmas lights strung through all the trees. The only sound was that of a mockingbird in a distant tree, mimicking a siren.

Right smack in the middle of downtown Pasadena every person within two blocks, including the entire police department, had been moved beyond a potential blast zone. Gabriel had stuck a thumb right in our eye by parking the Hyundai in front of the county court building and the police department. He was staking a claim that he could go anywhere, do anything. And what was most frightening was that I believed it.

A bomb squad robot was ten feet from the Hyundai,

its small video camera pointed at the face of the florist Breem. He was sitting in the passenger seat, his mouth covered with tape, his eyes wild with fear as they pleaded with the camera for help. We were a block to the south on the edge of the tree-lined plaza. Lacy's godfather, Chief Chavez, stared at the image on a small TV monitor, then shook his head.

'My God, I've never seen anything like this in my life.'

I stared at the monitor thinking the exact same thing. Whatever I might have thought I understood about Gabriel, it now seemed irrelevant.

'How much explosive is inside?' I asked.

Chavez shook his head. 'The first officer on scene backed off after he realized what the hell was going on.'

'Look at the rear tires,' Harrison said. 'The body is riding low, the fenders are almost touching. The trunk could be filled with a hundred pounds or more.'

'What happens if it goes off?' Chavez said.

'Let's just say none of us will be around long enough to hear the blast,' Harrison said.

'Do we know how it's wired?' I asked.

Harrison motioned to the tech officer controlling the robot.

I looked at the small video monitor that was receiving the image from the robot's camera as it panned off Breem's face to the door on the passenger side. There were two small objects placed on opposite sides of the door's opening.

'They look like window alarm sensors.'

'That's exactly what they are. We haven't seen the

other door, but it's safe to assume it's also wired. We open a door, break a window, that's it.'

He paused and looked at me.

'And that's just what we've seen. There could be a remote or motion sensors. I don't think we can rule anything out.'

'Can I talk to him through this?'

Harrison nodded. 'There's an open phone line on the robot.'

The camera made a jerky pass back onto Breem and zoomed in until his face filled the monitor again. He was breathing heavily; sweat covered the side of his face in long streaks.

'I don't know if he's capable of hearing you at this point,' Harrison said.

'Agent Hicks is on the way with the FBI's people. This is their ball game,' Chavez said.

'They're not going to ask him about my daughter.'

Chavez looked at the monitor for a moment, then nodded. 'Take as long as you need.'

Harrison motioned to the mike on the control panel. 'Just speak in a normal voice. He'll hear it.'

I nodded and Harrison flipped the mike's switch.

'Mr Breem, this is Lieutenant Alex Delillo. You remember me, I was at your flower shop? If you under-stand me, nod as much as you're able.'

A bead of sweat dripped down his forehead.

'He didn't hear you,' Harrison said.

'Mr Breem, if you can hear me, nod your head. There's a camera in the robot. Look at the robot and nod.'

Breem shook his head.

177

'Look at the camera and nod. I need to know that you can hear me.'

Breem slowly turned his head as if it were being restrained by a neck brace.

'I don't think he knows where he is,' Harrison whispered.

'We have the very best people here. You're going to be all right.'

Breem shook his head as if he knew something we didn't. His eyes were wide open but with the unfocused look of a blind man.

'Have you seen my daughter? She was a contestant in the pageant. You talked to her on the phone, Lacy Delillo. Do you know where Lacy Delillo is?'

He stared straight ahead. His eyes gathered focus as if searching out a memory, then he looked back at the camera.

'Lacy Delillo – do you know where she is?'

Lines appeared at the corners of his eyes, then they filled with tears.

Chavez's hand landed on my shoulder. I couldn't give it up. He knew something, he had to, otherwise he wouldn't be in that car.

'Mr Breem, have you seen my daughter?'

If he heard anything, he gave no sign of it. He looked straight ahead, his eyes retreating back into the nightmare he was living.

'He's gone. I don't think he even hears your voice,' Chavez said.

'He needs to see a face,' I said. 'He's alone and he's terrified.'

'Alex, don't even think—'

'He's lost. If he sees my face, if he thinks he isn't going to die . . .'

'You're not walking up there,' Chavez said.

'If he knows something about Lacy and we lose him . . .'

The air slipped out of my lungs, taking my voice with it. I tried to take another breath, but it was like breathing through a plastic bag. Finally, the words returned in a whisper.

'How do I live with that?'

Chavez looked at me like a stern father. 'His hands are bound, his mouth taped. Even if you get through to him, what are you going to learn?'

'All I need from him is a nod. If he makes a connection to Lacy then we know something we didn't know before.'

Chavez shook his head, looked over at Harrison.

'You're the explosives expert. Tell her why this is a bad idea.'

Harrison looked down the block at the Hyundai, glanced at me, then turned to Chavez. 'I don't have a daughter.'

Chavez shook his head and looked down the street toward the car.

'I have a daughter,' he said in a whisper. Then he turned to me. 'And I have a goddaughter.'

Harrison gave me a litany of things to look for in the car. The shape of the charge, was it bundled, how many circuits, where was the ground, source of ignition, how many fuses, what kind? If this wire or connection was present, was it intact? Was it broken? If it wasn't, I was all right. If it was, run or lie down, depending on the direction of the explosive wave. It sounded like a high-school science class twisted into the vocabulary of terror.

I'd walked this street outside headquarters for twenty years, but it was no longer familiar. Moving beyond the barriers felt like stepping onto the surface of the moon. It had the feel of one of those hideous blocks in Sarajevo where mothers ran past snipers just to buy bread for their family. With each foot gained, the ground became more and more suspect. Each step took me farther into a brave new world where the assumptions we held about right and wrong and justice were turning to dust.

I stopped just short of the robot as Harrison had said, then carefully looked around the base of the car for any pins of red light that indicated a laser motion detector.

'I don't see anything,' I said, the mike on the robot picking up my voice. Harrison had thought it best not to give me a radio. Triggers could be set to frequencies.

'Okay,' Harrison said. His voice sounded like it was coming from the other side of the planet instead of just two hundred yards away.

Breem was sitting bolt upright facing straight ahead, his eyes closed, his breathing as rapid as that of a woman in labor.

'Mr Breem?' I said in as casual a way as possible.

His eyes popped open like he was waking from a nightmare. He turned his head toward me without moving his body. There were deep circles under his eyes, his skin looked pale, as if he were being slowly drained of life.

'I'm going to stand here for a little bit so you're not alone. Do you remember me – Lieutenant Delillo?'

He stared at me for a moment, his eyes searching for a thread of memory, and then he nodded. I stepped up next to the car and looked inside. As Harrison had suspected, the window and door appeared to have been wired.

'You're going to be all right. We'll get you out of this.'

His eyes bore into me as if he were asking a question, then he looked down at his lap. My heart was in my throat. The fear of standing next to the car vanished and was replaced by a cold sense of dread. I was looking at the terror Harrison had talked about. There was no fighting this. Just seeing it, I had already lost. The strands that collectively hold all of us together as humanity had just been cut. I stepped back from the car, repressing an urge to vomit, then turned and spoke into the mike so Breem wouldn't hear me.

'His hands are sitting in his lap. They're not just bound, they're covered in a big ball of duct tape with wires coming out of each side.'

I looked down at the end of the block and could see Harrison turn toward Chavez and shake his head.

'Can you see what the wires are connected to?' Harrison asked.

'No, they go under the seat.'

There was a long silence on the other end. I looked down the street at Harrison. He was staring at the ground, working something out. The hair on my arms suddenly raised. I knew what Harrison was doing. He was trying to get into Gabriel's head. He was imagining the drawing of his face. The sharp features and dark hair. The small half-moon scar. The light eyes that even on paper had the power to look right through you. A 'strong man of God.' It was the perfect portrait of evil. Figure how Gabriel wanted this exercise in terror to end, and you have a window into how he had wired the device wrapped around Breem's hands.

I saw Harrison shake his head, then look up from the pavement and turn toward me.

'I think you should get out of there now. Just walk away,' he said.

'What do you think is—'

'Just walk away.'

'I have to ask him about Lacy.'

'Do as he says, Alex, walk,' Chavez said.

I glanced down the road, then turned back to Breem.

'Mr Breem, they're working out how to get you out of this.'

He looked back at me and then down at his hands.

'Do you know where my daughter is?'

He lifted his eyes toward me and then shook his head. He tried to say something but the tape muffled his attempt and he began to cry. Whatever hope was left inside him drained away.

From behind me on the speaker came Harrison's voice.

'Lieutenant, walk away. Walk away right now.'

Breem began to scream under the tape and shake his head violently back and forth.

'Get out of there, Alex!' Chavez yelled from down the block.

Breem's eyes paused just long enough for me to know that he had made a decision.

'No, we can get you out of this,' I said.

He shook his head and screamed under the tape. Down the street Chavez was yelling.

'Get out of there, Alex!'

I took a step back, then another and another as Breem's muffled wail became continuous. As I turned and started to run, I saw out of the corner of my eye Breem raise the ball of tape that covered his hands.

The concussion knocked me to my hands and knees like a hard slap from a giant hand. There was silence for a moment, and then the glass from the car's window began falling on the pavement around me like a dusting of snow. The echo of the explosion bounced off head-quarters across the street and broke the silence with a heavy thud. The concussion set off car alarms up and down the street. The thump of a helicopter became audible. The acrid smell of explosives blended with the sweet scent of night-blooming jasmine.

'Why?' I said, not entirely sure if I was having an internal conversation or speaking out loud. I began to shake my head. It didn't make sense. Why did he do that? I sat back on my feet and tried to determine if I was wounded. My legs were fine, my arms, head. Blood trickled from my mouth – I had bitten my tongue as I was knocked down.

Down the street, officers were running toward me. I turned and, to my surprise, saw that the car was still intact. The windows were all broken and some fabric hung down from the ceiling, but otherwise it appeared undamaged. Breem was still sitting in the passenger seat. His head was bent forward with his chin resting on his chest. Blood was dripping heavily from his nose. A strip of duct tape had been blown loose from around his mouth and hung like a torn piece of flesh. If he was alive, he was unconscious.

I rose unsteadily to my feet and walked toward the car and looked inside. Breem's hands were gone. All that was left was bone and torn muscle and the silvery sleeves of tendon.

I stumbled backward as two hands caught me by the shoulders and began to walk me away from the car. Voices were asking me questions, but I couldn't make out any of the words. I was aware of tears running down my face, but I felt no emotion. The hands around my shoulders guided me back down the street past the yellow tape and sat me down on the curb.

'Alex, are you hit anywhere?'

I looked up into the face of Chavez, who was kneeling in front of me.

'He set it off. I don't understand, he just set it off,' I said.

I shook my head in disbelief and ran my fingers through my hair. Tiny cubes of safety glass fell out like rice after a wedding.

I looked back down the street toward the car. Two bomb squad officers in full armored suits were pulling Breem's limp body out through the window and carrying him awkwardly toward some waiting paramedics.

'Terror,' I whispered.

'Alex?'

'Breem's eyes. He understood terror, he knew it.' I looked up at Chavez. 'He didn't know where Lacy was, but he knew she was kidnapped. He knew.'

'Someone want to tell me what the hell happened here?' said an angry voice.

Agent Hicks had arrived with the FBI's team and was standing behind Chavez. In the white, artificial light, I could see the flush of anger in his neck.

'I told you people to wait, to stay back and let us handle it. And what do you do? You let her walk in—'

' "Her" is the head of Homicide,' Chavez said defensively.

'Who just about got a witness blown up, brilliant work. Who do you think you're dealing with?'

'He set it off himself, Hicks,' Chavez said.

'Now, why the hell would he do that? You got an answer for that, Lieutenant?'

The gurney carrying Breem came clattering past with two paramedics working furiously. There was a tube down his throat to aid his breathing. Blood-soaked bandages covered the stumps of his arms. I could smell the explosives on him as he went by. It permeated his clothes like a rotting rose.

I replayed the events in my head. His screams under the gag. His shaking his head. He knew something. Terror. I suddenly understood. Harrison may have guessed it. It was why he told me to back away.

'Oh, my God,' I whispered.

Chavez took my hand. 'What?'

'I think Breem did it to save lives.'

'Come again,' Hicks said.

'I think there're more explosives in the trunk. He was given a choice. Gabriel gave him a choice.'

'What choice?'

'He could lose his hands. Or take the chance that others would die trying to save him. I think that's what he did.'

Hicks shook his head.

'All you know is that he panicked, and that you're lucky to be alive.'

'It wasn't panic I saw in his eyes, Hicks. He made a decision . . . an unimaginable decision.'

Harrison stepped up next to Chavez and knelt down.

'You okay?'

I nodded.

'The car is loaded with explosives. The charge on his hands took out the other triggers. If the full load had gone off, this would have looked like a street in Baghdad.'

'Jesus,' Chavez said.

'That car is ours,' Hicks said, getting out his cell phone. 'Get your people out of there.'

Chavez nodded and Hicks walked away, barking orders at other agents.

I looked at Harrison. He knew the truth about what Breem had just done as clearly as if he had been standing next to me. The horror of coming to a decision that cost him his own hands. How he sat in the car, running the possibilities through his head again and again. How he would have played out all the 'what ifs' and 'maybes' and 'prayers' only to come to the decision Gabriel had intended all along. The shock of it spread out like a wave from an explosion, leaving all who understood lessened and weaker.

'Tell me you can outthink him,' I said to Harrison.

The ambulance taking Breem away lit up its siren and sped off, wailing into the night like a wounded animal. Harrison watched it drive away.

'I don't know.'

'Screw it,' I said, angry at my weakness. 'He has my child. I will not give in to this. I won't do it.'

I reached out, taking Chavez's hand, and pulled myself to my feet.

'He's either already made a mistake or will make one. We just have to be smart enough to see it.'

I pushed past them both and started walking toward my car. More officers were arriving, but none of them understood, none of them had seen Breem's eyes. I glanced at my watch; it was nearly three A.M. Overhead, the stars that earlier had lit the night were gone. Dark, windblown clouds, heralding the arrival of another storm, now streaked the sky like coils of angry snakes.

'Fuck it,' I whispered to myself. It was what Lacy would say, and she would like that I was saying it. 'Fuck it.'

Breem was alive if you reordered your understanding of what life is. His breathing was being done through a tube and a respirator. At least sixty percent of his blood had been left in the Hyundai. What else he had lost in that car wouldn't be known until he regained consciousness. If there was a truly merciful God, Breem would be given as long a reprieve from consciousness and his new memories as possible.

In the hallway outside Emergency, Breem's wife sat with the dumbfounded look of a lost traveler in a bus depot. She was a small woman, pretty, with short brown hair, which she nervously kept brushing back behind her ears. She wore a white cotton sweater over khaki pants and a light tan shirt with coordinating socks and belt. It was not an outfit you just throw on unless there is a gene that some women have that allows them to properly match clothes without a second thought – a gene I apparently never got. She had even taken the time to put on appropriate lipstick for the occasion. Maybe it was how some women coped with stress; they dressed for it.

I held out the composite drawing of Gabriel for her to look at.

'Have you ever seen him?'

She studied it carefully and shook her head. 'Did he do this to my husband?'

I continued without committing either way. 'Do you know where he went this morning, or if he met someone?'

Again she shook her head. 'I told the other officers from before that I didn't. I told them everything. He was fine, everything was fine . . . I don't understand any of this.'

I removed a picture of Lacy from my pocket and handed it to her. 'Did you ever see her with him?'

She glanced at it without seeing it. 'My husband was not having an affair.'

I recognized something in the way she spoke that said her husband had not always been faithful.

'That's not what—'

'I'm sorry, I don't know why I said that.'

She glanced at it as if she wasn't really looking. Then I saw the flash of recognition in her eyes. 'Is she a contestant?'

I nodded. 'He telephoned my daughter three times. Do you know why?'

'He talked to all of them. He was making the corsages they were to wear in the parade.'

'Do you know if he was involved with any environmental groups?'

She looked at me as if she hadn't heard the question correctly or couldn't believe that I would ask it at a moment like this.

'You think the Sierra Club did this?' she said sarcastically.

That was it. Whatever secrets Evans Breem had, he had kept them from his wife. She looked away down the hallway toward the emergency room.

'The doctors haven't told me anything.'

She turned and looked at the bruises on my face from the door. 'Were you there? Do you know what happened to him?'

I looked down at my hands and saw the ball of explosives wrapped with silver tape. Then I saw Breem's eyes as he made his terrible decision. I looked at her, hoping she would never know what I did and wishing that I didn't.

'I don't know the specifics, I'm sorry.'

A few minutes later I walked out of Emergency and took an elevator up to the floor where my injured partner, Traver, was recovering from the explosion at Sweeny's bungalow. Even though I knew better, the one thing I assumed would always remain the same was Traver. And then Gabriel changed that. Just as easily as that. And now I had to find a way to tell him that my daughter had been kidnapped. I had to find a way to admit to him that I couldn't protect her. That I had failed. I couldn't do it. I couldn't bear the look in his eyes when he heard the news. I started to reach for the stop button, but the door opened and I was there.

The walls of the hallway were painted a washed-out yellow. From several of the rooms came the sound of ventilators rhythmically pumping air into weakened lungs. With each step I had the sense of walking back in time. I stopped at Room 308 without consciously realizing it. It was the room where Lacy's father had died. I had walked down this hallway and into this room with her every day for two weeks. The walls had been eggshell blue then, but everything else was exactly the same: the smell of disinfectant, the voice on the PA, the sound of a gurney's wheel wobbling on the lino-leum, the not quite natural silence of a hospital's hallways that had witnessed so many broken hearts.

It had all begun right here, Lacy's slipping away from me with each fading breath of her father. The first unspoken emotion, the first secret. The first step toward wherever she was now was taken right here. How could I have let it happen? It was my job to see the things that others couldn't. Why hadn't I seen that?

I stopped at the nurses' station and was told that it was more than a little past visiting hours, so I held up my badge and told her I'd just be a minute.

I stepped into Traver's room and hung next to the door for a moment. He looked smaller in the hospital bed. Fragile. There was a tube in his nose. His head was heavily bandaged from where they had drilled a hole to relieve pressure in his skull. His face was swollen and bruised. The doctors said he would recover fully, but you couldn't have convinced me of it at that moment.

I walked over to his bed and took hold of the steel handrails. On the nightstand was a photograph of the twins in matching panda bear suits.

'What time is it?' he said in an unrecognizable whisper. His eyes opened briefly and looked at me, then closed again. The fingers of his hands stretched out and I took hold of them.

'It's late.'

His chest rose under the sheets as he took a deep breath and then exhaled with an audible whoosh, as if it took all his strength to force the air out of his lungs.

'I've been hearing things,' he whispered. 'Are they true?'

'You just get better.'

He weakly squeezed my hand, then appeared to settle back into sleep. His breathing evened out into long, quiet breaths.

'Lace . . .' he whispered before his voice failed him. Then a single tear formed at the corner of his eye and trickled down his bruised cheek.

twelve

Harrison had been correct about the phone number we found in Lacy's journal. The address in Azusa was residential – a small Spanish bungalow on a street lined with tall palm trees and low-riders parked in driveways. But what were the phone number to a house twenty miles from her own home and the letter D doing in her journal? If D stood for Daniel Finley, and by proxy this house we were parked outside of, then a direct line had been drawn between my daughter's kidnapping and the bullet that went through the back of Finley's head in the flower shop. And if there was a connection to that murder, then there was a connection to every act of violence that Gabriel had perpetrated after that. And the acts of violence that were yet to come.

But if there was no connection? If the letter D stood for a cute boy she had met and nothing more, then we were wasting precious time that my daughter didn't have.

I opened the window and took a breath of the damp night air. Half a mile north, the dark canyon of the San Gabriel River rose up out of the pavement and sliced into what the Sheriff's Department called 'the ghetto of the National Forest System.'

I glanced at the cup of coffee from 7-Eleven sitting on the dash, then crumpled the remains of one of their ready-to-eat chicken sandwiches.

We had already called the house twice with no result. There were no lights on inside, no car in the driveway.

'Try it again,' I said.

Harrison punched in the number and let it ring ten times with no result, then hung up.

'What do you want to do? We don't have a warrant. A number in a journal isn't enough for cause,' Harrison said.

'Unless we find something.'

'In which case it may not be useable in court.'

'To hell with the court.'

We both sat silently for a moment. A few drops of rain landed on the windshield and slid down into the wipers. The ribbons of dark clouds had given way to a heavy, solid cover that was moving down the face of the San Gabriels above Azusa. Another raindrop landed on the windshield, then another. Maybe the rain would keep people away from the parade, I thought. Pray for rain, torrents of it, flash floods, mud slides, the works. Pray we would get lucky.

I saw something in the house out of the corner of my eye. Or at least I thought I saw something. I rubbed my eyes and stared at the window. I was beyond tired. It must have just been the reflection of a streetlight off the glass. Then it was there again.

'Look.' I motioned toward the house with a nod.

Harrison didn't see it and shook his head.

'Rear window on the right side.'

Nothing.

'I thought I saw—'

In the dark recess of the window, the orange glow of a cigarette burned a tiny hole through the darkness. Harrison stared at it for a moment, then tilted his head toward me.

'That's interesting.'

'What's your first thought when you hear a phone ring in the middle of the night?'

'Who died.'

I nodded. 'So why wouldn't you answer it?'

'I wouldn't want anyone to know I was there.'

'Because you're hiding something.'

'I'll buy that.'

The glow in the window appeared again for a moment and then faded back into the darkness.

'I think we just got cause to go in that door.'

We walked down the east side of the street and approached the house from the side opposite where the smoker had stood at the window. The front door was made of heavy oak, which would have been difficult to go through, so we slowly moved around toward the back. Shades were drawn on all the windows. Behind one of them, a candle appeared to be flickering inside. We reached the back corner of the house and stopped. Several yards away, a dog either heard us or picked up our scent and began to bark and pull against its chain, which rattled in the darkness like a Dickens ghost.

At the back of the house was a small landing – three steps to a flimsy screen door and then a standard home improvement plywood door beyond that. We moved under the windows, up the steps, and took positions on either side of the door.

I took my Glock in hand and Harrison followed suit with his 9mm. There were worry lines on his forehead. As cool as he was when faced with a bomb that could vaporize him, the prospect of an encounter with a living, breathing suspect scared the hell out of him. I couldn't argue with his logic. Going through doors was for adrenaline junkies, not forty-four-year-old mothers.

'I don't suppose we're going to knock,' Harrison whispered.

'You're fine,' I said.

Harrison half nodded, as if he had just grabbed hold of the fiction that he was fine and was being dragged along against his will.

'We don't know what's inside, so keep your weapon down. You kick the door and I'll go in first.'

I reached out and took hold of the screen door and pulled it open. The hinges creaked nearly as loud as a siren.

The light in the kitchen came on and I heard the fall of footsteps inside. Harrison looked at me with hesitation clearly in his eyes.

'Go,' I said.

His foot hit the door just beneath the handle, splintering the wood but not breaking the lock. He kicked it again and the dead bolt gave way completely, sending the door swinging wildly into the room. I stepped into the doorway and a can of Coke flew by my head and out the door, skidding off the landing out into the yard.

I yelled, 'Police,' but the figure was already disappearing back into the house.

'This is the police!'

I heard the suspect's footsteps retreating and the sound of a door closing.

There was a short hallway leading out of the kitchen and through an archway. Another open archway led into what appeared to be the living room on the left. Down the hall were two doors on the right and another one at the end. Harrison stepped past me and took a position in the archway leading into the living room.

I pointed to the light coming from under the door at the end of the hallway.

'Follow me and cover the doors on the right.'

Harrison nodded and I started down the dark hallway, holding on to my Glock like it was a safety line and I was just a step over the edge of a cliff. Harrison moved behind me, his gun trained on the doors on the right. I stopped and pulled open the first door. It was an empty closet. The second wasn't tightly closed and opened with a gentle push.

'Bathroom,' I whispered.

At the far end of the room, a dark shower curtain hung across the length of a tub. A sharp, metallic *ping* came from behind the curtain. I raised my gun and trained it on the center of the curtain. Harrison took two steps in, then slowly reached out, took hold of the curtain and yanked it open. A drop of water slipped from the shower head and fell onto the side of a metal wash pail that was overturned in the tub. Harrison glanced at me with a sigh of relief.

I swung around and trained my Glock on the door at the end of the hall. I could see the movement of a shadow from inside the room, breaking the line of light coming out from under the door. I motioned to Harrison, who slipped past me and took a position at the side of the door.

'This is the police. Come out of the door slowly with your hands in the air!'

Harrison's hand touched my shoulder.

'What is that smell?' he whispered.

I took a couple of breaths, testing the air.

'I don't smell—'

'Smoke.' He looked at the door. 'He's burning something.'

The high-pitched squeal of a smoke alarm let loose inside the room.

'Take the door,' I said.

Harrison rushed forward and hit the door with a powerful kick. The lock gave way with almost no resistance, flying open like it had been blown by a powerful gust of wind. I stepped inside and raised my weapon. A figure was crouched on the floor, madly fanning a small fire inside a wastebasket with a magazine.

'Put your hands in the air and drop the magazine, right now!'

The magazine fell out of his hands and he dropped to the floor, covering his head like he was doing a duck-and-cover drill from the sixties.

'Spread your hands!'

'I am not armed and am offering no resistance!' he yelled. 'I am not armed and am offering—'

'I have a gun pointed at your head. Now lie down flat with your hands and legs spread-eagle.'

He began to repeat his rehearsed statement.

'I am not armed—'

I pressed my Glock to the back of his head.

'Spread-eagle, now.'

He nodded and stretched out.

'I am unarmed and am not offering—'

'If you say that again, I'll shoot you.'

I put a knee into the middle of his back and holstered my weapon as Harrison took a position in front with his 9mm pointed at the suspect's head.

'Give me your right hand.'

He pulled his left hand back.

'That's not your right, but it will do.'

I put the cuff on his wrist, then drew his right hand back and clamped it tight behind his back.

Harrison moved over to the burning wastebasket, flipped it over, depriving the fire of oxygen, then walked over to the fire alarm above the door and shut it off. The silence felt like the immediate aftermath of a car accident when your perception of the world has just violently changed in a heartbeat. I stood up and took what felt like my first breath in over a minute.

The suspect was male, white, twenty-something, with

long dreadlocks that were spread out on the floor like the legs of a large, blond spider. His clothes were baggy and dark.

'Look at this,' Harrison said.

He was standing at two folding tables in the corner. Stacked on top were half a dozen large cardboard boxes. Harrison opened one of the boxes and removed a metal cylinder.

'Smoke grenades, Mexican military. I think we just connected another dot.'

I opened another box and removed a plastic one-gallon jug.

'Roundup.'

'Herbicide,' Harrison said.

I turned and looked around, then whispered the words Lacy had spoken. 'Direct action.'

'A call to arms,' Harrison said.

The room was a monument to environmental extremism. There were photographs of burned ski lodges, spiked old-growth trees, burned lumber trucks, ransacked college labs that were working on the best corn that altered genetics could produce. There were fake wanted posters for Monsanto, DuPont, and the secretary of the interior. A laptop computer that was turned off sat in the corner.

'You don't suppose Lacy got caught up in something and it has nothing to do with Gabriel's plan to attack the parade?' Harrison said.

I looked over at the kid lying facedown on the floor.

'You think a bunch of twenty-somethings trying to save the planet blew off Breem's hands?'

'No.'

'Neither do I.'

We both turned at the same time and looked at the upturned wastebasket.

'What was he trying to destroy?'

'I have rights. Unless you have a search warrant, you are trespassing,' the kid on the floor said.

He had a high, nasal voice with the soft gentle curves of Vermont or Massachusetts rounding his vowels. I imagined he had nice, liberal parents who wore jeans and L.L. Bean sweaters, and who at some point lost the ability to communicate with their son. I walked over and knelt next to him.

'You're under arrest on suspicion of kidnapping and attempted murder. You have the right to remain silent and the right to an attorney.'

'Murder?' he said weakly.

'You have no idea how much trouble you're in.'

'You're the one who's in trouble.'

Harrison picked up the wastebasket and its contents fell to the floor, along with flakes of ash from the burned edges of papers. He picked up a map out of the pile and spread it on the floor.

'Pasadena.'

'Assholes,' the kid said.

I walked over and knelt down to look at the map. The parade route along Colorado was highlighted in yellow.

'Look at the X's,' Harrison said.

Half a dozen red X's marked spots along the route at several-block intervals.

'Lacy was the warm-up act,' I said.

He nodded. 'Smoke grenades and Roundup.'

Harrison's finger moved to the top of the map. There was a small red dot from the marker where the roads sloped up into the foothills. It was barely noticeable, almost as if it was a mistake made by folding the map while the ink from the X's was still wet.

'That mean anything to you?'

I looked at it trying to find its place in the investigation, then a chill flushed through my body.

'Yes . . .' I stared at him silently for a second. 'That's my house.'

I rose unsteadily to my feet and took several deep breaths, resisting the urge to put my gun to the head of the kid on the floor and demand to know where my daughter was. My eye then caught something across the room. A page from the *Times* was tacked to the wall. I walked toward it until it was in focus, until it sent a jolt through my heart. It was a photograph of Lacy at the beauty pageant spraying the audience with herbicide. The same red marker that had made the dot on our house on the map had drawn a circle around my daughter.

Harrison stepped up next to me.

'Roll the kid over on his back,' I said.

I stared at the picture of Lacy as Harrison grabbed the kid by the arm and rolled him over onto his back.

'Ow!' he screamed in pain. 'My wrists! My wrists, assholes!'

I walked over and knelt next to him. Involuntarily, my hand drifted over to the handle of my gun.

'Where's my daughter?'

He stared defiantly at me for a moment, then smiled.

'Don't smile at me.'

'I want a lawyer.'

My hand drifted from my gun and I placed it on his chest. Beads of sweat were forming on his face.

'You can't touch me!'

I could feel his heart pounding in his chest like a drum.

'You know who Breem is, don't you?'

There was a flash of surprise in his eyes. 'I don't know anything.'

'Of course you do. You're a smart kid, probably went to a nice private college in the Green Mountains where you studied art and environmental science.'

'I'm not talking without a lawyer. And I will file abuse charges against you.'

'You smug little bastard.'

I grabbed him by his shirt, lifted him up off the floor and dropped him on his cuffed wrists. He shrieked from surprise as much as pain. It was one of the advantages of looking something like a suspect's mother – I could scare the hell out of them with the smallest gesture of violence. And then I realized I had seen him before.

'I know you.'

He shook his head.

'The night of the pageant. You jumped out of your seat and tripped right at my feet. You looked right into my face.'

Again he shook his head.

'You were supposed to be part of what Lacy did that

night, but you got scared and ran out of the auditorium without doing anything.'

'No, that's not—'

'I think yes. You left Lacy to do it by herself because you didn't have the balls.'

'I want a lawyer.'

'Did you put the gun to the back of Daniel Finley's head and shoot him at his flower shop? Did you have the balls for that?'

His eyes grew wide with surprise.

'On top of kidnapping, you're going to be charged with murder,' I pressed.

'No, we don't hurt people!'

'Who's we?'

'I'm not talking.'

'Do you know Gabriel?'

His eyes revealed nothing. He had either learned very quickly to be a better liar or the name was truly new to him.

'What about Finley's partner at the shop, Breem?'

Same result.

'A couple of hours ago Gabriel wrapped explosives around Breem's hands. He sat for hours staring at them, locked in a car, going mad, until he began screaming and they blew up. There was skin and bone and blood splattered across every inch of the inside of the car. A piece of a fingernail was stuck in his cheek. Where his hands had been, there was only bone sticking out and blood pumping over his legs like it was coming from a garden hose.'

As I spoke, his heart began to pound harder and

faster against my hand. Sweat ran down the side of his face.

'Gabriel is a terrorist. He's not trying to save the planet. He's going to kill people. He's going to place a bomb, not a smoke grenade, a real bomb, along the parade route and detonate it. Little kids in their parents' arms are going to be blown to pieces across Colorado Boulevard. Is that how you want to save the planet? Killing children?'

'We don't hurt people!'

'You can help me stop it. It's not too late.'

He shook his head.

'What's your name?'

I could feel my grip on self-control slipping away. All I needed was his name. If he gave me that, the rest would come. I looked at Harrison and shook my head.

'To hell with him, Lieutenant. He's a terrorist,' Harrison said loudly, for effect.

I looked at the kid. 'You're not a terrorist, and you're not a killer, either, are you?'

I stood up and walked over to the other side of the room.

'What do you want to do?' Harrison asked in a whisper.

I shook my head. 'Goddamnit, he knows where my daughter is, or he knows someone who knows.' He had to talk. One way or another, he had to. He wouldn't leave here until he did.

'If I ask you to leave the room, no arguments . . .' I said to Harrison.

Concern flashed in Harrison's eyes. 'Lieutenant—'

'I don't care what it costs me, I'm going to find out what he knows about Lacy. You understand?'

Harrison looked at me for a moment, then nodded.

'Eric Hanson,' the kid said.

It was barely a whisper, but it was as good as if he had shouted it from the rooftops. I walked over and knelt next to him.

'You're not a murderer, are you, Eric?'

He looked away from me and stared at the far wall.

'Then you have to help me stop it, or you're going to be charged with it.'

'You're not lying to me?' His voice sounded as if he were thirteen. I shook my head.

'No, I'm not lying, this is real.'

'We don't hurt people.'

'Gabriel does.'

'I don't know Gabriel.'

I took out the Xerox likeness of Gabriel and held it up. 'Have you ever seen him?'

Lines appeared around his eyes as he looked at it, then he looked away and shook his head. 'I've never seen him.'

'You know who I am? You know I'm Lacy's mother?'

He nodded.

'Where's my daughter?'

His eyes seemed to be searching inside himself for some foothold of reason to cling to.

'I don't know—'

'What don't you know?'

'We work in cells.'

'Was Lacy in yours?'

He began to shake his head. 'I want a lawyer—'

'A lawyer isn't going to stop Gabriel – you can. A lawyer isn't going to help someone who blew up children on Colorado Boulevard. And that's what you're a part of now.'

'No one was supposed to be hurt.'

'People already have been. People have been killed.'

'It wasn't us. It wasn't.'

I could see in his eyes that he was on the verge of tears. I glanced over at Harrison and motioned for him to help me get Eric to his feet. We picked him up and sat him in a chair, and then I knelt in front of him. Sitting up, the lines of stress disappeared from his face and he looked younger. He had a pimple on his neck. His green eyes had a youthful clarity that were clinging desperately to some recent, more innocent past.

'Was Lacy in your cell?'

He lowered his eyes and nodded.

'Who recruited her?'

He took a breath. 'I like Lacy, she's—'

'Who recruited her?'

He hesitated, still clinging to distrust like a life preserver.

'Eric,' I said softly, 'we're talking about my daughter's life.'

He closed his eyes as if that would make it all go away. 'I did. I met her at Starbucks. I was following Daniel's instructions.'

'Finley? Daniel Finley?'

He nodded sadly. 'They told me he was killed in a burglary.'

'Who told you?'

'His partner, Breem. I don't know the others. We don't use names . . . just letters.'

'Eric, it wasn't a burglary. He was killed because he knew who Gabriel was. Gabriel put a gun to the back of Daniel's head and pulled the trigger like he was a steer in a slaughterhouse. The bullet exploded inside his skull, killing him instantly.'

He shook his head and whispered, 'God.'

'Why was Lacy kidnapped?'

He had the appearance of a small child lost in a shopping mall.

'Why?'

'For the money.'

'Why Lacy?'

'After what she did at the pageant, Finley thought it would look like antienvironmentalists did it. No one would get hurt, it was just to raise money. If you didn't pay, she'd be released.'

I didn't want to ask the next question but I had to. It would have been worse to hear someone else ask it.

'Was Lacy part of it? Did she know?'

His chin dropped to his chest and he didn't answer. I grabbed him by the chin, raising his eyes to mine.

'Was Lacy a part of it?'

He sat silently for a moment, then shook his head.

'She didn't know. I wanted to tell her but . . . that wasn't the plan. Breem called her the night of the pageant. Told her to meet him somewhere the next day. That's when they took her.'

'Do you know where she is? Where they're keeping her.'

He shook his head. 'Only an e-mail address.'

'If you're withholding information from me—'

'I'm not, I swear.'

'Who else is in your cell?'

'It was just Finley and Lacy.'

'How many in the others?'

'I don't know. That's how it works. Finley and Breem were the only ones who knew.'

'Does the name Sweeny mean anything to you? He worked for Finley and Breem at the flower shop.'

He shook his head.

'What was your job in the cell?'

'I was in charge of the stuff for the parade.'

'How was it acquired?'

'Finley got it. I don't know where.'

'How were you to get the smoke grenades and the Roundup to the others?'

'I was going to receive a place and time by e-mail.'

'Did you receive it?'

'No.'

'Do you know the e-mail address you were supposed to get the message from?'

'Yeah.'

I stood and pulled Harrison to the other side of the room.

'Can we get a street address from an e-mail?'

'We would have to go through the service provider. That would take a court order.'

'We don't have time for that.'

'Hicks and the FBI could do it.'

I had an image of an FBI SWAT team storming a house with my daughter inside. It didn't sit very well. People who weren't supposed to tended to get shot.

'We could send a message from Eric's computer to the other e-mail address.'

Harrison nodded and finished the thought.

'Eric tells them the cops are watching this place and that he has to bring the grenades and Roundup to their location.'

'It's worth a try.'

'I think something's wrong,' Eric said.

We both turned.

'What do you mean?'

'I've sent them five e-mails over the last five hours and they haven't responded.'

I walked over and knelt in front of him, placing my hands on his knees.

'That's not supposed to happen, is it?'

He shook his head. 'No, someone is always supposed to be there.'

'Do you know if Finley's partner, Breem, was at the location you were e-mailing?'

'He ran the cell, I guess he might have been.'

'When did you last e-mail them?'

'About an hour ago.'

I could feel my heart beginning to beat faster. It was becoming one of those nightmares where you're trying to get somewhere, but every door you open takes you in the wrong direction.

'If Breem was at this e-mail location just before he was placed inside the car with a bomb on his lap, then it's possible the terrorist Gabriel was also there. Eric, if Gabriel knows that location, then everyone there is in great danger. You understand?'

He nodded.

'You must have had a prearranged signal to send if something went wrong, didn't you?' I asked.

He hesitated.

'Gabriel is a killer. He will not let anyone get in his way. Every one of your friends is in danger.'

'Everything is screwed – that's the signal.'

'What's the e-mail address?'

He looked at me. I could see in his eyes that some piece of him was still clinging to the eco-warrior image he had built for himself. Name, rank, and Sierra Club membership number only. Anything more than that and you were a traitor to the cause. No different from the lowliest oil company executive raping the planet.

His eyes fixed on me, and I could see him dig his heels into what was left of his eroding world.

'What if you're lying to me?'

'Your friends, and my daughter, may be dead already, but if they're not, the only thing that may save them is what you do right now.'

He looked down at his lap and the last of his resolve was expelled with a long, tired breath.

'I need your password, and the e-mail address to send the message to.'

He sat silently for a moment, and then the words slipped out of his mouth in the dull monotone of a witness naming names in front of a Senate committee.

'Hldtplnetgr.'

'Hold the planet green,' Harrison said.

Eric nodded.

Harrison sat down at the laptop and began logging on. The computer chimed and whistled and then connected to the 'net. The synthetic 'welcome' had an eerie, menacing quality to it. Like an automated voice in a cockpit repeating 'Pull up, pull up.'

'What's the e-mail address?'

'Keptplnetgrn@znet.com.'

Keep the planet green. Hold the planet green. Jesus. It had the sound of kids playing at being spies. Connecting it to real violence was unimaginable. Connecting my daughter to it was terrifying. How the hell had it gone so horribly wrong? How had Gabriel slipped into this? And why? What creates a person like that? How are we to understand a kind of thinking that is utterly foreign to us?

Harrison entered in the e-mail address, and then typed the message: 'Everything is screwed.'

I glanced at Eric. 'Anything else?'

He shook his head. 'Just that.'

'How are they supposed to respond?'

He shrugged. 'I don't know.'

I nodded to Harrison and he pressed send.

'If they don't answer—'

He left the question hanging, as if not really wanting to finish it. I stared at the screen silently, trying to will

212

an answer to our message. It was like the first night Lacy had ever stayed out well past the agreed time of her return. I had sat on the couch until three in the morning, staring out the window, waiting for her headlights to appear in the driveway. With each minute that passed, I created another scenario of disaster, another story of lost innocence. When she did return after three that morning, instead of telling her that I loved her and thought I had lost her, I told her that I knew too much about how horrible things can happen to people and that she was grounded. A brilliant piece of parenting. Push her away.

I glanced at my watch and began marking the minutes since we sent the mail, the same way I had counted them that night waiting for Lacy. Four minutes passed, then five, six . . . seven . . . nine . . . ten.

'How long—' Harrison stopped himself. 'Never mind.'

I turned from the computer and looked around the room. Eric was sitting slumped in the chair, his head hanging, eyes staring at the floor. He looked like a high-school kid who couldn't believe that he had just lost the big game.

I walked over and pulled up another folding chair in front of him.

'Tell me about Lacy.'

He looked up at me with either surprise or disbelief on his face. 'What do you mean?'

It was pathetic to have to ask a kid who helped kidnap my daughter who she was, but pride was the last thing I was worried about now. I wanted to know what she was passionate about, what she feared, loathed, dreamed. I wanted to know all the things I should, but didn't because I had stopped paying attention. I wanted to know who my daughter was.

'Why did she do this?' I asked.

A slight smile appeared on his lips. 'Oh, that . . . like how could my daughter do something so . . . yeah, right.'

He looked at me and shook his head as if in disbelief. 'How can you all be so clueless? You think we do what we do because we admire the world you've created?'

Right. Ask a foolish question of a twenty-year-old true believer and you may just hear the truth.

'I may have failed my daughter, but you betrayed her.'

He looked at me with the defiant eyes that he had when we first put him in cuffs.

'I did what I did because I believe in something. What's your excuse?' he said.

I stood up. 'Love is my excuse. Blind, stupid love.'

I walked over to Harrison, who was sitting in front of the computer with his eyes closed.

'Maybe we should cancel the parade,' I said.

He opened his eyes, as if woken from a deep sleep, and glanced over his shoulder at me.

'Can you do that?'

'I doubt it. Doesn't exactly send the right message, does it? First sign of trouble – cave, abandon tradition.'

'Not to mention millions of dollars in television revenue.'

'The greatest of all traditions.'

Harrison's eyes seemed to pick a thought out of the air. 'How much of the parade route is televised?'

I thought for a moment. 'Just the first few blocks.'

There was the answer. Or at least the answer that offered the most hope.

'We can forget the rest. He'll want it live and in color.'

Harrison nodded.

'Would you bet your family's life on that?' I asked.

'Not if he's willing to die.'

'So we find him before the parade.'

'It's the only way to eliminate all doubt.'

The chimes of an instant message came from the computer.

We both turned and looked at the screen.

'Somebody's alive,' Harrison said.

The message read: 'How screwed?'

Harrison looked at me for a response. I walked over to Eric.

'Did you have any other messages prearranged?'

He began shaking his head, the anger building in his eyes. 'You said everyone at the other location was dead. They're not dead. You assholes lied to me!'

'You want to keep them alive, you tell me what I want to know.'

'I'm not helping you anymore. Screw it.'

I walked back to Harrison.

'We need a reason for them to tell us where they are,' he said.

I looked over at the smoke grenades and the Roundup Eric and his friends on the other end of the e-mail had planned to use to disrupt the parade.

'Write "Everything is completely screwed. Need to

215

move the grenades and Roundup to your location or forget the parade." '

Harrison typed it and sent it. We waited thirty seconds, then a minute.

'They're talking about it,' I said.

The first minute stretched into another and still nothing came back.

'I don't think they're buying,' Harrison said.

'No kidding, you think we're stupid,' Eric whispered.

Harrison's fingers quivered over the keyboard as if they were impatient to type.

'What do you want to do, Lieutenant?'

'Give 'em a push.'

Harrison looked at the keyboard, then glanced at Eric as if he were snatching thoughts from his back pocket. His fingers typed out an imaginary response in the air then stopped moving and settled onto the keyboard and he sent another message: 'I have to move now, assholes! Where do I bring it. Give me an address.'

'Send it.'

He clicked on send and we waited for a response.

'It isn't going to work,' Eric said.

Nothing came back.

'I don't know,' Harrison said. 'You want to send something else?'

I shook my head. 'They either buy it or they don't.'

Harrison's hand patted his shirt pocket as if searching for a pack of cigarettes.

'How long ago did you quit?'

'Four years.'

'Took me eleven years before I stopped doing that—'

216

The chimes of a response came back and we both watched it come up on the screen like we were waiting for lottery numbers.

' "Make sure you're not followed, then bring the stuff to 1472 . . ." '

'It's an address,' Harrison said.

I was praying it was somewhere in Pasadena. Anywhere else meant other departments would have to be notified, and that meant control would slip from my hands.

'1472 Monte, Pasadena,' Harrison said. 'I think I know that.'

He moved over to the map spread out on the floor and found the address.

'That's just north of the 210, across the street from a park.'

'Assholes,' Eric whispered.

I took out my cell and called Chief Chavez as I started for the door. He answered on the first ring as if he was expecting the call.

'We may have found Lacy,' I said. 'Pasadena address. We'll need tactical to be ready, but I don't want anyone barging in. I don't think they'll hurt her.'

I stepped out the front door into the predawn light. A drizzle was falling now. The sweet citrus odor of a grapefruit tree hung in the moist air.

'Breem and Finley were the leaders of the environmental group that took her. And connecting her to them draws a line straight to Gabriel.'

The silence on Chavez's end of the phone lasted too long.

'What is it, Chief?'

'Breem died ten minutes ago. He lost too much blood.'

I took the phone away from my ear and took a breath. In my mind I saw Breem's eyes for a second. There had been a question in them, a terrible, simple question: Why? Why was this happening to me? It was the same question I wanted answered.

'What's the connection between a small group of idealists and a monster like Gabriel?' I asked Chavez.

'Maybe he needed Breem and Finley to smuggle in the explosives from Mexico and it ends there.'

'I don't know.'

'Alex, we don't have to understand him, we just have to stop him.'

I wasn't sure Chavez was right about that. Understanding Gabriel may be the only chance we had. But there were no reference points to understanding him. He was a book filled with blank pages.

Harrison stepped outside with Eric in tow.

'Breem's dead,' I said to him. I looked at Eric. 'He bled to death.'

Eric's mouth hung open as if he had lost the power of speech, then he looked down at his feet as if ashamed. Harrison started toward the car and I picked up the phone and continued with Chavez.

'Lacy may be at an address just north of the 210, 1472 Monte.'

'I'll set up a staging area.'

'And we'll need this house in Azusa sealed.'

'I'll take care of it,' Chavez said. Then he started to say something else but stopped.

'What is it?' I asked.

'Agent Hicks is blaming us for Breem's death. He wants you out of the loop.'

'What did you tell him?'

'I told him to go fuck himself.'

My big Chicano grandfather. I started to say thanks, but the words hung in my throat.

'Forget it,' Chavez said. 'He can still pull this out from under us, but until he does, we do it our way.'

I hung up and started for the car after Harrison. The rain was falling heavily now and had washed away the scent of grapefruit. The tops of the palm trees swung in the increasing wind like they were stuck on springs. My breath was visible as I exhaled. I looked west, along the sloping front of the San Gabriels toward Pasadena. The valley floor had once been Spanish land grants. The mountains above were home to gold mines and grizzly bears. Looking at the landscape now, with its suburban sprawl, it felt as unrecognizable as if I had turned back the calendar a century and a half. Everything had changed, everything.

thirteen

The house on Monte was a small stucco home with a detached garage in the back off the alley. The windows were barred, the front and back doors covered by heavy metal screen doors. The lot to the right was vacant. A storefront with an OUT OF BUSINESS sign in the window occupied the one on the left. It was the perfect address to go through a day unnoticed.

By the time we arrived from Azusa, Chavez had already set up the staging area a block away. A SWAT officer dressed as a homeless man was watching from across the street in the park. Another officer had an observation point in a second-floor window of a house directly behind it.

'There's been no movement inside, no lights, nothing,' Chavez said.

I looked toward the east. The first hint of dawn was showing over the mountains, but with the low clouds and rain, full light would be slow in coming. I glanced at my watch; it was five-thirty.

'We have about forty-five minutes before it's light,' I said. 'They're expecting someone to drive up and walk up to that front door. I think that's exactly what we should do.'

The SWAT commander named Peters nodded.

'We hit the back as soon as they answer the front door.'

With his black uniform, machine gun, body armor, and helmet, he had the look of a real-life action figure. Most of his team were ex-military. For fun, I imagined they took fifty cc's of adrenaline and injected it directly into their heart muscles. For excitement, I couldn't imagine what they did.

'There's no reason to expect that they're armed inside,' I said.

'Unless Gabriel is in there,' Chavez said.

'If Gabriel is inside, then he's made a mistake, and so far he hasn't made any.'

'There's another possibility,' Harrison said.

We all turned to him.

'He may have been here and left.'

He didn't have to finish the thought. We could all draw our own picture of the results of that one. If Gabriel had been there, what had he left behind? I turned to Chavez.

'How long did it take to get the first squads here after we talked on the phone?'

'The first unit was here five minutes after I talked to you in Azusa,' Chavez said.

I looked at the house on Monte where the e-mail had originated from and walked the time line back another step.

'And I received the e-mail from inside that house two minutes before I talked to you on the phone.'

I looked at Harrison. 'That's six or seven minutes for him to leave.'

'If he preset a device, he would have only needed one minute. We could be walking into anything.'

I looked down the block toward the corner and then turned toward the house. Rain was hitting the hard shell of the SWAT officer's helmet and bouncing off like repelled rounds of buckshot.

'I need a vest and a rain parka with a hood.'

Chavez started to shake his head.

'If someone answers that door, you go in the back,' I said, looking at the SWAT commander Peters. 'If no one answers, I go in alone.'

'They see your face, it's over right then,' Peters said.

'In this light, with my hood up, it will give you enough time to go through the back.'

'I don't want you stepping through that door,' Chavez said.

'If it explodes and Lacy's inside, I can't let anyone else be responsible for that. This is my call.'

Chavez glanced down the block and shook his head. 'Give her a vest and a rain parka.'

Peters rolled his eyes disapprovingly and motioned to another officer to bring a vest and a parka.

'If no one answers, I should go through that door first,' Harrison said.

'No,' I said.

'He's right,' Chavez said.

I started to shake my head.

'You don't know a bomb from a burrito,' Chavez said. 'Harrison does. End of discussion.'

A SWAT officer walked up with the vest and a rain jacket. I slipped the heavy armored vest over my shoulders, then pulled on the rain jacket.

'No one answers, you do not touch that door until Harrison is with you,' Chavez said.

I nodded, but my mind was already walking up the steps to the house.

'If the door does open, you take down whoever opens it,' Peters said. 'If you can't, we'll already be in the back door, so don't go charging in yourself.'

I took out my wallet, removed a photograph of Lacy, and handed it to Peters.

'Make sure everyone on your team knows exactly what Lacy looks like.'

He took it and nodded. 'I have a daughter, too, Lieutenant. We'll take care of her.'

He tucked the photograph into a pocket, then glanced at Chavez. 'I'll need five minutes to get my team in position.'

He turned and moved purposefully off into the gray light. I walked over to my Volvo and glanced at my watch. I heard Chavez step up behind me.

'Now, remember, you wait for Harrison if there's no answer,' Chavez said.

I nodded and looked down the street to the corner. The rain had raised oil on the pavement that glistened under the streetlight. The sound of raindrops hitting the leaves of banana trees and birds of paradise plants muffled the crackle of police radios. It was strangely peaceful, the kind of morning to huddle under the covers and hold off the dawn for as long as possible.

'Park in front of the vacant lot to the right of the house. That'll give us time to see if anything is wrong as you walk up,' Chavez said.

I glanced at Harrison, who was slipping on his vest and other equipment. Chavez reached out and took hold of my arm, squeezing it gently in concern. 'Alex, do you think Lacy's in there?'

A cold drop of rain hit my forehead and slid down my cheek. 'They answered the e-mail. Someone was or is in there.'

'But who?'

'We're going to find out.'

I walked around to the driver's side and opened the door. Half a block down behind the staging area, I noticed a paramedic unit pull up and stop. Chavez glanced at it, then turned away as if not wanting to acknowledge its presence.

'Now, you remember—'

'I remember, Ed,' I said, using his Christian name in hopes it would reassure him.

'If it's no good you get out of there.'

'Gabriel's had his opportunity to kill me already and he hasn't. I imagine there's a reason.'

'You could also just be goddamn lucky.'

' "Lucky" is not a word I would apply to the last twenty-four hours of my life.'

Harrison stepped up wearing the tools of the bomb squad. His wide-eyed look of a newly hatched homicide detective was gone. His eyes had a penetrating clarity that could chill a glass of water.

'If there's a doorbell, don't use it – knock.'

He reached out with a small radio and hooked it to my belt, then ran an earpiece and a mike up to my ear and slipped them on. Our eyes met briefly as his fingers touched my ear. It was strangely intimate, like a shared glance in a public space between two secret lovers.

'I'll be on the other end. It's an open line; I'll hear anything you say.'

His eyes held mine for a moment, then he stepped back and I slipped into the car and started it. Chavez raised his radio to his mouth.

'We're moving.'

I slipped the car into gear and pulled away from the staging area. Looking through the wet windshield, I had the sense of being submerged in an entirely new reality where the old rules no longer applied. What was up was no longer up; what was down was anyone's guess. Halfway down the block, I switched on the wipers and turned right onto Monte. Rounding the corner, my headlights swept across the park, briefly illuminating the SWAT officer dressed as a homeless man, crouching behind a tree. In the middle of the street, a crow sat picking at the remains of a McDonald's bag, tearing at it as if peeling back the skin of roadkill to get at the soggy Big Mac underneath.

Ahead on the right, next to the vacant lot, was the house. It was smaller than I had pictured. Shabbier. Even when new, it would have appeared cheap. I imagined a hard, steady rain could wash the whole thing away, board by board. But that was the thing about Southern California, wasn't it? Nothing was really permanent. A little rain, a shake of the ground, even a single idea appeared to hold the power to change everything.

I pulled up to the vacant lot and coasted to a stop. I hit the lights and turned off the engine. Rain began to gather on the windshield and run down onto the hood of the car in little streams.

'I'm getting out,' I said into the tiny mike clipped to my collar.

'Okay, Alex,' Chavez said. 'One step at a time.'

I pulled the hood of the jacket up over my head, stepped out, and started walking toward the front door. Up close, with its barred windows, the house had a distinctly lifeless quality, like something that was abandoned during a plague. The blackness inside the windows felt like the dark eyes of a predator, waiting for a flicker of weakness or hesitation. Dead climbing roses littered the foundation around the front steps like discarded bones.

'You okay?' Harrison whispered in my ear.

His voice sounded like a lover's.

'I'm okay,' I answered, using the exact same lie I had told my husband after the final intimate act before our breakup.

My hand brushed back across my hip and landed reassuringly on the weapon under my rain parka. I stepped up to the front door. The barred outside door was open, like an invitation to step inside.

'The steel door is ajar.'

'I don't like this,' Harrison said.

I reached out and took hold of the handle and pulled it gently open enough so I could knock on the wooden door. With the first knock, the door swung halfway open. No light penetrated the interior. I could make out nothing. At my feet, pooled against the threshold, was an unmistakable, dark, viscous liquid.

'No one moves,' I said urgently. 'Nobody moves!'

I pulled my weapon and trained it into the empty blackness in front of me.

'Lacy!' I yelled. 'Lacy, can you hear me?'

Nothing came back, not even an echo. The blackness inside seemed to swallow everything, including sound. I glanced at my feet. A small stream of blood trailed from the pool at the door back into the darkness, where it disappeared.

'Lacy!' I yelled again.

From down the street I could hear the gunning of an engine as Harrison and Chavez skidded around the corner. I took out a Maglite and shined the beam into the darkness, following the stream of blood across the wood floor to where it disappeared under another door.

'Do not go inside,' Harrison said.

Too late. I was already three steps in, moving toward the door that concealed the source of the blood. Ten feet into the room, a single tennis shoe lay upturned. I stopped, the tight beam of light illuminating the tennis shoe's bright yellow laces. It was my daughter's.

'Lacy!' I yelled.

I swung the beam around the room. There was some tattered furniture, a couch, an overstuffed chair, a coffee table, and a small television. The rest of the room was empty. I directed the beam back to the door where the blood disappeared. The darkness closed in around me as if I had been submerged in water. I had trouble finding enough air to take a breath. A voice in my head was saying, 'No, no, no.' I looked at my daughter's shoe, and my hand holding the flashlight began to tremble.

The same voice began to say, 'This is not happening, this is not happening.'

A rage I had never known took hold of every cell in my body and I started for the door. It was as if I were standing outside myself watching a stranger's actions, watching a mother grizzly. I seemed to enter into a tunnel that was taking me toward the door and the source of the blood.

'Stop, Lieutenant.'

I took two more steps and reached for the door handle.

'Lieutenant, please!' Harrison yelled.

I hesitated, thinking I had heard something, then continued the slide down the tunnel toward the door.

'This won't help her,' Harrison said quietly.

I stopped. The pounding of my heart was the only sound in the room. The walls of the tunnel caved. I looked at my hand. It was inches from the door handle, though I had no recollection of how it got there. I turned and looked at Harrison, who was standing in the entrance.

'That's Lacy's shoe,' I said.

My hand moved toward the door handle as if acting on its own.

'Lieutenant.'

'That's my daughter's shoe!' I yelled.

'This is not the way to do this.'

'I don't care.'

I turned back to the door, then took hold of the handle and flung the door open. Air rushed past me as if wanting to escape whatever was inside the room. I raised my weapon and the flashlight and followed the trail of blood deeper into the darkness toward the center of the room and the source of the blood.

Harrison stepped up beside me, his hand tightly wrapped around his weapon and flashlight.

The body was facedown, its hands taped behind its back. I didn't notice what it was wearing; I couldn't tell if it was a man or a woman. It had the limp, lifeless look of a rag doll. I couldn't bear to think that it was my daughter.

'Are there shoes on both feet?' I asked.

I closed my eyes, waiting for the answer, dreading it. Only a second or two passed but it had the emotional currency of hours.

'Yes,' Harrison said.

'Is the rest of the room clear?'

He swung his light across the room.

'There's a mattress, some magazines, but nothing else.'

I nodded, then reached out and placed my hand on his arm and took a deep breath. 'Can you clear the rest of the house?'

The flashing dome of squad cars outside the front door began to fill the room with red light.

'I need to just stand here for a second,' I said.

Harrison nodded, then moved past me and through the door to what I assumed was the kitchen. I looked down at my hand and realized I was still clutching my weapon, though I had no sense of holding it. I slipped it back into its holster, then looked at my daughter's shoe on the floor. Its yellow laces were untied and trailed out toward the stream of blood that passed by just inches away.

I turned and walked into the room where the victim lay. In death, a body surrenders to gravity. All definition is often lost. If the hands hadn't been taped behind the back, I would hardly know if the victim was face up or down. It was dressed in jeans and a loose gray sweater. I pointed my light on the back of the head. The hair was shiny and jet black, except for around a small entrance wound, where it was wet and matted with blood. I shined the light onto the side of the face that was visible. There was a short stubble of beard. An open, unfocused eye stared lifelessly into whatever hell his last moments had been. He was young, mid-twenties at the outside. Probably of Japanese descent.

My head felt light, and I moved back toward the doorway. God, he was just a child who looked into the wrong face. How could he possibly have understood what was happening to him? He was going to save the planet. And then this. I imagined him chaining himself to a redwood to keep it from being cut down. I turned away and looked back toward Lacy's shoe on the floor.

I walked over and picked it up. It was her left shoe. In my hand it felt almost weightless. She had a thing about keeping them as white as the day they came out of the box. I looked for any traces of blood but found none. There was a dark scuff mark on the left side as if it had been stepped on.

'Oh, God,' I whispered as I began to reconstruct what had transpired in these rooms.

She would probably have seen what happened, or if she was in another room, she would have heard it all. Either was unimaginable. Did she try to kick the killer? Did she try to run? He probably stepped on her foot as she tried to get away, which would explain the scuff mark. I closed my eyes, trying to shake the images in my head, but they persisted. I felt helpless. Gabriel had taken more than my daughter from me. Regardless of the cruelties I had witnessed as a cop, there was always that fundamental faith that in the end, good, no matter how bruised and battered, will survive. Now, that was gone.

I wrapped both hands around the shoe and clutched it to my chest. Dawn was gathering speed and light was beginning to filter through all the windows. The color of the blood on the floor was changing from dark chocolate to a deep red rose. I looked up and saw Chavez standing in the doorway.

'There's one dead in the other room. My guess is that it was a small caliber to the back of the head, just like Finley,' I said.

He took a deep breath that was a confused mix of relief and concern.

'Lacy was here,' I said. 'But we missed her.'

He glanced at the tennis shoe in my hands, and it was

clear no other explanation was necessary. He put his hand over his mouth and stared at the floor for a moment, gently shaking his head back and forth in disbelief.

'Son of a bitch' then slipped out like a monk's evening vespers.

Harrison stepped out from the other room.

'Rest of the house is clear – no explosives.'

I heard Harrison's words, but they were unimportant. My fingers were wrapped tightly around the laces of my daughter's shoe, as if I were trying to keep it from slipping from my hand – to keep her from slipping further away.

'I don't know what to do next,' I said helplessly.

Harrison glanced at Chavez. I could see the concern in their eyes. A grieving mother wasn't going to do anyone any good right now. The badge I wore was little more than an absurd prop. I should be home, like a good mother, helping my daughter get ready for school, fixing her breakfast. Telling her how pretty she looks. I glanced down at Lacy's shoe and let my fingers slip out of the laces.

Okay, I said to myself. Work it, think it out. I turned to Harrison and tried to find my way back to the present. 'Did you see a computer anywhere?'

'No.'

I took a breath. Small steps, one at a time.

'So he either took it, or he wasn't here when we e-mailed him.'

'I think he was already gone,' Harrison said.

I nodded in agreement.

'Which means he sent us here.'

'Jesus,' Chavez said. 'Jesus Chri—' The good Catholic in him kept him from finishing. 'Why?'

I glanced at Harrison and could see he was thinking exactly what I was.

'He's letting us know who's in charge,' I said.

'We're like goddamn puppets,' Chavez said angrily.

Loss of control was something Chavez was unaccustomed to. His eyes had the appearance of a bewildered monarch toppled from power.

I walked over and gripped his powerful forearm.

'We'll need a time of death as soon as possible,' I said. 'And I want to know if it was the same gun that killed Finley.'

His eyes refocused and he nodded. 'I'll get crime scene and the ME rolling.'

I looked down at the shoe in my hand, then tentatively held it out toward him.

'Can you bag this? Maybe we can get something useful from the scuff mark, or . . . maybe we'll get lucky.'

He nodded and took the shoe gently from my hand.

I had to get out of the house. The walls were closing in like soil filling a grave. I brushed past Chavez and stepped out into the open air. A dozen squads were now parked on the street. Most of the cops were staring in my direction like drivers passing the scene of an accident. Raindrops hit my face and slid down into the corners of my mouth. They had the strong saline taste of tears. I had been crying but hadn't realized it. I wiped them away with the back of my hand and glanced down the street. The crow that had been picking at the soggy

McDonald's bag now stood several feet away from it, indifferent to the remains.

From somewhere among the jumble of squad cars and the sound of radios, I heard the high-pitched *ping* of a cell phone. A uniformed officer walked up.

'A phone's been ringing in your car for a couple of minutes, Lieutenant.'

I turned to him, not hearing what he had said. 'I'm sorry?'

'Your phone's been ringing for a couple of—'

I was already moving before he finished. Call it a mother's intuition, or a woman's, or a cop's, but a phone ringing continuously at six A.M. at a murder scene sounded like a desperate plea. There was no such thing as coincidence anymore. Every moment, every second now had an urgency. I ran to the car, flung open the door, and reached across the seat to the phone on the center console.

'Delillo.'

I heard the click of the caller hanging up.

'Shit,' I said, tossing the phone back onto the seat. It could have been anything, it could have been nothing, but I had missed it, and I couldn't afford to miss anything.

Back at the house, Chavez was walking out, carrying Lacy's shoe in an evidence bag. He handed it to another officer, exchanged a few words, then looked my way.

The *ping* of the phone ringing again jolted me like the report of a gunshot. I stared at it, reluctant to answer. Terrified of what it might be or what it might not. On the fifth ring I did.

'Delillo.'

I heard over the line what sounded like the distant siren of a fire truck.

'This is Delillo.'

The voice that came back was quivering with fear and disorientation. 'Mom,' Lacy said. 'Mommy.'

I clutched the phone to my cheek. 'Lacy, where are you?'

Only silence.

'Lacy . . . Lacy, can you hear me?' I said, desperation spreading through me. 'Lacy, can you hear me? Are you hurt? Do you know where you are?'

'No . . . she doesn't.'

The voice sounded distorted, deep, with slightly slurred pronunciation, like it was coming from a surrealist painting in which reality is stretched and curved. I knew immediately it was Gabriel's voice.

'You bastard,' I said involuntarily.

'And you are nothing.'

The words reached through the phone like a hand grabbing my heart and squeezing it. He had all the power in the world at that moment. He could wield it with the touch of a finger or a single word like a mythological god. He was right. I felt like nothing.

'You're my partner now, Lieutenant. You're going to do exactly what I tell you to do. If you don't, your daughter will die.'

'I won't make deals with you.'

'Maybe not yet. But what will you do when I give you the choice of saving the life of a stranger, or your daughter?'

'You're out of your mind.'

'If you don't do everything I tell you, hell will fall on you.'

'Please don't do this. Don't hurt my daughter.'

I felt weak for saying the words, but there was no sense hiding it. I was weak. He had seen to that. I would do anything.

'Take me, not her, please.'

Only silence came back.

'Take me, damnit! Take me!'

'Mommy,' said Lacy.

The tears in her voice seemed to slip from the phone into my hand.

'I'm here, Lacy.'

The line went dead as abruptly as if she had just been yanked out of my arms. In the brief moment that my mind stayed clear, I tried to retrieve the number but it was blocked. I slumped against the car, then all the strength in my legs vanished and I sank to the wet pavement. I buried my face in my hands as the rain began to soak my hair.

Think, find something, replay Gabriel's words, the sounds in the background, anything, there must be something.

I opened my eyes and Chavez was kneeling in front of me.

'What is it, Alex?'

'I heard her voice.'

He glanced at the phone lying next to me on the pavement.

'Lacy? You talked to Lacy?'

I nodded. 'She was afraid . . . Oh, God, she was so frightened.'

He put his hands on my knees and gently squeezed them, trying to pull me back.

'Talk to me, Alex.'

I stared past him as if looking into the dark corner of a nondescript room at a teenage girl huddled in terror. There was the whoosh of wings as the black shape of a crow flew low overhead, as if guiding me back to the moment. I looked into Chavez's soft, dark eyes, then reached out and gripped his hand.

'What's happened?' he asked.

I looked up and let the rain fall on my face.

'She . . .' I lost the words.

'Alex, what happened?'

I closed my eyes and let the rain fall over me for another moment, hoping against hope that it would all be swept away like a terrible dream. If I told Chavez everything, would he be able to trust me? Could you trust any parent faced with the life of their child like this? Was that asking too much of anyone? And if I didn't tell him, could I trust myself to do the right thing? Was I strong enough? A cold, icy shiver went through my body. And I wondered if I had just become a partner in Gabriel's madness. I looked at Chavez.

'Talk to me, Alex.'

'Hell is falling down on me.'

fourteen

For an hour I sat in the car listening to the rain dance across the squad as crime-scene technicians and the coroner went over the house on Monte. Was there a miracle waiting to be found in a strand of hair or a fiber of fabric in the empty house? Was there a map in the contours of a fingerprint leading to Gabriel's hiding place and my daughter? The beating of my heart played out the answer like a primal drum message. No . . . no . . . no.

Chavez had told me to give it a rest for a few minutes, but whenever I tried closing my eyes for refuge and edged toward sleep, the sound of Lacy's voice on the phone brought me back to the cold, wet reality of the gathering dawn. 'Mom, Mommy.'

Jesus. No parent should ever hear that. Ever.

I looked out through the water streaking down the windshield. The scene being played out in front of me was as distorted as a fun-house mirror. Squads' flashing lights twisted and curved. Officers working the scene

239

seemed to appear and disappear as if stepping through holes in space. And through it all, one thought remained constant and threatened to overwhelm me: How could I have failed so terribly at protecting my daughter? How could I, a homicide cop, not have known what was hiding in the shadows? I wasn't a clueless suburban parent who only knew crime through the looking glass of television. I had lived with it for twenty years. I had held its bleeding, bewildered victims in my hands. I had seen it shatter families. I had watched it destroy hope and smother dreams. And still it happened in my house, to my child, shattering my illusion of safety. How could I have been so blind? How?

Harrison tapped on the window and waited for me to open the door, which I had apparently locked. I reached across and opened the driver's side and sat back as he slid in out of the rain. The scent of wet eucalyptus followed him in and filled the interior of the car.

'We may have caught a break,' he said flatly. The tone in his voice left no room for false hopes. 'A motel clerk on Colorado thinks Sweeny may be a guest.'

'Sweeny?' I said.

The events had taken on the quality of a raging river that I was watching pass from the riverbank. Somewhere in the torrent, my daughter had vanished and I now stood helpless, watching her drift away.

Harrison's fingers hovered just above the car horn as he waited patiently for me to catch up to the meaning of the words.

'Sweeny,' I said again.

I could feel the tug of events pulling me back toward

the investigation. The fog I had been left in after the phone conversation with Gabriel began to lift. I remembered Traver opening the door to the bungalow, the flash of explosion, the feel of glass hitting my face. Sweeny. Breem and Finley's employee.

'Okay,' I whispered, as if to steady myself in the flow of events. 'We located Sweeny in a motel on Colorado?'

'Yeah,' Harrison said.

'Do we have surveillance?'

He nodded as he started the car. 'An unmarked squad is watching it and won't move until you give the word.' He hesitated. 'That's at least something.'

'We already know what Gabriel looks like,' I said. 'We know what he plans to do. We know he has Lacy. What good is a two-bit check bouncer like Sweeny going to do for us?'

'Wouldn't you like to know what he was doing in Finley's house when he hit you with the door?'

'Would it change anything about the landscape we're in now? Unless Sweeny knows where my daughter is, or has a photograph of Gabriel . . . what good is he to us?'

Tiny lines formed around the corners of Harrison's eyes. That complicated head of his was still trying to work it out.

'If Gabriel is trying to eliminate everyone who can ID him, then it would be natural to assume that—'

'He would be looking for Sweeny, too,' I said, interrupting.

Harrison nodded. 'Maybe we can use that.'

I held the thought for a moment. 'Use Sweeny as bait.'

Harrison nodded.

'Put it out over every police frequency that we're watching Sweeny at a specific location and hope Gabriel is listening to a scanner. Let him come to us.'

It was a small chance at best, but it was at least worth a try.

'We talk to Sweeny first though,' I said.

'I was thinking,' Harrison said.

I looked at him, and he hesitated as if unsure of broaching a subject. 'We can talk about it later.'

'Go on. What is it?'

His index finger tapped the steering wheel as if he were keeping the beat to a song.

'I was thinking about the phone call from Gabriel.'

'What about it?'

'Why did he make it?'

'Part of his game,' I said, wondering if Harrison had guessed what Gabriel had said to me.

He nodded uncomfortably. I could see he didn't buy what I was saying.

'It's just that—'

'What are you saying?' I said, annoyed.

Harrison glanced down at his lap, then straight ahead, without making eye contact with me.

'I know what it is to lose someone, and I know that I would have done just about anything to change that if I could have.'

He had hit Gabriel's words right on the button. He knew. Maybe it was in my eyes. Maybe he recognized something in me that was familiar: a silent deal he had made with whatever power presided over the murder of his wife.

'I don't think anyone really knows what they would do until the moment happens.'

We looked at each other, the truth more or less on the table if not completely spelled out.

'Maybe you're stronger than you give yourself credit for,' he said.

Our eyes held for a moment, then he pulled the squad away from the curb and began to drive.

As we moved, I glanced one more time at the scene on Monte Street. Against the gray chill of the storm, the yellow crime-scene tape stood out like a row of bright sunflowers. Through the door of the house, the coroner emerged with the covered body of a boy who wanted to save us from ourselves. One of the gurney's wheels wobbled like a broken shopping cart's as it hit the sidewalk. A faint bloodstain on the sheet marked the spot where the bullet had entered the skull. I wondered how his parents had raised him. Did they love him, support him, or disapprove of him? Did they teach him to believe in the things that ultimately stole his life? Had they done a better job than I had? Did it matter?

'I can't help but wonder if he knew my daughter,' I said.

Harrison glanced at me, then turned south, heading toward Colorado four blocks away.

'In the squad,' he said hesitantly, 'you're taught to limit the imagination. It's kind of a rule. Stick with what's in front of you – the wiring, fuses, detonators.'

'Does it work?'

He nearly smiled at his attempt at advice. 'Not that I've noticed.'

I leaned back and closed my eyes as we headed for the Vista Palms Motel.

'I read the same thing in a parenting magazine when I was carrying Lacy,' I said.

'Any luck?'

'She was less than a day old when I imagined that the hospital had misplaced her, given her the wrong medication, and that she was dying all alone in her little bassinet.'

I glanced at Harrison, then looked out at the passing landscape without seeing any of it.

'I decided the writer of the article had never given birth.'

The Vista Palms Motel was one in a string of aging motels built in the sixties along East Colorado. The original owner figured he'd strike it rich because of its proximity to the Rose Bowl. He apparently didn't know how long football season is. Most of the motels were now owned by Indian immigrants who kept them up just enough to attract low-end tourists not willing to pay Marriott or Holiday Inn prices. For fifty bucks a night you got clean sheets, noisy air conditioners, and double locks on the door. No mints on the pillow, no conditioner in the shower. For whatever reason Sweeny had chosen this motel to hide from Gabriel in, it wasn't because he was used to the finer things in life.

Detective Foley, who had taken the call of the Mexican major floating in the casting pond, was parked across the street in a brown Crown Victoria. We pulled up behind him, and he stepped out into the rain and walked back holding a Dunkin' Donuts coffee cup in his hand. Out of the corner of my eye, I saw Harrison smile at the image, as if Foley had stepped out of an old movie. I rolled down my window and Foley leaned in. Some pink sprinkles from a glazed doughnut were stuck in his teeth and powdered sugar dusted his thin Gable mustache. He may have given the appearance of a slightly harmless cop waiting for retirement, but he was the perfect man for the job of questioning a former felon like Sweeny. Wipe the sugar off Foley's lip, and he could scare the Hell out of a corpse if he wanted to.

'Sweeny's upstairs in two-eleven at the far end with the curtains closed. There's another unit watching the back.'

'When did he check in?'

'The night after his bungalow blew up with you and Traver inside. Another customer called the clerk saying that he recognized his picture on TV.'

'He in there now?'

'Yeah. I sent a maid up to knock on the door. He was still in bed. You want to take him in or sit on him?'

'We have less than twenty-four hours until the parade. We don't have time to sit on him.'

'I'll get the key,' Foley said.

He walked back to his car, picking at his teeth, and we pulled across Colorado into the parking lot.

There were a number of beer cans littering the lot. Next to the curb's drain, the soggy remains of a pizza was inching its way through the grate. Half the cars had Washington Husky stickers on the bumpers for the big game New Year's day. One of the boosters had thrown up next to a blue Chevy Blazer.

Foley walked out of the office with the key, and the three of us started up the stairs.

'This the asshole who hit you with the door, Lieutenant?'

God, I had almost forgotten.

'Yeah, but he said he was sorry.'

We reached the door and Harrison moved to the other side.

'Don't get in front of the window,' I said.

He glanced nervously over his shoulder and took a half-step forward.

'How do you want to do this?' Foley asked.

'He thinks someone's trying to kill him. We go in unannounced, he might do something stupid.'

Foley pulled his weapon, then reached across the door and pounded three times.

'This is the Pasadena Police! Open the door!'

From inside I heard a heavy thud as if he had fallen out of bed.

'Sweeny, open the door!' Foley yelled.

I heard another thud inside the room, then a barely contained 'Shit, shit, shit!'

'I think we woke him up,' Foley said.

I heard muffled footsteps on the other side of the door. It sounded like he was pulling on his pants.

'Hold your badge up to the peephole,' came from inside.

Foley looked at the door, then over to me, and shook his head.

'There is no peephole in the door, asshole.'

'Then how do I know you're the police?'

'Because I'm the one you hit with the door!' I answered.

'Oh.'

There was a long pause.

'I'm sorry—'

'Open the door, Mr Sweeny, now!'

The chain slid open on the other side of the door and then the dead bolt clanked open. As the doorknob began to turn, Foley moved through the door as if it were a sheet hung out to dry on a line. Sweeny began to react, but Foley was already on top of him, pinning his cheek against the floor and driving his knee into the middle of Sweeny's back.

'Don't fucking move,' Foley said, in case there was still some doubt about who was in control.

'Okay,' slipped weakly out between Sweeny's lips, which were buried in the long strands of rust-colored shag carpet.

Foley clamped the cuffs on him as Harrison checked the bathroom to make sure we were alone. The room was stuffy and smelled of thirty years of accumulated cigarette smoke. A faded print of the Taj Mahal hung over the bed. There was a paper sack on the chest of drawers containing a toothbrush and toothpaste. A shirt was draped over the back of the only chair in the room. There was nothing else that appeared personal. Everything he owned had gone up in the bungalow explosion.

Foley got to his feet, leaving Sweeny staring into the carpet. I knelt down next to him.

'You're in a great deal of trouble.'

'I think you got me confused with—'

'If you bullshit me, I'll charge you with accessory to murder.'

'What!' he bellowed, his voice rising several octaves.

I glanced at Foley. 'Get him up.'

Foley grabbed him by an arm and lifted him onto the bed. Sweeny's eyes quickly took in the room with the rehearsed skill of a con man looking for a way out of a room in case the grift went south on him.

'I don't know nothing.'

'Stop,' I whispered. It had the effect of a shout.

'I need to know everything you know and everything you think you know. If you lie to me or play games, I will lock you away forever. You assaulted a cop, you're a loser, and I have no time to waste. You help me, I'll forget about the door you hit me with in your employer's house.'

'My what?'

'Your boss, Finley. You worked for him at the flower shop.'

The air slipped out of him like a dying balloon, and he looked up at the ceiling and nodded. I glanced at Harrison.

'Get the file from the car.'

He nodded and walked out.

'Why were you in Finley's house? What were you looking for?'

'Money. What else would I be looking for? My boss got killed and my house blew up. What the hell was I supposed to do?'

'You could get a job, asshole,' Foley said.

Sweeny glanced into my eyes, then looked away as if somewhere inside he harbored a long-simmering shame about his life or the fear that Mom was looking over his shoulder shaking her head in disappointment.

'I needed the money, okay? I didn't know you were a cop when I hit you with the door.'

That was his first lie, and I felt the blood rise inside me.

'I told you not to lie. You're going to jail.'

'Okay, okay . . . hold on. I knew you were a cop. I panicked. I'm sorry.'

'Tell me everything you know about Finley.'

'What would I know?'

'Answer the question!' Foley said, bending over and getting in his face.

Sweeny knew the routine. He sighed and shook his head.

'Not much. I just loaded the truck. The other guy hired me.'

'Breem?'

'Yeah.'

'He's dead,' I said matter-of-factly.

Surprise registered clearly on Sweeny's face, then just as quickly turned defensive.

'I didn't do it.'

'Shut up, asshole,' Foley said.

The door opened. Harrison walked in and handed me the file. I opened it and found myself looking at a picture of Lacy. It was a class photograph from school that she hated. She thought it made her look fat. I thought it made her look perfect. It had been taken pre-piercing. As I picked it up, my fingers trembled ever so slightly. I think Harrison noticed it because he looked away until my hand steadied.

'Have you ever seen this girl?'

I held it out for him to look at. His eyes passed over it, seeming to barely take notice.

'No—'

'Look at it!' I yelled.

Sweeny snapped to attention as if stung by a jolt of electricity. He nodded and his eyes fell on the picture of my daughter and began to study it. Having a con's eyes, even those as pitiful as Sweeny's, going over a photograph of Lacy felt strangely like violation.

'Is she that girl in the pageant thing? Yeah, I saw her on the news . . . right?'

He looked at me as if for confirmation.

'You never saw her except on television?'

'No, never. What the hell is going on?'

I slipped the picture carefully back in the file and took out a Polaroid of the kid murdered in the house on Monte. It was a shot of his face. His lifeless eyes were half-open, his face slightly distorted from the blood settling as he lay facedown.

'Have you ever seen him?' I said, holding it up.

Sweeny looked at it with a puzzled expression. 'What's wrong with him?'

'He has a bullet in his head.'

'Jesus Christ, what the hell is going on?'

'He was killed by the man who put a bomb in your house.'

'That was a bomb?'

'Don't be stupid,' Foley said. 'You think it blew up all by itself?'

'It happens.'

'And dogs have wings.'

'Have you ever seen him?'

'No, never.'

His voice cracked with fear for the first time. I showed him a Polaroid of the kid we arrested in Azusa and one of the dead Mexican soldier.

'I've never seen them either. You wanna tell me what the hell is going on?'

I took out the sketch of Gabriel and held it up.

'Tell me about him.'

Nothing passed in Sweeny's eyes. No recognition, no attempt to conceal. No fear. There was nothing there. I glanced at Harrison. He had seen the same thing and was just as puzzled as I was.

'Never seen him,' Sweeny said.

'Look at it.'

He took a breath and looked at it for another moment.

'No, I've never seen him.'

'Don't lie to us!' Foley demanded.

Sweeny looked at the drawing again. 'I've never seen him. I've never seen any of 'em. I swear it. I'm a nobody, I mean nothing to no one.'

It was as honest and as sad a self-assessment as I had ever heard. I would have pitied him if I had had any spare room in my heart to share with another person. I stuck the drawing back in the file. It felt like I was closing the door on the only hope left to me.

'Why were you hiding then?' Foley said.

' 'Cause my boss got shot, I hit a cop, and I'm a con. Jesus, what did you think? I'm scared of guns.'

'If you're lying . . .'

'He's not lying,' I said.

Foley looked at me disappointed. We were wasting our time and he knew it just as well as Harrison and I did.

'Is that the guy who blew up my apartment?'

I looked at Foley and motioned toward the door. 'Put him in my car.'

Foley grabbed him by the arm and pulled him off the bed.

'I want to know, is that the guy? 'Cause I got a problem with him.'

'Shut up,' Foley said.

'I got a right to know—'

Foley lifted Sweeny's cuffed arms just enough to send a twinge of pain through him and shut him up. As they reached the door, I thought of one last question.

'Did you ever meet Mrs Finley?'

There was nothing behind the question except instinct, which was possibly just another way of describing desperation. Foley spun Sweeny around with a yank so that he was facing me. It occurred to me while looking at him how pathetic it was that I was hanging even a thread of hope for my daughter's survival on a twenty-nine-year-old two-time loser wearing unbuttoned jeans, a Jim Beam T-shirt, and black socks with more holes than fabric.

'I saw her around . . . yeah.'

252

'Did you talk to her?'

'I guess.'

'Yes or no?'

He shrugged, his head moving side to side like a bobble-head doll. I imagined direct answers were something he had spent most of his life avoiding.

'Yeah.'

Foley gave the cuffs another tug.

'Yes,' Sweeny blurted in a high-pitched squeal.

'What did you talk about?'

'Nothing. She said hi, I said hi. Shit like that.'

I motioned to Foley and he took him out the door, leaving Harrison and I alone in the room.

'Why would Gabriel have tried to kill Sweeny if he never saw him?' Harrison said.

I shook my head and glanced at the print of the Taj Mahal above the bed. I hadn't noticed before, but there was no glass on it, and a former guest of the room had drawn McDonald's golden arches over the top of it, which the owner had apparently tried to erase. I turned and looked out the open door into the rain. There is nothing pretty or restful about rain in Southern California the way there is in New England or the Midwest. Something to do with all that pavement that just makes it cold and harsh and full of violence. I always thought that if Thoreau had been a resident of Los Angeles, Walden would have been about mud slides and flash floods.

'Clueless,' slipped out of my mouth.

'There's got to be some sense to it,' Harrison said.

I tried to put some order to it, but it eluded me.

'Is Sweeny lying?'

I shook my head. 'Didn't look like it.'

'Could we be wrong about the explosion at the bungalow?'

Could we be wrong? I tried to think about what we had been right about but came up empty-handed.

'Next question,' I said sarcastically.

'Maybe Sweeny just didn't remember meeting him?'

I thought about the drawing of Gabriel's face, the distinctive scar, the intense light eyes.

'Would you forget that face?'

'Unlikely.'

'Could Gabriel have made a mistake?'

'That would be a first.'

'What other possibility is there?'

'He was trying to kill someone else,' Harrison said.

'Such as . . .'

'You.'

I took a deep breath and exhaled heavily. 'I don't think so.'

'Why not?'

I stepped up to the door and watched the rain fall heavily on the street below. The water was beginning to pool on the road and passing cars were sending spray six feet into the air.

'Because he's trying to use me.'

Harrison stepped up to the other side of the door-jamb.

'The phone call?'

I nodded.

'He's counting on you doing what he says in order to save Lacy.'

'Yeah,' I said, feeling a confused mix of shame and God knows what else. 'I'm sorry, I should have said something.'

'I wouldn't have,' Harrison said without hesitation.

I glanced into his eyes as if to say thank you.

'It hardly matters,' I said. 'I don't think he intends to hold up his end of the . . .'

I let the thought drift away. Trying to step into Gabriel's mind was a losing proposition. He was a killer; to assume he would do anything other than continue to kill was foolish.

'If Gabriel is so sure that you're going to make a deal with him to save Lacy,' Harrison said, 'we do nothing to let him think otherwise. We get as close to him as he lets us and hope he makes a mistake.'

'I've been clinging to that very thought, but there's damn little to hold on to. He hasn't made a mistake yet.'

'When he does, we'll see it.'

'We have to,' I said grimly. 'I don't expect there'll be a second opportunity.'

We both stood silently for a moment.

'Why did you ask Sweeny about Mrs Finley?' Harrison asked.

'She said she never met him. Why would she lie about meeting Sweeny?'

'Maybe she didn't know his name. He was just a temp.'

'Possibly, but that's not good enough right now.'

'You want to ask her?'

I nodded. 'Yeah, I want to ask her.'

My cell rang and I slipped it out of my jacket pocket. 'Delillo.'

There was nothing on the other end for a second, and then he was there.

'Thank you,' Gabriel said in a voice entirely devoid of emotion or any connection to life at all.

'What—' I began to say, but the line went dead.

I turned to Harrison. 'It was him.'

'Gabriel?'

I nodded. 'He said thank you.'

'Nothing else?'

I shook my head. 'Just thank you.'

'For what?'

'I don't know.'

I looked down at the parking lot below. Foley was opening the door to his squad. Sweeny was sitting in the backseat of my car, fifteen feet away, his head bobbing as if he were playing a song in his mind.

'You think he was just playing more games?'

I shook my head.

'What's changed since I talked to him before?'

'We came here.'

'Oh, God,' I whispered.

I looked at Harrison and saw in his eyes the same horrible flash of recognition that was pulsing through me. He immediately began to sprint toward the stairs as I yelled to Foley.

'Get him out of the car!'

A truck passed by on the street shifting gears, smothering my words. Foley looked up and shook his head.

'What?' he yelled back.

Harrison rounded the first landing and started down the final steps toward the parking lot.

'Get him out of the—'

Under the car I saw a white flash of ignition reflect on the wet pavement. The blast moved silently up into the interior of the car, filling it with wispy blue fingers of flame that looked as unreal as the aurora borealis. I saw Sweeny look around in surprise as if a swarm of insects had just surrounded him. He began to shake his head violently, and then the interior of my car erupted in bright orange flames and he disappeared.

fifteen

The accelerant Gabriel had used burned hot enough to melt the steel frame of the car. Harrison and Foley both attempted to approach the doors when it erupted in flames but it was already burning too hot. There was nothing they could do. Sweeny had died in a matter of seconds without knowing how or why. He saw the thin blue flames dancing around him without feeling any of the heat yet. Then the air was sucked out of his lungs. Before he could even gasp for a desperate breath, he was gone.

I was sitting in the conference room at headquarters with a blanket over my shoulders to fight off the chill from the soaking rain I had stood in after the fire. Chavez walked in carrying a cup of tea and a sandwich wrapped in plastic.

'When was the last time you ate something?'

I shook my head; I hadn't a clue.

Chavez placed the food and drink in front of me then took a seat across from me. Behind him, Harrison stepped in and closed the door. It was nearly noon. Precious hours had slipped by as we secured the scene at the motel. And with every minute that ticked off, Lacy felt further from my grip.

'I led Gabriel right to him,' I said.

'You couldn't have known.'

'I should have. He was less than a block away. Lacy might have been in the car.'

Chavez looked at me. I could see a question forming in his eyes, one he was reluctant to ask.

'Why didn't you tell me about the rest of the conversation?'

'With Gabriel?'

He nodded.

'I suppose I didn't want you to think I couldn't be trusted.'

'I have no doubts about that,' Chavez said, unflinching.

'How did you find out?' I glanced at Harrison and he shook his head.

Before Chavez could answer, the door opened and Agent Hicks walked in with two other FBI suits who were unknown to me. I glanced at Chavez and he subtly nodded.

'Why did Gabriel say thank you when he called you at the motel?' Hicks asked.

I looked at Hicks at the end of the table, wondering what other surprises he had in store.

'You're listening to my cell phone,' I said.

Hicks removed a small cassette player from his pocket and hit play.

'You're my partner now, Lieutenant. You're going to do exactly what I tell you to do. If you don't, your daughter will die.'

Hicks turned it off and slipped it back in his pocket.

'Since you've been listening, you know why he said thank you,' I said.

'Yes, because you just led him to the last person who could identify him and who is now a piece of toast! Was that part of the deal you made?'

Chavez stood up, the veins in his neck swelling angrily.

'Back up, Hicks. You know damn well no deal was made.'

'Do I? How do we know there aren't other conversations that we haven't heard? What stronger motivation could the lieutenant possibly have than the life of her daughter? How can we be sure?'

'Because I would trust my own life with her,' Chavez said.

'How about the lives of the people on Colorado Boulevard? Do you trust her with their lives?'

'Yes.'

'I can't afford to.'

'There was no reason to kill Sweeny,' I said.

Hicks looked at me incredulously.

'Did you look at his remains? Because it sure looked like there was purpose behind it to me.'

'We showed Sweeny the drawing. He had never seen Gabriel.'

Hicks hesitated as if to measure my words. 'And you believed him?'

261

'About that, yes. He had nothing to gain by lying.'

'How do you know?'

'Because I was looking into his face. I'm a good cop.'

'If you were a good cop, Sweeny would be alive!'

Chavez took half a step to his left, blocking Hicks's view of me.

'As I remember, Hicks, you're the one who believed there was no connection between Lacy's abduction and Gabriel. I think you should choose your words more carefully. Lieutenant Delillo's daughter has been kidnapped by a madman. If you disrespect her again, you will no longer be a guest in this building, and I will have to get that door replaced.'

They stared at each other for a second, then Hicks took half a step back and rolled his shoulders. He glanced uncomfortably around the room, then looked at me.

Everybody plays games with the truth – every crook, cop, husband, wife, everyone, for every reason imaginable. The feds are particularly polished at it.

'I don't think we really know what Agent Hicks believes,' I said, fixing my eyes on him. 'Do we, Special Agent?'

'If I've given you the impression that I am not sorry about what's happened to your daughter, then I apologize. We put the surveillance on your phone last night because we have identified Gabriel through the French police.'

'Why didn't you say something before?'

'I have a daughter myself. I understand the pressure

you're under. I had to be certain that he hadn't manipulated you. He has some history with this.'

'History?'

Hicks nodded ominously.

'Was he on a terrorist watch list?' Chavez asked.

'No. He's on a wanted list.' Hicks turned and looked at me. 'The French detective I talked to called him a collector. They found what they described as a gallery of his work.'

'A gallery of what?'

'Victims. It's believed he's responsible for the murder of up to seven people in various . . . complicated scenarios. Gabriel disappeared nearly two years ago.'

'Scenarios?'

He hesitated. 'He's posed as a doctor, a handyman, even a policeman. And with each murder, the plots, for lack of a better word, became more and more complicated and elaborate . . . and more violent. He creates a story, a fiction, for each killing. Like a kid playacting.'

'You're not describing a terrorist,' I said.

Hicks shook his head. 'No.'

'What the hell are you describing?' Chavez asked.

'A serial killer,' I whispered.

'I'm afraid so,' Hicks said.

My heart sank. There wasn't enough air in the room to breathe. I got up from my chair, walked over to the window and slid it open. The heavy rain had now passed. Just a light mist dappled my face, gathering like tears on my cheeks.

'What does this mean?' Chavez asked.

263

I turned and looked back into the room. Glancing at Hicks, I saw by the look on his face that he knew just as I did what it meant. When you reach into the twisted psyche of a terrorist you still find a seed of a cause. A justification for their violence regardless of how twisted it has become. When you reach into the dark interior of a serial killer, there is nothing there but your worst imaginable nightmares.

'It means he's less predictable and far more dangerous than we previously thought,' Hicks said.

'He kills people. I don't see the difference,' Chavez said.

'A terrorist's acts are calculated to cause the most damage as an expression of a political goal. That opens the possibility that we can predict his actions because we know what he's trying to achieve. A serial killer has no political agenda. Killing isn't a means to an end for him. It is the end.'

'So why is he pretending to be a terrorist?'

'Because it's the biggest stage there is now. His greatest role.'

'Jesus, you talk as if he's an actor,' Chavez said.

'He is in a sense. As twisted as he may be, he still needs to take on the persona of another person in order to carry out his crimes. Many serial killers take on other personalities during the act of killing, just not to this extent. Whatever is broken inside him only feels right when he is playing another role.'

'And killing,' I said.

'Yeah.'

'You're telling us this guy is just a wack job who thinks he's gonna win a goddamn Oscar?'

'Not just a wack job. He's *the* wack job,' Hicks said.

'What do you know about the other murders?' I asked.

Hicks looked at me and hesitated – I recognized it as a parent's hesitation.

'Do you really want to know?'

'He took my daughter to get to me. The more I know, the better.'

Hicks turned to one of the other agents in the room, who handed him an open file.

'In 'ninety-eight he posed as a doctor in a hospital in Paris. For two nights he made rounds as if he was on the hospital staff. The one patient who had contact with him and survived claimed he was the best doctor he had ever had. Even several of the nurses thought he was the kind of doctor they wished there was more of.

'On the second night of making rounds, he gagged and bound three of the patients to their beds and operated on them. The doctors doing the autopsies on the victims estimated they were probably alive through much of what happened.'

Hicks took a crime-scene photograph out of the file and placed it on the table.

'Jesus' tears,' Chavez whispered.

'I could go on, but . . . they're all just as bad as this.'

I looked quickly at the photograph, then turned away. I could imagine all too easily my daughter's face in it, and that was not something I needed to see. I walked back to the window and looked out at the dull gray light.

'We don't have all the details on every killing,' Hicks said, 'but it appears that the one thing they have in common is that he exhibited great skill and knowledge of whatever role he was playing. When he was a cop, he was the best one people had ever met. Even made an arrest. When he was a handyman, he was the most skilled carpenter.'

'And now he's a terrorist,' I said, still looking out at the city. 'And a master bomb maker.'

'Exactly,' Hicks said.

I turned away from the window. 'When he was a carpenter, did he use weapons that were specific to the trade?'

Hicks nodded grimly. 'Like he was rebuilding a house.'

The room fell deathly silent as if words were no longer adequate to express what we were feeling. The weight of the information seemed to physically rest on my shoulders as if a shroud had been placed over me. I turned and looked back out the window. Panic began to swirl inside me like a storm trying to gather momentum and take shape. I thought I had understood what I was facing. I thought I knew who had my daughter and what I was up against. But now it was clear that I knew nothing.

Be a cop, that's all there is, work it.

'Do you have a photograph of him?' I asked.

'No. French police only had a drawing, but it was remarkably similar to ours.'

'So there's no doubt about the ID?'

'I'm afraid not. It's him. The only difference is they believed him to be a Frenchman. According to our witness Philippe, Gabriel's an American.'

266

'So which is he?' I asked.

'Philippe said Gabriel recently returned from Europe. That makes sense to us. But whether he is or isn't, the one thing we can be certain about is that Gabriel can become anyone he wants to be.'

'I want access to the French files.'

'You'll have a copy of what we get on your desk.'

'You said one of the patients at the hospital survived?' Hicks quickly scanned the file.

'Yeah, a man. That's where the drawing the French have comes from.'

The words hung in the air demanding attention. Why had Gabriel let someone live who had been in his hands? It was the same question I had been asking about Philippe's survival. Why hadn't Gabriel killed him? The existence of another surviving witness now gave me the answer.

'Then it's probably not a coincidence that Philippe survived,' I said.

'That's my guess.'

'What the hell does that mean?' Chavez said.

'He wants us to know it was him,' I said.

Chavez shook his head. 'I don't get it.'

'At some level, conscious or not, he can't commit these crimes without his audience knowing it was him. He craves the attention as much as he does the violence.'

'He wants the credit for his work,' Hicks said.

'Every actor does,' I said, as if describing a performance of Shakespeare in the park.

Harrison walked over and stood next to me looking out over the city. Somewhere below, a car horn blared.

A small flock of green parrots went rocketing past in a blur of wings and high-pitched squawks, sounding as if their fight against gravity had become one of desperation.

'I knew there were a million things I didn't understand about being a parent. Clueless, according to Lacy. But at least I thought I had learned everything there was about being a cop,' I said softly. 'Every assumption we've made about Gabriel so far has been wrong.'

Harrison looked down at the people filling the sidewalks, blissfully unaware of the events taking a choke hold on their city.

'You aren't wrong,' he said. 'There're just some things we aren't meant to ever know. Things no one should.'

I scanned the streets below for a moment. I could feel Gabriel's presence out there as surely as a hand brushing against the back of my neck.

'He could be watching us right now. And if he isn't, he has us thinking he could be. I wonder which is worse?'

Harrison shook his head. 'He's studied his role very thoroughly.'

Every imaginable emotion began churning inside me. Anger, fear, panic, frustration, and worst of all, hopelessness. Whether I had always understood it or not, Lacy was what defined me. Take motherhood away from me and I was just a cop, and that wasn't enough. I could feel her slipping away. If I lost her, I knew I would be lost without her. I turned and walked back to the conference table and took my seat across from Hicks.

'In your estimation, what does this mean for my daughter?'

'Do you really want to talk about this, Alex?' Chavez asked protectively.

'I'm not walking away from any part of this . . . I can't.'

Hicks took a long, deep breath to give him time to figure out how to respond.

'That he has used her as a bargaining chip indicates that there's a very good chance she's alive still, and is an integral part of his . . . play.'

'What would happen if we cancel the parade?' Chavez asked.

'My daughter will be killed, and he'll pick another target. One we would have no chance of stopping.'

'I agree,' Hicks said.

I stared at the file for a moment, thinking that I had missed something.

'Were any of his victims women?' I asked.

'No.'

'Then why did he take my daughter? Most serial killers at some level are working from sexual dysfunction. Killing for them is a form of power over whatever the victim represents in their damaged mind. If he's killed all men, then the need that is fulfilled in him when he murders may only be satisfied when he kills a male. So why did he take Lacy?'

'To get to you.'

Hicks was talking about the deal Gabriel believed he had made with me. I could save my daughter's life, or a stranger's.

'But why? I'm a woman, something would still be missing for him.'

'Maybe you and Lacy were never intended as victims. It's possible he has something else planned for you.'

'And what the hell is that?' Chavez said.

My heart began to race and I took a breath to slow it down. 'He needs the two of us for the end of his play to work.'

I looked at Hicks and he nodded.

'A serial killing live on television disguised as an act of terror. Somehow Lacy and I are a part of that.'

The room fell silent.

'That's not going to happen,' Hicks said. 'Security was already tight before this. Now it will be even tighter. We know what he looks like, and nothing that could hide a bomb is going to get anywhere near the route, particularly the first two blocks that are televised.'

'Maybe it will rain and keep people away,' Chavez said.

Hicks shook his head. 'The storm is supposed to be east by midnight. Tomorrow's going to be beautiful.'

'A picture-postcard day,' I said softly. 'What about the phone he called me on?'

'He used two different ones, both stolen. They're useless.'

'So what do we do in the next twenty hours?' Chavez asked.

'We have two things going for us,' Hicks said, looking at me.

I finished for him. 'One, he's going to use me, and

two, we know he has no intention of martyring himself for a cause that doesn't exist.'

'How do you know that?' Chavez said.

'Serial killers aren't suicidal. In fact they're usually afraid of their own mortality. Until they're caught, they'll do anything to survive.'

'There's another possibility,' I said reluctantly, as if the words had snuck out involuntarily. 'Regardless of what we think we know about Gabriel's previous crimes and their patterns, or what we actually learn about what his mother did to him or his father, or the next-door neighbor, or whoever damaged him as a child. One thing can render it all useless.'

'What is that,' Chavez said.

I glanced at Harrison and saw in his eyes that he knew what I was about to say. 'None of it matters if he's evolving, turning into something new with each act of violence.'

A cell phone rang in the room. Everyone reached to check theirs and then looked at the phone in my hand.

'If it's Gabriel, don't let on that we've identified him. If your daughter has any chance, it's by keeping this fiction of his going.'

I nodded, took a breath to gather myself, and then answered.

'Delillo.'

'Lieutenant, did you like the fire?'

Gabriel spoke in the same dispassionate voice, a voice that was the picture of well-measured reason or insanity. The result was the same either way. I felt as if I had just been lowered into an ice bath.

I glanced at everyone in the room and nodded.

'You didn't need to do that to him. He couldn't identify you.'

'One must be so careful.'

'He didn't need to die.'

He laughed, if you can call the sound he was making laughter. It escaped from a place in the soul that was the domain of fever dreams.

'Everyone needs to die.'

'Why?'

'Because you're weak and need to be punished.'

'I want to speak to my daughter.'

'No,' he said, dismissing me like an angry parent. 'Tell the FBI that they are children and that I've corrected all mistakes.'

The line went dead. Anger welled up inside me and I had to fight the impulse not to smash the phone on the table.

'What did he say?' Hicks asked.

I quickly replayed the words in my mind, trying to decipher their meaning.

'He said "I've corrected all mistakes." '

'What the hell does that mean?' Chavez said.

I looked at Harrison.

'What mistake?'

'Killing Sweeny, making up for missing him at the bungalow?'

' "Mistakes." It was plural. What's the other one?'

'If he's talking about something we don't know about, then it's meaningless to us.'

'He wouldn't have told me then. He wants us to

respond. He was boasting. He's done something else.'

Harrison searched his memory, working backward through the carnage of the past forty hours.

'Traver, could his survival have been considered a mistake?'

I shook my head. Gabriel didn't care about Traver. The bomb inside the bungalow had worked. The mistake wasn't on Gabriel's part. It was on Traver for walking through that door. It was something else that he had 'corrected'.

'There're two people alive who can identify Gabriel. He wasn't talking about Lacy – he wouldn't have missed the opportunity to wield his power over me. That leaves the Frenchman Philippe.'

'But if we're right about Philippe, Gabriel left him alive intentionally so we would have a description,' Harrison said.

So what were we missing? The logic we had been clinging to was sound, but I was missing something in the fine print of the facts. I looked at Harrison. 'What did you just say Gabriel wanted us to have?'

'A description—'

'That's it.'

'What's it?' Chavez said.

'A description, that's what Gabriel wanted us to have, and Philippe gave it to us.'

'And the point is?' Hicks said.

'Gabriel will get all the credit he wants for his crimes now. He's the poster boy of evil.'

Hicks nodded.

'But there's a big difference between getting credit, and

leaving a witness behind who can ID him. Philippe and Lacy are the only two alive we know of who could pick him out of a lineup. And we know he has other plans for my daughter. That leaves only Philippe.'

I turned to Hicks. 'Where do you have him?'

'Philippe's in a safe house in the valley where we house protected witnesses. We have agents watching him. He's safe.'

'Gabriel said the FBI are children. Why would he say that?'

'There's no way he could have found him, he's fine.'

'He found Sweeny.'

'There's no way—'

'Hicks, Gabriel's like the kid in an eighth-grade class with an IQ of two hundred. He thinks the students around him are there for his amusement to be played with and tortured like lab mice. He thinks his teachers are little more than village idiots who can be manipulated and driven to distraction to get just what he wants. You've seen what he can do. He kills because it gives him pleasure. He's proven he can be anyone and anything he wants to be. How much evidence do you need to know that we are way behind his learning curve.'

We stared at each other a moment.

'Are you sure Philippe is safe?'

The steely resolve of his eyes gave way just enough for him to maneuver. He nodded silently, then removed his phone and dialed a number.

'This is Hicks. I want to talk to Philippe . . . Well, get him out of the room . . . knock on the door and wake him up. Yes, right now.'

I started to walk over to the window to get some fresh air.

'What?' Hicks said, as if he had misunderstood something. I turned and saw Hicks's square-jawed confidence dissolve. His eyes had the look of someone who's just been told he has cancer.

'Oh God,' I whispered inaudibly.

'Do not go in. Seal it!' he yelled into the phone. 'Wait for an ordnance team . . . Yes, goddamnit, you heard me! Wait.'

He stood perfectly still as if unable to digest what he had just heard, then spoke to the room without making eye contact.

'His door was locked. One of the agents went outside and found an open window. Through a crack in the curtains, he could see part of the bed. It's covered with blood.'

He looked at me for a moment with a bewildered sense of surprise – a look you would see in the eyes of a child who has just seen something unimaginable and beyond his ability to comprehend.

'Philippe's gone.'

sixteen

Harrison and I drew an unmarked squad from the motor pool to replace my charred Volvo and started across the San Fernando Valley on the 101 freeway to the FBI's safe house. At Van Nuys Boulevard we turned north, passing block after block of car dealerships decorated with thousands of Christmas lights and enormous plastic Santa balloons floating above the cars, promising deals, deals, deals in English, Spanish, and Armenian. At one dealership three salesmen dressed as wise men stood outside trying to attract buyers with offers of no payments until Easter.

In a landscape that had clearly slipped off the track and created its own reality, I couldn't help but think that Gabriel had found the perfect home.

Three blocks from the last car dealership the endless suburban sprawl of the valley spread out in every direction until there was simply no more land to build on. Nearly a million and a half people lived here. It was the perfect place to house someone who didn't want to be found, or so the FBI had thought.

The safe house was a small, square rambler on a quiet tree-lined street. It had a wide, deep lawn, a picket fence, a rose bed, and a hedge of rosemary. A weeping willow shaded the front of the house where a curved brick walk led to the front door. Except for the presence of half a dozen FBI sedans in the driveway, it had the appearance of a house plucked straight from a small town in Indiana where nothing out of the ordinary ever happened.

Philippe had occupied a small bedroom in the back of the house. The room had two windows that looked out onto a fenced backyard with a kidney-shaped pool and an alley beyond that. One of the windows was open, the screen had been sliced in a large X. Two FBI agents had been in the house the entire night yet heard nothing.

I stepped in the room and looked around after the FBI bomb squad had declared it free of explosives. It had the appearance of a room that had once been occupied by a teenager, probably a boy. There were squares of masking tape left on the walls where posters had been. Holes from darts that had missed a board dotted the wall next to the closet. The generic rented furniture gave the impression of a motel rather than a home.

There was a blood smear on the sheets of the bed – a foot-long red swipe that looked as if it had been made by a hand with a wound in it – a defensive wound. Philippe's shoes were still next to the bed where he had taken them off to go to bed. It was the only thing of his left behind.

Gabriel's presence still cast a shadow over the room. He was here, a predator, stalking, playing a deadly game. I thought I understood violence. I'd seen husbands kill wives because dirty laundry had been left on the floor, friends murder friends, strangers point a gun and fire at someone they had never seen before because they held money in their hand. But this was a willful evil that was beyond my understanding. It wasn't based on hate or rage or love gone horribly wrong. None of the sadly ordinary reasons why we destroy each other applied. He was the nightmare in the car stopped next to you at a red light who you are afraid to make eye contact with – the faceless stranger walking toward you on a dark street. He was everywhere. He made me fear the things I didn't know. And dread the things I imagined.

Hicks stepped in next to me and looked around in frustration.

'How do you take someone out a window against their will with two FBI agents in the same house, and neither of them hears a thing? How, goddamnit, does that happen?'

I stared at the bloodstain and the slashed screen. A picture began to form in my mind as if flashbulbs were illuminating small pieces of the story in a dark room. I looked at the bed and saw Philippe trying to sleep, desperately seeking some escape from the horrors of what had happened to him earlier in the day. He would have been tossing and turning, occasionally drifting away but never for long. There was little relief. The night was like a fuse slowly burning down.

The sound of the plastic screen being cut would have been nearly silent – a distant zipper being opened in the darkness. If he heard it at all he would have ignored it, burying his head into the pillow. And then he detected the sweet scent of a cheap cologne. And he knew, right then. He tried to turn his head, he tried to scream, but he was frozen. His will had been stolen from him earlier in the day as cleanly as if a surgeon's blade had removed it.

Hicks walked over to the window, ran his finger along the cut in the screen, and then shook his head in disbelief.

'How the hell is this possible? Why didn't he scream?'

'I don't think he could,' I said.

'Why the hell not?'

'Terror,' I whispered.

Hicks turned around and searched the room, trying to find reason where none existed.

'He could have killed him right here. Why did he take him?'

I shook my head in wonder. 'To show us that he can.'

'You think too much of him.'

I shook my head. 'No, that's not it.'

'What then?'

'I'm afraid of him.'

Hicks looked at me and shook his head. Fear did not officially exist in the FBI's sanctioned vocabulary. Cops like me could be afraid. The FBI stood shoulder to shoulder with steely resolve to fight any foe. He turned and looked at the window.

'What is he going to do with him?'

I didn't want to think about that because the answer could be the same for my daughter. And to imagine that was unthinkable.

'He'll use him until he's finished using him,' I said.

Two technicians walked in and began to dust the window cases for prints. It was a useless gesture. We would find only the things that Gabriel wanted us to find. The bloody swipe of a hand on a white sheet, an open window, and an empty room.

'Who knew about the safe house?' I asked.

'No one knew. They're rented out anonymously and are only used once. The owners don't even know what they're used for.'

'Did Philippe call anyone?'

He shook his head. 'No calls.'

Hicks drew his hand tightly into a fist and pulled it back as if he were going to hit the wall.

'What happened here is not possible.'

'Agent Hicks, I've learned in the last twenty-four hours that the unimaginable and the possible are not so different from one another.'

Hicks glanced around the room shaking his head, then turned and looked back into the hallway.

'What time was he brought here?' I asked.

'A little after ten. He had a Coke and went to bed shortly after that.'

I hesitated at the door, realizing that there was something incomplete in how I had been seeing the scene. But what? It was like one of those kids' picture puzzles in *Highlights* magazines with images hidden inside images.

'Were there any other windows open in the rest of the house last night?'

'What does it matter? He came through this one.'

'Was it jimmied?'

Hicks shook his head. 'Doesn't appear that it was.'

'So it was already open?'

'What's your point?'

'It was cold last night. Why would he have the window open?'

'You don't sleep with a window open?'

'Yes, but I have blankets on my bed. His is still folded, it wasn't used.'

'Maybe he never went to bed.'

'Then why is the streak of blood on the sheet as if he was lying there?'

Hicks looked at the bed. The blood had begun to discolor, taking on the dark hues of coffee. He stared at it for a moment as if trying to decipher a delicate Japanese calligraphy.

'You're suggesting that he opened it for Gabriel?'

'I'm not suggesting anything, I'm just observing.'

'Why would he let a man into his room who hours earlier had strapped him with explosives and left him to die?'

'I don't know.'

I walked over to the window and looked out into the backyard. The small kidney-shaped pool was painted dark, giving the water the feel of a wound in the earth. It reminded me of the 'tar pits' in Hollywood that lure victims with the promise of water, only to slowly pull them down to their deaths. An icy chill shimmered across the skin on my arms. It was as if I was looking at a portrait of Gabriel. He was there, lurking just under the surface, waiting to pull me down.

seventeen.

seventeen

As the weathermen had predicted, the storm that had been laying down a dreary rain was moving east over the mountains and into the desert. Patches of pale blue sky were beginning to show like holes in a tattered blanket. Tomorrow would be perfect, the mountains covered in snow, Colorado Boulevard in dreams of every imaginable color.

Harrison stopped the car in front of Philippe's apartment building in Hollywood. Sheets of soaked newspaper and plastic bags littered the pavement. A Mexican street vendor who looked Mayan walked past carrying a pole with bags of cotton candy hanging from it like bright pink clusters of flowers.

Walking up the stairs of the building, life had returned to normal without missing a beat. The same smell of cooking spices drifted out from under doors. The same music pounded out its rhythm. The same angry voices in Armenian and Arabic and Spanish drifted through the dark hallways like a New World nightmare.

Philippe's door was sealed with FBI crime-scene tape that warned of prosecution should it be tampered with. A tagger had spray-painted his homeboy's name over the tape in fluorescent orange paint. I peeled back the tape, pushed the door open, and stepped inside.

The room had been turned upside down. Every piece of evidence linked to Gabriel had been removed. Everything that remained was covered in print dust. The only thing that appeared unchanged was the chair where Philippe had sat with explosives in his lap.

It was the only space we definitively knew of where Gabriel had spent some time. Knowing what we knew of him now I held out a faint hope that we would see some small detail that had been overlooked because we had thought we were looking for a terrorist instead of a serial killer. I replayed in my head what had happened in the room. Philippe had survived because Gabriel had wanted us to know it was him. But how could Gabriel have been so sure that someone like Harrison was going to walk through that door and be able to disarm the bomb in Philippe's lap? Gabriel was too smart to leave anything to chance.

'How do you guarantee that you get exactly the results that you want?'

'Simple,' Harrison said. 'You eliminate all other possibilities.'

'So how would Gabriel have done that in this room?'

We both looked around the room in silence.

'Do you think it's possible that Philippe was working with Gabriel?' I asked.

Harrison looked at me in surprise, then glanced at the chair as if replaying events in his head.

'You mean do I think it's possible from the way the bomb was constructed, or from the look in his eyes as the timer clicked down?'

'Both.'

He raised his hand to his upper lip as if he were fiddling with a phantom mustache.

'What I saw in his eyes looked real.'

'What about the bomb?'

'It was simply constructed,' he said.

'The bomb in Sweeny's bungalow wasn't, so why was this one?'

'There was less required of it. All it had to do was kill a single person sitting motionless in a chair.'

'Unless it was designed not to kill him.'

'How do you prove a negative?'

'You eliminate all the other possibilities.'

Harrison cocked his head as if to go at the thought from a different angle.

'Unless I cut that lead, it would have exploded.'

'If you hadn't walked in, could he have stopped it himself?'

Harrison shook his head. It was like trying to juggle melting ice cubes.

'That's like asking which are the stripes on a zebra,' he said, 'the black or the white. It all depends on how you look at it.'

'If he had the knowledge, would it be possible?'

'If he knew how . . . yes, it's possible. But that still doesn't answer why.'

'So we would get a description,' I said.

'Philippe could have given us the description without the explosives.'

'But would we have believed him? By turning Philippe into a human pipe bomb, he immediately gained complete credibility.'

'For what?'

I could see the answer to his own question appear in his eyes. 'A false description.'

I nodded. 'Except it matched the one from the French police.'

'So that leaves us right where we started,' Harrison said.

'Yeah . . . we got lucky.'

I looked around the sad little room. From somewhere in the building came the sound of a dog furiously barking and throwing itself against a door that someone was passing by.

I walked over to the corner of the room where Philippe had placed a thrift store dresser. The drawers had been pulled out and all the contents dumped on the floor. His scattered clothes gave nothing away other than he shopped at the Gap. Above the dresser, a mirror mounted on the wall had half a dozen snapshots of him stuck in the frame. I reached up and pulled one down. Philippe was standing in front of a large white building. On his face was the kind of smile the bearer of a secret would have. It reminded me of the photograph of Lacy in the sequoias. I reached up and took down the rest of the photographs and placed them in my pocket in case we needed them for an ID.

'If he's not dead by now, he probably wishes he was,' I said softly.

I walked over to the window and looked outside. The faint glow of the setting sun had begun to shine through the breaks in the clouds. A shaft of light was painting a soft, pink square over a window on the adjacent apartment building less than thirty feet away. Inside the apartment I could see a mother nursing a child in her arms, gently rocking it back and forth as if they were floating on water.

'How do you understand something that is only measurable by its loss?' I said.

Harrison glanced out the window at the mother and child in the apartment. He looked away almost immediately as if his intrusion into the moment made him uncomfortable. I imagined that even secondhand intimacy had been difficult for him since the murder of his wife.

'When my ex-husband died, the love had long since faded, but it was different for Lacy. I tried my best to understand what she had lost, but it just wasn't possible. And my inability to understand what she was feeling just pushed her further away.'

I glanced once more at the mother with her child, then turned and looked over Philippe's room.

'You would think someone whose job it is to investigate death would have understood better than I did.'

Harrison's eyes met mine briefly, then he looked over to the chair where Philippe had been sitting.

'I'm sorry, this isn't helping,' I said. 'It's just . . .' I let the thought drift.

He shook his head as if to say okay. His eyes searched out a distant point of memory. 'I don't think our understanding is ever equal to grief. I think it's that way by design.'

We were both silent for a moment. I tried to step back to the investigation to ground myself in the debris Gabriel had left behind in his rampage. It was already after five o'clock. Lacy had no more than fifteen hours left. If I was ever to hold her again, I needed to focus enough so that I could do my job. But it was difficult. I wanted to go back through her childhood, step by step, and fix all the mistakes I had made. A part of me wanted to believe that by reconstructing her life I could change the direction it had taken in the last twenty-four hours.

But I knew better. Standing in this room wouldn't allow it. If there were answers, they were here – the one place in the world that I understood better than all others. Crime scenes were one of the few places I had ever found there to be something approaching absolute clarity. It might not be immediately evident, but the evidence left behind in the wake of violence is as declarative a sentence as anyone has ever written. Blood, bone, skin, body temperature, hair, carpet fibers, DNA, the trajectory of a bullet, a forced lock, the angle of a wound, the position of a body . . . all of it spoke in truths that were undeniable.

I looked over the room one more time in hopes of seeing that one clue that had been missed. If it was here, it still eluded me.

'If you were to draw a profile of Gabriel right now with what we know, where would you begin?'

'His intelligence.'

I nodded. 'When we discovered that Gabriel wasn't a terrorist, it frightened me because I thought it made him more dangerous.'

'Yeah,' Harrison said.

'But it also made him fallible.'

'How?'

'Twenty to thirty percent of most homicides go unsolved. But with serial killers, less than ten percent of their crimes go unsolved.'

'Why?'

'What goes hand in hand with brilliance?'

Harrison thought for a beat.

'Ego.'

I nodded.

'Gabriel believes he's the absolute top of the food chain. He can kill anyone, at any time with absolute impunity. He knows as he walks among us that every face he looks into, every person passing on the street or driving in their car is a potential victim. They're only alive because he chooses to let them remain that way. Think of the feeling of power that must give him.'

'God's strongman,' Harrison said.

'We're his prey, and the last thing a predator with no rivals fears is the victim he's about to slaughter, and that's why at some point he'll make a mistake. He'll get careless exactly because he doesn't believe we're capable of recognizing it.'

'Gods don't make mistakes,' Harrison said.

That was what I had come back to this room for – it

wasn't to find a clue, it was to find something approximating hope.

'We know one thing that Gabriel doesn't, maybe the only thing,' I said.

'What?' Harrison asked.

'We know he's no god.'

Darkness was settling in when we stepped onto the late Daniel Finley's porch and rang the bell. Before Sweeny had died inside my car he told us in the motel room that he knew his late employer's wife – a detail so small that it would seem unimportant except that Mrs Finley had denied to us the very same fact the first time we met her at this house. If she had lied about something trivial, then I had to consider the possibility that she had also lied about something that would lead me to Lacy.

When she opened the heavily chained door, Mrs Finley had the pale wispy look of a nineteenth-century photograph that was beginning to fade into oblivion. Her exhausted, empty eyes looked at me, but I got the impression they were incapable of registering information.

'I would like to see some identification,' she said, her voice tense with fear.

I held my badge and ID up for her to see.

'We were here yesterday.'

Through the crack of the open door, I saw the dull steel of a machete gripped in her right hand. It looked comically large in her thin fingers. I doubted very much that she could summon the strength to slice an orange with it.

'Do you remember me?'

She nodded, her face not registering any change in demeanor.

'Would you put the weapon down and open the door so we can talk?'

She hesitated, then placed the machete in an umbrella stand, closed the door, and slid the chain off the lock.

Inside, the air had the stale, lifeless quality of a locked storage closet. The dining-room table was covered with empty files and drawers that the detectives had gone through. I noticed the windows behind the table had several large nails crudely pounded into the sashes in an attempt to seal them shut. The dark oak trim around them was marked with missed hammer strikes.

'I don't know why they didn't clean this up,' she said, looking at the mess on the table. She moved in continuous, small steps when she talked, as if standing still would place her in jeopardy.

'Are you afraid of something, Mrs Finley?' I asked.

Her eyes glanced toward the windows, then quickly away.

'There's nothing wrong with being safe.'

'You nailed your windows shut and you're walking around with a machete in your hand.'

She drew her arms in, clutching her chest.

'My husband was murdered,' she said softly, her eyes focusing on some distant, unseen spot.

'Not just your husband.'

She looked toward the floor and whispered, 'No.'

'Were you involved in any of the direct action with your husband?'

She continued to look at the floor without betraying any emotion.

'Mrs Finley, you may know something that can help us and not be aware of it. I need you to answer my questions.'

She closed her eyes as she took a breath like an exhausted runner.

'In college we did things, little things, stupid things. I stopped believing we could change the world a long time ago.'

'What about lately, Mrs Finley? Did you know about what he was involved in?'

'I've already answered these questions.'

'And you lied.'

She looked up at me; her eyes held the weight of something heavier than grief.

'Were you part of your husband's plans involving the parade?'

'I wasn't involved with my husband at all.'

I recognized the look in her eyes. I'd seen the same reflection in my husband's eyes once, a very long time ago. It was what love looks like when the light has been replaced by deceit.

'Tell me about the temporary employee Sweeny,' I said.

'I don't know what you're talking about.'

'Lying won't help either of them or you.'

She glanced at me defensively for a moment, trying to steel herself against the question, then the protective shell she was hiding in began to fracture and fall apart around her like a collapsing building.

'We were only together a few times . . . that's all.'

'When was the last time?'

She held back from answering, then an exhausted breath let out what was left of her resistance.

'Night before last.'

'Where was this?'

'Where we always went, a motel on Colorado.'

Harrison glanced at me.

'The Vista Palms.'

She nodded silently. 'I went to end it . . . that's why I went.'

Her eyes filled with tears and she buried her face in her hands. Apparently she had failed in her task.

'Was Sweeny a part of what your husband was doing?'

She shook her head.

'Why an affair with Sweeny?'

'Because he meant nothing to me, because I was angry. Because I wanted to hurt my husband. Do you need me to draw you a goddamn picture?'

She almost imperceptibly shook her head. 'What have I done?'

'Your husband wasn't killed because you slept with Sweeny,' I said.

Her haunted eyes had the look of an animal locked in a cage.

'How do you know . . . how do you know why anything happens?' she whispered.

I slipped a photograph of Lacy and the sketch of

Gabriel out of my pocket and laid them on the table in front of her.

'Have you seen either of them?'

She looked at them and shook her head.

'They already showed me those.'

She reached out and picked up the photograph of Lacy and stared at it. 'She's the girl who's missing.'

'She's my daughter.'

Her eyes met mine for a brief second, then she looked away as if in shame and covered her mouth with her free hand to suppress a gasp. I took her by the arm and sat her down.

'Do you know anything about your husband's involvement with the environmental group that can help me?'

'I . . .'

'Anything?'

Mrs Finley flinched as if I had just struck her with the back of my hand. She drew her knees up to her chest and began to rock gently back and forth in the chair. She began to say something, but the words silently slipped away.

I looked at Harrison, then returned the photograph of Lacy and the sketch of Gabriel to my pocket. I glanced around the shuttered house and anger began to rise inside me. I had wasted precious time chasing down a tawdry infidelity while a madman had my daughter. I wanted to grab Mrs Finley and shake her out of her stupor. She wasn't to blame for what was happening, but she was sitting in front of me and at the moment, that was enough.

I started toward the door but stopped.

'You can take the nails out of your windows, Mrs Finley. If you knew something that could have helped me, you would already be dead.'

Whether from the flush of anger or the stale, lifeless air, I felt light-headed and rushed out of the house onto the porch. I took several deep breaths trying to regain my equilibrium, but the ground still fell away from under my feet. Harrison's hand gently landed on my shoulder and guided me to the squad, where he sat me down and placed my head between my knees.

'Long, slow breaths,' he said softly.

With each breath the world began to settle back into place beneath me. I became conscious of his hand on my shoulder and his fingers gently stroking my neck. God . . . I couldn't remember the last time I had been touched by anyone. I wanted to lean into his hand and disappear into his touch. To be held and told that everything would be all right. I ached for it the way someone afraid of the dark craves the light. But instead, each stroke of his fingers was like a fresh wound opening in my heart, reminding me of what I had and what I was losing.

I slowly raised my head and sank back into the seat. Harrison withdrew his hand as if retrieving a long-lost heirloom that had been misplaced for many years.

I glanced back toward the house. The door was already bolted again. Mrs Finley's shadow passed across one of the windows. I imagined she was slowly walking from room to room, holding the machete in her hand, checking all the windows to make sure that the nails were in place.

'I wonder if she's protecting herself from death or from love,' I said softly.

Harrison glanced uneasily at me, though his eyes appeared to look no further than his own shuttered past.

'The impulses are not so distinguishable from one another,' he said.

He looked back at the house, seeing something entirely different.

'I was thinking,' he said, the skin around his eyes drawing into lines as he formed a thought. 'I was thinking it was Gabriel who tipped off the motel clerk about Sweeny. He knew about the affair, all he had to do was follow her right to him.'

I nodded in agreement.

'If you're right, he could have killed him anytime, but he let us deliver the bomb,' I said. 'We're toys to him, his private playthings.'

The ringing of my phone filled the car like a scream. I had never believed in the view that physical objects could embody evil, or good, for that matter. But the sound of the phone ringing now carried dread with it. It was as if he were reaching out to me, his fingers brushing the fabric of my blouse. I let it ring four times, taking a breath to settle my racing heart. Let the mother grizzly loose, I thought. Don't let him control this. I pressed the button and answered.

'Yes.'

'Lieutenant.'

Hearing his voice was like stepping back into a recurring nightmare. I closed my eyes. Every muscle in my body tensed as if I were desperately trying to stop myself from sliding over a cliff.

'You're going to be very busy tonight,' Gabriel said. 'I have great plans for you and your daughter.'

I felt the ground slip away beneath me as I slid over the edge and began to fall.

'You have eight minutes to get to the corner of Marengo and Wallis. There's a school there. If you're late, I'll sever one of your daughter's fingers. If you're not alone, I'll cut off two.'

His voice slipped away like a snake moving into the grass, then the line went dead.

'Get out of the car,' I said to Harrison.

He turned to me in surprise, then understanding appeared in his eyes like a rising sun.

'He wants you alone.'

I nodded.

'I have eight minutes.'

'This is a bad idea.'

'I'm not writing the rules. Now go, please.'

Harrison shook his head. 'I can't let you do this.'

'I don't have time for debate. Get out.'

Harrison opened the door and reluctantly stepped out. I slid behind the wheel and started the car as a surge of adrenaline raced through my body like a jolt of electricity. My heart began to pound against my chest like an angry fist on a table.

'Set up a three-block perimeter around the corner of Marengo and Wallis. Make sure there isn't a cop inside that line. If there is—' The rest of the words caught in my throat. 'You got that?'

'I'll take care of it,' Harrison said.

I glanced at my watch; thirty seconds had passed since the call. I hit the lights and the siren and stepped on the gas, spinning the car 180 degrees, and headed north. I was fourteen or fifteen blocks south of Wallis and four or six blocks east of Marengo, if I remembered my streets correctly.

I passed through intersections, barely taking notice of headlights swerving to the curb to avoid my flight. I was like a horse wearing blinders. Fragments of images sped past in a blur of color and vague shapes. A car horn pierced the din of the siren. I glanced right and saw the flash of a white sedan slide to a stop inches from the passenger door of my squad before it vanished into the rearview mirror.

Rounding the corner onto Marengo, I saw a woman pushing a shopping cart step out into a crosswalk. She was wearing a pink jacket, white pants, and bright red lipstick. Her skin was dark, cocoa brown, and she had the round, pleasant figure of a recent arrival from Mexico or El Salvador. There was no stopping.

'No, no!' I yelled, but she heard nothing.

By the time she saw what was about to happen, it was already set in stone. She raised a hand toward her mouth as the front right side of my squad tore the cart from her and sent it tumbling into the air. Time froze for an instant as I looked into her astonished face, then shot forward as a plastic shopping bag landed on the hood, splitting open, sending tiny white grains of rice skittering across the windshield like flakes of blowing snow.

I pressed my foot to the floor and silently counted out the blocks as they sped past. Five more . . . four.

Do it, go . . . go.

Three blocks south of Wallis I passed a squad setting up the perimeter at the intersection. Whatever sliver of hope I had that Gabriel had given me an opening vanished. A squad parked at an intersection was a useless gesture and I felt pathetic for the feebleness of my ability to strike back at him.

A blue pickup pulled out into the intersection in front of me and I let out a scream. The truck jerked to a sudden stop as I slid around it, my rear wheel bouncing off the opposite curb as I swerved back into the middle of Marengo.

'You son of a bitch!' I yelled, pounding on the steering wheel.

My resolve began to spiral away into the madness that was engulfing me. A single, careless driver, one misstep, and my daughter would be . . . I let it go.

At the corner of Wallis, I slid to a stop and turned off my lights and siren. I looked at my watch. Did I have time left? I couldn't remember. Fifteen seconds, maybe . . . maybe less.

'Please' slipped out like a prayer of thanks, and then I looked around to orient myself.

There were no pedestrians on the street, no one visible in a parked car. Across Marengo was a bus stop bench, and beyond that, the parking lot of the school. On my right, a city park extended for a square block. At the far end, a couple was walking a dog.

I felt alone and vulnerable. Why did he want me here?

I hadn't had time to consider it as I drove, but now I couldn't avoid the question. I looked up and down the block, searching for a reason for my presence. What was unique about this block? What was different about it from the one to the north or west? Nothing appeared out of place, nothing appeared to be anything other than ordinary.

The din of the sirens wailing began to lift and I heard the faint sound of a phone ringing in a phone booth across the street.

That was why I was here. He knew he was being listened to on my phone and he wanted to talk alone. The cat with its mouse.

I sprinted across the street and picked up the receiver. It was wet with heavy dew, cold like the hand of a corpse.

'You're late,' Gabriel said.

His voice held the sharp edge of annoyance.

'No!' I said desperately.

I glanced at my watch, trying to determine how long it had been ringing before I noticed it.

'I had the siren on, I couldn't hear it. I was here.'

'Are you pleading with me, Lieutenant?'

'I'll do anything you want.'

'You're a whore.'

'I'm a mother.'

'Is there a difference?'

There it was: the X on the map of his life that marked where it all began. God help us. If it were being played out on a stage, it would have the weight of a Greek tragedy instead of the horror of a nightmare.

'You wanted to talk to me alone?'

'I could kill you right this moment.'

I quickly scanned the windows of the school building. For an instant I could feel the crosshairs of a scope moving across my face, but the fear passed. He wasn't that kind of a killer. He was a preacher of death and I was part of the ritual. He wasn't finished with me.

'If that's what you want, go ahead.'

'We have a relationship. I wouldn't hurt you.'

'We don't have a relationship. You have my daughter.'

A strange animal-like laughter came through the phone. 'Look down at your feet.'

'What?'

'Look down.'

Dread spread through me like a raging virus.

'This is what happens to people who lie to me,' he whispered.

I looked down at my feet. In the dim light I could just make out the unmistakable shape of a human finger. I felt a horrible rising in my stomach and I put my hand to my mouth to suppress my shock.

'Oh, God,' I whispered as my eyes flooded with tears. No, no, no . . .

'It's not your daughter's, but it could be. I'm holding her hand right now.'

I squeezed the receiver trying not to scream. I tried not to picture his fingers wrapping around my daughter's hand, but I couldn't stop it. He had let loose a storm inside me. My knees buckled for a moment, and I reached out and took hold of the phone booth to steady myself.

'It belongs to the garbage I took from the FBI.'

'You—' I swallowed the rest of the words. Play his game, I said to myself, play it right to the end. Right to the moment when I kill him and send him back to the hell he crawled out of.

'Have you decided yet?' Gabriel said.

'Decided what?'

'Are we partners? Are you going to save your daughter's life, or a stranger who means nothing to you?'

I took a deep breath and exhaled heavily.

'Have you decided?'

'No,' I said in a barely audible whisper.

'You will.'

'No, I won't.'

He seemed to almost laugh, as if whatever I said to him he had already scripted.

'Lieutenant, you have no idea what you're going to do for me.'

The line went dead. The receiver fell from my hand and I stepped back to get away from the finger at my feet. I wanted to believe that I was trying not to contaminate evidence, but in truth I was just horrified. I quickly scanned my surroundings for any movement, but I already knew it was futile. He wasn't here. There were no crosshairs lining me up. He had wanted me alone for the sole purpose of escalating the terror. He had reduced me to a frightened woman alone on a dark street.

'You bastard,' I said, barely able to form the words. 'That's the last time . . .'

I stood for a moment on the verge of shaking with

anger. I took a breath and held it for a second, then another, and another.

I reached for my cell phone but stopped. My eyes drifted back to the severed finger. I was missing something. What had just happened here? Nothing Gabriel did was casual. Everything had a reason, even the smallest details. I replayed his words in my head . . . 'It belongs to the garbage I took from the FBI.'

I stepped toward the finger and knelt down to examine it. The cut at the base had the clean precision of a surgeon's knife. The wound was covered with a light layer of blood that had begun to thicken and dry. There was a line of dark dirt under the curve of the nail. It appeared to be an index finger. It was lying on the pavement as if pointing toward the school behind me. I turned around and looked into the schoolyard beyond the fence. Nothing presented itself, just an empty parking lot.

I walked over to the fence and began to follow it along the perimeter to a gate thirty yards to the right. It was closed, but the chain securing it hung limp, one of its heavy steel links severed as cleanly as the finger. I unlatched the gate and pushed it open. A hundred feet across the dark parking lot, the glow of a light that I couldn't see from the phone booth appeared between two buildings. I picked up my cell and called Harrison. He answered before the second ring.

'Are you all right?'

'Yeah. I don't think he's here, but hold the perimeter until I call you back.'

I hung up and started walking across the dark parking

lot toward the light. The sound of small bits of gravel under my shoes shouted my presence with each step as if I were walking on glass. From somewhere out of the darkness, a mockingbird let loose a series of repeating songs that sounded like a car alarm come alive. Involuntarily, my hand drifted to the handle of my Glock. At the edge of the light, the gap between the two buildings opened into an alley that ended at a service entrance fifty feet farther on. Illuminated under the bright halogen light at the end of the alley was a large green dumpster.

There were no windows in the buildings lining the alley. Aside from the door at the end, the only way in or out was where I stood.

'Garbage,' I whispered to myself, repeating Gabriel's words.

I started to reach for my phone but stopped as the *thump thump thump* of the department's helicopter pierced the night as it slowly began to circle in the darkness.

I pulled my weapon and started down the alley. As I approached the dumpster, several palmetto bugs the size of mice scurried out of the light and into drains that disappeared under the buildings. The sickly sweet odor of rotting garbage hung in a radius of about five feet around the dumpster. From inside I heard the faint sound of hundreds of tiny legs moving across paper and metal. I raised my weapon and reached for the plastic lid that hung unevenly around the top edge. As I raised it, something ran across the tips of my fingers. I flung it open, pointing my Glock inside. A flight of flies sped past my face as a wave of stench rose up, and I stepped back.

The floor of the dumpster appeared to be moving, alive with hundreds of roaches foraging in fast-food wrappers, soggy boxes of pizza, and cans of Coke and Mountain Dew.

The body was upright, sitting on its knees, slumped slightly forward, the arms tied behind its back, bound just above the elbow with silver duct tape. A large, open wound on the top of the neck exposed the tendons, muscles, and bones that used to connect to the victim's head, which had been taken. The index finger on his right hand was missing. There was little to no blood present on the dumpster's floor. He had been killed somewhere else and placed here. I recognized the blue T-shirt and jeans as those Philippe had been wearing. Through the moving carpet of insects, I could see that his feet were bare, just as they had been when Gabriel pulled him through the window of the safe house.

I stepped back and looked out through the alley toward the street. The sense of hope for Lacy that I had resolutely clung to vanished with the speed of a single heartbeat. I holstered my pistol and picked up the phone and called Harrison.

'I have a crime scene here,' I said before he could say anything. 'Philippe is dead.'

I hung up and started back toward the street but stopped before I got ten feet. Jesus. The image came to me like the faint glow of light in the east at sunrise, gradually turning the sky from night to day. I turned and looked back toward the dumpster. Was it possible? I couldn't be wrong. Not about this. I'm too good a cop.

I walked back to the container and looked inside at the tape binding the victim's arms. It wasn't possible. It just couldn't be. But I wasn't wrong. The dark echo of a previous horror rose like a muted scream in my memory. I had seen this before.

eighteen

Harrison eased himself up the side of the dumpster to look inside with the tentative steps of an acrophobe approaching the edge of a cliff. When he was sufficiently close to get a clear look over the lip, he leaned slightly forward and stared at Gabriel's work with the repelled curiosity of a viewer examining the gory tableau of a Hieronymus Bosch painting.

Nothing feels real about an incomplete human body. I always imagined it was a defense mechanism we keep hidden deep inside from some dark ancestral place that allows us to disconnect from the mayhem that was once a nearly daily experience.

'I've never seen . . .' Harrison said, letting the thought drift before picking it back up. 'It doesn't look real,' he said softly.

'Without eyes or a face, we share nearly nothing in common anymore. What's left is like an empty room that hasn't been lived in for years,' I said.

I noticed Harrison's eyes drift down the length of

Philippe's arms to his hands, one of which was still clenched in a fist as if the pain of death was so great the hand refused to let go of it.

'Except for the hands,' he said. 'We still share that.'

He was right. After sight, the next sensation that brings meaning to a life is touch. From a baby's gentle soft fingers, to the paper-thin wrinkly skin of a great-grandmother's hands. We hold, we touch, we create, we even destroy with them. And when our voices falter or words are insufficient, we speak with them.

Harrison turned away and looked over to me, his eyes narrowing into a question. 'You've seen something,' he said.

'Look at the way the arms are bound just above the elbows.'

His eyes moved back to the bright duct tape pinching the arms nearly together.

'There's something about that?'

Harrison studied the body for another moment, then turned and looked at me as he realized there was something else in my reaction.

'That means something to you, doesn't it?'

I nodded. 'I think it means Gabriel may have made his first mistake.'

He shook his head, not understanding. 'I'm not following.'

'Eighteen months ago we found the body of a transient in a wash at the base of the foothills. We never identified him. The case is still open under a John Doe.'

'You think there's a connection?'

'He was on his knees, his throat was cut, and his arms

310

were bound in the same way with duct tape. It was one of the things that never made sense about the case. Why execute a homeless man? But there was nothing that tied it to any other open cases.'

Harrison thought for a moment, as if trying to construct a bridge from one death to another over the course of nearly two years, then shook his head.

'According to Philippe, Gabriel arrived in the country just two weeks ago.'

'But he disappeared in France two years ago.'

'You think Philippe was wrong.'

'Or lied, or was lied to.'

'Just because of the way the arms are tied?'

I glanced back into the container at the body.

'I've investigated nearly two hundred homicides, maybe twenty of those involved the binding of the victims' hands together, and in every one of those cases, the hands were tied at the wrists.'

'Except for these two,' Harrison said.

I nodded.

'Two out of two hundred is not coincidence. I'd bet my career that Gabriel killed the transient.'

I turned from the dumpster and looked toward the flashing lights of the patrol cars on the street. The terrible truth of my life struck me in the chest, causing my heart to skip. How many nights had I stood on damp pavement combing through the remains of violence? How many moments had I missed with Lacy in exchange for the privilege of sorting through the last moments of a wife, beaten to death by a drunk husband's fists? Or a ten-old-year girl whose skull was splintered by a gang member's twisted sense of respect. What kind of person would choose this? What kind of a mother would trade kissing her daughter good night for that?

'I hate this,' I said silently.

I turned and realized Harrison was staring at me, waiting to ask a question.

'How does this help us?'

I pulled myself back to the present.

'A serial killer doesn't just turn off the impulse to kill. It's primary to their existence, it's how they find their place in the world. And his vanity couldn't let the killing of the transient go unrecognized. The tape on the arms is his way of staking a claim.'

I started walking back to the street with Harrison a step behind.

'You think he wanted you to know it was him?'

'In the nightmare he's living, he thinks of himself as an artist. The idea that someone else could take credit for something he's done would be an anathema to him.'

'So . . .'

'We go through everything from the transient's death: every interview, every location, every shred of evidence that by itself meant nothing. Maybe there'll be a connection.'

'There's something I'm not understanding, Lieutenant,' Harrison said.

I turned to him as he continued.

'We're assuming that nothing he's done has been an accident, or is random, that everything has a purpose.'

'I think that's a safe assumption,' I said.

'Then why didn't Gabriel leave the head in the dumpster?'

I took two more steps and stopped. Lord, I had missed that.

'He doesn't want us to ID him. Unless Philippe's fingerprints are on file, without a face, dental records, DNA's only useful if you have something to match it against; identification would be impossible.'

'I was thinking that, too,' Harrison said.

The implication hung in the space between us as though awaiting understanding.

'Something about Philippe is a threat to him, even in death. We figure out what that is, and . . .'

I didn't dare take the next leap of imagination. One step at a time. If I started thinking too far ahead, I might miss something and bypass it without notice. One missed step, and the entire house of cards could tumble. And I would lose my daughter.

'It's something, at least,' Harrison said.

I shook my head. 'It's more than something.'

I glanced at my watch. It was going on eleven P.M. The minutes were racing by as if they couldn't wait for the dawn. I looked back once more at the dumpster as a photographer's flash illuminated the scene in a brief explosion of white light.

It was more than just something; it might be everything.

nineteen

Driving through the garment and jewelry districts of downtown LA is like stepping back into a fifty-year-old Kodachrome home movie of Mexico City. Garish colors of cheap clothes and custom jewelry spill out of storefronts onto the sidewalks like a street festival. The sweet smells of corn tortillas and diesel fumes drift in the air. Salsa music competes with mariachi, which competes with sirens and street crime and broken dreams carried from dirt shacks south of the border. It's a place unknown to most inhabitants of the City of Angels, as distant from the gated homes of the Hollywood Hills as a Third World shantytown.

Four blocks north of the light and the music and the petty street crime, the streets turned darker and emptier and more dangerous. In doorways, cautious, bloodshot eyes kept track of any passing threat. A late-model sedan idled on a corner waiting to buy crack. Passing an alley, a prostitute stepped out in search of a customer, then disappeared when she made us out as cops.

Harrison pulled the squad to a stop outside the Brothers of Hope Mission, which occupied an empty storefront on San Pedro. A quick survey of the dead John Doe file had led us here, the last-known address where the transient was seen alive before he was bound by the arms and his throat was cut.

There was no one visible on the street when I stepped out. The curb and sidewalk in front of the mission were spotless, whereas the next storefront over was littered with broken bottles, empty cans of malt liquor, and syringes caked and stained from repeated use by addicts. Aside from the lights inside the mission, life appeared to have retreated from the block and taken shelter for the night.

In the distance to the east, the *pop, pop, pop* of a small-caliber pistol pierced the night.

'It must be getting close to midnight,' Harrison said. He turned to me and saw that I wasn't following. 'New Year's, Lieutenant.'

God, I'd forgotten. People were celebrating tonight. Resolutions and promises were being made that were going to change lives and fulfill dreams. In the Hills and suburbs, champagne was being poured. In the barrio, guns were being fired like party favors in a form of celebration that would make Pancho Villa proud.

'I forgot,' I said, as another faint *pop* sent a bullet into the air.

I couldn't imagine measuring time in spans of years again. My world had been reduced to the next eight hours. I had 480 minutes before the parade began and Gabriel's hell came tumbling down on me.

Inside the mission, half a dozen men sat around tables scattered throughout the room. A few were hunched over cups of coffee clutched in their hands, staring into the black liquid as if it contained a secret. Others just sat motionless, like pieces of machinery that had been abandoned once they ceased to function.

In the far corner, a single woman sat with bulging plastic garbage bags containing her possessions and several chairs gathered around her the way settlers circled their wagons at night for security on the frontier. Her eyes were the only ones that took notice of our entrance, scrutinizing us with the practiced caution of a hunted animal, evaluating the escalation in threat with quick, darting glances. New Year's Eve would pass unnoticed in this room, suffocated by the heavy odor of human sweat, stale coffee, and bleach.

From a small side office, a bearded man in his mid-fifties, wearing a white shirt and dark pants, stepped out and extended his hand. I recognized him as Father Paul, the same Franciscan I had questioned eighteen months before in the death of the transient. His forearms were the size of a dockworker's, the edge of a tattoo just visible below the rolled sleeve of his shirt belying a past that was far more complicated, and I imagined less pious, than the present. I introduced Harrison, then he escorted us into the small spare office. A crucifix adorned one wall. On the opposite, a blue Dodger pennant.

'I can't imagine that there is anything else I can tell you,' he said. 'I only remembered the man who was killed because he broke the rules and brought alcohol into the shelter. I had to forcibly remove him and ban

317

him from the shelter. I try to give people as many chances as possible, but he was too combative.'

I took out the drawing of Gabriel and laid it on the desk in front of Father Paul. He studied it for a moment with the practiced eye of someone whose safety depends on his ability to read the level of rage or despair behind a client's eyes.

'I would remember him,' he said, shaking his head. 'That's a face designed to not be forgotten. I don't think he was ever in here.'

I reached into my pocket and removed the photograph of Philippe I had taken from the mirror in his room.

'How about him?'

He gently picked up the photograph by the corner with his thick, muscular fingers. A question formed immediately in his eyes.

'There's something . . .'

He considered it for another moment, then recognition replaced the question in his eyes. 'Yes, I think . . .'

He laid it on the table and sat back, searching his memory. 'He volunteered here for a brief time, I'm almost certain.'

'Are you sure?'

He looked again and nodded. 'He rode with our outreach van for a few weeks. I remember because he was the only volunteer we've had who was from France.'

'When was this?'

'It's been quite a while.'

'Can you give me a date?'

He nodded and turned to a filing cabinet behind the desk and began flipping quickly through rows of folders.

'We keep addresses and phone numbers of volunteers in hopes they can be enticed to help out again. Most never do.'

'Did he?' Harrison asked.

'No,' Father Paul said, pulling out a dog-eared file.

He paged quickly through it and removed a five-by-seven index card.

'This is him,' he said. 'Jean, no last name.'

'Jean, you're certain?'

'Yes.'

He read our reaction the way a cop would have. 'You know him by a different name?'

I nodded. 'Philippe.'

'Why would a volunteer give me an alias? He have a warrant on him? Or have immigration problems?'

'Not that we know of.'

'Well, he didn't want someone to know he was here.'

He glanced at the drawing of Gabriel.

'Maybe it was him.'

'You should have been a cop, Father.'

'That's what a parole officer once said to me.'

'Can you give me a date you last saw him?' I asked.

'He was last here . . .' His finger traced a line on the card until he found what it was searching for. 'He last volunteered in April 2003.'

'A month before the transient was killed,' Harrison said.

'Is there an address?'

Father Paul glanced at me guardedly.

'We like to think these are confidential, unless there's a reason for it not to be.'

'Earlier this evening we found the man you know as Jean, and we know as Philippe murdered in a dumpster.'

Father Paul extended the card to me without saying a word. 'I'll pray for his soul.'

Next to his name was an address but no phone number. I studied it for a moment, then handed it to Harrison.

'That's in Pasadena, not Hollywood,' he said in surprise.

I stood up and reached out to shake the father's hand. He took it gently, looking into my eyes with a weariness that was constantly doing battle with his faith.

'I hope the first hours of the new year bring something better than the last few of the old one.'

'Thank you, Father.' I turned and started for the door.

'And I'll pray for you, Lieutenant.'

I glanced at my watch; ten of my 480 minutes had already vanished into the new year.

twenty

The address in Pasadena was a run-down eight-unit apartment building a block north of the 210 freeway on Villa. The outside was a dirty mustard-yellow color, and as was the practice in the early sixties when it was built, the complex was given a grand name in elaborate lettering above the entrance: The Villa Estates.

Two graffiti-covered palm trees framed the entrance like a couple of forgotten, aging doormen who had been left behind when the building began its downhill slide.

There was no interior central hallway in the building. Each unit had its own exterior entrance. Four downstairs, four up. The last apartment on the ground floor was the address given to Father Paul. The entrance was tucked in a far corner, secluded from the street and the other apartments by a row of large bushes.

'A person could come and go and never be noticed,' Harrison said.

It had one window that was curtained. Several flyers for Thai and Mexican food lay outside the door.

'We're either going to surprise the hell out of some illegal day laborer, or . . .' I looked at Harrison as he let the thought go. Standing here was an act of desperation. A two-year-old address of a dead man.

'He probably just moved,' I said.

Harrison nodded less than convincingly. 'And changed his name.'

I placed my hand on my weapon and motioned Harrison to knock on the door.

'This is the police. Open the door!'

Nothing stirred inside. I kept my eye on the curtains for any hint of movement, but nothing disturbed them.

'Again,' I said.

Harrison pounded on the door, but no one responded. I glanced at the flyers on the ground. My breath caught up short like a cotton sweater hung on a nail. The hot rush of air from the blast at Sweeny's flashed in my memory. I winced at an imagined shower of broken glass and involuntarily stepped back.

'There were flyers on the ground outside Sweeny's bungalow,' I said.

Harrison glanced at me, then began to meticulously run his hands over the door frame looking for any sign of explosives. Frustration and anger began to boil inside me. Once again, Gabriel had gotten inside my head. I felt like a frightened kid who had been told a ghost story.

'Screw it,' I said, reaching out and touching him on the shoulder.

He turned to me.

'We don't have time for this . . . Lacy doesn't have time for this. Kick it open.'

'Yeah, why not.'

For a man whose life depended on meticulously dismantling devices designed to kill, it was an enormous leap of either faith or wild abandon.

He stepped back and drove a foot powerfully against the door, which flung open like it had been hit with a blast of wind. I swung around and trained my Glock into the apartment. Nothing moved. The air inside carried the stale odor of cigarettes. I reached around the door, found the light switch, and flipped it on.

A small round coffee table sat in the living room with a large ashtray in the middle. Several large pillows were gathered around it. Add a TV, and there was nothing else in the room. I motioned toward the door to the bedroom, and Harrison moved across the living room and gently pushed it open. He swept the room with his weapon, then flipped on the light. He started to take a step inside but stopped, his eyes staring in wonder at something.

'I think you'd better look at this.'

I walked over to the door of the bedroom and stood next to Harrison. On the floor of the room was a single mattress neatly made with a sheet and blanket in tight military-style corners. On the floor next to the bed sat a laptop computer and a printer.

'Jesus,' Harrison whispered.

The walls of the room were lined with photographs. My eyes moved across them with the reluctance of a civilian who has just stumbled upon the aftermath of battle.

'It's his collection,' I said. 'They must have found something similar in France.'

I glanced at Harrison and saw the confused look of someone who had just wandered off the map of human understanding.

'Have you ever seen . . .' He didn't bother finishing the thought. He saw in my eyes that there was no need to. He shook his head in disbelief, then glanced uneasily into the room. One photograph after another of Gabriel's victims, all arranged as if in an exhibition at a gallery. Harrison turned to me in barely contained horror and blocked my path into the room.

'Maybe you should let me look first—'

I shook my head. My heart began to beat wildly against my chest.

'No.'

'Lieutenant—'

'She's not here.'

'Please, just let me look first.'

My eyes fixed on Harrison's, refusing to give in to the possibility. 'She can't be here. No goddamn way . . . no way.'

Harrison's eyes held mine for a moment, as if pleading.

'You're right, but just let me do this. For me, not you.'

He began to reach for my hand, then withdrew it. I saw that my own hand was trembling.

'You're just wasting our time.'

'I know.'

'Okay,' I said reluctantly, turning around and staring into the living room. 'But she's not here.'

I felt his hand gently fall on my shoulder and then slip away as he walked into the room. With each step he took, my heart rate jumped tenfold. I heard his breath catch and then rapidly pick up in pace. His movement around the room seemed to take forever. And with each second, each step he took, my resolve that Lacy was not up on one of those walls began to weaken. How had my world gone so utterly and completely insane? A voice inside my head began to whisper, 'I can't do this, I can't. I can't—' I was going to scream.

'She's not here, Lieutenant.'

I spun around, the wave of relief coursing through my body nearly buckling my knees. Harrison put his arms around me as I tried to regain control of my breathing.

'You're sure she's not?'

'Yeah, I'm sure.'

His arms held me for another moment, then slipped away as I took a deep breath.

'He was here this evening, maybe as little as an hour ago. There's a photograph of Philippe.'

I stepped past him into the room and began to take in the record of carnage: every horrible act displayed on the wall as if he were chronicling a summer vacation to Yellowstone and these were pictures of buffalo and mud pots. There was the headless body of Philippe in the dumpster. The Mexican major floating in the casting pool. Finley lying on the cold concrete floor among the flowers. Sweeny in the burning car. The eco-warrior with his hands tied behind his back who died in the house on Monte where I found Lacy's shoe. And then it got worse.

'Breem,' escaped my lips in horror.

His sunken, terrified eyes stared straight out at the camera – the same eyes I had seen in the car before the bomb went off. Tape covered his mouth, but I could see from the contorted muscles in his jaw that he was screaming underneath it. His hands, encased in the ball of explosives, were held up as if pleading for mercy.

'He couldn't photograph him after the explosion, so he did before,' Harrison said.

'I thought I understood who Gabriel was . . . I was wrong.'

I turned away, unable to look at those eyes any longer, but I could still feel them. I doubted they would ever entirely leave me.

'Did you see anything in the background of the photograph that would hint at a location?'

'No.'

'Neither did I.'

Next to the photograph of Breem was a picture of Colorado Boulevard. For a moment, I thought it was out of place until I realized why it was on the wall.

'Oh, God, the parade route.'

'Just east of Orange Grove and Colorado.'

'The block that's televised.'

Harrison studied the photograph for a moment, then shook his head.

'He's not going to be able to get anywhere near it. It's already been sealed, every float, streetlight, every bleacher's been searched. No one gets close to the parade without being screened.'

'Then how does he do it?'

runthe risk

'He can't.'

Even as he said it, I could see the conviction behind his words disappear. We all knew that there was no longer any such thing as 'It can't happen here.'

I turned around and looked across the room. On the far wall, a space, the size of a photograph, had been left blank.

'He's left room for another picture.'

I stared at it as if waiting for another image to appear out of the paint.

'That could mean anything or nothing,' Harrison said.

'It means someone else is going to die. It means we have to . . .'

My voice faltered and we both stared silently at the space on the wall. Harrison turned and looked at me, his eyes carrying the unspoken truth neither of us wanted to utter.

'Lieut— Alex.'

I shook my head and turned away.

'When he calls again and he gives you the choice to save your daughter or a stranger, you have to choose Lacy.'

I let the words pass as if I hadn't heard them.

'We need to go through every inch of this apartment, every file in the computer. There's got to be something that points to where he is.'

'Lieutenant, when he calls—'

'There's no point to this.'

'I think there is.'

I turned angrily. 'Did you see something in this room

327

that suggests Gabriel possesses the quality of mercy? Because I missed it.'

'It may buy time.'

'He's going to kill her. If I had any doubt of that, it's gone.'

I hadn't allowed myself to say it before, but now I did. The words carried a terrible finality, and I instantly realized why I had avoided using them before.

'She is all I have . . . all I ever wanted. I didn't know how to tell her that . . .'

'We're a step ahead of him now,' Harrison said.

All I could manage was a nod. Then I forced myself to say something else as if to purge the other hopeless words.

'A small step.'

I walked out of the room and called Chief Chavez to set up surveillance of the apartment. If Gabriel were to come back here, we would have him. But I also knew that if he came back, it would be to put that last picture up on the wall, and it would be too late.

When I finished with Chavez, I stepped outside to clear my head of the odor of stale cigarettes and the images of death. In the adjacent yard I noticed a lone lemon tree heavily laden with fruit the size of clenched fists. I tested the air to see if citrus flavored it, but there was nothing there. The moisture in the evening chill seemed to settle everything it touched into place for the night, even sound, as it was unnaturally quiet.

I exhaled heavily into the darkness and watched the steam rise from my breath. Somewhere down the block, several shouts of people still celebrating the new year interrupted the night's silence. I thought of the ice and snow of the Midwest and how millions would be up in the morning to watch the parade. The highest achievement in civic salesmanship. The ultimate 'Wish you were here' postcard.

I turned and looked back into Gabriel's shabby apartment. Exactly when had we let paradise slip through our fingers here? Was there a moment in the history of Los Angeles that we could point to and say, 'there it was lost, right there, right then.' Was it the first orange grove that disappeared under pavement? The first concrete laid on the first stretch of the Pasadena Freeway? The first subdivision, the hundredth, or the thousandth? Maybe it was the first seeding of a lawn in a desert. The stealing of the Owens Valley's water. The paving of the Los Angeles River, or Disney declaring that two acres of Orange County was the happiest place on earth. Maybe it all began and ended with the first frame of film in the first movie in a town based on illusion. Or maybe there isn't just one point. Maybe everyone who was ever born here or moved across a continent or traveled an ocean to live here has his own moment of finality. That demarcation point where the dream is no match for reality.

To the south the high-pitched cycle of a squad car's siren briefly pierced the night. I turned and walked back into the apartment. Harrison stepped to the door of the bedroom, made brief eye contact, then looked back into the room as if he'd left something behind. I joined him at the door.

'There's a journal, of sorts. It actually reads more like a novel – a bad novel. I think it begins with the very first killing he ever committed.'

'A journal?'

He nodded, then glanced at the notepad in his hand and began to read.

'I'm the boy in the third row of the class photograph that everyone's eyes pass over. No one remembers my name, the color of my hair, or the sound of my voice. I'm invisible.'

He slipped the pad into his pocket.

'That's how it begins.'

I started to walk into the bedroom and Harrison reached out and took hold of my arm. He hesitated, then looked at me, his eyes carrying the weight of what he'd read. The sudden high of hope I had felt began to bleed away like a severed artery.

'What is it?'

He took a shallow breath. 'He's already written the ending.'

My mind began to race. 'Lacy? What does it—'

He shook his head. 'I just skimmed the last couple of pages, but she wasn't mentioned.'

'What was?'

'You. You're in the ending, Lieutenant.'

'Me?'

'Maybe you'd better read it.'

I looked past him into the room toward the computer.

'Tell me what it is, Harrison.'

The muscles in his jaw tightened as if bracing for an

impact, then he looked at me with the finality of a lover's good-bye.

'You're walking down Colorado Boulevard during the parade . . . You're strapped with explosives.'

twenty-one

Harrison's words seemed to gather up the air in the room, making it hard to take a breath.

'You okay?' he said.

I nodded, though he knew as well as I did that it was all for show. The ground itself was falling apart beneath our feet.

'I'm his suicide bomber,' I whispered.

I struggled to take a deep breath, my body fighting the impulse as if instinctively not wanting any part of the space we were in.

'We wanted to know how he would do it. Now we do.'

I shuddered as I imagined the weight of the explosive-laden harness being fitted over my shoulders.

'Be careful what you wish for.'

'There's no way in hell he gets you to walk down Colorado boulevard into a crowd of people.'

'He has my daughter . . . He can get me to do anything he wants.'

Harrison's eyes fell on mine trying desperately not to

reveal the uncertainty that was just under the surface.

'Not that.'

'You said it yourself. I have to choose Lacy. And that's what I'm going to do.'

'We need to get you wired with a transmitter. You're not going anywhere without us knowing exactly where you are.'

I nodded. 'Call Hicks. They'll be better at it than we will.'

Harrison took out his phone and began to dial when my cell phone rang. I started to reach for it.

'No!' Harrison shouted. 'If it's him and he wants you moving . . . That can't happen until you're wired.'

'That could take half an hour.'

'It doesn't matter. You have to wait.'

I reached into my pocket, took it out, and let it ring in the palm of my hand. On the seventh ring I began to shake my head. The eighth ring felt like the recoil of a gun pointed at my daughter.

'I can't—'

'Don't.'

Harrison began to reach for my phone but I already had opened it.

'Delillo,' I said.

'Choose,' Gabriel said.

The word felt like the door slamming against my face. I looked at Harrison and nodded. He immediately stepped back and rang Hicks.

'I first want to hear my daughter's voice, or you can go straight to hell.'

'Interesting choice of words, Lieutenant.'

'Put her on, or this is how it ends, right here, right now. Is that what you want?'

Gabriel laughed, and then the line went silent but it wasn't cut off.

I looked at Harrison, who was across the room shaking his head in disbelief and nearly shouting into his phone.

'Get him on the line right now! I don't have two minutes . . . No, he cannot call me back. I need him now!'

Over my open line I heard what sounded like a chair sliding across a floor. I then heard several shallow breaths. I knew the sound. It was as if I were listening to a recording of my own heart. It was Lacy, there was no doubt. They were the same breaths I felt against my breast when I held her moments after she was born.

'Lacy,' I said.

Nothing came back.

'It's me, honey.'

'Mom,' she said.

'I'm right here.'

She started to say something, but her voice cracked with emotion.

'Talk to me, sweetheart.'

'This fucking asshole—'

The phone was yanked from her hands and fell to the floor.

'Lacy! . . . Lacy, can you hear me? Lacy!'

There was no sound on the other end. I pressed the phone to my ear as if I could somehow get closer to her.

'Lacy, can you hear me?' I said desperately. 'I love you. You'll be all right.'

Nothing.

'Lacy.'

I heard something slide across the floor.

'Lacy . . . Lac—'

'Choose.'

My breath left me for a moment as if I'd been punched in the stomach.

'You bastard. You know damn well what I choose.'

'Say it.'

He sounded like an angry teacher demanding respect from a student.

'Say it!' he shouted. He commanded.

'Lacy.'

'Be at the corner of Orange Grove and Altadena in six minutes. I see any other police, if I hear a helicopter, if I see someone walking a dog, I'll cut her throat. Do not hang up. Keep the line open. I want to listen to every word you say.'

I turned to Harrison and held my finger up to my lips, motioning for him to be silent, then gestured for a pen and paper. He reached into his pocket and took out a notepad and pen and handed them to me. I began to write furiously as I started walking toward the door.

Was Hicks listening?

He nodded and wrote down his answer on the pad.

Twenty minutes to get here and get you wired.

I shook my head and we began passing the notepad back and forth as we walked out toward the squad.

Six minutes to get to the corner of Orange Grove and Altadena.

I'm coming with you. I can hide in the back—

I shook my head as Harrison kept writing.

No, you—

I yanked the pad out of Harrison's hand.

Read the journal!!! I wrote with several exclamations. *It's got to tell where he has Lacy – find her.*

I underlined *find her* several times.

We reached the car and I opened the door. Harrison reached out and covered my phone with his hand.

'How do I find you?' he whispered.

Our eyes met for a moment, then slipped apart.

'He's written down exactly how he plans to do it,' I said. 'If we lose touch . . . you have to be a step ahead.'

Harrison shook his head in disapproval.

'This isn't fiction.'

'He believes the same thing about what he's written.'

I got in the car and placed my hand on his.

'Find my daughter.'

I started the engine and stepped on the gas, east toward Altadena.

The corner of Orange Grove and Altadena looked as if a slice of a small town had been misplaced. Lines were painted on the pavement for angle parking. There was a diner, fabric stores, secondhand furniture stores, a barbershop. The only giveaway that it wasn't Indiana was that the signs were all in Armenian and Spanish.

I pulled to a stop on the southwest corner. A single car drove north heading into the foothill neighborhoods. The driver was a young woman, her eyes focused straight ahead as if she had had too much to drink and was willing herself home. On the opposite corner the light in a Chevron station's sign blinked erratically on and off from an electrical short. That was it. The corner was deserted.

According to my watch, five and a half minutes had passed. Thirty seconds left. I scanned the street trying to anticipate what he would do next.

Twenty seconds.

Nothing presented itself. If I only knew what was in Gabriel's computer. Had he written everything down to the last detail? My sitting in the car right now, my next step, my first mistake. But wishing for something that was out of reach would do me no good. All I had was right in front of me. Or maybe, more correctly, what was behind me – the accumulated moments that had brought me to this place.

If what Harrison had read was correct, Gabriel would need to capture me. But how? Was the trap right in front of me? Do I just walk right in and give myself up at the sight of my daughter?

Ten seconds.

No, I won't do that. I see him, I kill him. My one chance. Lacy's one chance.

The last seconds ticked off.

'Lieutenant,' Gabriel said.

The sound of his voice was like a gunshot next to my ear. Reluctantly I picked up the phone.

'I'm here,' I said.

'You have one chance to follow my directions. Hesitate, I kill her. There's a phone booth next to the gas station. Leave your phone in the car and run to it, now!' he demanded.

338

Across the intersection I heard the first ring.

I got out of the car, leaving my phone on the seat and the door open. The fifty yards across the intersection felt as dangerous as if I were crossing a minefield. Each step took me deeper and deeper into the dark, twisted nightmare of Gabriel's mind and away from my only connection to the world, which sat on the seat back in my squad. By the time I reached the phone booth, I felt as naked and vulnerable as a child. He was cutting me off from the world, drawing me in. This is terror. A phone ringing, an empty street, the imagination spinning out of control.

I picked up the receiver, gasping for breath from the run and the adrenaline racing through my body. I tried to gather myself to mask the stress in my voice so he wouldn't fully know his advantage.

'I'm here,' I said between breaths.

'The brown car fifty feet in front of you. Get in it and drive north on Altadena. Run.'

I dropped the phone and sprinted to the car. It was an old model, at least ten years, and in need of paint. An Impala, I think. The interior smelled of cheap aftershave and stale beer. The backseat was littered with beer cans and a pile of dirty laundry. On the floor of the front seat were several receipts from a check-cashing service. It had probably belonged to a day laborer, probably an illegal. And, very likely now, dead. On the passenger seat was a cell phone that began to ring.

If I picked up and followed his next set of instructions, I would be stepping wholly into the nightmare that had swallowed my daughter. I glanced across the street toward my empty squad. I imagined Harrison was reading Gabriel's narrative of what I was about to do. I could almost hear his voice as he stared at the screen shaking his head saying, 'No, Lieutenant, no.'

'Lacy's there,' I said softly as if explaining to Harrison. 'I have to.' I started to reach for the phone but stopped as rage rolled over me like a wave.

'You fucking asshole!' I screamed into the empty car, using Lacy's words.

I put my hands to my face and clenched my jaw, trying to smother the anger.

'Lacy, Lacy, Lacy . . .' I whispered, trying to quiet my racing heart. I couldn't lose control, not now. I needed to be thinking clearly. That and a 9mm round I planned to put into his heart were all I had.

I whispered 'Lacy' one more time as if she could hear me; then I started the car and picked up the phone.

'I'm going north on Altadena.'

'I know.'

'How far—'

'Quiet,' he shouted. 'You'll talk when I tell you. You're nothing now, not a lieutenant, not a cop, not a mother. You're only what I decide you will be.'

'And what does that make you?'

There was a brief, ominous silence.

'Your future.'

I glanced in my mirror to see if I was being followed. Altadena was empty. Nothing pulled out from a side street and followed me. He hadn't been there. He had bluffed his way through it and I had followed his

instructions. I had just given up whatever control of the
situation I might still have had.

'Fuck you.'

He laughed at me.

'You're like your daughter.'

I tried to reply but couldn't. I hadn't heard anyone
say that other than my mother. And when she had said
it, I reacted angrily as if she were insulting me. Why had
I done that? Why had I been afraid to approve and love
my own daughter without any doubt, any judgment?
What was I afraid of? What did I think I would find out
about myself by accepting her for who she is?

'You are nothing but a stupid woman,' Gabriel
said.

There it was. My life as told to me by a serial killer.

'No longer,' I said.

Just past Washington, the road began to rise more
steadily as I headed into the more expensive homes of
the foothills. On either side, the streets began to twist
and curve as if in a dreamscape. The dark shapes of the
mountains rose above me and threatened to tumble
down and cover everything at their feet. With each block
the streets became darker and emptier. A coyote
stopped in the middle of the road a hundred yards
ahead and let loose a string of cries before disappearing
into the night.

'Turn left on Midwick. Go a block and a half and
stop,' Gabriel said.

I turned, my headlights cutting into the darkness
ahead. The eerie, red eyes and the ghostly gray shape of
a possum reflected briefly in the lights before vanishing

down a storm drain. There were no houses on the street, the hillsides being too steep. A block and a half up I pulled to the side and stopped. The nearest streetlight was another block and a half farther on. Beyond that, I could make out four cars parked on the street in the darkness. One of them, I assumed, contained Gabriel and maybe my daughter. He was that close. For whatever he had planned, he had picked a perfect spot. I was sitting on the dark side of the moon. The lights of Los Angeles spreading out below me may just as well have been the swath of lights of the Milky Way for my ability to contact one of them.

'Turn the engine and the lights off.'

My hand fought the impulse to follow the directions then reluctantly obeyed his command. The plunge into darkness was sudden and complete, and my eyes were slow to adjust. I checked all the mirrors for any movement in the darkness behind me, but nothing stirred that I could see. I reached down and slipped my Glock from my holster and set it on my lap. The silence I thought I was hearing wasn't silence at all but the white noise of rushing water plunging from the mountains in a nearby ravine. Something moved through the brush on the hillside below. I clicked off the safety on my weapon and placed my hand on the grip, but the movement in the brush stopped.

In the rearview I saw a beam of headlights heading up Altadena slice the darkness. As the car reached the corner and came into view, it slid to a stop in the middle of the street. I tightened my grip on my Glock and raised it into an upright shooting position. The headlights of the car swept across my mirror and slowly came toward me.

'What is that?' Gabriel said. There was tension in his voice that hadn't been there a moment before.

'I don't know.'

'You had them follow you—'

'No, I didn't.'

'If you're lying, I kill her right now.'

'No! I'm not lying.'

'Then what is that?'

'It's someone coming home from a party, that's all.'

Even as I said it, I realized it wasn't true. I recognized the profile of the roof lights coming toward me.

'It's a policeman.'

'No, it's not.'

'Your daughter's dead.'

'No,' I screamed into the phone. 'It's not a cop. It's private security, a rent-a-cop. All the neighborhoods have them up here. It's nothing.'

'Rent-a-cop? What is that?'

'They patrol neighborhoods, they're not police.'

'You said cop.'

'It's a figure of speech. They're paid seven bucks an hour to drive around. That's all they do!'

I held my hand up in front of the mirror so the headlights of the sedan wouldn't blind me. It pulled up behind, hesitated, then drove by, the driver glancing in my direction though I couldn't see his face in the darkness. On the side of the car, the company's name was spelled out in bold letters. ARMED RESPONSE.

'You see. It's nothing.'

343

'If you're lying to me . . .'

'I'm not lying.'

Seventy feet in front of me the rent-a-cop pulled to the curb and stopped, his red brake lights glowing in the darkness like two menacing eyes. I stared at it in disbelief. This wasn't happening, it couldn't be. The driver made no attempt to get out of the car. He just sat there, waiting. I felt as if I were standing on a plate-glass window spanning an abyss, my daughter's life hanging on what a wannabe cop with a GED was going to do next.

'Move,' I whispered. 'Just drive on.'

'Why did he stop?' Gabriel demanded.

'He thinks I'm a burglar. He's doing his job, that's all.'

'He followed you!' he shouted, on the edge of rage.

The glass under my feet began to crack.

'No!'

'I'm placing a knife to your daughter's throat.'

'I'll get rid of him!'

'He followed you!'

'No!'

'You lie!'

'No!' I pleaded.

Only silence came back.

'I swear it, I swear I'm not lying.'

Still nothing came over the phone.

'Please, don't hurt her.'

I closed my eyes. I could hear the sound of the glass beneath my feet begin to splinter.

'Please—'

'Get rid of him, now.'

I instantly stepped out of the squad, holstering my weapon and starting toward the rent-a-cop. The white noise of the rushing water was punctuated by what sounded like thunder. I glanced at the sky, but there wasn't a cloud in sight, no flashes of lightning. With each step I took toward the idling patrol car, the rumble grew louder as if I were walking into the eye of a storm. I felt a small tremor under my feet, and then the rumble became a cascade of violent reports, one after another. I realized that a piece of the mountain above had broken loose and was careening down the wash in the darkness, sending boulders the size of cars bouncing off the concrete walls, swallowing everything in its path.

'Take him,' I whispered, or prayed, or just blindly hoped that Gabriel was in its path. 'Sweep him away.'

But as quickly as it had approached, the slide passed, the rumble quickly fading until the night was once again eerily silent. No miracles, not tonight.

Twenty feet from the back of the patrol car, I could just make out the driver's hand reaching up to adjust the mirror to watch my approach. I removed my badge and held the gold shield out so it wouldn't be mistaken for a weapon. As I passed the back bumper the driver's window began to roll down.

'Police officer,' I said, holding out the badge. 'I need you to move from the area right now!'

As I stepped to the door, the driver turned, his face catching enough starlight to reflect briefly in the darkness. I saw his eyes just long enough for a dreadful sense of familiarity to hit me. I knew those eyes, and they were now measuring me like a predator.

The unmistakable shape of a shotgun barrel protruded out the window. I reached for my weapon, but it was already too late. My hand just touched the cool plastic of the grip when the muzzle flash lit up the darkness like heat lightning, and the whole world turned white.

twenty-two

There was no sound, no color, no smell, no touch. Was I falling? Standing? Lying down? How long had it been? An hour, a minute, or just a second? If I was breathing, I wasn't aware of it. A dull pain rose in my chest with each beat of my heart and traveled through my body like a spreading virus, deadening everything in its path. Was this how you die, inch by inch, cell by cell?

The faint light of the night sky gradually began to come into focus, moving and shifting as if in a fun-house mirror. I was on the ground next to the car. I could feel the grit of the pavement on the side of my face. A faint taste of oil played on my lips. There was movement around me, though it was too quick for my eyes to focus on. I heard the trunk of a car open and then the sound of footsteps on the gravel of the pavement.

I looked over to my right and saw my hand splayed out, holding my Glock as if it had no connection to the rest of my body. What had happened? I tried to replay the events, but unconsciousness began to rise like a cresting wave, and my hand began to dissolve into the pavement as if it were melting wax.

Fight it. Find something, remember something. Push it back, push it.

'Lacy,' faintly crossed my lips.

The wave began to settle and then retreat. I remembered walking up to the car, the blast of the shotgun.

Where had I been hit? Why didn't I feel the moisture of blood on my skin and shirt? It didn't make sense. Death would make sense. There was something else, just before the shotgun.

'The eyes,' I whispered.

I knew those eyes, but they weren't the eyes that stared out from the drawing of Gabriel. But whose? I tried to place them, but the face remained just out of focus.

The sound of the footsteps began to move in my direction. I looked at my hand holding my gun and tried to will it to move, to do something, but it was like trying to yell instructions across a vast canyon. The steps drew closer. One by one my fingers began to tighten around the grip of my weapon.

'Move, goddamnit, come on, come on,' I whispered, willing the gun up off the ground as the footsteps drew closer.

I tried to point it at the approaching figure, but my hand drifted uncontrollably in space as if I were lying on the rolling deck of a ship at sea.

'Lieutenant,' a voice said.

I tried to steady the weapon on the dark shape of the figure looming over me. The gun swung wildly back and forth across my field of fire.

'Steady it,' I told myself, fighting for control of my own hand.

The gun swung left, then back to the right.

'Steady.'

As it swept back across the shape of the figure, I began to pull the trigger.

'Now,' I commanded my hand. 'Now!'

The gun steadied and for an instant, I had a clear shot.

'No, Lieutenant,' Gabriel said.

His boot stepped on my wrist, pressing it painfully into the pavement, and the Glock slipped uselessly out of my hand.

'I have other plans, Lieutenant,' he said.

His hand was covering my mouth with a cloth.

'Breathe, Lieutenant. Take a deep breath.'

The cloth had a sharp, pungent odor like a cleaning fluid. I tried to pull away, but my strength was already fleeing.

'Don't fight it like your daughter.'

'Go to hell.'

I reached out toward him as if I could pull aside the fog of unconsciousness that was enveloping me and see his face. He pressed the cloth against my mouth, driving my head hard against the pavement.

'Breathe!' he said impatiently.

I fought for another second trying to resist the instinct, and then I gagged for want of oxygen and took in the bitter air contained in the cloth.

'There,' Gabriel said, his voice drifting into the distance. 'Take it in. Take it.'

I tried with the last of my strength to shake my head free of his hand, but I no longer had any control over my body to fight it.

'Lacy,' I said faintly, trying to cling to consciousness.

I saw my daughter's face hovering just above me. She was talking, but no sound was coming out of her mouth. In my mind I tried to ask where she was, but I couldn't form the words. Her eyes filled with the light of stars as she became part of the night sky. I tried to reach out to her but the ground beneath me gave way and I began to fall, and Lacy disappeared into the stars.

I was moving now, flying maybe. Images and sounds passed by me with astonishing speed. I was holding Lacy. I was being kissed by a young man who would become my husband. I was a girl, standing naked in front of a mirror. A dinner table. My mother sitting silently. The sound of a gunshot. A dismembered body. A hand. The shattering of glass. Sirens. Traver lying in the hospital bed, a bandage wrapped around his head, a tear in the corner of his eye. A red sweater floating in a pool. Breem's eyes pleading for help. Lacy's empty tennis shoe. A bed of roses, thousands of them, as far as the eye could see, the color of blood.

My head began to spin from the cascade and I felt the urge to vomit. No. Stop it, reach out, take hold. My fingers groped for a handhold and then slipped their grip and I began to slide. I didn't fight it. I just wanted to sleep, to let it happen. I picked up speed, the nausea passed. That's better, now go the rest of the way, let go . . . go. The images lost all color, then all definition, and I slipped back into the refuge of unconsciousness.

The movement was different now. The constant rhythm of *p-dum, p-dum, p-dum* played in the darkness like a dripping faucet. I opened my eyes, but there was no light. I tried to move my hands, but they refused. The pain in my chest was different now, like a hand pressing down, trying to force air out of my lungs. If there was a wound, I was not feeling it.

The cadence of the sound picked up speed, then seemed to fade away and come back without missing a beat. I knew this sound, I thought. I reached out to it as if it were a rope that would lead me back to understanding . . . *p-dum, p-dum, p-dum* . . .

I know that, it's—

The lightness of unconsciousness began to roll over me again.

'No,' I said desperately, trying to fight it off, trying to cling to consciousness.

The rhythm slowed a full measure. *P—dum* . . . *p—dum* . . .

I know it . . . I know . . .

P—dum.

'A car,' I whispered. The sound of tires on pavement. He was taking me somewhere. The rope began to slip through my hands. Who was taking me?

P—dum.

'Gabriel,' I whispered. He's finishing his book. I'm a part of it. The end of it.

The current of unconsciousness began to lift me off

my feet. I fought it for a moment, but I wasn't strong enough. The sound of the tires began to fade. I reached out one more time to try to hold on. For an instant I saw myself walking down Colorado Boulevard. That's it, hold on. I tried to reach out farther. The parade. I saw it. I was walking into the middle of a crowd.

'No . . . no.' I tried to yell, but I couldn't make a sound. A little girl reached her hand out toward me and began to smile.

twenty-three

'Lieutenant.'

The voice was calling from across a room, or a long hallway, as indistinct as a memory.

'Wake, Lieutenant.'

I felt the sharp sting on my cheek from a slap. A hand then gripped my face and shook it painfully.

'Wake!' he yelled.

Consciousness began to return like an amusement park ride, speeding and twisting in jarring jumps of time. The last rush was like the final drop of a roller coaster, faster and faster until it ended with the abruptness of hitting a wall, and I was thrown violently back into the world.

I raised my head. I was sitting upright in a chair. My eyes were covered with a blindfold, my hands and legs bound tightly to the chair. I felt his cold hand touch the side of my face and I pulled away.

'Good,' Gabriel said.

The odor of his cheap aftershave clung to him as he

moved behind me. I tried to orient myself, walk the events back to the first step that had brought me to this room. A flash of light in the darkness. The shotgun. The gravel on the pavement, the taste of oil on my lips. My shirt was dry, no blood.

'You shot me with a stun round?' I said.

Where the round had struck me felt as if a hot piece of charcoal was burning into my flesh.

'I could have killed you.'

But he didn't, and wouldn't until I had played my role in his drama properly. It was my only advantage, if you could consider knowing how you are supposed to die in the next few hours a point of leverage.

'Where's my daughter?' I asked.

He slapped the side of my head, cupping my ear, sending a wave of pain through me like I had hit a live wire.

'I could have killed you!' he repeated angrily, as if I didn't fully understand the gravity of my situation or his ability to control my fate.

I felt the warmth of his breath on my neck and I stiffened.

'You're very lucky,' he whispered in my ear.

His breath held the sweet taste of cinnamon and the bitterness of burned garlic. His hand slipped over the top of my shoulder and pressed on the welt where the round had struck me. I gasped, and all the air left my lungs. It felt as if his hand had reached in and taken hold of my heart.

'Tender?'

I tried to speak but couldn't get enough air to form

354

even a single word. His hand traveled up to my throat. The sharp nail of his index finger began to follow the outline of my chin. The pain in my chest began to subside, and I drew a breath.

'You pathetic bastard,' I said.

His hand withdrew, and I braced myself for another slap across the face, but none came. In my darkness I could sense him pull away from me like a snake retreating to its hole.

I tried to remember what I had seen in his eyes, what quality told me those eyes didn't belong to the drawing of Gabriel. They were light, piercing, like diamonds. They had looked at me with menace, but I could picture them differently. I could imagine them softer, pleading, possibly holding love or shedding tears, or even celebrating joy.

'A face designed to not be forgotten,' was how Father Paul had described the drawing of Gabriel. His were not those eyes. His were a chameleon's eyes . . . an actor's eyes. Eyes that could be anything, go anywhere. Everyman's eyes. Then I understood. It was so simple, perfect.

'You're not Gabriel, are you,' I said. 'There is no Gabriel. You've created him to hide behind so you can go out in the light.'

Only silence came back.

'Who are you?'

In the darkness I heard him move. He seemed to be circling me like an animal, studying, deciding where to strike.

Press it, I thought. Pick away at his fiction.

'I know about France,' I said. 'I know how you killed. You're not a terrorist. You don't believe in anything, you're not fighting for anything, there's no cause. You kill because you're sick and twisted and crave control. You've crawled out of some dark hole and need to be put back.'

The soft fall of his footsteps stopped behind me and didn't move. I tried to take a breath, but it was as if the air in the room had vanished. Had I gone too far? How far could I push it without unleashing the madness inside him?

His breath fell on the back of my neck, and every muscle in my body tightened in anticipation of another strike. Nothing came. In the darkness his breathing took on the sound and feel of an animal's. Primitive, atavistic, hiding nothing. Fearing nothing. The top of the food chain. I felt like prey dragged back to a den.

'You think you know me?' he whispered.

'I know you've never killed a woman. Why is that?'

He started to laugh. 'You don't know me.'

'I know enough—' I started to say.

'I killed my mother. I cut her throat.'

His fingers brushed my hair away from the side of my face. A new wave of panic coarsed through my body as I replayed his words in my head. 'I killed my mother . . . I killed my mother.'

'You didn't—'

'You will never know me,' he said in my ear.

'What did she do to you?' I said weakly.

'Everything,' he whispered.

I tried to fight off the fear and keep talking.

356

'You—'

'Can you feel the weight of the vest?' Gabriel said.

A chill of fear flushed through my body. I felt a presence on my shoulders that I hadn't noticed before. Like the grip of hands. The weight bore down and seemed to encircle me. I took a deep, cautious breath, afraid the air might reveal more than I was prepared to know. The vest pressed tightly against my chest. The bulk of the explosives felt like blocks of clay arranged in a neat row. Below the explosives were small pockets of sharper objects that pressed against my flesh as I breathed. Nails. Shrapnel. The rest was obvious. I would be a killing field.

He was right. I didn't know him, couldn't. I had just stepped fully into his nightmare, and his world was unrecognizable. Not the evidence of his cruelty or even the taking of my daughter had prepared me fully for where I now sat. My throat quivered with fear as I forced myself to breathe. I had to fight the urge to take refuge in the panic pumping through my body with each beat of my heart. It would be so easy to give in to it and retreat.

'Lacy,' I silently whispered. 'Lacy, Lacy, Lacy . . .'

She was my beacon. Bring me back. Help me.

I heard a quick *pop* and the bright flash of a camera dulled the darkness for a brief second under the blindfold. He took another shot, and another, and with each flash of light my breathing quickened and became less controlled. What was happening now was . . . I was becoming another piece of his collection.

I tried to find some foothold from which to fight it, to push away the panic.

SCOTT FROST

'You needed someone to bring in your explosives across the border, that's why you got involved with the florists Breem and Finley. And you needed someone who could walk through police lines at the parade with your bomb, so you took my daughter, to get to me.'

'I took your daughter because I like the sound of her voice.'

'I won't kill for you.'

'Mom,' my daughter said.

Her voice was trembling. She had probably thought I would be here to rescue her, and now look at me.

'Lacy,' I said, my voice breaking as tears welled up in my eyes. 'Are you all right?'

'That's up to you,' Gabriel said.

A high-pitched whimper of pain pierced the darkness and then opened a wound in my heart as cleanly as a scalpel.

'You son of a bitch!' I yelled, straining against my bindings. 'Leave her alone!'

She cried out again. 'No!'

'Stop it, stop it!' I screamed, my tears soaking into the cloth of the blindfold.

'No, Mom, no!' Lacy yelled. 'Fuck him!'

He was turning me into a victim, methodically, step by step, as if I were a piece of machinery he was deconstructing.

'Please,' I begged.

Across the room Lacy's cries had become nearly silent.

'I'll do whatever you want. Just leave her alone . . . just leave her . . . I'll do whatever you . . .'

358

My chin dropped to my chest and my voice failed.

'You are just like all of them. Weak. You always surrender. You're nothing.'

He was rubbing my face in it, having his moment of control. I took a breath, holding it just long enough to slow my racing heart. Then I took another and another, trying to find my way back. A faint voice called to me from what felt like another lifetime.

'Work it.'

At first I didn't hear it or wasn't capable of hearing it, then it called to me again.

'Work it.'

It was Traver's voice. Big Dave, Lacy's protector.

'He doesn't know what you know. Work it.'

'Okay,' I whispered.

A door opened and then Lacy desperately called out, 'Mom!'

She was fighting it, kicking him as he dragged her unwillingly across the floor.

'Lacy!'

'You fucking asshole!' she screamed.

Her defiance jolted me the same way her infant cries did the first night home from the hospital. I was instantly ashamed of my own weakness. She had been captive for nearly forty hours and he still hadn't been able to steal her strength.

'You fucking tell him, Lacy!' I yelled.

The door slammed shut and her voice trailed off. The sounds of her struggling against him lasted another few seconds, and then she was gone.

'Lacy!' I yelled.

The silence closed around me as if it were one of Gabriel's weapons that had to be fought before it seized the advantage.

'You're going to be all right, Lacy! You hear me. You're going to be okay!'

My heart pounded audibly against the explosives around my chest. The pockets of nails dug into my waist like claws.

The door creaked open and I felt his presence reinvade the room.

'He doesn't know what you know,' Traver whispered.

Gabriel moved slowly around behind me like a stalking cat.

'When I know my daughter's safe, I'll do what you want,' I said.

He replied with silence that was as unnerving as a scream.

Was this part of his plan? Was I walking into the thick of it, exactly where and how he wanted me to? Had I just dug our hole even deeper? How could I know? Was Harrison reading what was about to happen and saying, 'No, no, no'? How could I know? I couldn't. Screw it.

'You don't like it, kill me now,' I said.

He exhaled heavily with several quick breaths, sounding like a woman in labor.

'You wouldn't like that, would you? You kill me now, there will be no parade. And that's what you really want, isn't it? To feel that power. To have two hundred million people around the world watching your work. Feeling your terror. Thinking that every time they pass a stranger on the street at night it might be you.'

I pressed it.

'If you don't let Lacy go, then everything you've done will have been for nothing.'

The floorboards behind me creaked under his weight.

'It'll be like you've never existed. No one will care. You'll be just another killer, nothing, something to be forgotten with yesterday's news.'

He took two more quick animal breaths and then fell silent. His shadow seemed to pass over me, raising the hair on the back of my neck.

'That's the deal,' I said.

The blade of a knife pressed against my throat. The steel was warm, as if it were an extension of his hand. I felt the sharp sting like the edge of a piece of paper being drawn across my finger. I closed my eyes.

'I love you, Lacy,' silently crossed my lips.

The blade began to press harder against my skin. I opened my eyes, staring at the tiny specks of light through the blindfold as if they were all that was left of the world.

He pressed it against my throat, forcing my chin up. I closed my eyes and saw Lacy standing among the giant sequoias. Free, perfect.

I felt a slight quiver on the blade of the knife as his hand began to shake, and then it slipped silently from my throat.

'You're going to walk down Colorado Boulevard,' Gabriel said, breathless as if winded from a run. 'And disappear in a flash of creation.'

twenty-four

The dawn has a sound. In my blindfolded darkness I could hear it inching over the mountains and then sliding down into the basin. It came in the sudden silence of crickets, the shouting calls of mockingbirds and crows, the slap of a newspaper hitting pavement, and the faint, distant hum of cars, at first few, then gradually more and more until the white noise rose like an incoming tide.

'He'll be coming soon,' Traver whispered in my ear.

I reached out for him as if he were in the room.

'Tell me about where you are,' he said.

It was a line I had used on him when he was new to Homicide, a training device to recognize the things in a crime scene you hadn't realized you'd seen.

I tried to build a picture of my surroundings from the sounds I had heard.

'A room of ten by twelve, a window over the street looking south toward the freeway, no dogs barking, it's not residential, a low-rent, commercial street.'

'What about smells?'

I took a deep breath through the blindfold. There was a faint odor in the air. It wasn't a flower. The sweetness carried in it was sharp, like the first time you smell day-old death.

'I don't know.'

'Yes, you do. Work it.'

I took in the air, trying to imagine the smell as if it had color.

'It's bright, strong.'

'And . . .'

'Animal fat,' I whispered. There was something familiar in it that I wasn't recognizing.

'Break it down like a crime scene,' Traver said.

'It's New Year's,' I said.

'What happens on New Year's?'

'Parades . . . football . . . but that's not it.'

'No.'

I pushed against it as if it were one of the bindings around my legs and hands, but I failed to make a connection.

'I don't see it.'

'Yes, you do.'

'How?'

'Work it back.'

'I don't know how far.'

'It's obvious.'

'New Year's Eve.'

'Yes.'

'The morning after.'

'Yes.'

'Hangovers.'

'Yes.'

I shook my head. 'I don't see it.'

'Yes you do.'

'Hang— Menudo, someone's cooking tripe.'

I listened for a moment and heard a sound I had been missing, faint but still there.

'An exhaust fan.'

'Good,' Traver said.

'I'm near a Mexican restaurant.'

I looked into the darkness of the blindfold and began doing the math. The brief rush of discovery faded.

'Who am I kidding?' I whispered.

Every Mexican restaurant in town would be cooking menudo.

'That's not enough,' I said angrily.

'Tell me about Gabriel.'

I thought of his hand holding the cloth against my mouth and tried to build a picture.

'He's strong, about six feet, right-handed—'

'You're not telling me what's important.'

'The lives he takes are nothing to him, they're just characters, they're not even alive until he creates them.'

'Not his mother.'

The thought alone was enough to sear every nerve in my body. He had cut his own mother's throat.

'No, that was different.'

'How?'

'She was alive to him.'

'Why did he kill her?'

'I don't know.'

'Rage?'

That wasn't it. I hadn't seen anything resembling rage in Gabriel.

'He was saving her.'

'From what?'

'Herself – her imagined crimes, her real ones, God knows.'

'And after that?'

I thought for a moment.

'After that was when his life began. Reality becomes what he creates on his stage. Everything else, every life, is a lie.'

The sound of footsteps outside my door silenced Traver's voice, and I plunged back into the isolation of the blindfold. The door swung open and Gabriel stepped inside.

'It's beginning,' I whispered.

He silently moved behind me. He had showered. I could smell the scent of shampoo on him. And there was coffee on his breath, strong and laced with sugar.

'If you try to remove the vest it will explode,' he said. 'If you try to run from a crowd of people, a motion device will set it off.'

'Like Philippe,' I said.

I heard a short puff of air through his nostrils. He was smiling, laughing at the thought.

'If Harrison tries to disarm this, he'll fail and you'll both die.'

'I won't be able to get close to the parade with this vest on.'

'Your jacket will cover it. There'll be no scent for the

dogs. And you're a policeman. Who would stop you?'

I remembered about the Israeli explosives that had no scent – the perfect assassination tool.

'I like you, Lieutenant, I feel like I'm part of your family. I like that you understand what I'm doing. You understand power. When I kill you on Colorado it will be the most watched murder in history. Can you imagine all the families gathered around the television, all around the world, to see a parade of roses, and in a flash, I'll be in all their lives, in all their homes. I'll be what they fear when they close their eyes and try to sleep. I'll be walking behind them when they hear a car backfire and think it's an explosion. I'll be everywhere, because you've made me the portrait of fear. That will be your last gift to the world, Lieutenant, the thing you'll be remembered for – me.'

'You sick bastard. I'm going to kill you,' I said.

He ignored my words as if I hadn't spoken.

'When the parade begins, and the first band starts down the street, you walk out onto Colorado and join them. When I see you, the phone in the pocket of the vest will ring and your daughter will tell you that she is free.'

He untied the restraints holding my arms to the chair, leaving my wrists tied together behind my back.

'And then you'll feel the spark of ignition, a brief flicker of heat above your heart. The smell of carbon.'

'And if I say no?'

'Then I remove your blindfold, and you watch me slowly cut apart your daughter like a butchered calf while you listen to her screams.'

Just that quickly, he had control over me again.

'I want to see her—'

'You'll see the last beat of her heart as she looks into your eyes.'

'Stop—'

'If you're late, she dies. Change anything, use the phone in the vest, she dies, and I still detonate the bomb. Do you understand?'

'Go to hell—'

His hand closed around my throat.

'Say yes,' he commanded.

I felt his nails begin to press against my skin.

'Yes,' I said weakly.

'Good.'

His hand then covered my mouth, and I detected the same bitter scent I had smelled before.

'We've done this before . . . breathe.'

I instinctively resisted, refusing to take a breath. He wrapped his arm around my neck and increased the pressure.

'You're wasting time you don't have.'

I shook my head and he hit me in the stomach with his free hand, forcing the air out of my lungs, leaving me gasping for breath. I took the ether deeply into my lungs as if it were bottled oxygen.

'Do you remember everything I told you?' he whispered in my ear.

The fumes bit into the back of my throat, and then a chill began to move through my chest to the rest of my body. My fingers felt numb. I tried to speak but I couldn't make a sound. I began to slip back into the fog of the drug. Out of the darkness a kaleidoscope of colors began to rush toward me through the fabric of the blindfold.

'Make a mistake, she dies.'

I shook my head, or believed I was shaking my head.

'If you're late . . . she dies.'

Gabriel's words began to stretch and lose their shape as if they had a physical presence.

'If you fail me . . . she dies.'

The words dissolved, then briefly took shape, then were swept away into the stream of colors.

twenty-five

I was moving again or had been moving. Through the haze of the narcotic, I couldn't be sure. Time seemed to bend back on itself then spring forward in jarring leaps. The present drifted into the past. One moment I was lying down, the blur of road noise sounding like a distant jet. The next I was watching my partner Traver, holding his twins in his arms. The next I was in a room with all of Gabriel's victims staring at me, their eyes asking for help.

There was traffic noise now, enough so that the cadence of tires was lost in the collective din of hundreds of vehicles. I tried to focus on a single sound, hoping it would be a stepping-stone back to consciousness, but there were so many. A whistle was blowing in short, quick bursts. A car horn sounded. I heard voices edged with excitement but couldn't make out the words. And there was music in the distance, random and dissonant as if the notes had been swept off the sheet music and tossed into the air.

And then nothing. The sounds fell silent. The movement stilled. I tried counting my breaths to hold on to consciousness: one . . . two . . . I began to drift . . . three . . . three. I was standing over the open grave of Lacy's father. Then I felt myself falling as if in a dream where you tumble, flailing at the air. And then it stopped abruptly. I felt his hands reach under my arms and pick me up. Then the pressure of the blindfold slipped from my face. Light appeared as if a set of curtains had been opened to a gathering dawn. Patterns of grays and whites shifted in my field of vision, but I couldn't make out any detail.

'Breathe.'

A pungent rush of ammonia filled my nostrils and I reeled back. A few colors began to surface in the soft field of grays and whites. The outline of a face appeared for a moment, then drifted away.

'Breathe.'

Another wave of ammonia struck me like a slap to the face. His eyes came into focus, looking through me as if I no longer existed.

I looked down and saw the vague outline of my hand in my lap. I slowly lifted it to my face. I took a breath, then another and another.

My hand came into focus. Consciousness rushed toward me like a car out of control, weaving and turning as it careened toward a final impact. The urge to vomit welled in my stomach. My eyes drifted in and out of focus. My hand found the Glock in its holster, and I instinctively grabbed it, thrusting it to where Gabriel's outline had hovered before me – the car was empty. I lifted myself up in the seat and looked up and down the street. It was nearly empty, a few stragglers rushing toward the steady stream of people heading to the parade on the adjacent blocks. Gabriel had vanished.

I set my gun on my lap and took several deep breaths. My head pounded from the effects of the narcotics. My watch read a quarter to eight. The parade would begin in forty-five minutes. There were things, instructions I was supposed to remember, but the details eluded me.

And then I noticed the extra bulk under my jacket and the weight on my chest and shoulders. Carefully, I took hold of the zipper and slowly slid it down, revealing the vest. The brick-shaped explosives were in pockets arranged in a neat row around my chest. Wires appeared to encircle the vest and then gathered at a small terminal just above my heart. Below the explosives, shrapnel bulged against the nylon of the vest, the tips of nails poking through the fabric. The image I had formed while blindfolded was remarkably similar to what I was now looking at, except for one item: In the center of it all was a small glass cylinder with what looked like mercury inside – the motion device. Expose the wire just under the surface of the mercury to the charged atmosphere inside the cylinder and the circuit is completed. It didn't take an expert to figure out what would happen then. I exhaled heavily and watched the mercury in the tube quiver from the slight movement of my breath.

The pounding in my head immediately ceased, and I remembered every word Gabriel had spoken, every detail of how I was to die.

'Run, you die,' I whispered. I looked around the car. 'Stay, you die.'

I slid across the seat, then opened the door and carefully stepped outside. As I stood up, my knees buckled and the pavement rushed toward me. I lunged for the car door, my left hand slipping down the glass, my right grabbing the top of the door as if it were a ledge on the fiftieth floor of a high-rise. I glanced at the motion sensor. The mercury rolled back and forth, the thread of wire just becoming visible with each pass of the liquid.

'Fall, you die,' passed my lips. I closed my eyes and a shudder ran the course of my body. 'Lacy dies,' I whispered.

I tightly gripped the door until my legs steadied and my head cleared enough to stand unassisted. I looked up and down the street trying to locate where I was. There wasn't a cloud in the sky, not a breath of wind. The people heading south to my right had to be walking down Orange Grove. The mix of commercial and apartment buildings I was looking at put me on Walnut, north of Colorado and just outside the perimeter Chavez and the FBI would have established. Harrison would be looking for me, but where? How detailed had Gabriel's journal been? I had to find a cop, but to do that I would have to walk at least a block in the middle of the stream of people moving on Orange Grove. And if Gabriel got impatient or made a mistake, or if I tripped, a stupid, simple misstep off the curb or a bump from an overexcited eight-year-old, how many would die?

I eased away from the car, taking several small steps to test my equilibrium. My legs held. I reached down and carefully slid the zipper of my jacket back up, covering the bomb, then started walking toward the stream of people a block away.

Forty minutes left.

In the distance I could hear the sounds of bands warming up. A drum roll, a scale from a trumpet, the bright, mournful sound of a French horn.

Three blocks south, two police helicopters were moving slowly up and down the parade route. Looking for what? The enemy? I was the enemy.

'That won't help,' I said angrily.

With each step I took, every sound, every movement, every color became more vivid. The collective din of a hundred thousand spectators' voices began to fill the air like the hum of a generator as they took their places along the parade route. From somewhere I smelled the sweet scent of cotton candy, then it was coffee, then the perfume of thousands of flowers covering the dozens of floats a few blocks south. Was this what your last steps are like, or what they would be like if you knew the end was around the next corner – an animal-like awareness?

A hundred feet from Orange Grove, I stopped. The people walking to Colorado were no longer just a river of shapes and brightly colored clothes. They were individuals now, thousands of them. Single, distinct human beings, all different, all unique, every one of them with their own story, their own history. I could make out faces – old, young, parents pushing strollers, lovers holding hands, families walking in tight little groups, smiling, laughing, innocence. It was all there. A collective time-out from everyday worries and pain and the global insanity that had attacked our illusion of peace.

I took a tentative step, then another and another until I was on the edge of the crowd. I tried not to make eye contact, but it was impossible. I was drawn to the eyes, they demanded to be looked at, to be understood, to be given value.

I stepped into the crowd and joined them walking south. A young woman holding a small child in her arms looked at me. She began to smile, but it slipped away. I could see a change in her eyes. The flash of a question, of distrust. Her arms tightened around her child and she looked away. A horrible sense of betrayal spread through me like a virus. I didn't belong here. I was a traitor. Why had I even come this far? Why hadn't I stopped when I was alone and could hurt no one but myself and . . .

The memory of Gabriel's words intruded.

'Choose.'

A small Mexican girl with jet-black hair and dark brown eyes looked at me as if she were asking the same question. She disappeared into the crowd and another face replaced hers, then another face and another, all oblivious to the danger walking among them.

I now knew the answer. I would easily give my own life for my daughter's, but I wouldn't do this. They weren't strangers walking toward the parade. It was the one thing Gabriel didn't understand. We were all part of the same cloth, the same fabric that wove its fibers through our lives. We ignore it most of the time, pretend it doesn't exist. We hurt each other, steal, cheat, lie, and then a single moment reminds us, connects us. It never lasts. But it does exist. Lacy understood it, had voiced it more eloquently than I had realized.

'Fuck him,' I said silently.

A kid ran past, brushing my arm, but I maintained my balance. His mother yelled at him to come back, then glanced at me.

'I'm sorry,' she said in apology.

I tried to reply but couldn't. My voice hung in my throat. I began walking faster and faster. I couldn't be here, I had to get away from them, away from their dreams and laughter, from their still-normal lives. Ahead, the stream of people slowed and began to form a line.

A security checkpoint. Cops. I saw the roof lights of several squads blocking the road. I removed my badge from my pocket and began working my way around the outside of the crowd. The line of people was being pinched through a narrow set of stanchions just wide enough for two people to walk abreast. Every face was being scrutinized, every bag searched. No one was complaining, not anymore. It's how things are done now.

Two CHP officers and a uniformed officer from the PPD were on the flank where I was approaching. As I walked up, I recognized Officer James and saw the look of surprise register in her eyes. And then just a momentary hesitation as she settled back on her heels, her gaze planted firmly on the windbreaker covering the bomb strapped to my chest.

'Get me away from these people,' I said desperately.

'Everyone is looking for you—'

'Now! Do you understand? Right now.'

She hesitated for a second, then motioned to the two CHP officers, who cleared a path through the barricades and she began walking me away.

'I need to get to Harrison.'

She nodded nervously. 'We thought—'

'I don't have much time,' I said, pressing the point.

I glanced back at the crowd. A woman with a child in her arms was watching me suspiciously, sensing the danger. I could see it in her eyes. That stare. That understanding of how fragile it all really is.

James led me to a waiting squad and we quickly got in.

'They thought you were dead, Lieutenant.'

She hit the lights and siren and started south on Orange Grove.

'We need a place where no one else can get hurt,' I said, unzipping the windbreaker.

James stared at the bomb for a moment, unable to mask her shock.

'They've set it up down in the arroyo.'

Her eyes glanced nervously at me, then turned and focused on the road ahead.

I picked up the handset of the squad's radio.

'This is Lieutenant Delillo. I need to talk to Harrison.'

James stepped on the gas and swung around two other squads blocking the road, then cut west toward the arroyo.

'If you hit anything, Officer, we're both going to die.'

I noticed a faint flush of color in her cheeks, then she pulled back on the speed and tightly gripped the steering wheel with both hands. The squeal of feedback pierced the radio's speaker. Then Harrison's voice came through.

'Lieutenant, are you all right?' he said.

'Did the journal say where Lacy is?'

There was a pause on the other end.

'Harrison?'

'No . . . it didn't.'

The words took my breath away. I sank into the seat and let the mike lie on my lap. That was it. The only chance of finding Lacy was if Gabriel had told us. It couldn't be, it couldn't. Not like this. I had just been in a room with her, heard her voice. She had been just feet from me.

Maybe I had not made myself clear. Maybe he misunderstood.

'You're sure? You read everything?'

He hesitated. I pictured him looking at Chavez, searching for an answer.

'Are you sure?' I demanded.

'I'm sorry,' Harrison said.

I lost the sound of the siren. The faces of the people passing by became a blur. The color of the sky began to fade until the blue had vanished and all that was left were colorless shades of gray.

'Tell me about the bomb,' Harrison said. But I didn't hear him.

James turned onto Arroyo Boulevard and started

south along the edge of the canyon. The houses lining the street were perfect examples of nearly every architectural style that has tried to capture the California dream: Tudor, ramblers, Craftsman, Spanish. They looked like artifacts of a faded empire. It was no longer my landscape; I was a stranger now.

I picked up the radio and cued the mike.

'Did it say anything about Lacy?'

Only static came back for a moment.

'We need to focus on the bomb,' Harrison said.

'Damnit, tell me what it said.'

Chavez's voice came over the radio. 'Alex, we think she's gone.'

I closed my eyes and shook my head as he spoke.

'I don't believe that.'

'Alex—'

'No.'

I turned the radio off and caught a glimpse of the fifty-three floats lined up for the beginning of the five-and-a-half-mile parade. Block after block of what looked like animated Hallmark cards the size of semi trucks with every inch covered in flowers as if they had sprouted naturally as a result of the winter rains. It was the perfect symbol that all that was needed to make anything happen in California were dreams and water. And nothing had ever stopped the parade, not for 115 years.

We reached the turn to the arroyo and drove past the squad securing the entrance. Down below, a hundred feet from where the Mexican major had been found floating in the pool, a bomb disposal container sat in the center of the parking lot surrounded by a fifty-foot safe zone in case I . . . in case I went off.

James drove the squad past the waiting officers and into the center of the safety zone, then opened the door.

'You're supposed to wait here.'

I nodded.

'Good luck, Lieutenant. I hope they're wrong about your daughter.'

She walked away quickly as Harrison, carrying a bag, approached, wearing a large Kevlar vest and a helmet with a bulletproof visor. In the distance I could see Chavez and Hicks watching helplessly. I opened my door, placed my feet on the ground, and remained seated until Harrison crossed the fifty feet and knelt down in front of me. His eyes met mine.

'Are you okay?'

I nodded, such as it was.

His eyes moved to the bomb. There was none of the college whiz kid visible in his eyes when he saw what he was facing.

'This is more complicated than the other one,' he said matter-of-factly.

He reached up and slipped his helmet off and set it on the hood of the car.

'I wish you would put that back on.'

'If this goes off, that helmet won't help.'

He reached around his back and unfastened the Kevlar vest and slid that off, too.

'How much time do you think we have?' Harrison asked.

I looked at my watch.

y minutes.'

He shook his head. 'That's not enough.'

'He's expecting me to walk out onto Colorado when the first band rounds the corner at Orange Grove.'

He studied the vest for a moment, then shook his head at some private calculation.

'I need you to take off the windbreaker so I can see the back of it.'

I stood up, and he moved behind me and gently slid the jacket down my arms.

'How does it look from back there?'

'A lot like the front.'

He stepped back around and continued studying the wiring.

'Did he tape anything to you, or can you feel wires touching your skin?'

'I don't think so.'

'Good.'

'How good?'

'He could be running a low-voltage circuit through your body. Break the circuit . . . bang.'

He covered every inch of the device looking for a weakness, a flaw in the conception.

'I need you to tell me something,' I said.

His eyes paused momentarily in their search.

'Okay.'

'Did he say that he killed Lacy in the journal?'

He reluctantly nodded.

'Did he specify *when* in relation to the other events?'

He thought for a moment, working his way through the text. 'No.'

'Then she's still alive.'

Harrison looked up from the bomb.

'Okay,' he said, gently questioning.

'He won't kill Lacy until the phone call.'

'I don't follow.'

'When the parade begins and I walk out onto Colorado.'

Harrison nodded. 'That was in the journal.'

'The phone in the vest rings, and I'm supposed to hear that she's all right. That's when he would tell me she's about to die. I would hear her cry for . . . He wouldn't miss that opportunity to manipulate and control. He lives for it, needs it as much as we need air to breathe.'

Harrison thought about it for a second and then nodded in agreement.

'Godlike.'

'Not any god I know.'

We looked at each other in silence for a moment, then his eyes returned to the vest.

'I'm figuring there're at least four triggers. The motion sensor's one. All the wires wrapped around the vest are the second; one of those is attached to a detonator. We try to cut the vest, or slide it over your head . . .'

'And the other two?'

'The other two I'm not sure about. I need to check under your shirt to make sure there're no leads attached. Are you wearing a bra?'

'Is there some misinformation about my figure that's given you the impression I need one?'

Harrison's eyes softened for a moment and he nearly

smiled. He reached out and unbuttoned my pants, then carefully pulled my shirttails out as he stepped around behind me.

'Try not to move. This will be tight, but I think there's just enough room.'

He slid his hand under the shirt and gently felt his way up my back to my neck.

'Nothing back here.'

'If you say that about my chest, you're in big trouble.'

He stepped around in front and slipped his hand under my shirt and began walking his fingers up my stomach. Just below my breast, he stopped, and I felt the wire that I hadn't noticed before. My heart jumped and my breath came up short.

'Oh, God . . . Can you—'

'Just breathe normally.'

He looked into my eyes reassuringly. 'I have to find the other lead.'

I nodded and closed my eyes as his hand worked its way to just below my other breast, where it stopped on the other wire. He then slipped his hand out from under my shirt.

'Is this one a problem?'

He reached into an equipment bag and pulled out some clips and a wire. 'Only if I make a mistake.'

He slipped his hand back under my shirt and began to carefully attach the clips and the wire to the leads.

'I saw his eyes, Harrison.'

He continued to work to attach the clips to the leads.

'The drawing of Gabriel is a fabrication. He doesn't exist. It's how he's hidden.'

He finished attaching one of the clips then slipped his hand across my chest to the other.

'He befriends one of his victims to give us a description then kills them later.'

'Philippe,' Harrison said, without looking up.

I nodded.

'He must have done the same thing in France.'

The words hung uncomfortably in the air for a moment, though I wasn't sure why. I heard the faint click of the second clip being attached to the lead, then Harrison withdrew his hand, picked up a small wire cutter and eased it up under my shirt. The absurdity that it took a bomb to feel the thin, soft hair of a man's arm on my chest made me want to cry, or laugh, I wasn't sure which.

Harrison positioned the blades of the clippers against the wire. I could feel its cold steel just above the warmth of his hand.

'If I've made a mistake, neither of us will know it.'

He looked up at me and I nodded.

'Cut it,' I whispered.

The muscles of his hand contracted and the blades sliced through the wire without a sound. He closed his eyes for a moment, a prayer, maybe, then took a deep, thankful breath.

'You okay?' he asked.

I nodded.

He slid his hand out from under my shirt then settled his eyes grimly on the motion detector.

'Be very still,' he said softly as he moved in close to examine the sensor.

The words that I had left hanging surfaced again and demanded attention.

'What did I say about France?'

He glanced up from the bomb without having heard a word. 'I'm a little busy.'

I ran quickly back through it.

'He befriends a victim then kills them after they've given the description.'

Harrison reluctantly took his attention away from the device. 'Why is that important?'

I thought about it for a moment, but I had only gone through the report once, and that seemed like a lifetime ago.

'What's important is that . . .' The details slipped past my fingertips just out of reach.

'Shit.'

And then it settled right in front of me as if it were an answer in a trivia game.

'What's important is that it didn't happen.'

He looked at me, a question forming in his eyes. 'What didn't happen?'

'The victim who gave the description in France survived. He wasn't killed.'

'He was lucky.'

Even before he had finished saying the words, Harrison looked at me and shook his head. The words just didn't fit, didn't apply to Gabriel, not 'luck.'

'You don't believe that either?'

'No. He survived for a reason.'

'But what reason?'

'The simplest is always the best.'

'If you can see it.'

Harrison thought about it for a moment, but it eluded him.

I took a leap. 'Why did Gabriel cut off Philippe's head?'

The line around Harrison's eyes tightened as he pictured the scene in the dumpster.

'To scare the hell out of us.'

'He's already done that. Why else?'

'To make ID impossible.'

'But why? What doesn't he want us to know?'

Harrison shook his head.

'There's a picture in my shirt pocket. Can you reach under the vest and get it?'

Harrison gently eased his hand in between the vest and my shirt until he reached the pocket and slid the photograph out. He then inched his hand back out from under the vest, holding the photograph from Philippe's apartment.

I took it and looked at the eyes, but the detail wasn't there. It was too wide a shot.

'That doesn't help.'

I stared at the picture for another moment. He was standing in front of a large white building. There was writing above the entrance in French. There were cars, pedestrians, and—

'What are you looking for?'

'This.'

I held the photograph out and pointed to a blurry object moving in the background. Harrison studied it for a moment.

'An ambulance.'

'Look at the writing above the entrance. What is that?'

'I think it's a hospital.'

'Why would you take a snapshot in front of a hospital?'

'You don't—' He saw it. 'Oh, Jesus.'

'It's where he killed his first victim,' I said.

'The murders in the hospital.'

I nodded. 'This was the first picture for his collection.'

Harrison looked at me dumbfounded. 'Philippe is Gabriel.'

I thought about it a moment to be sure.

'When I was blindfolded, Gabriel knew your name, but I had never mentioned it. He knew you because you took the bomb off his lap in Philippe's apartment.'

The pieces tumbled together like building blocks.

'And he wasn't taken from the safe house. He just cut his own hand and climbed out the window.'

It all made sense in a way it hadn't before, and the understanding only made my feelings of personal failure more profound. To have had a killer in custody and to have released him is every cop's nightmare.

'The body in the dumpster is a security guard for Armed Response.'

'He had to know that we would eventually find that out.'

'But by then he'd be gone, so it wouldn't matter.'

We looked at each other in disbelief, and then tears filled my eyes.

'Goddamn, we had him.'

I buried my face in my hands and began to tremble with a flood of emotions.

'He fooled us all, not just you,' Harrison said.

I looked at him and shook my head.

'It's my case . . . mine.'

Harrison started to speak but held it. There was nothing to say, nothing more to understand.

'How much time is left?' I asked.

He glanced at his watch.

'Twenty minutes.'

I tried to refocus on the details, to think about anything other than how we had been Gabriel's partner in his deception.

'We don't have time to disarm all of these, do we?'

Harrison looked into my eyes and shook his head.

'No.'

Thinking you understand something and then hearing it said are two different things. I looked down at the vest, but all I could see was a clock running out of time.

'So, we . . .'

I began to lose my way. It was all too much. The weight of the vest was beginning to suffocate me. I wanted my daughter back. I wanted to hear her voice and hold her and never let go. I wanted not to know that I had released the man who was going to kill her.

'So we what?'

I looked at Harrison, hoping he could find a way out of the abyss I was slipping into.

'Some of these are just meant to delay, so we only worry about the trigger he's going to use. The only way he can do this is remotely,' Harrison said.

He reached up, opened a pocket of the vest just above the explosives and gently slid the phone out. His eyes recognized something that mine didn't.

'This isn't right,' Harrison said in a near-whisper.

I looked into his eyes, trying to read the level of fear, but if it was there, he had long ago found the ability to mask it, probably the same way he had found to hide from love since his wife's murder.

'What isn't right?'

He took out a small knife, pried open the back of the phone, and stared at the circuit boards.

'There's nothing here. It's just a phone.'

'Meaning?'

He stared at the vest for a moment, then reached out and sliced open one of the pockets containing the nails, which poured out onto the gravel like entrails.

'There is no goddamned remote trigger,' he said, flushed with anger.

He sliced open the rest of the pockets containing the shrapnel.

'I've wasted time.'

'What are you saying, Harrison?'

He looked into my eyes. 'Don't you see it?'

I shook my head.

'I shouldn't have been able to remove the shrapnel like that, not if his intention was to kill a lot of people.'

He stared at the pockets containing the explosives, looking for something, following the wires from place to place with his eyes. He carefully opened one of the pockets containing explosives. His fingers traced a wire, his eyes dissecting the meaning behind it.

'Son of a bitch.'

He pulled the brick of explosive out and yanked the detonator out of it, then squeezed the soft material in his fist.

'It's clay.'

He tossed it aside. He quickly opened three more pockets.

'It's just goddamn clay.'

He yanked them out and tossed them aside. I looked down at the one pocket he didn't touch.

'Except that one.'

Harrison nodded. 'Yeah.'

'That's for me.'

'And you're the trigger.'

'The motion detector.'

'In the journal, when he talks about you and Lacy dying, I just assumed that because you die on Colorado that others die with you.'

He stared at me for a moment.

'He could kill dozens, but it's just you he wants?' he said.

I thought for a moment. 'He doesn't need to kill anyone else other than me.'

'Why?'

'Television. It's how we experience everything now, isn't it. Two hundred million people will have invited him into their living rooms to watch a parade. Two hundred million people will fear him when they watch me die.'

I saw the whole horrible picture.

'Choose,' I whispered.

Harrison looked at me apprehensively.

'He couldn't take the chance that I wouldn't kill others, so he made the choice simpler, one I would make without hesitation. I could listen to my daughter's screams, or . . . stop them.'

I looked out toward the rim of the arroyo, which was lined with people walking to the parade. All of Gabriel's twisted needs suddenly came into focus.

'Serial killers need the act of violence to be intimate. Gabriel's going to kill with words, just words, whispering into my ear like a lover would. There's nothing more intimate than that. And millions of people are going to see it . . . and fear him. What could be more powerful? He gets everything he wants.'

We stared at each other trying to sort out the new landscape.

'Do you know where he took you?'

I shook my head.

'I don't think that's where he has her, though. He would take her to a place that means something to me, that would demonstrate how much more powerful he is than we are . . . One more reason for me to do what he wants.'

'But where?'

I looked around at the walls of the arroyo and the houses dotting the hillsides.

'Home,' I whispered, turning to Harrison. 'He said he felt like he was part of my family.'

Details were flying past me.

'Was Lacy's garage door opener in her car when we found it?'

He thought for a moment then shook his head.

'I don't remember it in the inventory. But there's an officer there.'

'Give me your phone.'

Harrison gave me his phone and I tried my number. The machine picked up after four rings. *'You've reached Alex and Lacy. Please leave a message.'*

The machine beeped, and there was only silence until the tape ran out and I hung up.

'He could be out in his squad,' Harrison said.

There was something else, though, lost in the tattered fabric of the last few days.

'The phone machine,' I said to myself.

'What about it?'

'Before Lacy was taken, I had called home and left a message. She said she never got it, and when I checked it, it wasn't there. I think he's already been inside my house. He erased it.'

I looked down at the vest. 'How long will it take to disarm the rest of this?'

Harrison shook his head. 'Too long.'

'So I just have to be careful.'

He looked at me, the possibilities being played out just under the surface of his eyes. 'Very careful.'

I looked up and saw Chavez step up behind Harrison. He tried to find something to say but couldn't manage it. He glanced at the vest, then looked at me, his eyes filled with concern.

'We're running out of time. You want me to delay the parade?'

'You do that, Lacy's dead.'

Surprise, then relief registered on his face.

'She's alive?'

I nodded. He looked at me for a moment, clinging to a certain amount of doubt, not because he didn't want to believe but because doubt's a constant companion after twenty years on the job.

I held the photograph out to him.

'Philippe's not dead. He's Gabriel.'

He stood for a moment like a tourist looking into the Grand Canyon for the first time.

'Gabriel's greatest role wasn't the terrorist, it was the victim,' I said. 'We've been chasing a piece of fiction.'

'You saw him?'

'No.'

'This is a hunch then?'

'I agree with her,' Harrison said.

I handed my windbreaker to Chavez.

'I need a female officer to walk out onto Colorado in my windbreaker.'

'No problem.'

'She'll need a phone for instructions and pants the same color as mine.'

He took it and nodded.

'Where's SWAT?'

'They're positioned along Colorado along with everybody else.'

'How many officers are available?'

He studied me for a moment, then it dawned on him what I was talking about.

'You don't think he's at the parade?'

I shook my head. 'I think he took her home.'

'You're sure?'

'No, I'm not. And if I'm wrong, I lose my daughter.'

'Alex? We're here, ready. This is our best shot.'

'So there are no officers available, that's what you're saying? Not for a hunch.'

Chavez glanced over his shoulder at Hicks, then took a breath.

'He's going to kill her, Ed. I have to follow this.'

Lacy's big Latino godfather took a breath as if it were a shot of tequila. *If I was wrong and something happened at the parade and he had pulled officers . . . Shit . . . that would be it for him. He would attend the funerals of all the victims. And then watch the finger-pointing as thirty years of work was destroyed. I couldn't ask that. Not for me. Not even for Lacy.*

'Harrison and I will check it,' I said.

He shook his head.

'I'm available,' Chavez said.

twenty-six

Harrison turned the corner on Mariposa and pulled the squad to the curb. Three-quarters of the way up on the left, my house sat atop the sloping grade of ivy and ice plants. On the street in front, the unmarked squad of the officer who hadn't answered the phone was empty.

'He's not sitting in his squad,' Harrison said.

He glanced at me. 'And the paper's still on the driveway.'

Chavez scanned the front of the house with binoculars. 'Curtains are closed on all the windows.'

'I left them open,' I said.

I stared at the house trying to recognize it as the place where I had conceived a child and then brought her home from the hospital, but it was no longer recognizable as mine. My house couldn't be this one. Not the fake shutters, not the yellow paint, not the pathetic bed of roses I had once planted in a misguided quest to be a normal suburban parent. Everything looked exactly as it had every morning for the last eighteen years. But the sameness only made it more frightening. Inside, the fever dream that hides in every child's nightmare had been let loose from under the bed.

'In two minutes we should hear four F-15s fly over the length of the parade route,' Chavez said. 'Two minutes after that the first band starts around the corner and begins the parade and a hundred thousand people will start to cheer.'

I could feel the momentum begin to gather speed. I wanted to slow it down, to catch my breath, but there was no stopping it.

'Four minutes,' I said, as if I needed to hear the words in order to believe them.

'How do you want to make entry?' the chief asked.

'There's a door on the north side of the garage,' I said. 'He won't be able to hear from inside the house. He has her in either my bedroom or hers. Probably hers.'

I glanced down at the motion sensor strapped to my chest.

'How many feet do I need to be clear of everyone else if this . . .' I let it go.

Harrison and Chavez glanced uneasily at each other, then Harrison's eyes moved over the bomb, quickly calculating its destructive force.

'Out in the open, anyone within ten feet would be severely injured. Inside a house, that changes. It becomes more dangerous with objects flying.'

I pictured Dave disappearing in the debris at Sweeny's.

'Glass and doors,' I said.

Harrison had the look you see on people's faces at funerals where finality is for the first time measurable.

'Every object in a house becomes a weapon: a spoon, pen, coffee cup . . . everything.'

I glanced at my watch, which now took on the appearance of a weapon. I quickly began to fumble with the buckle, desperately trying to get it off. Chavez's big, thick hand clamped down gently on my wrist. His eyes met mine with the same assuredness they had held when he told me I was to be the head of Homicide.

'Please, don't do that,' he said softly.

In the distance, the faint roar of the F-15s began to rumble like a gathering storm, threatening to sweep up everything in its path. I let my fingers slip from the watch and started to reach out for Chavez's hand, but I couldn't touch him.

'Ten feet,' I said silently to myself, pulling my hand away. I was no longer a part of his world, even one as already jaded as a cop's. And nothing anyone could do or say would ever wholly reinstate me in it.

'He'll be calling,' I said.

Chavez watched my hand withdraw and sadly nodded as if sensing the gulf that now existed between us.

'Officer James volunteered to walk out onto Colorado. She'll do whatever I relay to her.'

'As soon as I start talking to him, we go through the door.'

Harrison began driving up the block toward the end

of the cul-de-sac. As we passed the third house on the right, the real estate agent my husband had had the affair with walked out in a blue bathrobe and yellow slippers to retrieve her paper. Her face was pale and her eyes strained against the morning light as if she were hungover. She glanced in our direction but quickly looked away when she saw me, as had been her practice since the day I discovered the affair. I like to think it was guilt that fueled her behavior, or even better, shame. But in truth I think she just wanted to pretend it never happened. And if she never looked at me, then it didn't for her.

Nothing of the outside of my house gave any hint of the events that might be taking place within. You could exchange it with any of the other houses on the block. They were all just different enough so that none appeared out of place. A three-bedroom, country rambler, next to the four-bedroom, next to the split-level. They were part of a time that seemed so distant now, part of a sense of community that no longer existed for me.

Harrison swung around the cul-de-sac and stopped in front of the second house north of mine. We stepped out, withdrawing our weapons, lowering them casually to our sides, and began to make our way across the ivy and lawns toward the side of the garage.

From the valley below, the sound of the jets making their pass over the parade route built and rose like thunder, until the glass of the windows in my neighbors' houses shook. I stepped across the split-rail fence that marked my property line, one eye on the fence, the other on the quivering liquid inside the motion detector. Four steps across a spit of grass and we were against the wall of the garage.

I was breathing as if I had sprinted a mile. My heart pounded against the brick of explosive strapped to my chest. I took two deep breaths then looked up toward the mountains that were dusted with snow five thousand feet up.

'It was a perfect morning,' I whispered.

Harrison turned to me not understanding.

'It's what they always seem to say about the morning of a disaster.'

Harrison glanced at me for a moment, then looked at some distant point on the horizon.

'Not always. Sometimes it rains,' he said softly.

The thunder of the jets reached its peak then faded into the distance, leaving behind an uneasy silence. There was no birdsong, no cars, no music, not even the collective white noise of nine million lives in the city spread out below. I took out my key and slipped it silently into the lock.

'I go through the door first,' I said.

Chavez shook his head. 'No way.'

'If we surprise him and he sees me, he'll hesitate because of the bomb.'

Chavez looked doubtfully at me.

'His nightmare is losing control, one of his victims turning the tables on him.'

'You.'

I nodded.

'There'll be a moment of advantage, but no more.

You take care of Lacy.' I glanced at Harrison. 'Both of you . . . whatever happens.'

They reluctantly agreed. I reached up and removed the phone from the pocket of the vest as Chavez rang James, who answered on the first ring. They exchanged several words, then he turned to me.

'Less than a minute to the start.'

My stomach began to tighten into a knot. I tried to take a deep breath but my lungs seemed to actively repel the fresh air. I looked down at the motion detector and the wires wrapped around the vest. Each breath, each step I took felt borrowed. I started to look one more time at the mountains rising above, then noticed a deer standing motionless on a lawn across the street. A dried slash of crimson across its back led to its left rear leg, which appeared broken where it had been hit by a car. Its eyes had a familiar quality to them, one that I would recognize if I looked in a mirror. I closed my eyes and managed to force a breath into my lungs, and when I looked up again, the deer was gone.

'Our window is going to be very short,' I said, pressing the point. 'As soon as James begins to run and there's no explosion, he'll kill her.'

As if on cue, the phone in my hand began to ring.

'To hell with him,' I whispered.

I waited until the sixth ring, then answered.

'Are you ready, Lieutenant?' Gabriel said.

I took hold of the key in the door and slowly disengaged the lock.

'I'm there.'

'Can you hear the music?'

'The music?'

Chavez asked James if she heard the music, then looked at me and nodded.

'It's just beginning,' I said.

I eased the door open and looked into the garage. All the familiar odors were there – the sweetness of the gardening tools, the sharpness of the trash. But there was something else, something new, something that carried death with it.

'There's been gunfire,' I whispered.

It took a moment for my eyes to adjust to the darkness, and then I saw the Armed Response patrol car parked in Lacy's space. I swept the garage with my weapon – nothing.

'I want to speak to Lacy.'

'You will.'

On the opposite side of the garage, the door to the house was ajar several inches, sending a slice of light like a blade into the darkness. I moved around the patrol car to the door as Harrison and Chavez took positions on the other side. From inside the house I could hear the sound of television from a distant room.

'What song are they playing, Lieutenant?' he asked testing me.

I knew from memory that it was the same every year.

' "The Marine Corps Hymn." '

'Hold the phone out. Let me hear it.'

I covered the mouthpiece.

'Tell James to hold the phone out toward the music.'

Chavez gave her the instructions, then held his phone out toward me. I could hear the tiny strains of the band music. I pressed my phone against the other earpiece just long enough for him to hear it, but not so long that he would understand that something was wrong.

'Satisfied?'

There was silence on the other end.

'What else do you want?' I asked.

Still nothing. I looked at Chavez and shook my head. 'I don't know if he's buying it.'

I put my hand on the door to the kitchen to push it open, then noticed a thin line of blood, no wider than a pencil, streaming out from inside, gathering in a small pool against the threshold and dripping down onto the first step. My heart was in my throat. It can't be, it can't. I quickly pushed it open, but it jammed halfway into the room. I raised my weapon, waiting for a response from the other side, but there was none.

'What do you want me to do?' I said into the phone.

Nothing came back but the faint sound of the band music from the television.

I eased around the door and into my kitchen and saw the sole of a boot blocking the door. The young uniformed officer who had not answered the phone was lying on his back, one leg bent awkwardly beneath him, his lidded eyes staring up at the ceiling. A hole smaller than a dime penetrated his skull just above the right eyebrow. There was no need to check for a pulse. I doubt he ever saw the face of his killer. Bored, and upset about guarding an empty house, he would have heard the garage door open and casually walked out to investigate. A burst of light from the muzzle flash might have registered, and then nothing. Not the sound of the shot

404

that killed him, no understanding of what just happened. I recognized him as the young officer named Baker, who had taken the call at Breem's flower shop. A kid who liked to talk like a TV cop.

Chavez stepped in behind me and stared in disbelief at the fallen. He had lost only one other cop in his tenure as chief, and now, seeing a second one, the heartbreak registered in his eyes instantly. His shoulders slumped and he closed his eyes and crossed himself.

I looked away and noticed that one of the burners on the stovetop was on, its blue flame glowing in the half-light, warming nothing, the hiss of the gas sounding like the warning of a snake coiled to strike.

I stared at it for a moment, then looked out through the passageway toward the dining and living rooms. I stepped past the body and moved to the edge of the tiled kitchen floor. The only light in the living room came from a faint glow through the curtains. Instead of the warmth of the morning light I had always felt in this room, violence had transformed it into something gro-tesque. The light seemed designed to draw me farther in, the furniture in the room, props to disguise the house's real purpose. Harrison stepped up beside me. His eyes were wide with adrenaline. His temple damp with sweat.

'I don't like this,' he said.

I looked into the living room, past the high-back reading chairs and the mission couch toward the dark hallway at the other end, where I could hear the faint sound of the TV. I knew everything there was to know about the room, but it was as if I had never been in it before.

'What you don't like is that this feels like a trap,' I whispered.

I'd seen it in other houses, other living rooms and kitchens and bedrooms. I'd seen it in the eyes of battered women whose homes had become a nightmare to escape from.

'Walk out onto Colorado,' Gabriel said.

I looked over at Chavez, who was kneeling next to Baker. He looked up, then got to his feet. I nodded.

'Start her.'

He gave James her instructions. I took a breath and tightened my fingers around my Glock.

'I'm walking.'

I stepped onto the carpet of the dining room and glanced back into the kitchen. Chavez was staring at the blue flame of the burner.

'There's something I want you to hear,' Gabriel said.

'What?'

'I want you to hear your daughter die.'

'No.'

'Run.'

I turned to Chavez, who was reaching out to turn off the burner.

'Tell James,' I said urgently.

He turned off the burner and the blue flame disappeared with a clicking sound.

'Faster,' Gabriel said. 'Faster.'

As I started into the living room, Chavez began to follow, then turned and looked back toward the stove as if he had heard something. Harrison started to raise his hand and then shake his head. From down the hallway I heard a cry of pain.

'No, Mom,' Lacy screamed.

Harrison started to move back toward Chavez, gesturing with his hand, shaking his head. 'No, no no.'

'Oh, God,' Chavez said in surprise.

He turned and looked at me. Then the kitchen disappeared in the flash of an explosion that swallowed him up in its brilliant white light. Harrison was in the air, tumbling backward over the dining-room chairs. Instinctively, I started to turn as blue fingers of burning natural gas reached out across the room and touched my face like a warm Santa Ana wind, burning into my eyes as if I had stared unprotected at the sun. The only sound I heard was dishes falling out of the cupboards and breaking on the floor like a hard rain.

I dropped the phone and reached for the motion detector on my chest to protect it from the flying debris, but by then it was over. I could hear Harrison on the floor, tangled up in upturned chairs, moving as if caught in a spiderweb. A fine dust was drifting out from the kitchen and covering everything like a snowfall. I was on my knees, though I didn't remember falling. I looked down at the motion detector on my vest, but all I could see in the center of my vision was a dull, round disk of faint light, as if a heavy gauze had been put over my eyes. There was no detail. I couldn't see the motion detector. I couldn't see my hand in front of my face. On the edges of my vision, I could make out dull shapes and colors, but the center . . . there was no center, just dull gray light.

I touched the glass of the motion detector and my

fingers caught on the uneven edge of a crack. I waited for another flash of ignition and a rush into oblivion, but it didn't come. A trickle of moisture slid down my cheek, and I reached up to find blood draining from my ear that was facing the blast.

I looked toward where I had seen Harrison tangled in the chairs.

'I can't see,' I said, though I couldn't even hear my own words.

If Harrison responded, I didn't hear it.

I pulled myself to my feet, then turned and looked down the hallway leading to the bedrooms. It had the appearance of a cave descending into the earth. All I could see was a circle of darkness with a halo of faint light around it.

Something moved in the darkness.

'I'll fire,' I yelled, raising my Glock.

The darkness seemed to pulsate, but nothing moved out from it.

I tried to picture the hallway from memory. A dozen steps. I took a step. My legs started to buckle, then stiffened and held. The gun felt impossibly heavy, and my hand began to tremble as I tried to point it into the blackness ahead.

One step, then another. My foot slipped on a piece of debris on the floor and the weight of the vest on my shoulders began to pull me over until I regained my balance.

I gripped the gun with both hands and worked my way along the wall, staring into the blackness.

A breath, then another.

I stepped up to the bathroom door and pushed it open. On the edges of my vision, the faint shape of the pale yellow shower curtain hung as if suspended in air. I swung the gun back and forth, my free hand groping into the blank space in the center of my vision.

The room was empty.

I turned and raised my Glock toward Lacy's room. At the bottom of my vision I could just make out a dull line of light at the base of the door. The faint blue flicker of a TV inside the room, maybe. I reached out until my hand found the handle, then I flung the door open with as much force as I could gather. The dull glow of the TV appeared to sit in the center of the room. I swung the gun back and forth trying to focus on the edges of my sight. Nothing moved. There was no sound, though I didn't know if that was because I couldn't hear anything or because there was nothing there. I took a step and my foot tangled up in something on the floor. My heart began to race.

'Lacy,' I whispered. I knelt straight down so as to not change the angle inside the motion detector on the vest and reached out until I touched it. Taffeta. It was her dress from the pageant. I started to gather it up in my hand as if I could protect her by gathering up all her things then I stopped and let it slip from my hand.

I backed out and moved toward my bedroom door at the end of the hall. The walls on the right were covered with family pictures. I counted them with one hand as I held the gun with the other, each step taking me further back into family history. The blood from my ear ran down my chin and dripped onto my shirt. Sweat filled with tiny particles of dust from the explosion fell, stinging my eyes. The hallway appeared to fall away from me, tumbling into complete blackness.

I reached out my hand to find the door, but it vanished into the darkness as if it had been severed. I pressed my back against the wall and tried to wipe the sweat and dust from my eyes, but it did no good.

Breathe. Take a breath, then move.

I could feel the frame of a picture against my back. I knew from its shape that it was a picture of Lacy as a child, sitting atop her father's shoulders.

I heard the sound of my heart beating like the pounding of a fist against a wall. I reached up to the motion detector and felt the vibration of my heart beating through it like a lit fuse.

'I'm still here, you son of a bitch,' I whispered.

In the darkness something seemed to pass inches from my face. I swept my gun across the darkness. It was like passing it through ink. Nothing was there.

I groped along the wall until my hand found the door frame, and then the handle. How much time had passed? Thirty seconds? A minute? Too much.

In one motion I turned the handle and threw myself at the darkness in front of me. The door flew open and a faint sheet of light rushed at me. The bedroom was little more than a pale field of gray with a corona of light around the edges. I swept the room with my Glock, searching for a hint of movement or color, anything that would give away Gabriel's position.

'Lacy!' I shouted.

I heard a voice and swung to my right. The blurry glow of the TV floated in the air several feet away.

'Lacy, where are you?'

A muffled cry rose from behind me. I turned and moved toward the sound, stretching my hand out to find what my eyes couldn't. I took a step, and then another, but my hand found nothing.

'Lacy, make a sound if you can.'

A barely audible shriek tried to escape its gag.

'Lacy, try again.'

It was fainter this time.

I took a step toward it then felt the warm air of a breath on the back of my neck. I spun around raising my Glock into the murky gray field in front of me.

'I know who you are, Gabriel, or would you rather I call you Philippe?' I said. 'Give it up. The house will be surrounded in minutes.'

I saw a break in the field of vision to my right and squeezed the trigger, firing a shot. The tube of the TV exploded with a shattering of glass and a rush of air.

I took a step back, swinging the gun to the left. 'Harrison!' I yelled.

The scent of Gabriel's cheap aftershave drifted past me. I spun on it, but my eyes could find nothing.

Fingers brushed the side of my cheek.

I started to turn but already knew I was too late. I had moved the wrong way. He was behind me, the cold skin of one hand tightening around my throat, the other taking hold of my hand holding the gun.

'You never chose,' he whispered in my ear.

His hand tightened around my throat. I could feel the sharp edges of his fingernails biting into my skin.

'Is it true what they say about blindness? Are all your other senses exploding with stimuli? What does fear smell like? Does it get lonely in the dark?'

'Go to hell.'

'Hell is where you make it, Lieutenant. A bedroom, a kitchen, a dumpster . . . Hospitals are particularly suited to it.'

'You're going to die and nothing will have worked out the way you saw it, the way you wrote it in your pathetic journal. The whole world doesn't fear you. They don't even know your name. You've failed.'

His hand tightened around my throat.

'What do you know of me? . . . Nothing!' His voice quivered with anger.

'I know you.'

He took two quick breaths like an animal standing over fallen prey. He was stronger than I realized. He bent my hand holding the gun back over my shoulder and placed the barrel against his own head.

'Kill me. Squeeze the trigger, hell is waiting.'

I started to tighten my finger around the trigger, but stopped. It couldn't be that simple, that clean. What game was he playing now?

'No,' I said.

He pulled me tightly against him and whispered in my ear, 'Do you know how easy it is to take life? How willingly most people beg for it?'

I tightened my hand around the grip of the gun and pressed it hard against his temple.

'There're three wires on the timer strapped to your daughter.'

I could feel the pulse in his neck pressing against my cheek. It was slow, barely elevated, like that of a reptile.

'Pull the correct one, she lives. Pull the wrong one, you've killed your own daughter.'

I pressed the gun even harder against his head.

'You want to, don't you? You want to feel it. You want the power. We all do . . . Kill me . . . Put the bullet in my head . . . I'd welcome the company.'

My finger slowly tightened on the trigger.

'I won't play any more games. Which wire?'

He shook his head. 'What kind of a mother are you?'

There it was, the one question I had no answer to.

'Tell me which wire, or—'

'You'll kill your own child.'

'Why should I trust you?'

'Because I've liked being a part of your family.'

'You're not part of my family.'

My finger slipped off the trigger.

'There're two minutes left on the timer . . . Now there's less than two minutes.'

'I'll find you,' I whispered.

I felt the muscles on his jaw tighten.

'But who will I be?'

He was smiling. 'I'll call Lacy's princess phone with the answer when you have thirty seconds.'

His hands slipped away from my wrist and throat.

'Of course, you could shoot me as I walk away . . . It's up to you.'

He pressed himself against me for a moment, then

slipped away. I stood frozen for a second, his words swirling around in my head. I spun around and raised my Glock. The dull field of my damaged vision shimmered like a curtain rustling in a breeze. I listened for a sound but heard none. I tested the air, searching for the sweet odor of Brut, but it was as gray and empty as my vision.

I pointed my weapon toward the darkness of the hallway and began to squeeze the trigger.

'Gabriel!' I yelled.

I aimed into the center of the soft, dark circle of the hallway.

Nothing.

I held on it for another moment, waiting for the creak of a floorboard, a shift in the pattern of light. My hand tensed, then I took a breath and lowered the Glock.

He was gone.

I held on the hallway for a moment, then turned my attention to the room.

'Lacy?'

If anything, my eyesight was getting worse. The blurry corona of sight on the borders of my vision was now filled with prisms of glaring color.

'I need you to make a sound if you can.'

I heard the faint creak of wood as if she was straining against her bindings. I reached out my hand and began to walk forward. A scent I didn't remember smelling since she was an infant filled the air. My child's sweet, perfect scent.

I started to rush and caught my foot on something on the floor and began to stumble. I had forgotten all about the vest over my shoulders. I reached out, expecting to fall, when instead my hand found the corner bedpost and held on. I held my breath, waiting to see if the liquid in the sensor had uncovered the wire, waiting for a flash, and then emptiness.

'Please,' I whispered as if it were a prayer and I was devout, which hadn't been the case in more years than I could remember. Belief was easy, a form of infatuation. Faith, on the other hand, was more like love. It required trust in something there was no physical evidence of.

I took a breath. The wire was still covered.

My hand released its grip on the turned wood of the post, and I groped my way slowly around to the other side of the bed.

'Where are you, honey?' I said softly.

I swept my hand out across the bed and found the familiar touch of her denim jeans just above the knee where her legs were bound with duct tape.

I quickly ran my hands up along her slender figure until I found the small brick of explosives and the detonating device. I froze. Upon touching it, my hand began to tremble. I thought there was nothing more I could possibly learn about fear or terror, but I was wrong. It was taped and wired around her neck like a medieval collar. I tried to say something but my voice caught. I could feel her trembling with fear.

'It will be okay. I'll get this off.'

I ran my hand along the side of her face until I found the tape that covered her mouth. A tear slid down her cheek and across my fingers. I worked my way around the edge of the tape to make sure there were no wires

415

protruding, then I slid a fingernail under the edge until I had enough tape to pull it off. Lacy tried to speak, but sobs overwhelmed her.

'Mommy.'

I wanted to hold her, pull her to me, but I couldn't. I brushed her hair off her forehead and caressed her.

'Get it off . . . get it off me!' she pleaded, as if it were a parasite that had attached itself to her.

'We will. But I can't see, so you have to help me . . . okay?'

I felt her body shudder with a sob then stiffen as she weakly nodded.

'Ass . . . hole.'

'Yeah . . . fucking asshole.'

Her body heaved with another cry and then settled into a series of short, quick breaths. I placed a hand on her chest like I had done so many nights when she was a child and her lungs had filled with asthma.

'You have to slow down, okay? Just one breath, just one . . . one . . . one.'

The rhythm slowed and she began to take in air.

'That's better. Now, I'm going to look at this, and you tell me what I'm feeling.'

'Okay,' she whispered, barely managing even that.

I ran my hands down to the device. Tape covered most of it, but I found the square shape of what must have been the timing device. Two wires ran out of one side, one on the other.

'Can you see this?'

Her breathing began to quicken again.

'Slow down. Try to tell me what I'm holding.'

416

'I can't see it . . .' She tried to say more but couldn't.

'Okay, it's okay. I found the wires. That's all that matters.'

'What is that?'

I felt her eyes on me, staring at the bomb strapped to me.

'That's nothing to worry about.'

'It's another bomb . . . Oh God.'

She began to tremble and I lied.

'It's been taken care of. We have to worry about you, that's all. Okay?'

The phone began to ring in Lacy's room.

'Oh God, oh God. Hurry . . . Hurry.'

Lacy's voice was on the edge of panic. I started toward the hallway as fast as my vision allowed. He had said he would call with thirty seconds left. My hand followed along the dresser until I found the doorway. The flashes of light at the edges of my vision made it more difficult to walk and keep my balance, so I closed my eyes and ran my hand against the wall until I found Lacy's door.

The phone was across the room on the other side of the bed. I steered around the TV that was in the middle of the room. My foot hung up in her dress on the floor, and I dragged it until it caught on the foot of the bed.

No, no, no.

I kicked my leg and heard the tearing of fabric as I pulled free.

How many seconds had passed? Too many, slipping away, and I could do nothing about it.

I rushed around the bed and reached for the phone.

417

My hand hit it with a jolt, and it slid from my grasp and fell off the bed table onto the floor. I started to bend down and then realized I would uncover the detonation wire in the motion detector if I did that. I dropped straight down to my knees and searched the floor until my hand found the cord and then the receiver.

'Which one?'

'You should have about twenty seconds,' Gabriel said.

'Which one?'

'The blue one.'

'The blue – I'm blind!'

'I know . . . Good-bye, Lieutenant. Fifteen seconds.'

I dropped the phone and rushed across the room to Lacy's dresser. She kept a hand mirror on it – had bought it as part of her transformation into a beauty pageant contestant. If it was still there . . .

I swept my hand across the top of the dresser, knocking aside the other props she had acquired for her role, until I found the smooth surface of a ten-inch hand mirror. I blindly rushed out of the room and down the hall toward my bedroom.

The seconds ticked away in my head. Fifteen, fourteen, thirteen.

In the darkness I felt myself approaching the edge of an abyss.

I hit the bed hard with my knee, and then my hand found her leg. Through my blindness I tried to position the mirror to reflect the device where Lacy could see it.

'Which of the wires is blue?'

'I can't—' she shouted like a person in free fall, trying to be heard over the rush of air.

'Just tell me. It's all right.'

'I can't see it – the wrong side, turn it around!'

I spun the mirror in my hand.

'Tilt it up.'

I twisted it in my hand.

She shuddered and cried.

'Lacy, which one is blue?'

'Ten, nine . . .'

'Oh, God.'

'Lacy!'

Her voice carried the sound of defeat.

'They're all fucking blue.'

I felt her body heave as terror took control of her. I dropped the mirror and fumbled in my darkness until I had the three wires in my fingers.

Which one?

I tried picturing Harrison and how he would interpret each wire's function. Which was the ground, which was the trigger, which was the . . . I was clueless.

Eight . . . seven . . .

In the dark I heard Lacy hyperventilating.

Think. Work it. There was something there. The blue one, what about it?

Six . . . five . . .

'Mommm!' Lacy cried. 'No . . . no.'

I tried to run it through my head. How would Gabriel do it? How would he play this? His greatest role wasn't as a terrorist, it was as the victim Philippe, sitting with a bomb in his lap, looking at me as Harrison dismantled the timer. There was laughter in those eyes. The player. Nothing was real for him. We had him in our hands, but we didn't know it. It was a game to him. A deadly carny trick. Three wires, all blue . . . Choose.

Four . . . three . . .

In the distance I heard the shrill sound of sirens heading in our direction. I gripped the wires in my hand.

'I don't want to die,' Lacy cried.

Two . . .

'I love you, sweetheart.'

I closed my eyes against the confusion of my damaged sight. I saw Lacy in a yellow dress, running toward me with her arms outstretched. She was ten years old, then five, then . . . She was calling my name, holding something in her hands to share with me. A discovery, a mystery. A gift.

'The blue one,' I whispered.

One . . .

The room seemed to empty of all sound, even those of memory. I tightened my grip, then pulled all three wires at once.

One . . . one . . . one . . .

I waited for the blinding flash of ignition. An instant of searing heat before death overtook us. Nothing. One second passed, then another and another in silence. Was this just another twist in Gabriel's play? A few seconds of relief and hope as the delayed fuse ticked down? By pulling the three wires had I sealed our fate, or saved it? Which was it? How could I know? Or was this the genius psychopath perpetrating one more cruel joke on his lab mice? My fear no longer belonged to me, it was his to do with what he wanted.

'I think it's over,' I said.

'What's that sound?' Lacy whispered.

'I don't—'

Then I heard a high-pitched whistle of rushing air.

'Can you tell where that's coming from?'

'It— Oh, God!' Lacy cried.

'Where is it?'

'On the bomb, get it off, get it off.'

The whistle of rushing air grew louder.

'No!' Lacy screamed.

I reached out and felt the skin of a balloon rising out of the device around her neck. A child's toy, growing bigger and bigger like some final, terrible joke that sets off the device when it bursts. I put both hands over it to try to force the air back out of it, but the balloon continued to grow, the whistle of air getting louder and louder.

Lacy's breathing began to cycle out of control. She was trying to say something but couldn't get enough air. The balloon began to press tight against my hands, and then to stretch to the breaking point.

'We're not your playthings,' I yelled.

I felt the bed shudder as Lacy began to shake uncontrollably.

'No,' I started to say. And then I started to scream, 'You son of a bitch!'

The sharp bang of the balloon filled the room for a deafening instant and then it was silent. A horrible, expectant silence. I took a breath, then another, and braced myself for the second and final blast that would end it.

Nothing happened.

A faint odor of latex hung in the air. Pieces of the balloon clung to my wrist like strips of skin tissue. I counted to five, and then to ten just to be sure that it was really over. Nothing else happened.

Gabriel's play was over. His final act, the bursting of a balloon, a reminder that everything he touched, even a toy, was filled with terror. Were we alive because I had chosen correctly? Or because he had chosen for us? There was no way to know, any more than there was to understand where he had come from, or what had made him what he was.

I reached out for my daughter until I found her and cradled her in my arms. Lacy began to cry with relief and shake as if she were cold.

'Assho—' she began to say, but the word disappeared into another cycle of sobs.

I touched the soft skin of her face.

'It's okay,' I said. 'He can't hurt us anymore.'

The muscles of her shoulders tensed and she shook her head.

'There's something dripping from that glass thing on your chest.'

I reached up and touched the motion detector. A thick drop of mercury rolled down my finger and across the palm of my hand.

'Oh, God, that's bad, isn't it,' Lacy said, her voice beginning to tremble again.

I tried to tell her that it wasn't, but my voice faltered. I tried to take a breath but the vest seemed to fight the air I was trying to take in. I reached out and touched Lacy's cheek and then pulled away.

422

'Don't leave me here.'

'I have to—'

'No!' she pleaded. 'Don't leave me!'

I felt another drop of mercury seep out of the cracked glass of the motion detector as I rose from the bed. I was the only danger to her now. I was the only thing that could harm her.

'I have to go into the other room.'

'No, stay with me.'

I moved toward the door and Lacy began to cry. 'Mom.'

'I love you,' I said.

'No!' she yelled.

'It's going to be fine.'

'Don't leave me, don't leave me.'

'I have . . .'

The words slipped silently away from me as I turned my back on my daughter and started toward the dark shape of the hallway.

'Mom!' Lacy screamed. 'Don't leave me . . . don't . . . don't.'

My hand found the door frame to the hallway and I guided myself away from the bedroom as quickly as I could. Lacy screamed for me again and then all I heard was her faint cries. My fingers passed over the family photographs on the wall as I moved toward the dull light of the living room. I tried to remember how big a blast area Harrison had estimated the charge would destroy. How far did I have to be away from my daughter to know she was safe? Ten feet, or was it twenty? How many walls did I need between us? I passed Lacy's bedroom and stepped into the living room. After the darkness of the hallway the light filtering in through the windows was like looking into a blinding sun. The sharp odor of explosive still filled the room.

'Harrison!'

Nothing came back.

'I need your help,' I pleaded.

Still silence. I took a step toward the dining room, where I had seen him disappear into the flash of the first explosion. The floor was littered with pieces of china from the cabinets in the kitchen. I took one step, then another, each one like walking on a shattered pane of glass. For an instant I thought I smelled the scent of Gabriel's aftershave, but just as quickly it seemed to vanish. I started to reach for my Glock and realized I had left it in the bedroom, and then a hand took hold of my leg.

'Lieutenant.'

Harrison was on the floor at my feet where he had crawled after the explosion. I knelt down and reached out toward him. He was slumped on his knees like an exhausted marathoner. The right side of his face was covered with blood and small pieces of debris.

'I need your help,' I said.

'I can't hear so good,' he said weakly.

I reached out until I found one of his hands and I guided it up to the motion detector. His fingers felt lifeless and clumsy for a moment and then they seemed to come alive as they began to gently study the glass of the detector.

'It's cracked.'

I nodded. 'Is the wire exposed?'

He studied it for a minute.

'Yes.'

'How much?'

'Almost entirely.'

He drew a heavy breath, spitting blood out of his mouth as he exhaled.

'There's a tool kit in the squad. You need to find some tape and seal the crack.'

'I can't see.'

Nothing came back for a moment.

'I'm blind. I can't go to the squad.'

He took a labored breath, then another. 'We'll do it another way.'

I reached up and felt another drip of mercury forming on the detector. 'How?'

The act of forming a plan seemed to draw the last of his strength. 'I need you to move right next to me like we're embracing.'

His breath caught up short and he rested for a moment.

'The wire from the detector connects on the inside of the vest. I have to reach it from underneath.'

I slid over next to him. The blood on the side of his face slid across my cheek. The odor of his singed hair clung to his scalp.

'Now raise your arms . . .' his voice faltered again. 'Put them around my neck so I can reach under the . . .'

His voice weakened and slipped away.

'Go on,' he whispered.

I started to but stopped and shook my head. 'I can't ask you to do this.'

I started to pull away but he held me with what little strength he had.

'You're not asking . . . I am. And I need to do it now or we're both dead.'

I started to shake my head and he reach up and gently touched the side of my face.

'Please, let me do this.'

I raised my arms and put them around Harrison's neck. He slipped a hand under the vest and eased it up behind the pocket of explosive until he found what he was looking for.

'Jesus,' he whispered.

'What?'

His head dropped forward for a moment as if in defeat.

'There're five wires here, but I can't follow where they go. There could be a secondary fuse I haven't found.'

'I don't think so,' I said.

'Why?'

'He's playing with us again.'

'I've got to be certain.'

'Cut them all,' I whispered.

Harrison shook his head. 'I can't do that. There could be a sequencer, I cut the wrong lead, I do it in the wrong order.'

'Give me the clippers. I'll do it.'

Harrison took a breath, and I felt the muscles in his shoulder tense. 'I'm not letting you do that.'

I leaned into the side of his face.

'I don't have time. It's not your fault . . . Let me go.'

He raised his head slightly and whispered in my ear, 'Hold me as tight as you can.'

'No.'

I felt his fingers find all five wires and guide them into the clipper blades.

'It'll be okay,' he said gently.

'Don't,' I pleaded.

'As tight as you can. Do it now.'

I wrapped my arms around his neck and pulled his face to mine. I felt the stubble of his beard on my cheek, the taste of blood on my lips. I reached up and placed my hand on the back of his neck and closed my eyes.

'Now,' I whispered.

He nodded silently and gently exhaled, then I felt the muscles of his hand tighten around the grip of the cutters, and heard the faint metallic click of the wires as the blades sliced through them.

Like the end of a recurring nightmare, a second passed and then another, expecting it to return, but it didn't.

Harrison eased his hand out from under the vest and I heard the clippers fall to the floor. He put his arms around me and we clung to the rhythm of our breathing.

'Thank you,' I whispered into his damaged ear, but he didn't hear me.

His arms began to relax, and then he slumped into unconsciousness in my arms. Outside I heard the sound of the first squad's siren as it turned onto the block and headed for my house. I opened my eyes and looked into the blurry light filtering through the windows in the kitchen where Chavez lay wounded and a young patrolman was dead.

It was over. My daughter was safe. A few miles to the south in the heart of Pasadena the parade was moving safely down Colorado Boulevard, just as it had done for 115 years. And around the world two hundred million people would be watching, safe and happy, staring in wonder at the power of the imagination to create such beautiful things.

'They don't know,' I whispered.

twenty-seven

'**I** want you to tell me what you see,' the doctor said as he began to slip the bandages from my eyes.

A week had passed since Gabriel had plunged me into darkness. The doctor assured me that the eyes were one of the quickest-healing organs in the body. 'Miracles of nature, really,' he called them. But he couldn't do anything about what they had already witnessed. Would my world ever look the same after Gabriel had walked through it? He'd taken my daughter from me. He had played with me like a cat tossing a mouse around a living-room floor. He killed seven people. He nearly killed Traver, Harrison, and Chief Chavez, and then I let him go. I set him free to get my daughter back. I let him walk away. A cop's worst nightmare.

'You had a gun to his head.'

It was the voice that whispered in my ear as I lay blinded in my bed at night. I could have ended it, but I didn't. Maybe I wasn't strong enough. Maybe I just wasn't a good enough cop. Or maybe the part of me that didn't pull the trigger when I had the chance was the only part that Gabriel had not touched – that hidden *querencia* of the soul where love exists separate from the rest of daily life and the injuries it inflicts. The part that loves Lacy, and would give everything for her to live. Even Gabriel's freedom.

That was his gift to me. I would watch my daughter become a woman. I would have a chance to undo all the missteps I had made as her mother in her first seventeen years of life. I would be better. And in return for this gift, I'll carry a burning ember in my heart that knows wherever Gabriel goes, whomever he touches, whomever he tortures, he did because I chose it.

What happened to Gabriel?

What I knew for certain was that he drove away from my house in the dead officer's cruiser and parked it three blocks from the parade route on Colorado Boulevard. One witness placed him watching the parade, waving to the passing floats and taking pictures. Another report sighted him at the Long Beach airport. Neither was confirmed. He had vanished.

The French consulate had no record of one of their citizens entering the country matching his description. No passport record exists. No visa, no work permit, nothing. The partial prints we had of him matched no record on file with the FBI or any state agency in the country. School records across the country were searched. Arrests, military, and birth records, even fishing licenses. Every possible paper trail was studied and they led nowhere.

He was, as he told us in his journal, the boy in the

class photograph whose name and face we've all forgotten. And until the last day that he takes a breath on this earth I will never be finished with him. Every time the telephone rings with the report of a body, I will wonder. Every time I detect a familiar aftershave passing in a crowd, I will turn. Every time I hear cries of victims' families, I will remember.

I will always be looking for him. And I will always feel his eyes watching, waiting for the moment he whispers a single, terrible word in my ear.

Tell me what you see? You don't want to know what I see.

The doctor gently took hold of the last bandage and lifted it off my face.

'Now open your eyes,' he said.

I hesitated for a moment, the bandages' phantom presence lingering as if they were a permanent part of my anatomy. Then I slowly let the light back into my life. The colors and light were muted as if I were caught halfway between a dream and consciousness. Then gradually the room began to come into focus and I saw my daughter's face.

'Mom,' Lacy said.

I stared at her, examining every feature on her face, looking for the baby I had held in my arms, and the girl I had watched grow, but she was gone. The face I was looking into was that of a young woman. The soft contours of childhood had been drawn tight and carried the burden of her ordeal.

'I'm here, Mom,' she said.

I looked into her eyes and saw that Gabriel had not

touched everything. Her fierce strength burned as intensely as ever.

'Fuck him,' she whispered.

I felt my heart skip a beat and knew instantly that she would be all right, just as I knew that she was no longer the same. For better or worse, this was where we begin our new lives together and leave behind the mother and daughter we had once been.

'Remember us,' said a voice behind her.

Traver, my old partner, was leaning over Lacy's shoulder. Big Dave, my protector. A bandage still covered portions of his head, his face carried dark blue streaks of bruises and swelling, but his great strength and spirit were clearly intact. To his left Chief Chavez sat in a wheelchair, his face red and swollen, his burned hands covered in bandages, an IV taped to his arm. But he was smiling. He would be all right, too.

I looked over Lacy's right shoulder and there stood Harrison.

Our eyes met and I started to say his name but words left me. We were back in my house, my arms wrapped around him as he saved my life. I could feel the steadiness of his hands as they undid Gabriel's terrible handiwork. No act of love had ever been as intimate or more powerful. I held his eyes for another moment. Who were we to each other now? In saving me was he also saving his young murdered wife, whom he not been able to protect? Or had he just saved his own life, and given himself the future that had until that moment eluded him?

Was he my partner? Or was he to be more than that?

I noticed a subtle spasm of pain in the corners of his eyes and I quickly looked over the rest of his body for signs of injuries. A wound, drawn like a contour on a map, ran from his ear down along the line of his jaw. Another, the shape of a crescent moon, touched the corner of his left eye. He appeared to favor the right side of his body slightly. A faint tremor in the fingers of his right hand gave away the presence of more unseen damage.

'Alex,' he said gently, using my Christian name for the first time.

His voice nearly took my breath away and I closed my eyes trying to breathe, but I couldn't. The doctor slid his chair over in front of me and shined a small light briefly into each of my eyes.

'Now tell me what you see, Lieutenant.'

Tears slid out of the corners of my eyes and down my cheeks. I glanced at the three men who had stood by me and risked everything to be there.

'What do you see?' the doctor repeated.

I reached out, took hold of Lacy's hand, and looked into her beautiful face.

'I see everything,' I said softly.

This work would not have been possible without the assistance of a number of people. Kathryn Hall, with her fine ear and sharp pencil. Beth Bohn, Steve Fisher, and Gregg Almquist, with their continued belief and support. Elaine Koster, whom I can simply never thank enough. And David Highfill at Putnam, who took the leap with Delillo.

Creepers

David Morrell

'Creepers.'

That's what they call themselves. Urban explorers who illegally enter sealed buildings – many of which have been abandoned for years. Exploring one is like going into a time capsule, as the building's secrets are unveiled.

One chilly October night in New Jersey, a group of creepers enters the Paragon, a hotel designed and built by a reclusive millionaire. The once magnificent structure is now a decrepit, boarded-up edifice marked for demolition and has a disturbing history. Soon after the group enters it becomes clear that this decaying seven-storey building holds more secrets than they could have imagined in their worst nightmares. Danger, terror and death wait for them in a place ravaged by time and redolent of evil.

With customary brilliance, David Morrell, the father of the modern high-action thriller, inexorably draws you in to CREEPERS – a story that will haunt you for nights to come.

Praise for CREEPERS:

'*Creepers* is a good old-fashioned chiller, as the pages turn the tension increases, almost to breaking-point. Terrific' *Independent on Sunday*

'A gripping story that demands to be read in a single sitting . . . Morrell delivers first-rate, suspenseful story-telling once again' *Publishers Weekly*

0 7553 2748 9 (Super A format)

0 7553 3135 4 (A format)

headline

Thorn

Vena Cork

In the city's open spaces, there is time to kill . . .

A tragedy has changed Rosa Thorn's life for ever. Now she has to start again with a new job, a new school for her children and some empty space in her life. But strange things start to happen . . .

When a growing sense of unease turns into sudden violence, Rosa fears for her safety and even more so for the wellbeing of her children. For her daughter is the subject of someone's demented infatuation. But like a diseased town fox, the real threat stalks the shadows, in the night-black recesses of the under-growth, not just of the city, but of the human mind . . .

Vena Cork's astonishing, thrilling debut novel is as shocking as it is unputdownable – a brilliant, menacing, psychological thriller that takes you to the edge of darkness.

'One of those rare and energetic books you can't put down yet don't want to end' *The Times*

'An outstanding debut' *Time Out*

0 7553 2394 7

headline

Now you can buy any of these other
bestselling Headline books from your
bookshop or *direct from the publisher*.

FREE P&P AND UK DELIVERY
(Overseas and Ireland £3.50 per book)

Straight Into Darkness	Faye Kellerman	£6.99
Jacquot and the Angel	Martin O'Brien	£6.99
Creepers	David Morrell	£6.99
Immoral	Brian Freeman	£6.99
Double Tap	Steve Martini	£6.99
Hen's Teeth	Manda Scott	£7.99
The Patriots' Club	Christopher Reich	£6.99
Double Homicide	Faye & Jonathan Kellerman	£6.99
Mandrake	Paul Eddy	£6.99

TO ORDER SIMPLY CALL THIS NUMBER

01235 400 414

or visit our website: www.madaboutbooks.com

Prices and availability subject to change without notice.